THE
GOLDEN
JOURNEY

THE
GOLDEN
JOURNEY

AGNES SLIGH TURNBULL

HOUGHTON MIFFLIN COMPANY BOSTON
The Riverside Press Cambridge

To my husband, James Lyall Turnbull,
for his unfailing interest, encouragement
and critical assistance through the years.

I

&§ THE GREAT CURVING STAIRWAY hung delicately between the floors like an unsupported cloud as though designed only for light, happy, unladen feet; but the two men, with no thought of the beauty of its architecture, descended it now heavily and without speaking. They crossed the wide hall, still in silence, and entered the library at the rear of the house which James Kirkland, the host, indicated by the slight direction of his finger.

Once within the room, which now in the late March afternoon was filled with the young, golden light of spring, they faced each other as two bare souls freed from all bodily limitations might conceivably stand to demand and to deliver the truth.

The second man, Dr. Hertzog, was short and stout, built with a large head, lined face, tight lips which looked hard when closed but with merciful dark eyes behind his thick glasses.

Kirkland waited, his tall body and aquiline features rigid. He swallowed with difficulty, his own eyes fixed upon the other as though the man before him held life and death within his power of giving.

"Mr. Kirkland," the doctor began, "you brought me to this country a week ago at great cost to see if I could help your daughter. In that time I have met with the other physicians who have had charge of the case; I have heard every detail of the accident and of all the treatments given since. I have made my own examinations and tests ending with these I have just finished here in her own room in the last hope that she might under those circumstances be more completely relaxed. I have left undone nothing which all my training and experience could suggest. And I must sadly now report to you that I am forced to concur with the American doctors who have for these last months been working upon the problem."

Kirkland sank into the chair behind him as though all strength and volition had gone out of him.

"You too," he whispered. "My God, is there then no hope at all?"

"There is complete hope that in all other respects she will remain a healthy and normal girl. But I cannot hold out any honest assurance that she will ever walk again."

He paused, watching the stricken man before him. His English was excellent but the heavy accent seemed to put additional emotion into his words.

"I am a doctor, yes, but I am not what you call a cold professional. I have feeling for all my patients, but I tell you now with honesty I have never so greatly wished to help anyone as I have to help your daughter. She is your only child?"

Kirkland nodded. "All I have in the world."

"She is beautiful, *very* beautiful and with a mind as well."

Kirkland's face worked convulsively.

"She has everything, doctor, everything for her life's fulfillment. She graduated from college a year ago with honors, she has beauty as you can see and a fineness of spirit which I know better than anyone else. And now, now at twenty-two she's condemned for life. . . ." A terrible sound broke from him. "I could curse God and die!"

The doctor had not sat down, though neither was conscious of the fact. He paced now slowly back and forth, his heavy head low, his hands behind his back. The lines on his face had gone deeper.

"No, Mr. Kirkland," he spoke slowly, calmly, "you will not do that. You are thinking *small*. We must never think small. I may speak so to you for I have seen much tragedy. More than you can even imagine. We in Europe these last years have had to learn to bear, to endure and to try not to—how shall I say it simply?—put the blame on God. Who of us little people can know what are his powers or his limitations? Perhaps the heart of the Eternal suffers with us, no?"

James Kirkland straightened, his face now composed but gray.

"I am ashamed of my outburst," he said, "but I am her father and I've never until now given up. Surely you can see. . . ."

The other nodded. "I know. I see all too well. As I tell you, I would give much, much to be able to help her. My full diagnosis will be sent to your own physician later. To you I say this. Like the others I find no actual physical reason for this paralysis of the limbs. It is caused by some subtle, some undetectable nerve injury which evades us but which, I am convinced, is deep and permanent. I would to God I could feel otherwise. And now, Mr. Kirkland, I must take my leave of you."

Kirkland rose and drew an envelope from his pocket.

"You have been kind," he said, handing it to the other. "Your coming at all was a very great favor. I deeply appreciate it."

The other fingered the envelope without opening it.

"It is a very large sum. I feel, now, a little embarrassed. When I set my fee I had expected—you must not think I speak in vanity, but it has happened that I have had a large measure of success—I had hoped to be able to render a commensurate service."

Kirkland waved away his reluctance stiffly.

"Do not think of that. You have done all you could. The money is of no consideration."

"In that you are fortunate," the doctor replied gravely. "You will be able to make her life more happy or, shall we say, more bearable and full. One more thing before I go. You will not have to tell your daughter of my report."

"She knows?"

The other nodded. "She asked me for the truth. I told her. She has courage. She . . . she smiled and thanked me. It moved me greatly. I shall always remember her, always."

He wrung Kirkland's hand, and walked quickly into the hall and on toward the outer door.

Suddenly he stopped, stood for a full minute as though considering and then, looking up at Kirkland, who was watching him closely, made a sign again toward the library. When they had re-entered it Dr. Hertzog seemed visibly agitated; he stood upon the hearth rug, looking at Kirkland uncertainly.

"I am about to do a thing which I feel is very unwise. All my professional judgment is against it. Yet I will be haunted always by your face . . . and your daughter's. This that I will tell you is an unrelated fact merely. You will now make me your promise you will take it as such."

Kirkland assented, his strained face surprised and intent.

"So!" said the doctor. "Many years ago I had a patient in the hospital in Vienna, a young woman, married only a few months. She had had a bad accident in climbing a mountain and was brought in for dead. Gradually she recovered except that her legs were paralyzed. I did all I knew, to no avail. She went home, as we believed, never to walk again."

Kirkland was scarcely breathing.

"Yes?" he prompted as the other hesitated.

The great doctor spoke with more difficulty.

"Later her husband reported to me that she was going to have a child. It was born in our hospital. I was in close touch with the case. While she was in desperate labor she stood up, quite unconscious that she was doing so, and walked across the room with the nurse's help. Some subtle nerve block in the brain had apparently been released. Afterwards her legs functioned normally."

Dr. Hertzog moved toward Kirkland and caught him by the shoulders.

"I was somehow constrained to tell you this but I must insist that you accept it, as I said before, as an unrelated fact. Even if your daughter were now married, even if she some time were to have a child, there would be no slightest reason to expect a similar result. In these so delicate nerve injuries each is different from every other. You understand, do you not?"

Kirkland's voice was harsh in its intensity.

"I must get this straight. I must be completely clear. Please answer my questions. Was the condition of this other girl similar, in your opinion, to that of my daughter?"

"Outwardly, as far as one could judge, I should say, yes, but only outwardly. I must insist. . . ."

"All right, let us go on from there. After the birth of her child that young woman regained the use of her legs."

"That is so."

"Beyond those two facts you will say nothing?"

"I will not," said the doctor, "because I dare not. And I pray your forgiveness for saying what I have."

Kirkland held out his hand.

"Thank you," he said.

The two men looked deeply into each other's eyes for a long moment, then with no further word spoken, Dr. Hertzog hurriedly took his leave, and James Kirkland walked back toward the stairs.

He stood, looking up at their fragile, curving beauty. When he and Alice, his wife, had planned the house twenty years before, the stairway had been her dearest wish.

"I want to see Anne coming down it one day in her wedding gown!" she had said. "So it must be the most beautifully ethereal staircase in the world!"

He had laughed at her then, tenderly, as a man laughs at the woman he loves but even as he teased her, his own inner mind had suddenly held the vision of a young girl in filmy, flowing white with Alice's bright hair and eager face, descending the stairs as he, her father, waited below for his share in the joyous, crowning hour!

A surge of bitterness like a relentless, overwhelming physical wave of the sea beat upon him as he bowed his head against the carved newel. Alice was dead. And Anne. . . . He straightened, at last, pulled himself together with a hard effort, and started up. Even though she knew the truth he must get to her without more delay. As to the last, incredibly strange conversation with Dr. Hertzog, he must keep that to himself, to gnaw, to tear at alone later in his own heart.

Anne's room was on the second floor at the back of the house, where, even though the city surrounded it, there had always been a garden. She was sitting beside the window now, and looked up as her father entered, shaking back her hair and forcing a smile.

"Jimmy," she began, "you needn't tell me. I know already and I wasn't surprised. I really didn't have the confidence you did in the outcome. Oh, I admit I had a tiny bit of hope"—she was controlling her voice well—"but not much. So we're no worse off than before, and let's just forget Dr. Hertzog. Professionally, I mean. Otherwise he's a perfect darling. I liked him tremendously. He talked sense to me. All the other doctors seem to feel because I'm small and blond that I must be treated like a six-year-old! Now he . . ."

Kirkland lifted her face in his hand and kissed it.

"You needn't run on, Mouchie. We understand each other, don't we?"

Her smile faded. "Yes."

"Then we'll . . . manage." In spite of himself his voice caught on the last syllable.

She looked up at him, her beautiful eyes sad beyond words. "I feel almost worse for you than I do for myself. Try not to . . . not to . . . Does Gran know?"

"Not yet. Would you rather I called her?"

"Yes, if you will." She sighed. "You know all the details." Then she spoke again quickly. "Listen, Jimmy, why don't you go over and have dinner with Gran? That will make it better for her. You can both talk freely then. And really—now don't think I'm morbid for I'm perfectly all right, but I'd rather be alone. That is, it's better for us to be apart tonight."

"You may be right," he agreed heavily, "but I hate to leave you."

"It'll be a relief," she said, trying to make her voice natural. "We're not good for each other right now. Tomorrow we'll both have our second wind. Besides, we ought to think of Gran tonight, too."

"But what will you do? Oh, I can't leave you alone, that's all there is to it."

"I won't be alone later. I'll have dinner up here and eat it while

I finish this mystery. I'm half through and it's a corker. I'll round up three of the girls who aren't doing anything and we'll play cutthroat bridge down in the library afterwards. We'll probably still be at it when you get back. No, go, Jimmy, please. This is the way I want it."

He kissed her again tenderly. "There's a meeting I ought to be at later."

"Wonderful! Now, you're all set. Give my love to Gran and tell her I've decided to be a poet. We considered art last week, but paints are too messy. Now, writing is nice clean work, and from a lot of the stuff I read, I think a child could do it."

Her banter stopped abruptly. "Make up a good story for Gran, won't you, Jimmy? She'll be pretty hard hit. She somehow expected a miracle from Dr. Hertzog—like you. Can you hold her up, do you think, when you're with her?"

"You know Gran. It will probably be the other way round. But I'll do my best."

"Stout fellah!" She waved him out of the room, smiling again until the door was closed. Then she picked up the house phone beside her and called her nurse in her room down the hall.

"Davy, I want to rest until seven and then have a perfectly fabulous dinner up here. Something different and frilly and, oh, you know, tempting to the appetite! Just tell Perth to let herself go on it. And could you call up some of the girls, and ask three for bridge tonight? Any three you can get."

There was a hesitant question over the wire.

"Yes, we have the report, Davy. It's no dice. I just want to be alone for a little to pick up the pieces. You understand? I'll be all right. I won't need you till seven, and thanks, Davy."

She set down the phone carefully and leaned back in the tall chair. Outside her window a fountain was sending ecstatic rainbow plumes into the sunny air. The lilac hedge at the back of the garden was in bright leaf and masses of daffodil buds were crowding the border beds. A robin sang in the rowan tree. It was spring.

Anne sat staring at the bedroom wall, her body immobile, rigid. Then slowly the tears began. She made no effort to staunch them. They rolled down the white, saddened cheeks while great shuddering breaths came faster and faster. They were the stillborn sobs of quiet and utter despair.

Kirkland rang the bell at his mother-in-law's apartment at a quarter to seven, feeling the same mixture of pain and eagerness he always experienced as he approached her presence. Both emotions were caused by the fact that Mrs. Catherby even at eighty had the unconscious power of calling up her daughter's presence. In a dozen small ways—in their physical attitudes, their voices, their opinions, in their laughter—mother and daughter had closely resembled each other.

She looked up now, the fine, beautiful bones of her face sharpened and drawn with anxiety.

"Jimmy! Tell me at once. Don't spare me. I knew from your voice on the phone that the news is not good. It's not—hopeless?"

Kirkland nodded.

She gave a small moan and her face went white.

"Somehow I felt that this man, this doctor would know just what to do. He didn't suggest operating?"

"On the contrary, he was opposed to it."

The old woman wrung her thin hands until, Kirkland thought, the diamonds must have cut the flesh.

"I *prayed*," she said, "harder than I ever prayed in all my life. And there came over me such a confidence, an assurance—I can't describe it, but my heart has felt lighter this week than at any time since the accident."

"I know. In a way, so has mine. And in spite of what she says I think Anne felt the same. Also, though you may not believe it, I prayed myself, harder than I ever did. I don't believe, however," he added with cold bitterness, "that my own prayers have much weight."

"Tell me exactly to the letter what he said, if you can remember."

"Remember? I wish to God I could forget." He repeated Dr. Hertzog's diagnosis, and they both sat silent.

"I was to cheer you up," Kirkland said at last with a grim smile. "Anne's idea." Then in a rush the words burst from him.

"If I were a man of moderate means I honestly believe I could bear this better. It's the thought of all the money, useless, *useless* that drives me mad. Why did I sweat and struggle and work to get it all? Why did success come to me when so many men miss it? It didn't save Alice. Now, it can't save Anne."

He got up and strode back and forth, his emanation of strength filling the room.

"And it's not only the money. I've got power too. I go to a meeting from here where we'll decide on the next candidate for governor.

I will decide. *My* word will settle it. I'm boss of this state. And what good is it?" He all but shouted the words. "What good is any of it to me now? Nothing but a bitterness."

Suddenly he stopped short in his pacing, his head raised, his whole attitude dynamic.

"Unless. . . ." His voice dropped. "Unless. . . ."

Mrs. Catherby was still working with her hands.

"Don't, Jimmy," she said earnestly. "Don't torture yourself. Success just came to you. It's like that in life.

> *By right or wrong*
> *Lands and goods go to the strong.*

And you're strong. I'm afraid you'll have to lend that strength now to all of us. We'll need it!"

Dinner was announced and he helped her in to the table. They talked then of indifferent matters until Mrs. Catherby looked at him searchingly.

"Jimmy," she said, "there's something you're not telling me. Your mind's off a mile away. Is it politics now?"

"I guess you'd call it that. Forgive me, Ellie. I've been poor company for you. But you've done *me* good, if that's any consolation to you. I always get ideas somehow when I'm with you. I think you're magic. I remember once when you were explaining your requirements for a new butler I suddenly thought of the perfect man for State Senator! Never occurred to me before. We got him elected, too," he added.

"It would seem to me," the old lady said sadly, "that there are more important matters for us to think of tonight than even senators or governors."

Oddly enough Kirkland smiled back at her, unashamed. "Be patient with me," he said. "My mind works in devious ways. But no matter what I seem to be thinking about, it's always Anne, underneath."

Back in the living room they spoke little. Kirkland resumed his pacing the floor, stopping occasionally, hands in pockets, to stare out of the window at the lights of the city. Mrs. Catherby, knowing his moods, knitted quietly. All at once he went to the hall, seized the telephone and dialed a number.

"Arno?" he questioned. "This is Kirkland. I can't be there tonight . . . I know. I'm sorry, but it's impossible." The words were curt and final. "Can you get the boys together for Friday instead? . . . All

right. Things going okay? Listen, Arno. What do you know about
young Devereux? . . . I mean personal, professional, everything
. . . You can? Fine. Call me at home tonight between nine and ten
. . . Good. Thanks, Arno."

He hung up, sat still thinking deeply for a moment, then went
back to his mother-in-law.

"What was that, Ellie, you were quoting before dinner about the
strong?"

"Oh, that! Some lines from Emerson. I have a feeling that I'm
one of the very few who still read his verse. I take his 'Terminus'
every morning now with my breakfast to bolster me up about being
old. When you get to be eighty, Jimmy, read it. Don't forget."

"You and your poetry!" He said it in the same teasing tone he had
used with Alice, half scornful, half wistful.

The old lady looked at him tenderly. She had told him often to
his face that she could never understand him, that in fact she disap-
proved of him, yet loved him in spite of it. So it had been with her
daughter.

"Say the lines again," he demanded.

"They are from another poem you wouldn't care for at all, as a
whole. But these particular words always make me think of you.

> As garment draws the garment's hem,
> Men their fortunes bring with them,
> By right or wrong,
> Lands and goods go to the strong."

She paused and then added softly as though to herself:

> "Nor less the eternal poles
> Of tendency distribute souls."

But Kirkland had caught it. His head flashed up and he gazed
at her with piercing intentness.

"What was that last? What does that mean?" The questions were
sharp and peremptory.

She laughed a little. "Don't bite me, Jimmy. You ought to read
more and then you could interpret poetry for yourself. But I'll explain if I can. I think it means souls are mysteriously drawn to each
other—or they aren't. You can't *force* people to be friends. You can't
compel young folks to fall in love. It's 'the eternal poles of tendency'
at work that does it. That's all."

"I know," he said heavily. "I've thought of that. But," he muttered, half under his breath, "I've got to take the chance."

It was Mrs. Catherby's turn to question.

"What are you talking about? What chance?"

He was at once his controlled and inscrutable self.

"Nothing," he smiled. "Nothing, really. Just politics again."

She brought the conversation back to Anne.

"I overheard you on the phone. I'm glad you're going back home from here. I'll go over tomorrow if I can make it. We must try to think of something new and different just now to take up her mind. I talked to her last week about painting lessons. She might develop some talent. She's so clever at everything."

"Oh, I forgot. She sent you a message to the effect that paints were a bit messy and she thought she'd try writing. Clean, easy work, she said."

They laughed in spite of themselves.

"I've got a man working on a specially designed piano," he went on. "Some device to take the place of foot pedaling. Hope he strikes it right. That would mean more to her than anything. And of course her new car's ready for her but she doesn't seem . . . and I can't. . . ."

"No!" Mrs. Catherby cried out. "Not the car yet. None of us could stand the thought of that for a while."

Kirkland rose abruptly and, with one of his rare caresses to her, bent and kissed her forehead.

"I must go, Ellie. Thanks for everything. Sorry I've not been a brighter guest but you've done me good—maybe more than meets the eye."

"I'm glad you came," she said simply. "Just tell Anne I sent my love. She'll know the rest."

She waved him off, smiling, fighting back the tears.

Kirkland stopped at the front door as he always did to confer with Hawley, and slip a bill into his seamed hand.

"Take good care of her," he said. "Call me anytime, day or night, if she should not be well. She's not so young now."

The old colored man was serious in his devotion.

"I know, Mistah Kirkland, an' I watches her like a hawk. You can trust me an' thank you, suh."

Kirkland got into his car and drove home more slowly than was his wont. A light rain was falling and even though it was chill there was in it the delicate, insistent presence of spring. Indescribable, this essence, but present, penetrating the senses, far beyond man's power to manipulate, to force or to retard. Subtly, commandingly, the world was young again.

Kirkland felt this without words, and the knowledge made his determination grim and impregnable. This very night he must face the startling thought that had come to him in Ellie's quiet living room, come with the force of an exploding bomb and torn through his mind with a flash of incredible potential. This very night he would settle the matter with himself, at least. He stepped on the accelerator and the car sped forward.

Once in the hall at home he was greeted by a burst of laughter, and then silence. He walked down to the library and stood at the door unobserved. The room looked brighter now than it had even in the afternoon sun when he and Dr. Hertzog had stood here together; for a fire crackled gaily on the hearth and great bowls of yellow daffodils stood about. In the center four young girls sat at a card table, intent upon their game. Anne's chair (one of the many he had had made for her) was just like the others, above the table, at least. She looked up now suddenly and called out to him.

"Quiet, Jimmy. I've bid six spades doubled and I think I'm going to make them!"

"Go ahead. I'm not going to bother you. Just looked in. Gran sent her love," he added.

The others greeted him with varying degrees of familiarity and Anne blew him a kiss. He nodded to Miss Davis, sitting unobtrusively with her knitting in a far corner of the room. It was well. Davy would look after everything. He had been wise to comb both America and Britain to find her. Nurse, companion, friend—just what Anne needed. He would go on now to his own study across the hall and not see Anne again that night. It was better so.

Once in the study he closed the door and sat down at his desk, where a light was always kept burning for his return. In this spot he did his real planning, received and made his most important political phone calls, and saw visitors whom he did not care to have come to his downtown office, and was never, never disturbed by extraneous matters.

With the intensity of concentration of which he was capable, he now set himself to review his thinking of the last few hours. He was a man accustomed to swift and irrevocable decisions. So, now, the greatest, most important of his life must be made without delay.

The money was useless. Even he, ruthless and unscrupulous as he was in its use, had been at once bitterly aware of that. The delicacy —strange for him—which had controlled his intimate relations with Alice held still in his consuming love for his daughter. But the thought that had struck him with violence at Ellie's was that he held in his hands another negotiable asset; less sordid, less crass, more fluid, more compelling to the right person even than money. And simultaneously with the thought there had appeared in his mind the face of a young man, strong even as his own, with keen gray eyes and determined chin. It was Paul Devereux who was looking up at the ladder whose heights Kirkland himself controlled.

Sentence by sentence—graven as they were upon his brain—he went over again now the last conversation with Hertzog. The anguish of mortal uncertainty lay upon each word. And yet that faint, evanescent possibility, too dim to be called even a hope, in connection with Anne must not be disregarded; must not even be postponed.

When the call came at nine-thirty, he was ready. He thought, as he answered, that Arno never failed him. Kirkland with his usual unerring eye for ability had picked him up as a grubby messenger boy, fifteen years before, and had made him into his own right hand. Arno had now become not only the peerless secretary but even adviser in political matters, for by this time he was wise in the ways of the *haut monde* as well as the gutter.

"Chief?"

"Go ahead, Arno."

"Well, I went through the files on the precinct workers and here's what I have on young Devereux. Lawyer with the firm of Hartwell & Harvey; thirty, unmarried, lives at a rooming house on the north side. And I might add just on my own opinion, ambitious as the devil. That's all at the moment."

"Okay. Get in touch with him the first thing in the morning and ask him if he'll have lunch with me at the Down Town Club at one, and be prepared to spend an hour afterwards with me in my office. If he can't make it tomorrow, then the next day."

"I rather think he'll be able to make it," Arno drawled. "And I believe you've got a right hunch, Chief, about that young fellah. I heard him too, you know, at that Young Politicians' Club."

"That's right. You did. Well, thanks, Arno. Goodnight."

Kirkland sat looking into space, avoiding the eyes of the two pictures which stood upon his desk. Nothing, *nothing* could be predicted until after their talk. There were plenty of general matters he could discuss if he didn't like the young fellow at close range. If he did. . . .

It was very late, and the house quiet when he rose, put out the light and left the room. He walked past the elevator concealed in the paneling, which always smote his heart with a physical pain by its tragic significance. He went on slowly and heavily to the staircase and there he stopped, as though the decision were all to be made anew.

For the terrifying possibilities of the course to which he was committed again overcame him. A wrenching doubt assailed him, the like of which he had never known before; a shattering doubt of himself, of his judgment, of his power. Was it ever possible to tamper with impunity with those poles of tendency of which the poet had written?

An alien fear settled upon him, a weakness that drained his very members. His head sank on his breast, his hand clutched for the newel, as the tortured words beat within his brain.

Who am I to do this thing? I am not God!

When he looked up at last he saw the curving steps where Anne's feet had been used to go so lightly, so fleetly up and down. His lips, though white, became once more firm and implacable.

"But I am her father," he said aloud.

2

◄§ KIRKLAND SLEPT late after a restless night, but even when he was dressed and ready to go downstairs there was still no sound from Anne's room as he paused tensely outside to listen. This quiet was ominous, for as a rule her door was open and she was sitting propped up in bed, eager for a chat when he came by. They even breakfasted together sometimes by her window. He realized he had hoped for that this morning.

But the closed door and the silence meant that for her too the dark night had been heavy with bitter fruit, and only ultimate exhaustion had released her from the weight. There was no sign of Miss Davis either and he felt a sharp twinge of jealousy as he thought that perhaps she had shared those hidden hours of anguish instead of himself.

He went slowly down the stairs to the dining room, where Hackett was holding his chair. He managed the brief morning amenities, scanned the newspaper headlines, drank his coffee eagerly, but found he could do little with breakfast. The burden upon his heart was so heavy that he felt he could not set forth upon the day without more human companionship than Hackett's austere presence offered. He decided to call Ellie. She was sure to be up.

He gave the number to Hackett and in a moment the extension phone was in his hand.

"Oh, Ellie?"

"Good morning, Jimmy. I'm glad you called me."

"Are you all right?"

"Yes, of course. How is Anne?"

"She's still asleep. They probably played bridge until all hours last night, but still . . . it's so late now. . . ."

"Yes," the old woman's voice was drowned in sadness, "she would not feel the whole force of it until she was finally alone and quiet in bed."

"That's what I thought. I have to get to the office now, but you'll call her later on?"

"Of course. I've been trying to think of something new and startling to take her out of herself at once. I'll keep on."

"Ellie?"

"Yes."

"Did you ever settle something in your own mind after the best thought you could put on it, and then waver? Decide and doubt. Doubt and decide. Did you?"

For answer Mrs. Catherby laughed, a musical sound that belied her years.

"You ask *a woman* that? I never came to an important decision in my life that I didn't make and unmake it a dozen times. That's the way the feminine mind works. But I'll tell you something, Jimmy."

"What?"

"I've come to believe in the Law of the First Intention. At least that's what I call it."

"How do you mean?"

"Well, I think your first impulse may not be the *wisest* from certain points of view but is likely to be the best in the long run."

"You really think so?"

"I do."

"Thanks, Ellie. I've got to go, but you've been a help as usual. Take care of yourself now."

"I never know what you're up to, Jimmy, but if it's good, God bless you with it."

"I need some blessing. Well, goodbye."

He felt better as he left the house, though there was still no sign of life on the second floor. When he reached the office, his usual confidence was taking possession of him. He felt more secure at his desk here than in his study at home. It boldly represented the accomplishment of the years—this massively carved and polished piece of furniture which might have stood in a king's council chamber. To Kirkland it was a symbol of the victory that had crowned the struggle. He rang for Arno and the man was instantly beside him.

He was of medium height with an extraordinary breadth of shoulders. Anne's one-time laughing comment, "There but for the grace of you, Dad, goes a gangster of the first water," seemed borne out by the heavy features and the sharp, enigmatic black eyes. As though to complete the look sinister a scar, innocently enough come by in a boyish fight, ran across one cheek. When he smiled, however, this somewhat malevolent expression was dispelled. The lines of intensity did not leave his face, but the forcefulness then was a friendly one. Men as a rule liked Arno, and as he often said brusquely, he had no time for women.

"Well, Chief," he began now as Kirkland leafed through the letters before him, "I got young Devereux this morning on the phone. It was like I thought. He jumped at the chance of lunch with you. One o'clock, I told him, at the Down Town Club and perhaps an hour here later. He's got a lot on the ball, that fellah. What's on your mind about him?"

"Oh, just want to size him up a little. Material for something, maybe, some time."

Arno watched the older man worshipfully.

"Yeah, when you pick 'em you really pick 'em. I fixed the meeting up for Friday night at Barney's, too. Okay?"

Kirkland nodded. "I haven't too much time before lunch. Better send Miss Sayles in and I'll get at this mail."

"Those are the most important ones." He paused, glancing at the photograph on the desk of a young laughing girl, her face raised to the sun.

"And . . . Miss Anne?"

Kirkland shook his head. "Nothing," he said. "Dr. Hertzog has gone. I can't talk about it."

Arno went out without a word and in a moment Miss Sayles, tailored, efficient, inscrutable and not so young, entered.

"She's as restful to me as a live Buddha," Kirkland had once told his mother-in-law. "With most people you get tangled up in their personalities somehow, and it's distracting. But with Sayles I can concentrate as well as though I were looking at a blank wall."

"As sexless as that?" Ellie had asked smiling.

"Absolutely. I wouldn't be surprised one day to see the typewriter growing right out of the ends of her fingers. One machine."

"I'd like to meet her," Mrs. Catherby had said.

"Well, if anybody could humanize her you could. But don't you dare," he had added. "I want her as she is."

She took his dictation now with amazing speed, sometimes stopping him with "I can finish that, I think," or merely nodding assent when he said, "Reply to this one in the usual way."

When the first stack of letters was finished he turned to another group, his brows contracting. The coal business he knew thoroughly. His father as a young man had left the collieries in Scotland to come to the New World, hoping to make his fortune in a different fashion.

But the old had claimed him even in the midst of the new and he had gone to work again in the mines, though this time in an American setting. So the young James had grown up in the shadow of the tipple and the coke ovens. The "works" had been his college until he had mastered the industry. Then at twenty-five, with his savings in his pocket and a relentless ambition pointing up his native sagacity, he had taken a chance on buying an option on a hitherto overlooked farm. The veins of coal he had suspected had been there. His climb up had begun.

It had been a long, rugged way but to him the struggle was part of the prize. Now, when he was sixty, his own works stretched for miles along the valley and the hills beyond the city. The coal business, then, held for him no surprises, and at this point relatively few problems except the normal ones of administration. It was the other great interest that had curiously overtaken him along the way, which now gave to him the compelling zest of the eternally devious and challenging.

He picked up a letter and stared through Miss Sayles and beyond before he began, more slowly, to give the name and address. "My dear Senator," he went on. "As it looks now, we will be able to nominate Halsey for governor. I am quite confident he can be elected if the Barker interests don't get the upper hand. I count upon you to use all the influence you can muster to prevent that. Needless to say our organization here is doing its utmost. Halsey still seems to me the best man. His record will sound good, he's proved himself a strong campaigner, he has popular appeal, and yet will be open to—shall we say suggestion—as he goes along. I'm glad you concur in all this. I will be happy to receive any suggestions you may have. I can even make it convenient to take a trip to the capital if a conference seems advisable at this point. Very truly yours. Mark the envelope 'Personal,' Miss Sayles."

It was nearing one and the nervousness he had felt at breakfast was now again gripping him hard. He dismissed Sayles, pulled himself together and prepared to start out.

"I've ordered a table for you, Chief," Arno said, coming in again. "Place gets pretty crowded about this time."

"I wonder if I'll know Devereux? I've never talked to him except in a group. All at once I can't remember him too clearly."

Arno looked at his boss keenly. This last remark was out of character. The chief remembered everybody he wanted to remember after a single meeting! Could recall them years after. What had hit him now about young Devereux?

"Oh, you couldn't miss him," he said carelessly. "Tall, brown hair, pretty neat dresser. Anyway he'll know you for sure."

"When we get back here, I do not want any interruptions of any nature," Kirkland said. "That goes for you too, Arno."

Once again Arno's black eyes looked puzzled.

"Okay, Chief. I'll see to it."

As Kirkland drove to the club he felt a cold sweat breaking upon him, along with a faint touch of nausea. In spite of himself his hands kept straining and clenching each other while a weakness seemed to creep up from his legs to his head.

"Should have eaten a proper breakfast," he muttered. "Need food, that's all."

Once at the club there was no difficulty in locating his guest. The young man was already in the lobby, watching the door. He came forward eagerly and Kirkland had a swift, pleasurable impression. Devereux was tall, as Arno had said, with a slender face, brown hair, gray eyes, and a strong cleft chin.

"Mr. Kirkland! This is a pleasure." Good smile he's got, the older man was thinking.

"Ah, Devereux! Nice of you to join me today. Wait till I get rid of this hat. . . ."

The headwaiter was obsequious.

"Mr. Kirkland! This way, please. We kept a quiet spot for you . . . here in the alcove."

They sat down at the table in a tall bay window that looked off to the river and the hills beyond.

"Cocktail, Devereux?"

"No thanks. Not at lunch, if you don't mind, sir."

"Good! Never do myself then unless I have to. Makes me fuzzy somehow for the afternoon. Well, find something you like. I'll start with soup—any kind so long as it's good and hot, Wilson," he added to the waiter.

"I'll join you with that."

They finished ordering in that light accord which comes of congenial tastes in food, and then, as was his custom, Kirkland started directly, almost brusquely, upon his questioning.

"So, Devereux, I am to assume you're interested in politics, eh?"

"Yes, sir," the young man replied levelly, "I am."

"Why?"

After the sharp monosyllable they sat looking at each other as though taking measure. Devereux's gray eyes grew cold and keen. Kirkland stared back at him with the penetration and intensity of years of experience showing under the half-closed lids.

"Why?" he repeated.

"I suppose you want the truth?"

"Naturally."

"I think," Devereux said slowly, "that there is a direct relation between ego and a certain kind of ambition. There are men who want quiet, even-tenored lives. They do not want to be bothered by any interests outside their work and their families. There are others who crave power. They want a part in manipulating men and events to their will. I am one of the latter."

"And you think this is . . . *ego?*"

"Well, I've come to believe that the man who is ambitious for power usually thinks rather highly of himself. If he doesn't he'll never get anywhere. You see, I'm being honest."

For a minute there was silence. Then Kirkland shot another question.

"You're not married?"

"No, sir."

"Are your affections engaged in any way?"

The young man smiled even as a faint reserve crept into his voice.

"No, they are not at the present, though I certainly do not intend to live a celibate life. The thing is that I've stuck pretty closely to my work and so far I haven't met. . . ."

"All right! You'll understand later I wasn't prying. Have you a political goal already set for yourself?"

"Yes. I would like some day to be governor of this state."

"Why stop there?"

They both laughed a little.

"The ultimate always beckons but after all, there must be milestones on every journey!" Devereux replied.

Kirkland suddenly looked immensely gratified. For long years he had been accustomed to sizing men up almost at sight with an uncanny accuracy.

"I like your straightforwardness and your honesty. I like your whole getup, young man. Well, let's get on with our lunch and then go back to my office. I want to talk to you privately."

For the rest of the meal he spoke with almost a lightness of spirit about other things, coming back occasionally to the personal.

"By the way, where do you hail from? City-bred?"

Devereux shook his head. "No, I come of country stock. Northwestern end of the state. On my paternal side they were practically all farmers. On my mother's there were some professional men, but I'm country-born myself."

"Um-hm. Well, a rural background never did a politician any harm. The fact is it's a big asset. The common touch, you know. A country-bred man can always learn to get on with city people, but a town-bred fellah never gets the real hang of the country. You can put city polish *on* a man, but by golly, it seems you can't ever rub it off him. Well, if you're finished, let's be going."

On the way back to the office Kirkland was silent. Now that he liked the young man unreservedly he was struck by the possibility that Devereux might be entirely averse to the strange suggestion about to be presented to him. In proportion to his desirability there grew the shattering fear of his refusal. It was characteristic of Kirkland that his doubts before had been of his own judgment and of the findings of his opinion, never of the other's acquiescence.

Once in the office, with the doors closed, Kirkland motioned Devereux to sit down, then took his own place and plunged at once, with heedless disregard of the weight in his breast, into speech.

"You must have wondered why I got in touch with you today when I hardly know you. You will be more surprised when you learn the truth. For I am going to make you a proposition which I hope with all my soul you will agree to."

He paused. "I have made some strange *deals* in my time but this is by far the strangest."

He reached for the photograph on the desk and turned it to face the young man.

"My daughter," he said.

An instant feeling of approval crossed Kirkland's troubled mind. Devereux inclined his head slightly as though acknowledging an introduction but made no comment. Instead, a look of withdrawal, of dignified wariness passed over his face. Kirkland liked this. The man then had independence and integrity of spirit. A small or *cheap* man would have given some sign of gratification as he leaped to a rather obvious conclusion.

"My only child," Kirkland went on. "She is twenty-two. Wellesley, last year, with a *Magna Cum*. Eight months ago she was in an automobile accident. She has not walked since. She may never walk . . . again."

He swallowed slowly.

"I have just had a European specialist over to confer. He gave no hope. None of the doctors do, though they can find no actual cause for the paralysis. They are all convinced that it is not caused by nervous shock or hysteria and yet there is just one chance in a million that it may be."

He told him then, averting his eyes, of Dr. Hertzog's last conversation with him; then the air about them grew suddenly heavy with suspense.

"What I am about to propose to you is this: if you can succeed in winning my daughter's interest to the extent of her being willing to marry you, if you will become her husband for a period of—say, three years, I will support you in your political career to the fullest extent of my ability. I suppose you know what that is."

Paul Devereux looked like a man who had received a blow full on the face. The color had left it, so that the prominent cheekbones seemed apparent through the skin. His lips above the long, cleft chin were drawn in as though from pain and his eyes were narrowed and strained.

"Why the three years?" he asked huskily.

Kirkland leaned forward. "Because I consider it only fair that if after that period of marriage nothing has happened to change her condition, you should be free. I would have some sort of instrument drawn up and signed that this was our sworn agreement."

"And she—your daughter—would she also sign it?"

Kirkland leaped from his chair. "Good God, man, have I omitted the *sine qua non* of the whole thing? My daughter must never by word or look from you know the truth! She must be made to feel you are in love with her. If she doubted you, there would be no marriage. Can't you see that? You must court her as any man would court a young woman, try to win her affection, go through with it on that basis. It's the only way it can be done."

"And then," Devereux moistened his lips, "after conceivably getting her to care for me, I would be free to leave her in three years' time, regardless of her feelings?"

It was Kirkland's turn to pale. The anguish on his face was hard to witness. When he answered his voice was harsh with the stress of his pain.

"I have thought of everything. Last night I lived through every possible situation that might arise. I still feel I must take this chance if you will agree to it."

Devereux's answer was immediate and decisive.

"I am sorry, Mr. Kirkland, but I cannot undertake to do what you ask."

Kirkland sat very still for a full minute. Then he spoke again.

"It is hard for me to lay bare my soul to you. It is not easy for me to plead with anyone. I have never done it before in my life. But now I beg, I plead with you to do one thing. Come to my home, meet Anne, and then after that take time to consider. Think over carefully the advantages to yourself. No one can be sure of anything in this world, least of all in politics. But I am in a position to do more to advance you than any other man in the state. . . ."

As the young man before him started to speak, Kirkland stopped him.

"Will you do this one thing, which of course carries no obligation whatsoever? Come to dinner at my home. Will you do that much for me?"

"Of . . . of course," Devereux stammered, plainly moved by Kirkland's appeal. "If you understand that I. . . ."

"I understand perfectly. Suppose we pretend none of this conversation has taken place. Suppose we begin at this present moment. Are you free tonight, Devereux? Could you dine with us?"

"*Tonight?*" His voice was amazed.

"Tonight, at seven. Can you come?"

"Why . . . yes, I'm free. Yes . . . thank you, I can come." He still sounded dazed.

"Good. We'll see you then. I'll send the car for you. And Devereux?"

"Yes."

Kirkland stood before him, his features suddenly like iron.

"Will you give me your word of honor that nothing that has been spoken here today will ever be repeated by you to Anne? No matter what happens?"

Devereux's eyes met his in a straight line.

"I can promise you that, sir, with all my heart."

"Swear it?"

Devereux raised his hand. "I swear it," he said.

As he was going out the door, Kirkland called after him. "Oh, by the way, black tie, if you don't mind. Anne doesn't have much chance to dress now!"

"Of course," Devereux answered. "I understand."

When he was gone Kirkland picked up the phone and called his home. Hackett answered.

"Is Miss Anne resting?"

"I'll find out, sir."

In a minute Anne's voice came, light, buoyant, natural.

"So you sneaked out on me this morning. Was that nice?"

"I thought you were asleep."

"Well, as a matter of fact I was. I thought those girls never would leave last night. What a game!"

"Did you make your bid? That what-you-may-call-it, doubled?"

"Oh, that. No, they set us, the dogs. Down one. Well, how's the big outside world today?"

"So-so. I've asked a man to dinner tonight. Tell Perth to scare up a good one."

"What's his type? Roast beef or truffles?"

"Oh, I don't know. Anything. Just thought I'd better tell you in advance, though, to keep Perth in a good humor."

Anne groaned slightly. "I'll talk to her. And I hope this one won't be as deadly as that last one you brought. You know, Jimmy, every time one of your candidates gets elected you should display a banner reading, 'Anne did her part.'"

Her father laughed. "I'll do that. Well, do your hostess stuff tonight. None can do it better. And dress up."

"For the man? Is he so important?"

"For me. I like to look at you."

"Flatterer. All right, I'll give him the works and you too."

Suddenly her voice dropped its banter. "Jimmy?"

"Yes?"

"Come home early if you can. I haven't seen you in a long time." She hung up abruptly.

Kirkland wiped his eyes, rang for Arno, and settled himself to work.

At two minutes to seven that evening Paul Devereux was deposited at the Kirkland home. He had never seen this section and before he rang he stood on the pillared portico looking about him. Here on West Hill resided those who had made their wealth in the mills and factories and surrounding mines which gave the city its fame across the world, and then, like ungrateful sons, had retired as far as was practically possible from the industries which nourished them. Here were not only wide lawns but wooded estates. Here, around the great houses of stone or many cupolaed brown shingles, spring could pour her alembic and the smoke and smog become clear, perfume-laden air. There was fine planting on the Kirkland lawns: the dozen white birches trembled with delicate new green; the flowering japonicas by the wall were all ablush, and the dogwood budding white. The larger trees were pregnant with swelling buds and the grass an intensely living green.

Paul drew a long breath, partly from appreciation of the beauty, partly because of the nervous tension in his chest. The latter had been increasing all the way out from the city. If he had dared, he would have stopped the car at several points and, upon some pretext, sent the chauffeur on his way and would himself have gone back to his furnished room on the other side of the city. He was embarrassed, he was puzzled, he was afraid. For, in spite of Kirkland's assurances, there was the danger that some obligation might attach to him because of this dinner.

Suddenly from the nearby maple came a sound that since his boyhood had stirred him with indefinable longing: it was the spring twilight note of a robin. He had not heard it for several years, but it had its old power to move him with an inner desire for a far, fulfilled bliss—a bliss which this evening might in some strange way threaten. He stood listening, the weight of a portent falling upon him; and yet he could not now turn back. With a slow gesture he rang the bell.

The door opened at once and Hackett took his coat and hat.

"Mr. Kirkland is not down yet, sir," he said in a low voice, "but he told me to ask you to step along the hall to the library at the back. Miss Anne is there, sir, and expects you. The last door, to the right."

There was no other way. He walked along toward the room indicated, the deep velvet carpet swallowing up his footfalls. There was, indeed, an oppressive silence all around. Why couldn't the butler fellow have come along and announced him? he thought. This business of barging in on the girl, *alone,* was intolerable. He hesitated and glanced behind him but the butler had now disappeared. What should he do when he reached the door, or even before that, to inform the girl of his approach? It was all so damned awkward. Kirkland had no right to leave him like this.

He tried to cough slightly but his throat felt frozen and no sound came. Still the silence. He went on until he stood at the doorway itself. Here, rooted, he remained.

Beside the fire sat a young woman, her head supported by her hand, as she leaned on the arm of her chair, watching the flaming logs. Alone, as she felt herself to be, there was no conventional mask upon her face; instead, an unutterable sadness lay open upon her features, a still, subdued anguish of soul far, far beyond her years.

She wore a yellow gown that matched in color the daffodils and forsythia on table and desk, and rendered at once more vivid and more incredible the blond gold of her hair. The deep neckline and tight bodice of the dress showed the lovely young curves of her body; the skirt fell billowing around the chair. Her face, though now half averted, seemed to Paul the most beautiful he had ever seen.

Suddenly she drew her breath in a sigh as of irremediable grief. And as he heard it Paul also seemed to hear again the note of the robin. Once more he felt the old inner longing but now it had become a yearning over the girl sitting so near to him but unconscious of his presence or even of his being. All his man's strength leaped within him in an urge to comfort her, protect her from her sorrow. Instinctively he moved back into the hall, startled by the force of his pity.

He looked anxiously toward the stairs but there was still no sign of Kirkland. It came over him then that his reception was premeditated. His host had wanted him to see the girl before she saw him. If so, the plan had fulfilled itself. He realized, though, that he could not stand silently here much longer; he must go to meet her and he knew that now the duty accorded with his own desire. He spoke suddenly aloud as though to Hackett.

"This way? The room to the right? Thank you. I'll find it."

When he stood again in the doorway, the girl was sitting erect, her features set in a fixed smile which changed to a look of surprise as he went forward.

"I'm Paul Devereux. I hope you're expecting me. Mr. Kirkland asked me to dinner and I was told to come on in here. . . ."

"Of course, Mr. Devereux. We are expecting you." She reached her hand cordially. "It is only that you gave me a slight shock. You see, most of the guests my father brings home are his own contemporaries . . . or at least on the very middle-aged side."

Paul smiled. "I'm afraid I'm not hoary either in head or wisdom but I'm glad he made an exception of me."

"So am I. Do sit down. I'll ring for Hackett and get him to call Father. He's probably taking a nap. He often does before dinner."

"Why disturb him, then?" He moved to the sofa near her chair and sat down. "When I'm wakened suddenly I'm apt to be horribly cross. If he should react like that he might change his mind and send me away."

They laughed together over the foolish words and as they did so, Paul was acutely aware of a certain radiant quality in her face. There was, as she laughed, a brightness like dawn itself in her eyes. This, he thought, is the way she must have looked all the time before the accident.

"It's delightful to see a wood fire," he said aloud, somewhat at random. "So few people have them nowadays. I wonder why?"

"Because," Anne said promptly, "they think only of the warmth which they don't need with modern heating. They forget all the other things that go with an open fire. Cheerfulness, for instance, and companionship. Burning logs can carry on quite a conversation!"

"Oh, can't they, though! Have you ever heard apple wood talking? It's the most loquacious of all. You really can't get a word in edgeways."

They smiled at each other in the sudden delight of matching minds, then looked up as Kirkland entered the room.

"Good evening, Devereux. I see you and Anne have made each other's acquaintance. I told Hackett to show you in here if I wasn't down."

When the men were seated Hackett appeared with a tray and a pleasant relaxation fell upon them in spite of undercurrents.

"This young fellah thinks he'd like a political career, Anne," Kirkland said a little later. "You might give him your views on the subject."

Anne made a small *moue.*

"My sex inhibits my language unfortunately. What I think of politics I can't say."

Paul looked at her in surprise. "Why, you do feel strongly about it. What's the matter with politics? Somebody has to run things."

"I know. That's the trouble. It's heady business. Men get drunk on it. Take Jimmy here. He was a nice, modest, sober businessman once, I'm told, with enough to do to run his coal mines, but he had to get mixed up in politics. Now he'd like to run the universe."

She looked roguishly at Paul and lowered her voice. "And with just a *little* help from God he probably could."

The men chuckled and Kirkland looked at her proudly.

"Now tell him the *besides,* Anne. That's when you always get the truth from a woman, Devereux."

"Well," the girl said, *"besides,* then, I get tired entertaining the kind of politicians he brings home—the kind I supposed *you* were," she nodded to Paul. "Then if it were only the mines he had on his mind he could retire now and have some fun instead of wearing himself out over who gets which office. It makes me very mad," she added. "So senseless!"

Paul threw back his head and laughed with relief.

"I'll remember that *besides.* It's very illuminating. But we'll have to convince her yet, Mr. Kirkland, of the value of politics per se, won't we?"

Hackett announced dinner and there was a second of embarrassment as a quick shadow fell upon Anne's face. Kirkland started over toward her but Paul, as he stood now, caught sight of the narrow bar on the back of the girl's chair and with a few steps was there before him, grasping it.

"Please let me," he said, beginning to move her gently. "This makes me think I'm a boy again. I knew a little girl back home who had a small red sleigh with a handbar like this. I used to be proud as Punch when she'd let me push her."

Anne turned her head quickly and looked up at him. There was a mist in her eyes.

"You're sweet," she whispered, huskily.

As they traversed the long hall she made a brief explanation.

"I have a wheel chair, of course, for daytime, but this type which Father had made for me does seem a little more dress-up for evenings."

When they reached the dining room doorway, Paul gave an involuntary exclamation of pleasure. Anne looked up quickly.

"You like it?"

"It's the loveliest room I've ever seen!" he answered with feeling.

"I'm glad you said that. You know, we rather judge people by their reaction to it. Now, we can tell him all the story, can't we, Jimmy?"

Kirkland nodded, though, Paul thought, with some slight reluctance.

"It was like this," Anne went on eagerly as they took their places at the table. "My mother held very definite views about a dining room. She believed the Arabs were right about the sacredness of breaking bread together, and she felt that it is at mealtime that a family is always united and perhaps as children grow older, the only time they are. So, she always said that the dining room was the heart of the home and should be the most beautiful room in it."

Paul's eyes moved to the chandelier above the gleaming table. Its crystals fell like a shower of iridescent raindrops. Anne's glance followed him.

"That was made to order in a little town in Czechoslovakia. It came over in tiny pieces, each wrapped in cotton and tissue paper. I can remember the thrill of seeing it assembled. The oak paneling came from England and the carving above it with the little animals was done in Switzerland, according to Mother's own sketches. The mantel motto was done by the same people."

"I've been looking at that," Paul said, "but my Latin is pretty rusty, I'm afraid, except for legal terms."

"It's *Benedictus benedicat,* an old form of Grace before a meal. I've always liked it. *May the Blessed One bless,*" she translated in a low voice with a faint catch in it.

And yet, Paul was thinking, she seems free from bitterness. How can she accept this fate? How can she be gay and conversational and natural in the face of the cruel sentence of yesterday? If he had not heard that heartbreaking sigh earlier when she felt she was quite alone, he would not have realized the effort behind her light words. A brave girl. Yes, a fine, beautiful, brave girl!

"I think," Kirkland was saying now, "that you've given enough details, haven't you?"

"I know," Anne laughed. "It's in shockingly poor taste but he really brought it on himself. You see I caught his look and it was *honest!* The admiration. Wasn't it?" She appealed to Devereux.

"It could not have been more so. And you're paying me a great compliment, you know, by telling me all this. I'm quite aware of it. Won't you go on?"

"That's kind of you. I'll tell you just one more thing and then I'll stop. You can look closer at the carvings after dinner if you wish. We have a different color of hangings for each season. Sort of like the ecclesiastical changes," she laughed, "only ours are purely secular. Yellow for spring, green for summer, a rosy rust for autumn, and bright red for winter. It's a nice idea, don't you think? It was hers, also. Now that's all. It's someone else's turn to talk."

It became a gay meal, as far as Paul and Anne were concerned. It was as though they had both buried for the time being the disturbing secrets of their hearts and were rejoicing in the bright, transitory surface play of youth. Paul exerted himself to the utmost to be entertaining and conversation became momentarily easier, touching upon a dozen themes. They laughed a great deal, too, trying always to draw Kirkland into the circle of their mirth. He, watching keenly under his heavy, graying brows, eating little because of his taut nerves, forced a smile now and then but that was all. To himself, however, he kept repeating over and over: *They're getting on together. They're really getting on.*

When the leisurely dinner was finished, Paul again took possession of her chair as Hackett approached it.

"No, please let me. I like to. Besides, I would like to make the rounds of the carvings."

At close range the delicate, whimsical charm of the designs became more apparent. They moved slowly from wall to wall, with Anne pointing out to him her favorites: the rabbit, the squirrel, the Brownie under a mayapple umbrella, the tiny leprechauns, the spirited little pony with its flying mane. ("She copied that from a merry-go-round," Anne explained.)

"It's perfectly fascinating!" Paul said. "How you must love it all, having grown up with it."

He paused before the fireplace, reading aloud slowly the words carved along the mantel front, and then looked up to the portrait hanging above it. It was of a young woman with dark, bright eyes and lightly smiling lips. The hair, the expression and the shape of the face were the same as Anne's. Only the dark eyes and the evidence of height were different.

"It was sensitive of you not to speak of the picture at dinner," Anne said. "I didn't mention it for I know it hurts Father yet to talk about it. It was painted from a photograph but it's an excellent likeness, the best we have. We thought this room was the place for it. Now come, I'll show you my final pet."

It proved to be a small monkey carved as though in glee by the artist, his small face shrewd and appealing as he extended a tiny cap clutched in his paw.

Paul examined him with delight. "He's my favorite of them all!" he exclaimed. "Has he a name?"

Anne looked up as though startled. "Yes, but how did you guess?"

"Oh, because he's so real. Not that they all aren't, but this little chap looks as if he might jump on your shoulder any minute. What do you call him, or is it a secret?"

"No," said Anne, "not really. It's just that nobody ever asked before. I named him Binkie, I don't know why."

"Suits him perfectly." Paul extracted a penny from his pocket and laid it solemnly in the tiny cap where it lodged.

"He probably expected a dime," he added whimsically.

"Oh, you mustn't spoil him," Anne laughed.

The trip back to the library was made to seem almost natural by their light chatter.

When coffee was finished Kirkland was called to the telephone. There was a decidedly obvious quality in the arrangement that followed but Paul heard his words with no sense of panic.

"I find I have to spend a little time in the study," Kirkland announced nervously. "It's unfortunate just this evening, but some things have come up. Would you mind dropping in on me there later, Devereux? Just across the hall. No hurry, of course, but I would like to discuss a few matters with you. Maybe you young folks can find something to talk about meanwhile."

"I wouldn't be surprised," Paul answered, smiling, and then he and Anne were once more alone.

He put a fresh log on the fire, stirred it to new blaze, then having lighted her cigarette and his own, dropped to the hearth rug.

"Do you mind if I sit here," he asked. "I always used to at home. With the cat."

"The cat?" Anne echoed in surprise.

"Oh, yes, we always had one. Haven't you?"

Anne shook her head. "Never. I don't believe the thought of one ever entered anyone's head, here."

"But wouldn't you like one? It would be a great pet for you. Sit on your knee while you read and. . . ."

"On *my knee?*" The slight catch in her voice smote his heart but he went on lightly.

"Absolutely. You'd have to push it off when you tired of it. They like to be close to people. I'll tell you! Couldn't I send you a kitten? Instead of flowers, for instance," he asked, laughing.

She was looking at him with a peculiar intentness.

"You are the strangest young man I've ever met," she said gently. "But I love your choice of a gift. I know it would give me a lot of pleasure."

"Good. I'll start hunting right away, for this must be a very superior feline. It may take a little time, though."

"I'll be looking forward to it and I'll name it for you. Let's see . . . oh, I know! Devvie, short for Devereux. How's that?"

"Fine, for if he gets to be a nuisance it could stand for *Devil*, too."

They laughed again, as it was easy for them to do, then slowly drifted into reminiscences of their childhood—always a dangerous theme if the conversation is to remain impersonal. In swift flashes now they saw into each other's hearts.

"My parents are both gone. My father was quite an old bachelor when he married and my mother wasn't young herself when I was born. We lived on a farm but it wasn't a hard-scrabble kind. We were pretty comfortable as country life goes. The fellows from college were always begging to come along home for vacations. I love the old place and I still own it, though it's probably not good business to keep it. . . ."

She told him of her little girlhood and of her mother, bringing forth small memories to lay before him, at first hesitantly, then with assurance as she looked into the warmth of his eyes. The past of each lost its blankness for the other and became clear and living between them. They reviewed college days and the congeniality of certain courses. He told her of his present work in the law firm of Hartwell & Harvey, drawing an amusing but affectionate portrait of old Harrison Hartwell, the senior member.

"You would like Gran," she said impulsively. "And when she knows you are actually fond of poetry she'll give you the accolade! That is her absolute diet. She's eighty but she's wonderful. You really must meet her soon. . . ."

Her quick, eager voice suddenly dropped and a look of embarrassment came over her face. He divined the reason, spoke naturally in reply, and then went on talking to cover the small painful break. As he did so his heart felt again the sharp stab of pity which had struck him as he heard from the doorway her unconscious sigh. In addition to this he was increasingly conscious of her beauty and of a certain rare sweetness of spirit. Just as he also realized that their minds met with an immediacy he had not before experienced with any other girl.

"Oh, yes," he heard himself saying in answer to a question, "I have plenty of faults, heaven knows! All the evil passions man is heir to, I guess. Of course I try to keep them caged but I hear them growling sometimes."

"And ambition is one, isn't it? I mean the kind that never lets you rest, that is driving you headlong into politics, for instance?"

"You call that a fault?" His tone was quick and surprised.

"If it's too intense," she answered. "I've watched Jimmy." She stopped and looked into the fire for a moment, then went on, slowly.

"If a man is ambitious in order to accomplish some great good he can't very well make a mistake. But if he only wants to play the big game in order to have his own way in moving the pawns . . . well, I'm not so sure."

He sat, quiet, watching her, considering how he might be honest with her and yet stand up for his own longing for power. The light that illumined her face when she laughed, brightened now.

"That wasn't very polite of me. You did right not to answer. Maybe, as Gran says, all women are unconsciously a little jealous of men. They, the women, you know, are rather left behind when the men make their journeys to Samarkand."

"I'm afraid I don't recognize the allusion. Stupid of me."

"Oh, no! It's from a poem—a play rather—that isn't too familiar. It's Gran who often quotes from it. I think Samarkand stands for the masculine goal, the big quest, you know, that the strong men, the ambitious ones are always setting out upon."

She made a light gesture. "Well, anyhow, good luck for the journey."

He rose to his feet. "Thank you. I'll not forget that. I know it must be getting late and I've promised to stop in your father's study. I've had a wonderful evening, Miss Kirkland—Anne. May I call again?"

For a second it was as though a stone had been hurled into a smooth and silent pool. The room seemed a-tremor with vibrations. When Anne replied, however, her voice was controlled and natural.

"Of course," she said. "Father will be glad to have you. It was too bad he was busy tonight."

He looked at her steadily.

"When would you be free?"

She glanced down at her hands and her lips were unsteady.

"Father may have told you that I am of necessity free most of the time now."

"He did tell me," he answered. "What night would be convenient for me to come?"

Slowly the color rose in her throat, her cheeks, until her face was suffused with it.

"Two weeks from tonight, perhaps?"

"Fine! I'll be here around eight-thirty if that isn't too early. Well, goodnight, and thanks again for a delightful evening! Oh, and if a box should be delivered to you meanwhile, open it carefully. It won't be violets, you know!"

They parted on a laughing note.

He went out quickly, and as he had done earlier, stood still in the long quiet hall. This time also, his heart was beating hard from inner tension. In a few moments he must seek Kirkland, and although he knew he would not be pressed for an immediate answer the eyes of the older man would pierce him to the marrow with their desperate urgency.

He looked slowly about him at the elegance of the massive furnishings: the carved chairs, the golden mirror, the paintings, the stairway that curved upward in white grace like an unsubstantial dream. Everything here represented wealth at its best. In the room he had just quitted was a girl whose attractiveness no one could question; in the study to which he must soon go, was a man whose power, influence, and tried experience could advance him in the career of his choice. Why should he hesitate? Why should he stop to analyze the situation further or to demand the future to stand and deliver upon every point? Why should he probe into or dissect his own emotions? Why not accept this opportunity which fate had so strangely presented to him?

> *There is a tide in the affairs of men,*
> *Which, taken at the flood . . .*

Why not go with the tide, trust it, let it bear him on?

There was in him, as in Kirkland, a strong predilection for prompt decisions. His mind grasped facts quickly, organized them logically and then formed judgment without delay. So now with a swift feeling of certitude he walked toward the study and tapped lightly on the door.

Kirkland opened it and then closed it at once and, as Paul had suspected, looked at him in haggard questioning.

"Well?" he said, as though the monosyllable had been forced out of him against his will.

"Mr. Kirkland," Paul said, "since meeting your daughter I have completely changed my mind in regard to the matter you discussed with me. I shall do all in my power to make her willing to marry me."

The older man stared, half incredulously, and then sank down upon a chair.

"Thank God!" he said brokenly. "I had thought that as you came to know her you might reconsider and accept my plan, but I had not dared to hope for a favorable decision at once. My boy . . ."

He paused and wiped his eyes.

"I can only promise that I will dedicate myself from this point on to advancing you in every way possible. I'm not sure I can talk any more tonight. I'm a little shaken. You must excuse me. But, shall we say lunch again tomorrow? No, I forgot, I have to be out of town. A week from today, then?"

Paul assented.

"We must start at once to make plans. There are men I want you to meet soon."

Paul rose. "I think I had better be going now. It is much later than I thought. Thank you for everything."

"I'll call the car."

"No, please don't. I would really rather walk for a while. I can pick up a cab when I get tired."

"As you wish." Kirkland grasped the young man's hand and wrung it hard.

"One thing," Paul added gravely, "we must not forget. I have told you merely of my own decision. What your daughter's will ultimately be is something we cannot tell."

"I watched you both at dinner," Kirkland said. "I know Anne. I could see she liked you. Very much. So that's a start. But be sure to go slow. Anything precipitous might throw it all off. She is . . . lovely, isn't she?"

"Very," Paul agreed, trying to make his voice even.

After a final handshake at the front door and an exchange of casual goodnights, which might drift back to the library, Paul found himself out again in the cool spring darkness. He walked down the drive and made his way along the wide quiet street. A half-moon hung lightly in its heavenly pastures with a flock of small clouds, like lambs following it. The scent of the waking gardens near at hand drifted delicately upon the air while the young budding leaves wrought magic tracery just overhead.

It was a night to stir a man's senses, but as Paul walked slowly on he knew that he was more deeply moved than these physical aspects would warrant. Something had happened to him. Something of such magnitude that he was not now the same person who had entered the Kirkland house a few hours earlier. Although he had made his swift decision in the hallway and reported it to Anne's father, he had not then pretended to plumb his own heart. Rather, he had refused to admit that his emotions might actually be involved. The judgment, he felt, should be based upon other considerations; it should be reasonable, but quickly and lightly arrived at, as a bold man chances his all upon the throw of the dice. Kirkland had made his amazing offer; he, Paul, after meeting his daughter, had accepted it. Let that suffice for the moment.

But, somehow, now in the cool detachment of darkness, his heart would not remain a mere reasonable ally to the plan. Whether he would or not, he had to listen to the findings of its review.

He was now thirty years old. Outside of the callow infatuations of his very early years he had never been in love. He had often wondered about this, thinking that perhaps like his father before him he would remain a bachelor until late in life. For in spite of having a fairly normal social experience since college he had never met a girl who attracted him strongly enough to make him desire to marry her.

There had been beauty often for his appraisal, brains many times, and occasionally a peculiar sweetness of nature; but never all three combined in such appealing proportions for him, at least, until. . . . Well, admit it, he urged himself, never, until he had met Anne tonight.

But, while he knew beyond any doubt that his calm emotional life had been shaken by this girl's beauty and personality, he felt obligated to hold himself in check. There was the unreal and mechanical situation into which they were all tending; there was the barrier of her helplessness which, if he had met her in an ordinary fashion, would probably have dissuaded him at once from seeing her further; there was the strange possibility that this new fire which kept leaping within him was born only of pity.

He walked on, alone with himself and the soft, encompassing spring night. Was it possible, he pondered, for a man's heart to be suddenly ravished, even as a woman's body? And if so, could the tenderness of compassion alone beat down its ramparts for love itself to enter? Could desire seize upon a man when his first craving was only the power to protect and cherish? He was not sure, although something deep in his own flesh tried to give an answer.

As he stopped at last to hail a cab, there was only one thing of which he was certain. This was that *the journey*, the one of which Anne had spoken, had begun.

3

✒§ ARNO SHARED one habit with his chief. He woke early and lay for a time sorting out conflicting plans and tangling problems before he rose to begin the active day. On this morning, a week following Paul's dinner at the Kirkland home, he watched the sun gain the height of the brick chimneys upon which his bedroom window faced, and considered—of all things—himself. Without knowing why, he suddenly opened to the full contemplation of his mind an inner chamber he usually kept closed, fearing that even the conscious admission of certain facts would lessen the profoundness of their secrecy.

He was in reality two men, and the great complication of his life was that part of each must remain a mystery to the other. At least for the present. When Kirkland had discovered him, a sharp-eyed youth of eighteen, he had then been a whole personality. He had lived with his family, eldest of eight, in three small rooms behind his father's fruit shop on Water Street; and he had known life in that section of the city so completely that the thoroughness of his proficiency had lent him a faint swagger as he walked the dirty pavements.

But once under Kirkland's wing, strange new horizons had opened. Incredibly perceptive, gifted to a remarkable degree with the imitative faculty, and suddenly and fiercely ambitious for a way of life before undreamed of, he had studied not only the details of the tasks assigned him but the man who set them. In two years' time he had mastered the outward technique of a gentleman's behavior; this a much more difficult accomplishment than the work at night school which he had doggedly pursued and conquered. Besides all this, and even more important, he had learned to know his employer himself. He knew his strength, he knew his weaknesses; he knew the relentless drive of his power; he knew those delicate and illogical nuances of business and political ethics which guided his actions: just what he himself would do to achieve an end, just what he would delegate to a subordinate to accomplish while he, the master planner, looked the other way.

The coal business had from the first held only a superficial interest for Arno. Besides, it was thoroughly organized before he came upon the scene. What captured his imagination from the start was the great game of politics in which Kirkland at that time was just emerging as a state leader. There came a day later on when Kirkland called him into his office and set before him certain facts which faced the men who were running for office under his auspices. These facts had to do with a world Arno knew well, the one indeed to which he had been born. There were other men who had served Kirkland before as a link between that world and his own, but with an unerring instinct he had guessed that Arno would be able to carry this liaison to a smooth and safe perfection.

This had been accomplished. Now it was only necessary for Kirkland to say with a casual lift of the eyebrow, "How about Micky Orlando?"

"He's fixed, Chief. I saw him last night."

"And Camponelli?"

"He's okay."

"Sure?"

"Sure, Chief."

It was clever also of Arno to suspect from the first that the money which came from these hidden sources should not be discussed openly between them. Instead, some typed figures appeared on Kirkland's desk from time to time. Campaign funds were swelled; and in several small banks the savings of Arno Mallotte (he had substituted the *e* for the final *i* long before) kept growing out of proportion to his salary, which was in itself very good. For Arno intended to be a rich man one day.

He had first seen Anne Kirkland when she was sixteen. She had come bounding into the office one spring afternoon, laughing and golden and lovely and Arno had stood dumb before her.

"Isn't Mr. Kirkland in?" she had asked him. "I'm his daughter and you must be Arno, aren't you? Father often speaks of you."

All his hard-acquired poise, his superficial *savoir-faire* deserted him. He became again young Arno Mallotti of Water Street as he stumbled over his words in reply.

And even after her father had come in and the two had gone out together, Arno could not work. His soul had drunk fire. He had been once to the Kirkland house on a winter night when Anne was home from college at the holidays. He and the Chief had been to a meeting. When it was over, the hour was very late and they were both tired to the point of exhaustion.

"Come on up to the house, Arno, and we'll dig up something to eat," Kirkland had said with an impulsiveness rare to him.

When they entered the front door, Anne in a red dress had come running down the stairs, her bright hair curling to her shoulders, her eyes like stars. She had made them coffee and sandwiches and had sat leaning upon the table, chin in hands, talking eagerly as they ate.

Arno had been vaguely sensible of the beauty of the great house, but he had carried away in his mind one picture so vivid that it had power to stir him if his thoughts merely glanced upon it. He was no dreamer, Arno. He was a hardheaded and sharply practical dealer with life as he knew it to be. He hugged no illusions to his breast. He knew that between him and the Chief's daughter an uncrossable gulf was fixed. This in spite of the fact that he knew also that he possessed an attraction to certain women. He had discovered this long ago on Water Street. Even now—well, there was Sayles in the office. Ten years older, she must be, and with as much sex appeal as a burnt match, and yet her fool hands went shaky when he got close to her. He'd seen it. He knew.

But all this did not alter his own status with relation to those facts which he rarely allowed his heart to face. His was a strange, strong, set nature with which he never broke faith, but as he was fond of remarking, he always knew the score.

The reason on this morning that he was considering himself as he was doing, he suddenly admitted, was the confession the Chief had briefly made that day last week. Anne's case was hopeless. She would never walk again. So the normal fulfillment of her life would not take place. The big wedding in one of the biggest churches, the newspapers running pictures and write-ups and featuring everything like mad from the engagement on—all this which he had steeled himself to face when it came would never happen.

Arno lay, a slow, hot flush rising to his cheeks. No man, not even a low dog of a fortune hunter would want to marry her now. Not likely. Anne's world then, in a few short months, had changed utterly. And by this strange circumstance, so had his.

Across the city as the sun rose higher, men and women everywhere opened their eyes upon the new day. Kirkland himself woke as he had each morning for a week with a feeling of relief so profound as to be almost physically sensible. The first step toward his all but impossible goal had been taken. Given back to him, like a gift from heaven, had been the ability to hope.

Paul in his turn, roused himself from uneasy slumber, and fairly leaped from bed. A tremulous excitement now filled him. He felt constantly a compulsion to be alert, active, in complete possession of all his faculties in order to test his decision, to weigh it against all odds, to be sure that the magic of a fire-lit evening and a beautiful girl had not overcome his sober judgment. In this clear, appraising morning light he was *not* sure. He was, in fact, afraid that he had committed himself to a course which he might bitterly regret.

He stopped short in his dressing. One thing at least was certain. He had made no rash promise to Anne herself. He could retract the other to her father if he felt compelled to do so. But he would go to lunch with him again today according to arrangement. He could hear the initial plans for "the journey," as Anne had called it. A man could always turn back, even after setting out, couldn't he?

Anne herself was still asleep when her father left the house, but not as she had been a week ago, exhausted from anguish, her face set and white and stained with tears. This morning she lay relaxed, her cheek pillowed on her hand, the skin warm with color, breathing softly and half smiling in her dreams as she had been wont to do in the happy years before disaster had overtaken her.

Kirkland had set one o'clock again for lunch but this time the place was different. Paul had met him in the office and they had gone out at once to the street. Kirkland hailed a taxi.

"I'm going to take you to a spot that's hard to get into," he said, smiling. "It's really just a small restaurant which a group of men have taken over. Men who for one reason or another are interested in making things *tick*. I want you to meet most of them as fast as it's decently possible. Our political opponents in these parts call it the D. D. Club—damned dictators," he added grinning.

"It's not all politics here," Kirkland was saying after they ordered. "It's business too, and finance. Some of that can go a long way. But now," his tone growing more incisive, "let's get down to you. As I see it, we can either try to put you on the state ticket, or I can run you for State Senator from our district. I have a hunch the latter may be more to your liking. Tell me about the speechmaking. You're good, you know. I heard you once. How did you arrive at it?"

Paul smiled. "I suppose it's really a long story. My mother studied 'elocution' when she was a girl. She gave readings all her life at the local affairs. She was *really* good, I think, looking back on it. When I came along she taught me recitations when I was knee-high."

He stopped, laughing. "I believe I could stand up this minute and say 'Horatius at the Bridge' if there was a demand for it! So I've always been used to *spouting*, as my father called it. In college I went in for debating, of course, and the plays, so—that's how it is."

"You *like* to speak then?"

"Yes, I do. You see," he leaned forward, "there's a tremendous thrill in really *getting* your audience. Feeling them come out to you and then holding them in the palm of your hand. It's queer, it's like a physical and mental transference. Well, since between us there are no punches pulled, I'll admit I not only like to speak, I love it. I've wished sometimes I'd taken a try at the stage instead of law. That must seem to you quite a confession."

"Um-hm." Kirkland was studying him intently and there was the light of discovery in his eyes.

"That settles it," he said. "The idea then, as I see it, is for you to speak at every possible opportunity. Get yourself known round the city and outside if you can. Get yourself talked about. No matter where you're invited to make a speech, *go*, even if it's the Annual meeting of the Mothers' Sewing Society. And every time you open your mouth let the eagle scream a little. *You* know—our great heritage, our flag, our Constitution—America the Beautiful. I'll see to it you meet the right men round here and get some bigger engagements and you can do the cracker-barrel stuff yourself, can't you?"

"Cracker barrel?"

"Rural, small town, all that."

"Oh, yes," Paul said, "that comes easy to me."

Kirkland smiled a strange, satisfied smile later as he picked up the bill.

"I never have been given to early predictions, not in this game, but I think, Paul, you may be a *natural* for it."

It was the first time he had used the Christian name and something in the way he said it sent a warm glow over Paul. That and the prediction itself coupled with the method of the initial attack. Nothing could be more congenial to him. And to aim at once for State Senator! He felt hot with excitement. Of course he would still have a private talk with Kirkland when they got back to his office and tell him—tell him what? That now just when the political wheels were being set in motion he was unsure about the other part of the bargain? Unsure about—Anne?

It was absurd, he knew in the moment, even to think of retracting. He had given his word. Come good, come ill he must stand upon it.

Kirkland had risen and was piloting him toward the back of the room. He stopped beside a table.

"Hello, Brennen," he said to a heavy-set man with a gray mustache. "Glad we ran into you. I want to introduce a young protégé of mine, Paul Devereux. Paul, this is our County Chairman."

The two shook hands and exchanged greetings, the older man eying him keenly; but this was all and Paul followed again as Kirkland moved on. He was stopped by a dark handsome man in his sixties who called out from a table at which, curiously, he sat alone.

"Hey, Kirk, why don't you sit down? Haven't seen you in weeks. What have you been up to?"

He pushed some papers aside and signed to them to sit.

"How are you, Jack? Want to introduce Paul Devereux. Mr. Bovard."

The latter shook hands pleasantly but did not give him Brennen's close scrutiny. He turned back to Kirkland.

"How are things with you? Pretty quiet?"

"We're running all right. If we could just get rid of a few damned competitors."

Bovard laughed easily.

"Don't be a hog. You can't own all the coal in the state. Say," he lowered his voice, "I got a tip that Old Bill is getting the wind up again. Blast his hide. Nothing due before fall, but I'm afraid we'll be in for it, then. I want another strike about the way I want to go to bed with a rattlesnake. Can't you get at him, anyway, Kirk?"

Kirkland squinted across the table, but did not answer the question. Instead he said, "This young fellah here is quite a speaker. If you ever hear of any organization that wants one . . ."

"*Speaker!*" Bovard interrupted. "Say you're sent from heaven! Here I've been racking my brain like murder the whole lunchtime and all I could dig up was a preacher or two whom I don't want, the President of the Elks, who's seventy, and old Judge Whipple, who's always too long-winded. I want someone young and peppy. Look, I'll tell you what I need and then you can tell me how you feel. Here's the layout."

He leaned nearer. "You know my boy Johnny is in the business with me now and he's as full of ideas as a fish is full of eggs. Lots of them crazy. I have to sit on him. But he's come up with this one I think may be worth something. He says why not give a big picnic

Memorial Day for the whole works out at Redstone. Make it big stuff. Roast an ox, let the beer run, have races and a ball game like the big shindigs of the old days. But he says we ought to have a *speech* too."

Bovard studied Paul now with interest. "Tell you what we want. A little flag-waving, of course, then country of opportunity and all that. Their children's chance to go as far as they want, and so forth. Then, just smooched in nice and delicate-like, something about the brotherhood of man and the employer's good will to his employees and how all must work together for the common good. Get the idea? You see, an employer can't talk to his own men, damn it, without danger of getting into trouble, but *somebody else* can. See? Well, how about it, young man? Is he really good, Kirk?"

"He is," Kirkland pronounced solemnly. "What do you say, Paul?"

"I would like to try this, Mr. Bovard. If you wish I'll make out a sort of outline for you. I'll hunt up some jokes they can understand, too. Yes, I'll be glad to do it."

"By crickey, this is luck. I'll get Johnny at you, Devereux. He's the ringleader of this. Where could he get in touch with you?"

"I'm with Hartwell & Harvey. He can reach me there any day."

"Good enough. And thanks meantime. Give old Hartwell my regards. Great old guy, that. If you're in his office I guess you're all right. Well, bring me luck again, Kirk,"—as they all got up—"and don't undersell me behind my back, you hog!"

Once in a cab again, Kirkland smiled. "Jack Bovard and I have been friends for years even though it's often been dog-eat-dog between us. Somehow you can't get mad at Jack. Well, you've got your first chance, and a good one it is. They've all got votes, those hunkies, and they won't forget you. By the way, how is all this going to affect your law practice? You'd better tell your firm soon about your plans."

"I will," Paul said soberly. "I'll do it today."

"I'll be no help to you there," Kirkland said brusquely. "Old Hartwell doesn't like me, since I'm a 'devious and unscrupulous' politician. His words." He gave a short laugh. "I'd advise you to play me down, though the—ah—connection will come out someday. We hope."

He paused and then looked straight ahead. "Your decision was very suddenly made last week. As of today, do you wish to reconsider?" His lips looked thin and almost pale as he brought out the words.

Paul was amazed at his own response. It came strongly and with no hesitation, as though another man were speaking.

"My decision stands," he said.

"Thank God," Kirkland muttered. "Let me out here and take the cab on to your office." He gave the driver a bill and waved stiffly to Paul as the taxi sprang forward.

When he reached his own small office Paul gave way to an over-mastering impulse. He found a number, dialed and then waited, his heart beating faster. A woman answered.

"This is Mr. Devereux. May I speak to Miss Kirkland?"

In a moment he heard her voice with its peculiar warm vibrancy.

"Hello."

"Hello. This is Paul. How are you?"

"Just fine! I've been thinking all morning about the kitten. Do you really suppose you can find one?"

"Sure of it. I've been pretty busy this week but I'll look today. When I do locate one, though, I've been wondering . . ."

"Yes?" As she said it, the syllable was sweetly provocative.

"I really think I should bring it up myself, don't you?"

She laughed then, and the sound went into all the corners of his heart. She did not answer.

"I would be a little uneasy to let a messenger boy take it. Besides a week from tonight is a *very* long way off."

There was a pause and then she said calmly, casually, "It was so pleasant having company that night you were here, for I *was* rather blue. You see, I had just learned the day before that my present condition is quite hopeless, that is, permanent."

"I'm more sorry than I can possibly say. But about coming again. I may need to consult with you about types of kittens. Colors, and so on. In fact the more I think of it, it seems quite essential. Could I drop in just for a few minutes? Tonight? I'd feel safer about making the choice, then."

And now she laughed with a strange catch in her breath as though tears might be near also.

"What a persistent young man you are!"

"One has to be in the law. It's all right then? Tonight?"

"Of course we shouldn't make a mistake about the kitten," she said slowly.

"But definitely not. Thanks so much. I'll report soon."

Her reply was almost inaudible. He leaned back for a moment, and the feeling of that first evening with her came sweeping over him again. Some lines of Meredith returned to him from college years.

Let me hear her laughter, I would have her ever
Cool as dew in twilight, the lark above the flowers.

He plunged into the work before him, trying fiercely to concentrate. At four he pushed back the papers, rose and pulled himself together, then went slowly toward the office of the senior partner. Never before had he gone toward Hartwell reluctantly. In fact he had been wont to make excuses for visits, so greatly did he like the old man and respect him. Now he went forward soberly in response to his "come in."

"Ah, Paul!" Hartwell smiled with pleasure and adjusted the eyeglasses on their black ribbon which somehow gave the effect of a monocle. His eyes were startlingly blue for his sex and bright for his years; his nose was large and below it he wore a somewhat ragged gray mustache, the ends of which he twisted downward instead of outward, especially when engrossed.

"Yes, my boy, what's the problem?"

Paul's face grew more grave.

"I'm afraid it's me, this time. I have come to a decision and it affects my position here. I want to talk it over with you."

"Go ahead."

"I have always been interested in politics."

"Ah! Not unusual in a young lawyer. Rather like whooping cough. Get it early. Have it behind you."

"The point is I've decided to try for a political career." It was harder than he had expected, to say this.

"Just how do you expect to go about it?" Hartwell asked dryly.

"Well, I'm going to start by making speeches everywhere I can. I have a little flair for that. By doing this I will become known to a good many people in different walks of life . . . I will. . . ." His voice trailed off.

"Ah-huh. Speeches. Well, they're certainly part of a politician's stock in trade. I'd advise you to read all of Winston Churchill's. Might as well study from a master when you're at it. Ever meet a man named Kirkland? If you haven't run into him, you will."

"I've met him."

"Oh ho! Don't tell me he's backing you?"

"In a sense—well, yes, that is true."

Hartwell pulled at his mustache until the ends framed his chin.

"I don't like that, Paul. I don't trust Kirkland round a stump. He's a *devious, unscrupulous* politician. I've told him that to his face."

Paul tried not to smile.

"How did he ever discover you?"

"He heard me speak once."

"Well, my boy, my advice is to have no hookup with him. If you do, you'll get the worst of it. I've known him for years. Used to be a client of ours for his coal business. We ran into something with him once that was distinctly *odorous*. We dropped him. Now, if you want to go into politics, go ahead. God knows we need good men more now than ever. Things are in a bad way. Of course they always are. But fight your own battles. Be honest. Keep out of Kirkland's machine. Build up one of your own. Well?"

Paul did not answer.

"I take it you are not going to accept my advice?"

"I'm afraid I can't sir."

"So." His eyes were on the ceiling. He sat as though considering all sides of the problem. "What about that man's daughter?" he asked suddenly. "Was in an accident, wasn't she? I seem to remember the papers. . . ."

"Yes, that is so."

"Recover?"

"No, sir."

"What do you mean? Did she die?"

"No, she's very well, except that . . . she cannot walk."

Suddenly the bright blue eyes pierced Paul through and through.

"You have not told me all the story of your relations with Kirkland?"

Paul swallowed hard.

"No, sir, not entirely."

"You can't tell me more, I take it?"

"I'm sorry, sir."

There was a long pause.

"Naturally I will say nothing to anybody. I suppose this speech-making of yours will be largely done at night?"

"I fancy so. I thought I could do my preparations then, too."

"What office are you heading for? Confidentially, that is."

"State Senator."

"Highty-tighty! Starting fairly high, at that! Well, my boy, I'll talk to Harvey, but as I see it this will be our position. We like you, we need a young man here. You've done excellent work. We want to keep you. Go ahead and as long as you can still do a fair amount of business for us we'll make no change. Even if you get to be a senator, eventually, they only sit in session three months of the year, I believe."

"That is correct."

"You would still need to practice. A senator's salary is pretty small. So, let's go ahead together and see how it works out. One thing, though."

Once again the blue eyes made Paul feel as though there had been a *touché*.

"As long as you do an honest job in your politics we'll do everything we can to co-operate. If you ever descend to Kirkland's tactics, we'll break at once. Is that clear?"

Paul rose, his head rather high.

"Not only clear but completely satisfactory. And thank you, Mr. Hartwell, very much indeed for your kindness to me."

Paul put his desk to rights and left his office at five. He had the feeling of a small craft being borne on by a mighty current. In one short week, the course of his life had been changed with entire unexpectedness. But was not that the way of life? Suddenly in the midst of the familiar, the habitual, the routine scene, there came the blinding flash, the thunder, and *perhaps*—the rainbow. It was this very possibility of the unexpected that kept the race of men busy and half content with the eternal gamble of existence, wasn't it? It was this quality which kept hope alive in the human heart. So why should he be startled by the suddenness of what had befallen him? The thing to do was accept it and go along with it. There was something about it too big, too destiny-laden, for him to laugh off, or brush aside. No, he was committed. Utterly. And with the thought there came a young upleaping in his heart. Without actually admitting it, still, in a measure fearing it, and distrusting it, he knew that he had many of the symptoms of a young man in love.

He called at several pet shops, making humorous notes on an envelope as to pedigree, colors, size, age and disposition of various small felines, then went on out to his rooming house on the other side of the river. It was a solid brick house on a quiet street. He had found the place through Mr. Hartwell, who knew the owner. Mrs. MacLeod was elderly, Scotch and quite alone. She wanted the feel of someone else in the house, especially at night, so gladly gave Paul a bedroom and sitting room on the second floor. He enjoyed their brief encounters and felt himself fortunate, for in addition to his general comfort he found buttons replaced and socks neatly darned.

In his room now he went to the bookshelves and picked out an anthology. The Meredith poem under his eyes carried him away as it always had done with its feeling and its sheer music. "From 'Love in the Valley,'" the title read. Would he dare take it along tonight and show it to Anne? Why not? They had discussed poetry that first night. I'll be casual, he thought. Just happened to recall a line of it today and looked it up. Just like that.

He dressed with greater care even than last week, and after calling to Mrs. MacLeod that he wouldn't be too late, he went out into the March evening. Even here on the solid brick street there was the delicate throb of budding life in the air. He thought of the farm with a sharp yearning. His boyhood scenes rose before him, all his senses replete with remembrance.

Happy, happy time, when the white star hovers
Low over dim fields fresh with bloomy dew . . .

The Meredith poem again. He touched the book that he had fitted into his pocket, and went on to the small restaurant where he usually ate. Dinner was an effort tonight for some reason, so he sat smoking nervously over his coffee, until after many glances at his watch he decided he might reasonably start out for the West Hill, making the trip by trolley this time, with perhaps a cab at the end.

He had tried to time himself to arrive at eight-thirty sharp but was annoyed to find when he stood again on the large portico that it was already nine. He rang quickly and was admitted at once.

"Miss Anne is expecting you," Hackett said, smiling. "She's in her own sitting room. I'll show you up."

Paul had a distinct feeling of warmth in the air this time as the old man escorted him up the stairs, and also that the steps beneath his feet were made of nothing more substantial than cloud, so ethereal did their beauty seem.

The room he entered was large and full of light. In the wide bay window at the back Anne was seated on a sofa, with a chair opposite and a low coffee table between. The windows were open a little and the unseasonably warm air blew in with fresh sweetness. He went toward her eagerly and took her hand.

"Hello," she said smiling.

"You were good to let me come tonight, and I'm laden with statistics. Oh, what a chance for a pun!"

"You should have gone ahead and said it. I love puns. They simply set me up for hours. I thought it would be pleasanter perhaps here this evening."

"It's delightful. What a charming room!"

"You like it? This is my very own. I planned all the furnishings. I think it does look a little *younger* than the rooms downstairs."

Paul's eyes took it in admiringly. There was originality and zest in the chintz patterns, the colors of wall and pictures, but with it all a harmony and an easy comfort. A man, he thought, could relax here, as well as be entertained. He glimpsed the long bookshelves, the cabinet of records and the television set in one corner.

With only a glance at the big chair he sat down beside her on the sofa.

"I know you want to hear about the kittens. It's amazing what a demand there is for them. When I think of the numbers I drowned at the farm . . ."

"Oh Paul, you *didn't!*" Anne's face was full of horror.

"Well, you see we always had several cats at the barn as well as a house pet, and sometimes production ran high. We couldn't give them away there, so steps had to be taken. Hard necessity. But don't think about that. Let's consider the matter in hand. Now here's what I found this afternoon."

He produced his notations and read them carefully, as Anne listened and laughed at the wording. They both agreed after some debate upon a very young tiger-striped animal which had especially taken Paul's fancy.

"He's playful as the dickens and has a nice pert little personality. Now, I don't want to overinfluence you if you'd rather have the Persian, for instance. I don't care so much for the fancy breeds myself, but you might."

Anne shook her head. "No, I think I'd like the little tiger. I've always loved the big cats at the zoo. In fact, one of my suppressed desires is to stroke a lion's nose. So, you see, this may be my *fulfillment*," she said, laughing.

"Fine. I'll go the first thing in the morning and have the man hold it for me. I have to go to a meeting tomorrow night, but maybe the next one. . . ."

"I'm having some girls in then."

"Could we make it Saturday?"

"I think so. Yes, that would be fine."

"But please don't think I'm relinquishing my date for next week, for I'm not."

The soft quick flush rose again to her cheeks and her beauty overwhelmed him. He spoke at random to put her at ease and in a few minutes they had relaxed again into the interesting mental give and take of their first meeting. Before he left he produced the book. He had thought of a likely way to introduce it.

"You spoke of your grandmother's fondness for poetry and of course as I told you I'm something of a bug on it myself. I just remembered today a poem I think is pretty special. I brought it along for you to lend to her if you think she'd like it."

He opened the book at the page. "It's from George Meredith's 'Love in the Valley' and I think for pure music and sentiment too it can't be beaten."

With sudden courage he began to read.

> *"Under yonder beech-tree single on the green-sward,*
> *Couch'd with her arms behind her golden head,*
> *Knees and tresses folded to slip and ripple idly,*
> *Lies my young love sleeping in the shade.*
> *Had I the heart to slide an arm beneath her,*
> *Press her parting lips as her waist I gather slow,*
> *Waking in amazement she could not but embrace me:*
> *Then would she hold me and never let me go?"*

He knew he was reading well. His mother's gift woke freely in him. He went on through the next stanza without looking up.

> *"She whom I love is hard to catch and conquer,*
> *Hard, but O the glory of the winning were she won!"*

Only once as he proceeded did she interrupt.

"Please read those last lines over," she begged, "I want to feel them again."

> *"Lovely are the curves of the white owl sweeping*
> *Wavy in the dusk lit by one large star."*

When he was finished they sat silent a moment.

"It's so beautiful I'm a bit breathless," she said at last. "It is pure music, as you said. Gran will love it. But how marvelously well you read! Did you ever think of the stage?"

He laughed. "Oh, a little. Like all young fellows who have the lead in the college plays. I should show up better than I do, though, for I have an inheritance."

He told her then of his mother.

"I think she would have made an actress and a fine one if she had been born under different circumstances. Instead she was a country schoolteacher and farmer's wife and gave readings at the Grange meetings and church sociables!"

There was a hint of bitterness in his voice.

"As I look back now I think her wonderful gifts were wasted."

"Oh, not when she had you!" Anne said quickly.

And then they were looking deep into each other's eyes while a hammer pounded in his pulse. It was only by the strongest effort of control that he kept from taking her in his arms.

She recovered first.

"But you are going to use that inheritance in another way. Father says as a speaker you are a *natural* and I can understand that now."

"Your father told you, then?"

"Yes, tonight at dinner. I knew when he had you up last week that he had some plan for you. That's the way he always works. But I never dreamed you were headed for anything so soon. But that's also Father's method. And if he sets out to make you a senator, you can pretty well count on it. I'm awfully pleased. I'll follow your campaign and cheer you on to victory."

"You had just better. I'll need advice on my speeches, too. How to wangle the woman's vote, you know. But as to your father, he does move like lightning, doesn't he? I'll always be running to catch up, I'm afraid."

"Have you met Arno? In the office?"

"Just barely."

"What do you think of him?"

"He looks like a thug till he smiles. Then, he's really rather attractive. Why?"

"Oh, I don't know. I've never liked him, somehow. It bothers me to have Father depend on him so much. As you get to know him better keep an eye on him and tell me what you think. There's never been anyone before I could confess this to."

When he rose to go at last, he bent down a little and took both her hands in his.

"Thank you again for a wonderful evening. You know, I've just discovered something. I believe I've been abysmally lonely."

"Oh, that's dreadful," Anne cried. "Haven't you met any young people? Why, I'll do something about that! I'll see you get to know some girls and . . ."

"Do me a big favor?" he asked, smiling.

"Why . . . why of course." There was a set look upon her face.

"Then let me pick my own friends, most *especially* girls," he said.

The set look vanished and she was all alight as they laughed together. Never, he thought, in all his life had he so madly wanted to kiss a girl as he now desired to. Instead, he pressed her hands close in his own and took his leave.

Once again he walked slowly under the stars, attempting with an almost judicial exactness to evaluate his own emotions. He thought of a remark his father had once made to him when he was growing up.

"I decided the first time I met your mother that I wanted to marry her, and I'd never felt that way about any woman before." He had paused, eying his young son steadily. "There's a big difference," he said, "between wanting a girl, and wanting to marry her. Bear that in mind."

He had never forgotten. The advice had saved him when he was close to one fatal early blunder and checked him as he approached several others. Now, for the first time, he completely understood the difference of which his father had spoken. Never before had he actually craved marriage. What he had known had been only transient desire. Now, every fiber of him yearned for that closest of all relationships with this girl he had met only a week ago. There was the physical enslavement of course, as his hot senses acknowledged. But now he not only longed to sleep with this girl in his arms, he yearned to wake to her smile, her voice, her laughter. He craved her constant companionship. He wanted to rush home from the office to tell her all that the day had brought; to discuss the little affairs of life and the greater ones with her; to share with her all the secret thoughts of his own heart and listen to hers in return. He wanted to be *one* with her, one flesh, one spirit.

This, then, was love, the true love for which he had long been waiting. Soberly now, he put behind him all former questionings and doubts of himself. The time, one short week, seemed brief indeed for such complete assurance. Yet had time anything to do with the origin of love? None whatever. The passions might ignite explosively in a second, or grow gradually from tiny spark to blazing flame. Time was never a cause then, but merely an accompaniment, so its brevity in his case could be discounted.

Once sure of himself, however, there was the question of Anne's own feelings. Paul was not given to undue personal vanity. He had indeed a new and profound humility as he thought of his beloved. Yet in that sudden moment when she had cried out concerning his mother, *"Oh, not when she had you!"* and their eyes had met and clung, he had been conscious of a mutual confession. He told himself he must not overestimate what he had read in her unguarded look, but he believed she might be at least beginning to care for him.

When he reached his own room at last, he prepared for bed and then in dressing gown and slippers sat smoking and thinking his own thoughts on into the night. His imagination had never been livelier. As the hours passed he found himself picturing in detail the life he and Anne might lead if they were married; he found himself inventing situation after situation in which she could find pleasure even with her handicap. He would dedicate himself to making her happy, to making up to her for what she must still miss of normal pleasure. He was smiling to himself as he finally put out the light.

It was not until he was sinking to sleep that a thought struck him with such shocking impact that he sat bolt upright, his hands clenched upon the covers. Why, he gritted between his teeth, had he been such a blind fool that this had not been plain to him before? In all his dreaming he had been seeing Anne, *even as his wife,* against her present background, her incapacity ameliorated at least by the wealth and luxurious comfort which surrounded her. Where in this picture did he, a strong, able-bodied young man of thirty, fit in? If the marriage took place was he as well as his wife to eat the bread and dwell under the roof of his father-in-law?

A bitter pride rose within him, a fierce feeling of revulsion. When Kirkland had first made his fantastic proposition he had called it, of his own accord, a *deal.* Within that framework Paul's own independence would have remained intact. Now, all was changed. He wanted to marry Anne for the same reasons any man wanted to marry a woman. Therefore how could he surrender his integrity of spirit to the extent of having his wife, and himself also in large part, financially dependent upon her father? Would it not make of him merely a glorified. . . . He tried not even to think the word *gigolo,* but it kept rising in his consciousness.

If Anne were normally active and well, he could support her in at least the type of modest comfort in which countless young couples started their marriage careers. He was doing well in the law office, as such things went, his prospects were excellent for the future, and he had besides a few investments and the old farm which he had inherited. He had enough to ask a girl to marry him, that is, any girl except Anne. It was her tragic situation which changed it all. For she needed, indeed *had to have* the care now bestowed upon her by "Davy" and a staff of trained servants. Even cutting it to the bone she needed Davy and at least one domestic. This would be impossible for him to provide for her on his present salary.

He sat on the edge of the bed, his chin in his hands, a cold sweat breaking over him, wrestling with the problem which now overshadowed and nullified all his previous assurance.

Once he straightened up telling himself roughly there was no need to tear his emotions to shreds over a situation at present imaginary. But this easement was short-lived. Again, with a searing native honesty he demanded an answer for the cleansing of his soul.

He heard Mrs. MacLeod's old clock in the lower hall strike and strike again before he began with a sort of still, logical desperation to array the facts in two opposing mental columns. On the one side he saw with bitter clarity all the mitigating advantages which the Kirkland wealth could bestow. But, slowly, doggedly, he saw the other column mount also. All that he had a few hours ago been planning for the joyous fulfillment of Anne's life with him found its place here. And as he contemplated it, he knew that if the marriage took place only his *pride* might suffer, but not his integrity. For if she should come to love him as he now loved her, he would be bringing to her as she would to him, gifts immeasurable. Did the rest matter?

He finally rolled back into bed, weary and shaken as though from physical exercise, but he had purged his heart of the last doubt. When the time came for it he felt he could honestly ask Anne to marry him.

His last thoughts were, "I could buy her clothes, perhaps pay Davy's salary too. The rest I would take with my chin up."

The next day he received a phone call from Johnny Bovard.

"Oh, I say, Devereux, my father tells me you're going to do this Memorial Day speech for us! I've been kicking up the dust about that, so I'm enormously relieved. Listen, could we meet somewhere and talk it over? Would lunch be easiest?"

"I believe it would. I could make it tomorrow."

"Fine. Shall we say one o'clock at the Down Town? I'll be in the lobby. Nondescript looking little guy. You can't miss me."

Paul liked him on sight and oddly enough recognized him from his own description. He did not have either his father's height or his handsome features, but there was a pleasant radiation of good health and good spirits about him. When they were seated and had ordered, Johnny began at once, his features strengthening under his earnestness.

"You see, Devereux, this speech is my idea and it means a lot to me. Some day, I'm supposed to inherit the business and I'm trying to learn it from the ground up." He smiled. "No humor intended. And I'm studying the people, too. I'm trying to make friends with them. My theory is there needn't *be* an eternal conflict between capital and labor, but I can damned well see how it's all come about."

He leaned nearer.

"I'm crazy about my father. Funny remark for a son to make, maybe, but that's the truth. So is everyone who knows him. Even Kirkland, his biggest rival, hobnobs with him. But in spite of my admiration for him in most things I know as sure as shootin' that if there weren't an organized union those hunkies out there in our mines wouldn't have a leg to stand on. These coal operators aren't in business for their health. They're out to make money—and they should up to a point—but if they hadn't been so greedy years ago, there wouldn't have been any unions now. Wouldn't have needed them. That's not such an original statement, but funny thing is you seldom hear it nowadays."

"May I ask if you're a Socialist?" Paul put in.

Johnny grinned. "No, I'm just an ordinary guy, trying to figure things out. I had a crazy idea the other day. Utterly loony. But just suppose once in a while when business has been good we as operators would go to the union and suggest we give a raise before they asked for it? We'd get the drop on them for once, wouldn't we? Take the wind right out of their sails, eh?"

He stroked his chin wistfully.

"But try to get my Dad to see *that* one! Well, now let's talk about the speech. I hope you don't think I'm completely screwball," he added earnestly.

Paul laughed. "Quite the contrary. I'm more interested than you think. Your father gave me a general idea of what you want me to say. . . ."

"Now, that's just it. I know what *he* wants, but it's not quite what *I* want. His idea is just a lot of nice hot air with a few allusions to the employer as the Big White Papa. Now what I have in mind is different. You see—I just happen to believe heart and soul in the future of America. I know it gets a little muddy and messy round the edges, but what doesn't? At the core it's as sound as Abe Lincoln himself. You agree?"

"I agree."

"Well, you know there's plenty of loose talk going round. Now, more than ever. God knows what may be brewing out there in the coal works that we don't know anything about. I'd like to counteract that. I'd like you to talk about America in a way they've maybe never heard of before."

He paused, studying Paul's face. "And I believe you can do it! Now here's the idea. Oh . . . In War Two, I suppose?"

Paul nodded. "Infantry. Europe."

"I was in the Marines in the Pacific. One day at Bougainville when things were pretty . . . rugged, I thought I was going off my rocker. Thinking about home, about America as it is, didn't do any good when I was wading knee-deep in jungle mud with snipers pot-shotting at me. All at once I thought of the stories I'd heard of my great-great-grandparents. They were pioneers. I suppose yours were too?"

Paul nodded assent.

"Well, I thought of them. Young like me when the Indians burned the cabin they'd built with their own hands, fired their cornfield, brained their baby against a tree under their eyes. And what did they do? They moved right on west into the Ohio wilderness and started up again. You know *that* was what kept me going out in that hell of a place."

Paul did not speak. He only waited.

"So, this occurred to me. I'll bet you no one in all Europe today ever stops to think about the way America was made! Most of them don't even *know*. They feel it just somehow sprang up like a mushroom, rich, easygoing country—money growing on trees—all that. They don't realize what went before, how the ground is soaked with the blood and the sweat of the pioneers. That's what I'd like you to tell in your speech. Make it *real* to those folks out at Redstone. Tell them it's their country now but it's been bought with a damned high price. You see what I mean? Land of opportunity now for them, and their kids, because of all this, but it's up to them to appreciate it and do their part and teach their kids to love and respect it. Well, what do you think? Sounds pretty old-fashioned, maybe?"

Paul was grave. He had been deeply moved by Johnny's talk.

"You make this a challenge," he said. "But I'll do my best. I come from the same kind of stock as you. I guess we're all inclined to forget what we owe the past. And it's certainly not a very *far* past at that, as countries go. I tell you what I'd like to do. I'll think this over pretty hard, then I'll sketch a rough draft and let you see it. I'd like to be sure I'm heading in the right direction. I really do get your idea," he added, "if I can only do it justice."

"You will," Johnny returned confidently. "Look! We forgot to eat. Let's fall to. Say, I'm sorry if your lunch is cold. Oh, by the way, Dad says he met you with Kirkland. May I ask how you got to know him?"

"Well," Paul said, "he heard me make a speech and found I was interested in politics."

"Oh, *that's* it! By golly, if I weren't tied up in the business I'd like to take a crack at that myself. I'd never get far, though," he laughed. "I'd be always bucking the machine. But good luck to *you!*"

"Thanks," Paul said. "I'm just a novice now. I've got an awful lot to learn. As a matter of fact I think you're one person whose viewpoint I would like to get from time to time."

"Advice free as air," Johnny said, "and probably as empty! Say, have you ever met Anne Kirkland?"

"Yes, I have." Paul hoped his color was not rising.

"Ghastly thing about her, isn't it? I never knew her well. She went with a younger crowd, of course, but I've met her at the big shindigs now and then. Boy, what a beauty! Young Lamson seemed to be making the best time there before the accident. He's the son of Lamson Steel, Ink. You know. *Only* son. What a tie-up of fortunes that would have been if it had come off. Well, it's pretty tough. My sister says Anne's plucky as the devil about it all. Of course she probably still hopes . . ." He broke off, looking keenly at Paul who still remained silent, then started quickly to change the subject.

As Paul walked back to the office he thought of Johnny's shrewd scrutiny and wondered if his own secret was written in his eyes as plainly as he feared. He must watch out for that. As to Johnny, he had a feeling beyond mere liking when he thought of him. A grand guy, that. In spite of his light casualness there was deep wisdom in him. He would make a valuable friend.

There was no word from Kirkland all that day nor the next until late afternoon. Then the call came.

"Paul? Could you stop in at my office when you're through today? I'll be alone here, working late."

"Of course," Paul replied. "I can get there about five-thirty."

"Good. See you then."

He hung up and Paul pitched furiously into the work upon his desk, trying to conquer the nervousness that kept recurring. He left at five, and was at Kirkland's office by the half-hour. Kirkland himself showed signs of agitation and Paul's certainty increased that the reason for this meeting was not politics but Anne.

The older man plunged in at once.

"There is one phase of our plan which I have taken most seriously from the start. I told you when I first proposed it to you that I, personally, would hold you free to withdraw from the—marriage if after three years Anne's condition is unchanged. I am taking an enormous risk in tampering with her life. But it is a calculated one. I have pursued every untoward possibility to its bitter conclusion. I have faced up to all that may happen. Or may not happen."

He paused and Paul's heart began to beat uncomfortably. It would seem so logical, so simple to tell this man the truth: that by some miraculous chance he was in love with Anne; that as far as he himself was concerned there was now no deal, no bargain involved. He could even tell him of his own inner struggle of the night before and of his triumphant issue from it. But this was for him not only distasteful but impossible. His love was so new, so inviolable that he could share the verity with Anne alone. Certainly with no other before her.

There was the danger also of some shade of unbelief, some hint of scepticism in Kirkland's eyes, if the confession were made, even while he would accept the news with joy. If this happened Paul knew he would shrink from the shadow of it, as though the wonder and the brightness of the miracle had suffered soil. No, he could not tell him.

Kirkland was speaking again, slowly, weighing each word.

"You have made a quick, I might almost say *hasty* decision to go on with this, due, as I believe, to my daughter's attractiveness. But as an older man I realize more than you what may ensue as time goes on if there should be no improvement in her case. You are young, strong, virile, active. You may come to feel restless and dissatisfied, even *trapped* by such a marriage. It is this situation which *I will not permit Anne to face.* I know her pride. I also have my own."

Paul started to speak but the other silenced him.

"It is to insure the preservation of my daughter's dignity that I wish this to be clearly understood between us. In fact, I have decided to commit it to writing so there will be no question ever as to the exact intent of our agreement."

"I would never put my name to such a paper!" Paul's tone was harsh.

"You don't need to. It's my name that's important. I'm the one making the statement. All I want you to do is to keep the paper and remain conscious of having it. I suppose I might as well admit that I believe there is a psychology involved. I don't think you will be as likely to feel trapped at any time if you know this written agreement is in your possession. Here it is. Read it for yourself."

Paul slowly picked up the sheet.

To Paul Devereux: If after a period of three years the plan decided upon between us has produced no change in physical conditions, you are free of all obligation to me to continue in that status if you desire to be released therefrom.

JAMES KIRKLAND

"Remember," Kirkland was saying, "this is no legal document. It is never to be seen by anyone but ourselves. But it *will* be a definite reminder to you in case you should ever feel uncomfortably indebted to me, that I hold you entirely free after . . ."

"But look here!" Paul burst out. "This is absurd. What about Anne in all this?"

Kirkland's face suddenly seemed to thin and whiten to that of an old man. His voice when he spoke was like steel.

"I thought I had made it clear that the first chance, which represents the only hope in the world for her, I *must take*. The second chance I will not."

There was silence and then Paul said slowly, "And what if we should eventually be in love with each other?"

"Ah," said Kirkland in a long drawn breath. "Ah—*that!*" He smiled for the first time during the interview. "Ah . . ." he breathed again.

Then as though he did not dare to comment upon this possibility he said briskly, "After three years you can destroy the paper. No matter what comes it will then have served its purpose. I have a copy. It will remain with my private papers."

Paul picked up the sheet gingerly.

"And put it where it won't blow away, my boy. You have a deposit box? Get one if you haven't."

Paul nodded.

"Best place for it. And don't worry about things. That's my business. I'm not good at saying what I feel but I guess you know. There's a change in Anne already. Brighter, more like her old self. I have a strong hope she may—well, good luck with everything! I'm getting some things lined up with Brennen and one or two others. Next week we'll get together and talk politics in earnest. No use in delays. Well —thanks, Paul."

He wrung the young man's hand.

When Paul reached his room, he closed the door carefully, took the paper from his inside pocket, held it over an ash tray, lighted a match under it and watched it burn to nothing.

"And that," he said aloud, "is that!"

Then he turned quickly to the telephone and dialed a number. All at once the entangling forces which were gathering in upon him from all sides fell away. He was only a young man in love, eager, listening, waiting to hear the one voice which rang in his heart.

4

◄§ As MARCH moved into the budding promise of April, a number of things happened to Paul. For one, he found himself now a professional speechmaker listed on the Speaker's Bureau, ready to do active campaigning for his party whenever the occasion arose. In his first real conference with Arno, during which they sat alone in the back office and quite patently liked each other, the latter gave him a rough outline of the months ahead.

"The Chief thought I might be of some use to you," he said, with a smile that changed the sinister expression to one of friendly candor. "I've been with him for a good many years now and I sort of know the score. Usually, that is."

"I'll appreciate your help," Paul said earnestly. "I'm horribly green. I've been concentrating pretty heavily on law, you know, even while I had my eye on a political career eventually."

"Well, that's all to the good, the law end of it. That's the way most of them start and if you please old Hartwell, I guess you know your stuff." His eyes narrowed suddenly. "By the way, how is he taking your new plans? Make any fuss about them?"

"No, not really. He was very kind, as a matter of fact. Gave me some advice."

"I'll bet he did! He doesn't like the Chief, that's for sure. Don't believe all he tells you. He gets ideas in his hair. Well, now, here's the way things are going. You knew the Chief was at the capital this week?"

Paul nodded.

"He's having a conference with Senator Hunt about Halsey—for governor. The Chief feels sure he can be nominated, but we have to step lively. The Barker interests are backing Dunham. I suppose you know what that means?"

"We have business dealings with the Barker Bank, of course, but naturally I have had no reason so far to know more than that."

"Well, that's all most people know. But the bank is just the front. Behind it there's a hookup with about every big financial concern in the country. Utilities, insurance companies, railroads, and so on.

They've got plenty of power all right, of a kind, but they don't always know how to use it. That's where the Chief outsmarts them. I think he'd rather beat old Barker than anything else in the world. And he's after him this time all right! No punches pulled!"

Arno grinned appreciatively.

"If Halsey gets the nomination, and I always bet on the Chief, then the idea is for you to start right in with your speeches boosting him for governor. You'll hear from the Bureau more and more as time goes on, but use every chance you get to talk him up. See? Of course the Chief's killing two birds with one stone. Campaigning for Halsey and getting you in the public eye."

Paul laughed. "He's pretty clever, isn't he? Well, I'll do my best to work for Halsey and myself at the same time. Since the word sort of got around that I'm available as a speaker, it's amazing how many invitations have already come in. All kinds. It seems as if an awful lot of people are eager to be lectured at. Funny, isn't it?"

"Great American pastime," Arno said. "Sit still and relax and let the other fellow feed you the ideas! Well, it suits our game all right. From now on up to the primaries next month get around to the different precincts as much as you can. If there's no chance for real speeches just put in a good word here and there. I'll give you a list of a few spots you might cover. Say, do you mind if I ask you something?"

"Of course not," Paul said, a shade too heartily to cover his sudden fear that Arno's question might be embarrassing.

"Well, I'm just curious. Did the Chief really never see you between the time he heard you speak at that Young Politicians' Club and the day he had you meet him here to have lunch with him?"

"No," Paul said, "he didn't."

"That's straight?" Arno persisted.

Paul flushed. "I'm accustomed to telling the truth," he said shortly.

Arno merely grinned. "Don't get sore. I wasn't calling you a liar. When you're in politics a while you'll learn you have to sort of turn facts around to suit the occasion. You know the old gag about a diplomat. The Chief always gets a rap out of it. If a diplomat says *yes,* he means *perhaps.* If he says *perhaps* he means *no.* And if he says *no,* he's the hell of a diplomat."

Paul managed a laugh and Arno seemed satisfied. "The Chief says that goes for a politician too. But what I was talking about is I can't figure out how he picked you practically out of the air and started backing you with all he's got before he even knew you. He's a smart picker and he works fast, but I've never known him to do anything like *this* before. Weren't you surprised yourself?"

"Very," Paul answered.

Arno waited as though expecting further explanation, then shrugged his shoulders.

"Well, he doesn't often make mistakes so you can consider yourself . . ."

There was a discreet knock on the door. Arno looked irritated. "Come in."

Miss Sayles appeared. This time she was not "icily regular, splendidly null," as Paul had always mentally described her. Her face was flushed and her manner agitated.

"C is in there," she said in a stage whisper.

Arno jumped to his feet. "You're crazy," he hissed. "He's never been here in his life!"

"I'm telling you he's in the Chief's office right now and he's mad. Arno . . ."—her eyes suddenly gave her secret away—"Arno, I'm scared for you. Watch your step. Be careful."

"What in the devil are you talking about?" he said fiercely. "Don't be a fool. I was going to see this fellah today anyhow," he said turning to Paul, "and he's just come to save me the trouble, I guess. Sorry to stop our talk but I'll have to get on in there. You mind going out with Sayles through the reception room? Well, so long. Be seein' you."

In a flash he had pushed her unconsciously restraining hand aside and was gone through the door.

Paul got up to leave and then stopped.

"Miss Sayles," he said, "what's going on? Is there likely to be trouble in there? I'm pretty husky. Hadn't I better stick around?"

She tried to look calm. "Oh, no, I'm sure everything is all right. This man makes me nervous, that's all. He . . . has such a temper. I'll show you out."

"Who is he?" Paul asked as they reached the outer room.

"Oh, just a . . . a sort of politician. There are all kinds, you know. Goodbye, Mr. Devereux."

Paul went slowly through the hall toward the elevator. He had an extremely uncomfortable feeling. Sayles's fright had been genuine, no matter how she tried to cover it now. Arno had been startled and upset and had gone to the caller with a speed that betokened his importance. These were the only facts to go upon at the moment.

On the first floor he left the elevator and took his station across the lobby where he could see all who came down. He pulled some papers from his pocket and made pretense of reading them. He decided to wait for fifteen minutes and then phone to make sure everything was all right. When he finally rang up from the lobby booth and asked for Arno, Miss Sayles's voice was reassuringly cold.

"He's been in conference until a moment ago but I'll put him right on."

When Arno answered, Paul thought of an ostensible reason for his call.

"You spoke of a list of places you were going to give me," he said. "Could you just mail it to my office?"

"Righto." Arno sounded rather complacent. "Sorry to leave you so abruptly but you know how things come up!"

"Sure," Paul said. "Goodbye, and thanks."

As he turned from the booth one of the elevators clanged and a man got out. He was short, heavily built and swarthy of face. He wore a brown suit and hat, brown topcoat and tan shoes. He glanced sharply toward Paul—the only other person in the lobby—and then walked swiftly out, into a waiting car, and drove off with another man behind the wheel. With an electric intuition Paul was sure this was the mysterious C.

Once back in his own office he had an overpowering urge to talk to old Hartwell. He went in before closing time and found the old man sitting staring at the ceiling and twisting the ends of his mustache.

"Never grow old, Paul," he began characteristically, "or if you do, be sure to have a family about you. This thing of being a bachelor in the city is a lonesome business. *Magna civitas magna solitudo.* I'm beginning to hate to leave my office at night."

"I'm only in sort of bachelor rooms, sir, but if you'd ever be willing to spend an evening with me it would be doing me the greatest favor! The woman where I stay would serve us a little supper there. Do consider it!"

The very real affection Paul felt for the old man showed in the warmth of his voice.

"I wasn't hinting," Hartwell smiled, "but I'll take you up on that sometime, my boy, and thanks." He sounded moved. "Now, what's on your mind?"

"Well," Paul began, "I just wondered what you knew about this man Halsey, or Dunham either, for that matter. I'm for Halsey and am to do a little campaigning for him if he's nominated. I just wondered how you stood."

Hartwell laughed shortly. "It's like the old story of the ass and the mule: not much to choose between them. I'm voting for Halsey because I don't like the reason for Dunham's being put up at all. You can't use this in your speeches but I'll tell you if you want to know."

"I do."

"Well, it's like this. In the Barker Bank, you know, there's Barker Senior, about my age or older, and Barker Junior, in his early fifties. Junior is presumably a solid, upstanding citizen, fine wife from one of our best families, and a family of grown children."

Hartwell paused and sighed. "Wouldn't you think that would satisfy a man? But every now and then he goes a-roving and this last time nearly put an end to it. He had a girl out at some roadhouse back in the country. It was a bad night and the car skidded on a curve and ran into a tree. When a motor policeman found them Junior was still half drunk and the girl pretty badly hurt."

Paul whistled.

"Not a nice story. Well, old Barker got busy, managed to keep it out of the headlines, and hired Dunham to do the rest. He was State Senator then but of course he still practices here. Considered the shrewdest lawyer in the state. I don't know yet how he did it, but he got Junior out of the mess with no publicity. Of course old Barker would pay him well but Dunham wanted something more. He wanted to be governor. Well, there you have it. That's why I'm going to vote for Halsey."

"You feel he's a good man, then?"

"Not especially. He's a pleasant fellow. I've known him slightly for years. He'll make a fine impression on the public and if he's elected he'll probably do about what he's told."

Hartwell fumbled in one of his desk drawers.

"Ever look up a definition of politics, Paul?" he asked.

"No," Paul smiled, "I'm afraid I never have. It's one of the words we usually take for granted somehow."

"I've got a note or so here for you. I copied these out of an old dictionary that I still hang on to."

He read, "*Politics: the administration of public affairs in the interest of the peace, prosperity and safety of the state.*

"Then listen to this. It's a quotation underneath supposed to illustrate and illumine the definition.

"*I regard politics also as the principles by which nations should be governed and regulated, as only a branch of ethics; or rather as a special application of the principles of morality and religion.*

"There, my boy," he said, handing Paul the slip of paper, "put that in your pipe and smoke it as you think of your own career. Well, good luck to you."

Paul recognized the signal and left at once. He put the paper carefully in his inside pocket, smiling faintly as he did so. For a hardheaded, successful lawyer old Hartwell held some pretty idealistic views. It would be interesting, though, to discuss them with Anne tonight, since he was to see her at dinner.

As a matter of fact his friendship with Anne was growing beyond his fondest hopes, and he knew also that Kirkland was inwardly jubilant over his progress. His calls had become steadily more frequent until now he was dropping in several times a week, often at her invitation or Kirkland's, to dinner. On some evenings when he had work he stayed for perhaps an hour only. This was possible because he was now the owner of an automobile. It had become clear to him that a car was a necessity both for his courtship and for his speechmaking, and he had lost no time in making the purchase. Johnny Bovard, who knew everything and everybody, had steered him to a really good model which a friend of his wanted to sell.

Paul was amused at his own somewhat boyish reactions. He had never owned a car before. During college and law school he had driven the family one at vacations; during these last years of living in the city he had considered a car a needless luxury. Now he felt an absurd delight and importance in the knowledge that this sleek and powerful creature belonged to him. His great desire was to get Anne into it; but so far she had turned off his tentative suggestions.

He drove up to the big house that evening at six-thirty, his usual eagerness intensified by Anne's promise of a surprise. "*Two* of them," she had amended.

The sudden glimpse of a large car parked a little way beyond where he himself came to a stop gave him a feeling of disappointment. In Kirkland's absence he had looked forward to dining alone with Anne. Now, apparently, this was not to be.

Hackett, who was already his sworn friend, received him with a broad smile and showed him toward the library. From the doorway he saw an old lady with a beautiful, thin, patrician face, sitting opposite Anne.

"Surprise!" Anne cried as soon as he had entered. "I've talked so much about you, Gran, that I'm sure Paul will recognize you on sight!"

"It seems to me," the old lady said with a twinkle as he bowed over her hand, "that I've heard occasionally of you, too."

As he went over to Anne he saw that the kitten was curled up, asleep on her knees.

"Just as you predicted," she said stroking the small tiger gently. "He's here most of the time and I love it, especially when he purrs. Davy says, though, that we like animals only because they flatter us by *their* affection. Do you think that's so? It seems so disillusioning."

"That may be part of it," Mrs. Catherby returned, "but you could carry that idea on logically into the world of humans and I should *not* like that."

"Heavens no!" Paul said. "That would put emotion on a very low level indeed. But I don't believe it's true in relation to animals either. We had a colt once when I was a boy that was the most cantankerous young beast ever born. We simply couldn't break him. He snapped every time I tried to bridle him and threw me off a dozen times, I suppose, and yet I was crazy about him. I was terribly upset when Father finally sold him. There, does that comfort you?" he asked Anne.

"Very much. My love for Devvie is now justified, a hundred per cent pure! I believe dinner is announced," she added, as Hackett appeared. "We're skipping cocktails since Gran doesn't take them. Will you help her in, Paul?"

As they moved slowly through the hall, Mrs. Catherby looked up at him.

"I'm very much interested in what Anne told me of your political ambitions," she said. "I don't know much about such things, but from the news in the papers every day it would seem that we could use some good young men in government. May I ask if you're a crusader?"

"I'm afraid not," Paul laughed. "I'm just an ordinary fellow who hopes someday to run for office. Of course," he added, "if I ever reach any goal of that sort I'll try to do an honest job."

"Doesn't it amount to the same thing?" she asked seriously, as they reached the table.

Paul turned to Anne as he sat down. "Your grandmother is trying to make me out a reformer, when I'm not in the least. You must tell her how earthy my ambition really is."

Anne leaned forward, her lovely face animated with interest.

"I'll tell you what we'll do. Since we have Gran here we must talk sense. Let's have a dinner 'topic' as the French do. How about *the perfect state and how to arrive at it?*"

"Excellent," said Mrs. Catherby. "The idea of perfection always gives one a chance to talk without knowing facts. Where do we start?"

"Why not at the bottom with the individual," Paul said, "and build up from there?"

They argued and wrangled happily through the courses, with Paul watching Mrs. Catherby with more and more respect.

As they sat over dessert she made a summary.

"Well, we have now arrived in our rosy fancy at a society of perfect citizens who freely elect perfect representatives who on all levels administer government perfectly. How, though, do we move into Utopia?"

"And might it be boring after all?" Anne asked thoughtfully. "Are human beings so conditioned to imperfection that any other state would seem a trifle flat to them? And does good really only shine out in contrast to evil?"

"Aren't you negating heaven itself, then?" Paul asked smiling.

"Oh, no! I was only thinking of earth. Such a funny, tragic little ball as it is. I believe, though, that we chose a wrong topic tonight. It's been fun—all the discussion—but maybe we should have been more practical. Maybe we should have considered how a young man entering politics"—she glanced shyly at Paul—"can improve conditions as they already exist."

"First, get himself elected to office," Paul said promptly. Then he suddenly remembered the slip of paper in his pocket.

"Say, I have something apropos to all this right here. I forgot about it. Mr. Hartwell, our senior partner, gave it to me this afternoon and I brought it along. Definition of politics."

He read the statements and then paused for comment.

Mrs. Catherby's face was grave.

"*A branch of ethics,*" she repeated slowly, "*a special application of the principles of morality and religion.* The quotation is even more startling than the definition. I wish—sometime—you would show that to Mr. Kirkland."

An uncomfortable silence fell, each knowing that if Kirkland had been present the conversation would not have taken place.

To break the embarrassment Paul said suddenly, "By the way, wasn't I promised two surprises tonight? There couldn't be a second as delightful as the first," bowing to Mrs. Catherby, "but even so, I'm curious."

Anne gave the signal to rise and Hackett was instantly at her chair.

"I'll show you, right away, even though it isn't strictly good form," she said. "The music room, Hackett."

It was a part of the house Paul had not been in before—a beautiful room of tall leaded windows and soft green satin chairs and sofas. There was some fine sculpture here and there, and a large and handsome piano in one corner. Hackett moved Anne's chair toward it. She laughed over her shoulder at them as she settled to the keyboard.

"You'll have to suffer for a while, I'm afraid, for I can't keep away from this, ever since it arrived. Father had it specially built, Paul, to compensate partly at least for the lack of pedal action. Don't expect too much, though."

She began to play. From where he sat he could watch her profile, with the light shining on her golden hair. He saw fully for the first time the character in her face. Behind the delicacy of feature there was strength. It showed in the firm line of the lips, the chin, in the intentness of the eyes, as she concentrated completely upon the music.

He was amazed at the brilliance of her playing, and felt himself caught up in a joint heaven of love and melody. Once in a while Mrs. Catherby asked for a favorite, and once Anne stopped suddenly and shook her head with a small tragic gesture.

"It's not the same, without real pedaling. But," she added quickly, "it's wonderful to be able to get any effect at all."

When she stopped at last, Paul felt strangely tongue-tied. The ordinary words of compliment would sound wooden compared to the depth of feeling in his heart. He remained silent while Mrs. Catherby spoke her pleasure and then rose to her feet.

"I must be going now," she said. "It's been a delightful evening, Anne, and Paul, it's been so very nice meeting you. I've been reveling in the book you lent me. May I keep it a little longer? I'm hoping," she added with a smile, "that sometime you'll read the Meredith poem aloud to me. Will you?"

"If it would give you the least pleasure, I would be glad to," Paul said, "though I'm afraid Anne has been exaggerating my small accomplishment. It's been wonderful meeting you, Mrs. Catherby.

I've been looking forward to it very much. May I be of any help to you going back?"

"No, thank you. Hawley watches over me like a hen with one chick. Here he comes now. He always seems to sense when I'm ready to go. It could be," she added smiling, "because I always leave at practically the same time."

When she had gone Paul pushed Anne's chair back to the library and they settled to themselves.

"She's all you described her," Paul said warmly, "and more. She's amazing! Such a mind! Such a personality! But Anne, the biggest surprise was your playing. I said nothing before because I couldn't find the words. I was too much moved by it. Is there *anything* you can't do?" he burst out.

She smiled her thanks and then a shadow like a cloud fell upon her. Her lips quivered.

"There are several things I can't do," she said huskily.

His heart ached for her and he cursed himself for the thoughtless question. He moved nearer and tried, however, to speak casually.

"I've been wanting to ask you something. You know this new play that's running at the Empire? Johnny Bovard tells me it's very amusing and full of meat, too. Would you go with me some evening, perhaps Saturday of next week, if I can get the tickets?"

She turned her face toward him with a look of horror.

"What do you mean?" she asked in a low, unsteady voice.

"Just what I say. It would be very simple. Here am I strong as an ox. Here are you, a mere featherweight. I could carry you to the car. We would have aisle seats, go in just after the curtain goes up, then at the end we could sit and chat a few minutes till the theater empties. Perhaps instead of my car we could use one of your father's, then it could be drawn up just ready for us when we go out. You see? As easy as that. What do you say, Anne? I want terribly to take you!"

She still sat, her face frozen and drawn as with shock.

"What do you say?" he begged eagerly.

"I couldn't possibly," she managed at last.

"But why? You need diversion. Have you really never been away from the house since . . . . it all happened?"

"Just to the hospital in an ambulance."

"There! That's what I mean. You must get out and see things and do things. This would be such a simple, easy way to begin. Besides,

I want so much to have the pleasure of taking you. I'll arrange everything. Please say *yes!*"

Her hands, he could see, were trembling in her lap.

"I'm not ungrateful," she said painfully. "Thank you very much. I'll . . . I'll think it over."

"No!" The word exploded from him. He caught her small shaking hands in his strong ones, holding them tightly. "That is just what you must not do. You'll think up all kinds of foolish obstacles. I want your promise *now* that you'll go. Nothing except cowardice would make you refuse. And you're certainly no coward."

He leaned over her. His voice was tender but commanding. "Anne, do as I ask this once. I won't urge you against your will again."

She was looking up at him dazedly. "You wouldn't be . . . embarrassed?"

"*Embarrassed!*" He repeated the word with a great upstanding vehemence. Then he waited for a moment as though considering how to answer. At last he put a hand on each arm of her chair and bent toward her until his face was near hers.

"Do you suppose," he asked very low, "that I would not *like* to carry you, to feel you in my arms?"

Then quickly he straightened and assumed his usual tone.

"I must be going. I'm always keeping you up too late. I'll see about tickets tomorrow and let you know. There's quite a run on this show I hear. Well, it's been a beautiful evening. Thanks for everything and . . . goodnight."

He walked quickly to the doorway, afraid she might break the unspoken promise with a word. But she did not speak again, only watched him with a strange expression in her eyes as he turned, waved his hand and went out.

Once back in his room, he put on his dressing gown, lighted the gas logs in his fireplace and sat down to think. He had never felt more completely and richly awake. There was first of all, to consider, the thrill of winning Anne's consent to go to the theater, for he knew from her eyes that it *was* consent. His heart beat faster at the thought of having her beside him in the car, at the play, just like any other girl. If this first experiment was successful there could be all sorts of delightful ones to follow. Perhaps before too long he could confess his love itself. She must surely guess something of his feelings from what he had said tonight.

He thought of her playing and the sweet clear strength of her face as he had watched it in profile from his vantage spot. She was a girl in ten thousand! Old Mrs. Catherby was a prize, too. He felt he would get on well with her. His thoughts drifted to the talk at the dinner table. He went over it, bit by bit. How bright and sparkling and *literate* it had been on the part of the two women; and with a tinge of complacent pride he felt he had done rather well himself in keeping the conversational ball in the air!

Then steadily, devastatingly, as water pushes through a barrier, there began to flow over him the realization that all he had said that evening with reference to politics had been insignificant and *shallow*. And the reason for this was that he, himself, had up to this point been shallow in his thinking and in his ambition. This was what old Hartwell must have sensed as he pierced him with his blue eagle eyes and handed him the slip of paper.

Suppose he took stock of himself, what would he find? A fairly clever, hard-working young fellow, with a desire to get into the Big Game someday, he scarcely knew why. Where were his convictions? Where was his unselfish patriotism? Where the determination that leads to reform? These qualities were not present. If, as Kirkland's man, he was ever elected to office might he not merely fulfill the description Hartwell had given him of Halsey, the would-be candidate for governor? *Pleasant, likable fellow making a good impression upon the electorate, and doing what the bosses told him to do.*

Paul sat forward, his head in his hands. He had to think about this thing. He had to penetrate to the bottom of this force of which he had rather blindly wished to become a part. For a long time he pondered, his mind seeking, questioning, probing. At long last, like a light, a concept suddenly came to him. He sat up, thinking it through again, eagerly. Why, this was it! Thus was the crux, the core of it all.

As sex was to the individual, upsurging, creative, dominant, so was government to society. The same compelling impulse rising from the mass of men to insure continuity, not of the race but of civilization. There was the necessity, the trust, unconsciously recognized and obeyed. And if government (as sex) was clean and honest, then the present was protected and enriched and the future preserved; if corrupt, the pillars of society fell and with them civilization itself. It was as simple and as fundamental as that.

And if he held tightly to this concept, then perhaps his own position with regard to it would have a chance to emerge with clarity. Meanwhile, at the moment, he felt as exhausted as he had on that other night when he had wrestled with the question of his own personal integrity in the event of his marriage to Anne. He got into bed, drawing a long sigh as he put out the light. The complications of his life had certainly multiplied in the last weeks. In spite of them, however, and with a last young thought of the coming theater date, he fell instantly to sleep.

The next day, as happened now once a week, he was lunching with Johnny Bovard.

"I'm taking you to a dive," the latter announced as they drove in his car. "Little joint down on Third Street, but they've got the best Italian food in the city. We might see a *hood* or two. Not that I'm personally acquainted with them."

"A *what?*" Paul queried.

"Hood. Short for hoodlum, gangster, underworlder, or whatever. You know, I suppose, that we've got a few in this fair city. And they pretty damned near run it, too. Oh, here we are."

They went down steps to a basement restaurant where Johnny greeted the proprietor.

"Hi, Nick. How's the ravioli today? Say, this is a good friend of mine, Bill Smith. What a gang here! Can you give me a table?"

Nick patted Johnny's shoulder. "Always a table for you, Mr. Bovard. Right this way."

"You know," Johnny remarked when they were seated. "I always have more of a feeling of being among the big shots when I'm here than when I'm with Father at his D. D. Club. That's bad."

"What made you give me an alias?" Paul asked curiously.

"Oh, I don't know. Just hit me that if you're going into politics you'd better keep your nose clean all round—if it's possible. How's the speech coming?"

"Nearly done, but I'm not satisfied with the end. I've been working like a dog on it. Maybe next week I can have it ready for you to look over. Of course it will sound better, I hope, as I give it."

"I think the whole jamboree's going to go over big. I'm seeing to the ox roast. Seems there hasn't been one round these parts for thirty years. Good old custom. Ought to be revived. You know what I'd do if Dad would let me? Invite the *Union,* too. Old Bill himself. And I'll bet he'd come. I've still got a hunch that if we got together sometimes in between strikes it would be a smart idea. Oh, say," he leaned closer, "to coin a phrase, don't look now, but behind us at the corner table is the Kingpin himself."

"Who?"

"Why Camponelli! He's head of the numbers racket and Lord High Everything Else in this burg. He's the one in brown."

When they got up to go, Paul glanced around, and his face stiffened. The man in brown was the same one who had stepped out of the elevator the day before in Kirkland's office building. His name, then, began with C. The pieces of the puzzle fit.

Kirkland returned two days later from the capital and immediately sent for Paul. The older man breathed power and near-jubilation.

"How are you, my boy? Well, the news is good right down the line. I'm sure Halsey's going to get the nomination. As soon as that is fact I'll have the two of you to lunch and you can get acquainted. Then until fall election you can campaign in earnest and get the feel of it. Like the prospect?"

"Very much, sir."

"But I've heard good news since I got back. Anne tells me she's going to the theater with you!"

"Yes. She finally agreed. I got the tickets yesterday. I'm certainly looking forward to it."

Kirkland's face looked almost young in its pleasure.

"The whole plan, Paul, is proceeding beyond my wildest hopes. She has resolutely refused to go out before. She is proud and terribly sensitive, of course. Now, that she has consented to *go to the theater with you* is nothing short of a miracle. I simply can't tell you how happy I am! Don't rush her, of course, about—the other, but so many small things point to the fact that she will ultimately consent. You've handled it all wonderfully, my boy. Wonderfully!"

Paul smiled and thanked him and then turned serious.

"Mr. Kirkland, there's something I want to discuss with you, if you'll allow me. It has nothing to do with Anne."

At once Kirkland's usual guard was up.

"Of course," he said crisply.

"The other day while I was talking with Arno in his office, Miss Sayles came in greatly agitated. She said C was here. Arno said it was impossible, but she insisted he was and that he was mad. Arno tried to cover, but it was clear he was upset too. He left his office like a shot to confer with this man, who I have reason to believe was Camponelli, the numbers racketeer. Can you explain what connection he would have with this office?"

Kirkland's face had undergone no change of expression. Not a muscle showed undue reaction. Only his eyes, Paul thought, had narrowed warily behind their lids. His voice when he spoke was composed and casual.

"Arno's quite a character," he began with a reminiscent flavor. "Never really told you about him, did I? Well, he grew up, one of eight, in three rooms on Water Street, toughest part of the city. His father had a little green-grocer shop. You never can tell where kids like that get brains, but Arno had them all right. I ran into him when he was a messenger boy for Western Union. Don't know why I took a fancy to the kid, but I did."

He paused and lighted a cigarette.

"He's been with me ever since and heaven only knows what I'd do without him. But, you see, he's got a lot of friends from the old background. I never pry into his personal life. I've no idea what he does when he leaves here. Do you see what I'm getting at? If this fellow came to see him, it's none of my business. Naturally Sayles wouldn't approve that kind of caller!"

"It was not merely disapproval. She was scared white. Her hands shook."

Kirkland laughed. "Oh, come now, Paul. You're making a movie out of this. Let Arno run his own affairs. It's possible he's been writing some numbers on the side, himself. He's a born gambler. You just forget the whole thing. Well, I see my desk looks as if I'd been away."

Paul rose at once. Kirkland stood also and grasped his shoulders affectionately.

"My boy, let me tell you again that my heart feels lighter than it's done since Anne's accident. Count on me for anything, *anything!*"

"Thank you, sir," Paul said gravely. "If the trip to the theater turns out all right, I'll try to think of other things we can do. She needs to get out of the house. I must be running along now. It's good to see you back."

Paul moved slowly through the hall toward the elevator, thinking. He was not completely satisfied with Kirkland's explanation of Camponelli's visit to the office, yet it all sounded plausible enough. He knew it would be wise to drop it from his mind for the present.

As a matter of fact, while he did his daily work faithfully and labored most evenings in polishing up and practicing the Memorial Day speech, his thoughts reverted constantly to the coming date with Anne.

The evening itself, when it came, could not have been finer. There was a light warm breeze blowing, and a faint melting tinge of rose left in the west as he drove out. The delicate hint of fragrance from early leaf and bud had become now the appreciable incense of spring in bloom. He could detect the scent of lilacs as he turned up the drive, and he heard the robin's twilight song again with an ecstasy of longing.

It had already been arranged that the large Kirkland car with the chauffeur would be waiting at the front door, so Paul parked his own at the back and went, with a vast sense of trepidation and fear, into the small morning room to the left of the front door and nearest to it. This, Anne had planned.

She was seated on a small sofa, and he gave an exclamation of pleasure as he saw her, for she was wearing a coat of light pink wool which apparently matched the dress underneath. It buttoned simply to the neck with a small round collar which gave her the appearance of a little girl. Close to her face she wore the violets he had sent earlier.

"I never saw you look so lovely!" Paul cried. "Are you as excited as I am?"

He caught her hands in a firm grip and sat down beside her. "Let me just take you in, for a minute."

Anne laughed shakily and ignored his compliment. "Excited!" she said. "Why, I haven't been able to sleep for thinking about it. I didn't know how terribly I wanted to go out until I'd actually made up my mind to go. I'm still a little hysterical over it, so be prepared for a flood of tears at any moment. Happy ones, of course. And oh, I *love* my violets."

"My mother always taught me to carry two handkerchiefs," Paul returned, "so I'm prepared, if there's a flood! Let's get started, shall we? There's no telling about traffic and if we get to the theater too early, we'll sit in the car until curtain time."

He stood, and then quite easily lifted her in his arms.

"Are you sure I've got you?" he asked, laughing. "I can't feel a thing!"

But he did, though, and his heart beat fast. He felt her soft hair against his cheek; he felt her tender body against his own.

"Put your hand around my neck. It will be more comfortable for you."

In the hall Kirkland was waiting with the supreme grace of casualness to see them off as Hackett, smiling broadly, opened the door.

"Goodbye, Mouchie. Have fun! Goodbye, Paul. Hope you like the show."

Just as he'd seen her off a hundred times before!

Morley, the chauffeur, opened the car door impassively. Paul set her gently on the seat, hurried around the car, and climbed in beside her. They were off! They did not speak until they were down the drive and out upon the wide street. Then Anne, watching intently from the window, drew a long quivering breath.

"It's more wonderful than I can ever tell you, to be doing this! I think I have been a coward, and a vain one at that. But really," she added innocently turning toward him, "it *is* different going out with you this way than it would have been with Father."

"I hope so!" Paul said.

And then suddenly the tension broke and they laughed immoderately together. Paul put his arm through hers and held her hand while they went on with complete ease to talk of inconsequential things.

When they drew up before the theater it was exactly the hour for the show to begin. Morley had done his timing to perfection. In spite of a spattering of latecomers in the outer lobby, the place looked deserted.

"Here, you take these," Paul said, putting the tickets in Anne's hand. He got out quickly, took her again in his arms, and then in the briefest of moments they were in the already darkened theater. The usher led the flashlit path to aisle seats halfway down; they were in their places, Anne's coat unbuttoned and draped behind her, her violets pinned to her dress, and their bodies instinctively leaning toward each other as their eyes fastened upon the stage. So easy, so uncomplicated it had all been.

When the lights came on, Anne turned toward Paul full of animation about the play.

"I love it!" she exclaimed. "It's beautiful and yet completely realistic. It has . . ."

The young man directly in front of Paul turned suddenly around in his seat, his eyes wild with surprise.

"Anne!" he said. "*Anne!* Where did you . . . how did you . . . I didn't know you were . . ."

Anne's voice broke in very calmly and, as it seemed to Paul, coolly. "Oh, hello, Bill, how are you? This is Paul Devereux. Bill Lamson."

"And Sally McBride, Anne. I think you've met."

"Of course," Anne said pleasantly. "It was after a game once at a frat party. I remember we all had a lot of fun."

The introductions were completed, but Paul noted the constraint in the air. The girl named Sally looked distantly at Anne as through the far end of a telescope, the young man named Bill quite evidently took the close view and could not tear his eyes from it. Poor devil, Paul thought, he's loved her too. Turned down suitor, probably.

When Anne finally leaned back in her seat as though to terminate the conversation, Bill still persisted.

"How are you, really, Anne? I haven't seen you round. Nobody's told me a thing. I'm completely in the dark."

"I haven't been around, Bill. This is my first sortie. I'm still not automotive, but," with the lightest possible side glance toward Paul, "I'm finding life extremely interesting, even so."

This time young Lamson colored crimson for some reason and turned abruptly around as the lights again went out. Anne leaned closer to Paul.

"Do forgive me for that, but I had reason. I'll tell you about it later," she whispered.

"You couldn't have said a nicer thing, reason or not," he whispered back, and though she seemed to hesitate, he managed to capture her hand again.

Through the next act Paul kept wondering about the young man in front of him. *Lamson.* He had heard that name somewhere. Suddenly it came back to him. It was Johnny Bovard who had spoken of him that first day at lunch as he had inquired about Anne. *Young Lamson seemed to be making the best time there before the accident, son of Lamson Steel, Ink.,* he had said. So that was it. Paul felt more than ever curious but soon found himself lost again in the play.

When it was all over they sat still. Anne chatted on brightly as the people just beyond passed out in front of them and the aisles became crowded. Paul saw young Lamson pause as he stood up, trying to catch Anne's eye but she was looking elsewhere. They sat on comfortably, with small feeling of being observed until, in an incredibly short time the theater was empty. He helped her into her coat, eying again the low-cut pink wool dress that matched it.

"I think this is the prettiest outfit I ever saw," Paul remarked, "and the most becoming I've seen you wear. That's saying quite something."

"I'm glad you like it," Anne smiled. "It was exciting to have a real reason for buying something new."

"Shall we go now?" Paul asked. "I imagine Morley will be waiting."

He picked her up again easily and in a few minutes they were in the car. When they were out of the worst traffic, Anne turned toward him.

"Paul," she said, and her voice broke a little, "I simply haven't words to tell you how much this evening has meant to me! I can't thank you enough for planning it and making me go."

"It's meant even more to me," he answered, "and if it made you happy, I'm infinitely more so."

They rode on in silence for some time while waves of tenderness seemed to lap them round.

"I must explain about Bill Lamson," she said at last. "It was all very awkward and yet I'm wicked enough to be glad he saw me there. You see we were practically engaged before my accident."

"So that was it," Paul said slowly.

"I know now," Anne went on, "that I didn't really love him, but I was fond of him, I'd known him since dancing-class days, and it seemed rather inevitable. I had not accepted a ring, but it was all rather . . . settled."

She was looking away from him out of the window.

"When I was hurt, no one could see me for several weeks. Of course Bill telephoned then and sent flowers. But when the word got out that I couldn't walk and might never again, he stopped calling up and he never once came to see me. I think he was scared to death for fear in some way he might be involved . . ."

"The dog!" Paul gritted between his teeth.

"No," Anne said slowly, "he's young, and extremely athletic. Most of the time we spent together we were doing something active— you know—golf, tennis, skating, dancing. I loved doing them all so much, too." Her voice caught in spite of herself.

"At first it hurt unmercifully, but gradually I began to realize that a marriage with him would have been the greatest possible mistake. We really had nothing in common but these things I've mentioned. So it was best that he broke clean. Oh, he kept on sending red roses! Wagonloads of them. I still hate the sight of them. Davy used to send them straight to the hospitals! But you see how it was to-night. I'd never seen him since I was hurt, and it did my pride good somehow to meet him out, like any other girl, with an escort—oh, you don't think too badly of me, do you, for that?"

For answer he drew her close. His throat was too choked to answer. The tragic little sentence, *I loved doing them all so much, too*, rang in his heart like a knell. Never until this moment of her confession had he felt the full weight of her enforced renunciation. He saw it all now so plainly: Anne, dancing in gay ballrooms, the very essence of young, flying grace; skating, with scarlet cheeks, on the winter ice; running fleetly over a tennis court on summer days; swinging uphill, down dale over a golf course. All this and so much more swept away from her in a moment! How could she accept the tragedy as she had done? Was the inner strength he had sensed in her great enough to account for the courage, the lack of bitterness, the outward smiling grace with which she met the days? His heart yearned toward her with an overpowering burst of pity and love.

"And then," she was saying, "that last little innuendo I used, dragging you in, as it were. You must forgive me for that under the circumstances."

He spoke then. "You mean it was not true?"

Anne laughed. "Oh, the witness refuses to answer on the grounds that she may . . . why, here we are at home! The ride went so fast."

The car had stopped and Morley was holding the door. Paul went around to Anne's side, picked her up again and went in.

"To the library?" he asked.

"If you can hold out that far."

Once in the quiet room, Paul stood, making no move to put her down. His face was so close to the sweet beauty of hers; his arms clasped her body against his own. It was too much. He pressed his lips to hers with all the strength of his passion. Again and again with long, merciless ardor.

Then he set her gently down. Speech was impossible. He saw that under her drooping lids the tears had started. His own eyes were blinded with them as he walked to the door, through the long hallway and out again into the night. As he drove back he felt his hands trembling on the wheel, and his body shaken with emotion by what had passed. What then later on, would be the full consummation of his love? Drunk with his desire and his hopes, he shouted his triumph to the stars.

The letter came to his desk by special messenger the next day. He glanced at the handwriting and then opened it with ecstatic haste.

Dear Paul:

I have had some anxious moments before, but after last night it is necessary that I make my position entirely clear. Our friendship has given me much pleasure but it cannot ever lead to any normal climax. Therefore it is best that it should not continue. I cannot see you again. And if you are as kind as I think, you will make no effort of any kind to communicate with me. It would be useless to do so, for my mind is unalterably set, knowing as I do, much better than you, the full circumstances involved. This is a final goodbye. May God bless you always.

Sincerely and gratefully,

ANNE

5

◄§ PAUL SAT STUNNED, holding the small note before him. The minutes passed; then with a reactive wave of second thought he grasped the telephone and dialed Anne's number. His heart was still thudding but his lips were relaxed. The thing to do was to refuse to take it seriously, even for a moment. Light, joking phrases flashed through his mind. *Did you actually think I would pay any attention to this crazy message? Or perhaps, I can't decipher a line of this letter but I'm coming out tonight to reply in person!*

"Hello," said the quiet voice of Miss Davis.

"Oh, this is Paul Devereux. May I speak to Anne, please?"

"I'm sorry. I'm afraid you can't."

"Why not? Is she ill?"

"No." Miss Davis seemed to be having difficulty with her reply. "It is . . . I mean . . . she does not wish to speak to you."

"I don't believe it!" Paul burst out, then added quickly, "I'm sorry, Davy, but I simply *have* to talk to her."

"Her orders are definite, Mr. Devereux. I cannot go against them."

There was a pause, and then Paul said, "Will you please give her a message then?"

"I can't even do that. She does not wish to communicate with you in any way whatever, and oh, Mr. Devereux, if you are wise and kind you will accept this intention at once."

"Wise," Paul echoed, "*kind!*" And, unable to say more, he hung up the phone.

He was well disciplined. A brief had to be prepared before tomorrow, and gritting his teeth he went at it. He did not dare consider his personal concerns further until after five o'clock that night. He worked straight through the lunch hour for a heaviness in the region of his heart took away all appetite. As he was settling his desk for the night, a message came from Hartwell. When Paul went in to his office the old man eyed him shrewdly.

"What's wrong, Paul? You look rather white round the gills."

"A little tired, maybe, and I did skip lunch." He forced a smile.

"Well, a good dinner may fettle you, as the Scotch say. And about the invitation you gave the other day? Does it still stand?"

"It certainly does. When could you come?"

"Tomorrow evening, perhaps?"

"I'll consult my landlady tonight and report in the morning. It's almost sure to be all right with her. That will be fine, sir!" He tried to make his voice hearty. He couldn't possibly put the old man off and yet he desperately wanted to keep the next evenings free for attempts of every kind to break through the barrier Anne had imposed.

He paused again in his own office beside his desk. The impulse to call Kirkland was overpowering; and yet he felt it might be better to wait a little longer. He went on home drearily enough, hope alternating with despair within him. If it was merely her own condition which had prompted Anne's letter, he felt sure he could convince her of the absolute feasibility of their marriage along with the joy he pictured at the very thought of it. But suppose in contrast to his hopes she felt none of the emotion for him that he did for her? Suppose he had been a rash, presuming fool? No girl could receive such a kiss as he had given her the night before without being aware that a man's passionate heart lay behind it. If this passion was unacceptable to her, she would then put a stop to the friendship. And since she could not, like other girls, plead other engagements to graduate the blow, it would have to be dealt summarily.

So, his painful thoughts ran as he choked down an unappetizing dinner in the restaurant and went back to his room. Old Hartwell's visit had to be arranged for. He found Mrs. MacLeod in her small Victorian parlor and broached the matter. She was at once enthusiastic.

"It'll be no trouble in the least. In fact it will do me good to have something special to do. How would a nice bit of roast beef and Yorkshire pudding be? With a light custard for a finish since the pudding's so rich?"

Her blue eyes brightened, her gray bangs quivered, and all her neat, plump, capable small body seemed to come alive with anticipation.

"And as to serving it upstairs, I can manage nicely with setting up the table before you come home—maybe you'd just clear it off tonight since I wouldn't want to mislay anything—and then, would you want a first course?"

"I think not. He's an old man and I fancy the simpler we keep it all, the more to his liking. Do you have any wine glasses?"

"Aye. For port, would it be? That's a nice old gentleman's drink. Oh, I've got some glasses. Left over from the good old days. And a couple bottles of port too, mind you, if you want them?"

"Thanks just the same, but you may need them yourself. I'll pick up a bottle tomorrow. I do appreciate all this, Mrs. MacLeod, and now, I'll leave the rest to you."

He managed to get away after a few more details had pursued him up the stairs. In his own room he sat down at his desk and started a letter.

Anne darling, he wrote with a hand not too steady.

Then he crumpled the sheet and threw it away. That might strike her as being as presumptuous as his kiss. He wrote simply at last,

Dear Anne:

I am utterly at a loss to understand the finality of your letter. That I must have deeply offended you by my action last night is apparent. I can only beg you to forgive me and let me come as soon as you possibly can to explain the reason for my behavior. You are too kind, too just, to deny me this privilege. I need hardly tell you that I am desperately unhappy until I hear from you. I will telephone when you have had time to receive this.

Yours, always,
PAUL

He sealed it after several rereadings and propped it before him to give him hope. He would send it tomorrow from the office by special messenger. No, he suddenly thought, the regular mail would be more sure to reach her. He opened the envelope, selected a fresh one, and disguised his hand as he once again addressed it. It seemed a cheap enough little trick but the necessity was heavy.

He tried to work on the big Memorial Day speech but the string would not pull. He decided to read but poetry hurt; it was too closely linked with his own feelings and with his conversations with Anne. He settled at last to a book on Abraham Lincoln which Hartwell had given him some weeks ago. Better scan it now before tomorrow night's visit. As he leafed it through, sensing its value for deeper study, he found a passage Hartwell had marked. It contained some notes for a law lecture which Lincoln had once drawn up.

The leading rule for a lawyer, as for the man in every other calling, is diligence. Leaving nothing for tomorrow which can be done today. Never let your correspondence fall behind. Whatever piece of business you have in hand, before stopping, do all the labor pertaining to it which can then be done . . . Extemporaneous speaking should be practiced and cultivated. It is the lawyer's avenue to the public . . . There is a vague popular belief that lawyers are necessarily dishonest . . . Let no young man choosing the law for a calling for a moment yield to the popular belief—resolve to be honest at all events; and if in your own judgment you cannot be an honest lawyer, resolve to be honest without being a lawyer. Choose some other occupation, rather than one in the choosing of which you do, in advance, consent to be a knave.

Strong, forthright words with the weight of one of the world's greatest men behind them. The advice about the public speaking pleased him greatly. That was in direct line with his inclination and his plans. As to the honesty—of course he expected to be honest. Only—he sat thinking intently of Kirkland, of Arno, of the mysterious connection existing between the latter and the numbers racketeer. Was Kirkland himself in any way involved? Would he, Paul, find the delicate line between dishonesty and expediency hard to distinguish if his political career developed?

He closed the book, and picked up his letter. He would put it in the mailbox at the corner for early morning collection. His lips twisted in a forlorn attempt at a smile. At least, even as Mr. Lincoln urged, he had not let his correspondence fall behind.

The next day was arid and empty after a sleepless night. No sign from Anne; no reply to his phone call; no word from Kirkland, this latter seeming even more ominous at this point than the other; but it would still be best, Paul felt, to wait for the older man to open up the subject. It was, strictly speaking, his own and Anne's affair and he would leave it so until Kirkland made a move. Hartwell had showed real pleasure as he heard that the plan for that evening was settled and had promised to be at Paul's rooms by seven.

When he reached home at six he found Mrs. MacLeod had outdone herself in preparation. His sitting room looked almost festive with the table already laid and a bowl of spring flowers gracing it.

"I never thought of flowers," Paul told her as she surveyed the scene proudly, "but it's a fine touch."

"There's nothing like a bit posy to give an air to a table," she said, "and I've set a decanter and glasses there on the desk for you. Now I'll go back to the kitchen and you just call when you're ready. I don't think you'll be ashamed of the dinner!"

Paul patted her shoulder and thanked her again as she bustled off. His heavy heart lightened a little as he filled the decanter from the bottle he had brought and placed a box of fresh stogies beside the most comfortable chair. He was glad, after all, that he was not to be alone tonight and glad especially that it was Hartwell who was joining him. There was definitely a bond between them, and a very real affection on his own part at least.

When the old gentleman arrived, very elegant and immaculate as to black suit and linen, his delight was touching.

"Why have I lived all my years in a hotel room?" he demanded. "I have no knack at making myself comfortable. Back of that inability, though, there is the fact that, behind my office front, I'm a shy, sensitive, ingrown creature. I've lived with my profession all day and my books at night and thought I liked the impersonal atmosphere of a hotel best. Well—this looks more than cozy and I'm glad I'm here!"

They sat down to the excellent dinner, talking only lightly as they ate, each feeling real conversation belonged later, when there would be no interruption. When Mrs. MacLeod had made her final exit, laden with praise, they settled into the easy chairs and Paul poured the port.

"Just my drink," Hartwell commended, "and I see you remembered my smoke!"

He picked a thin cigar from the box, lighted and drew on it appreciatively, took a sip of port and then stroked his snug-fitting vest.

"A child could play with me now," he observed whimsically.

Paul laughed as he lit his cigarette. Even to him, though, the sound seemed strained in spite of his satisfaction in the old man's pleasure, for he found the effort of playing host a heavy one. Hartwell, he saw, was looking at him with fondness.

"Well, now that we're alone at last with an evening before us we can talk to some purpose. All our chats in the office have had to be brief. I might as well tell you one thing before we start. From the first time we met I have felt strongly drawn to you. I'm not a man given to sentimentality but I have grown to think of you to myself almost as a son. I hope you don't mind."

"I'm more honored than I can say. And I've had the same sort of feeling about you. I was thinking of it before you came tonight. My family, sadly enough, is gone and I feel that you more than any other person do stand *in loco parentis* to me. I can't tell you how I appreciate it. And," he added smiling, "you must always feel free to take me in hand, set me straight and give me advice whenever you see that I need it."

Hartwell was moved. He touched his eyes gingerly with a lean forefinger, blew his nose and then drew hard on his stogie as he looked off across the room.

"I have some things I've been wanting to say, though you may not be interested. I realize that the state senatorship, with perhaps a governor's chair someday and beyond that Washington beckoning, is the most glamorous daydream for a young man who is politically minded, especially the highest type of young man. But I happen to hold some odd ideas about the place to start. Mind if I enlarge on this a little?"

"You know I would welcome it," Paul said earnestly.

"Well, it's rather a roundabout approach," the old man said, "and it has to do with *cities*. I've always had a particular interest in cities. The ultimate units of civilization. The nerve ganglia of a nation. Now, we're not 'Athenians before we're Greeks' of course, but every man loves his own city. Did you ever look up the root meaning of the word? 'Pertaining to the clan; *dear.*' Significant that, I think."

He drew slowly on the stogie.

"Now the situation in America is different from that of other nations of the world in relation to its city centralization. As you know, we have no capital like London or Paris or Rome or Moscow or Berlin as it once was. Washington is an administrative center for politics and diplomacy. A dozen other cities scattered over the country are the centers of art and culture as well as industry. This comes, I suppose, of our being such a young country and such a huge one. But to my way of thinking it increases enormously the importance of the individual cities. Do you follow me at all?"

"I think so," Paul said. "Do go on."

"Well, now to the point. Something has been happening to our city governments over the years. There has always been too much corruption in them but now it's changing from bad hands to worse. Back in Boss Tweed's day in New York, graft was certainly rampant." He chuckled, "You know he once charged the city seven thousand five hundred dollars for three thermometers? But," he went on seriously, "bad as that was, the particular evil was centered chiefly in one man, it was known, it was held up to public censure by Nast and others, and was finally for the time at least, eradicated. Now, instead of the old-time bosses like Tweed, the gangsters have taken over."

"Ah," Paul breathed, "I've had occasion lately to think of that."

"It's time we all did some thinking. It's a strange, vicious, elusive, organized dictatorship. They never run for office. They just want to control the politicians, beginning on the lowest levels." He drew a long sigh. "I love my country passionately but I often grieve for her!"

Paul waited.

"We opened our arms wide in the spirit of liberty. Big, new country! Europe overpopulated! Well, they came, all right! All kinds. And what has been our reward? Plenty of stabs in the back. God grant they never prove fatal. I don't mean to sound too melancholy, but this business about our cities has me worried."

"You wouldn't be telling me this, if you hadn't thought of a possible solution," Paul said.

The old man smiled grimly. "The solution is so simple that it has never been tried and may never be. It's just this. If one city government from mayor down were completely honest, determined and incorruptible, they could run out every organized vice ring in six months."

"You think so?"

"I know it." He leaned forward, his eyes fixed on Paul's face. "And if I were a young man again, I'd take a try at it."

Paul looked very uncomfortable. "I'm more than interested in all you've said and you've given me a lot to think about, but I still believe, in my own case. . . ."

"Of course," Hartwell said gently, relaxing again in his chair, "you have your plans and your ambitions already set. I just couldn't resist airing one of my pet ideas."

"You see," Paul went on earnestly, "I am rather committed to Mr. Kirkland. I have started on this course with the other aim in view —it may end suddenly, though, I don't know. . . ."

All at once the weight of his trouble fell with full force again upon him. Hartwell eyed him keenly.

"My boy," he said, "a blind man could see that you've not been yourself the last few days. Far be it from me to press you, but if it would help to have a confidant, I'm as safe as a sealed tomb—aside from the fact that I care very deeply about all that concerns you."

Paul sat for a moment silent, and then said slowly, "I am extremely unhappy. It would be an enormous relief to tell you everything from the beginning. I believe I will."

Hartwell did not look at him as he talked. In the briefest possible words Paul told of Kirkland's original plan, of his own first refusal, of his later meeting with Anne and its strange result. Once started, it seemed easy to confess all, even his love. It was like unburdening himself to a father and any young man could do that with honor. Besides there might now be removed from Hartwell's eyes the question which had been there ever since he had first known of Paul's connection with Kirkland.

When he stopped, there was a brief silence. Then Hartwell spoke slowly.

"You are truly in love then with this girl?"

"I am."

"And this is completely independent of your affairs with Kirkland?"

"Completely. Utterly."

"Then, your path seems to me very blessed and fortunate, if she feels the same."

"But I haven't told you all. It seems she doesn't. At least she sent word two days ago that she did not wish to see me again."

Hartwell drew a long breath.

"Is there anyone else, do you know?"

"I'm sure there is not."

"Not likely, in her situation. I think, Paul, there is more to that message than meets the eye. She may only be afraid to let herself go on with this. She will see all the obstacles ahead in a marriage more clearly than you do. Women are wise. As to falling in love with you—I don't see how she could resist you!"

Paul gave a short bitter laugh. "I'm certainly no prize, compared to her. Well, it has helped to talk about it anyway. I've been pretty pent up. Now, just forget all my problems. I'll let you know if things get straightened out, and I'm really very grateful to you for listening —and caring."

"You did me an honor," the old man said. "I'll just add one thing more. Don't give up. 'By trying the Greeks got into Troy,' you know. You are innately a modest man. Don't let that get in your way now. And good luck to you!"

They began then, as though nothing had been said, to talk of other things: the Lincoln book, a case they were handling in the office, and at the last, for the old man left early, their mutual pleasure in the evening.

"We must do this often," Paul said warmly. "It's just what I've been needing. You will come again, won't you?"

"My dear boy, don't ask me if you don't want me. This has been my happiest evening in years!"

When he was alone, Paul wondered to himself why the one thing on his mind he had left unsaid was the episode of C and Arno. It was exactly in line with Hartwell's conversation, and yet—he had held it back. Perhaps the reason was an instinctive desire to be sure before he spoke. As for the rest, what he had told Hartwell had somehow relaxed the tight feeling about his heart. At least, now he would never be alone, as long as the old man lived.

For the next week Paul worked by day and followed Arno's list as well as he could in the evenings, putting in a good word for Halsey in those groups into which he quietly insinuated himself. He found himself loafing in corner drugstores, in garages, in pool rooms, in saloons. The pattern was not difficult to arrive at after a few feelers as to party line.

"Well, have you decided who you want for governor on our ticket?"

This could be put casually, but he always allowed his voice to carry.

"I'm for Halsey myself," he would go on. "Tell you why. The big money's behind Dunham. *You* know! Barker interests. If they get him elected, big business is going to run this state. Now *I* want a man who's for the *people*. Think it over, buddy. Might make a big difference to all of us! Hope you're enrolled so you can vote in the primaries! Don't forget! April twenty-fifth, you know!"

He learned what he had always vaguely known, that he could be all things to all men. The common touch, so to speak, was his possession. It would be even more apparent in the country than in the city. The cracker-barrel stuff, as Kirkland had called it, was part of his birthright.

And each day he wrote to Anne; each day he phoned without success; twice he had gone to the house, to be met by Hackett, who eyed him strangely and with a set face told him Miss Anne was not at home.

By Friday he could endure it no longer. He called Kirkland but was forced to give Miss Sayles the message. Her voice sounded more icy than ever as she reported that Mr. Kirkland would see him at four-thirty.

When he entered the familiar office, Kirkland rose and greeted him stiffly. His face looked haggard and old and gray.

"You've been ill, sir?" The question leaped from Paul's lips.

"No, not ill. Sit down. I've been waiting for you to come. I thought at least an explanation was due me."

"But I can't explain it," Paul said despairingly. "I'm as much in the dark as you are. I've wanted to come to you ever since I got her letter, but I was waiting for you to make some sign. Today I felt I couldn't stand it any longer without talking to you . . ."

Kirkland's eyes were piercing him. His face was frozen with amazement.

"You mean Anne . . . you mean it was not you who broke with her?"

"Good God, no! Is that what you thought?"

"What else could I think? The day after you took her to the theater she told me she wouldn't be seeing you again and didn't want to hear your name mentioned. It was only natural for me to think you had found out that night—taking her out in her condition—that you couldn't go on with the whole thing and had somehow made her understand it. Don't you see how it looked to me?"

It was Paul's turn to be amazed.

"I do see, but you couldn't be more wrong. The evening went much more smoothly, much more naturally than even I had expected. I gave Anne plenty of evidence of how much I enjoyed it. Too much," he added under his breath. "And I was sure she enjoyed it too. The next day her note came. No explanation, but definitely final. I've telephoned every day and oftener, I've written her, I've gone to the house. I simply can't get through to her, and I'm about as sunk as a man can get."

Kirkland sat as though dazed, watching Paul and at intervals saying "So! So!" in a low voice.

"Well," he said at last, "I feel as though a weight—one big weight —was removed. The thing left now is to find out why she did this. She has seemed up to this point so, shall we say, amenable to your attentions, hasn't she?"

"I was sure of it," Paul said. "I was perhaps *too* sure of myself, or rather of her."

"Did anything happen at the theater that would have upset her? Was she embarrassed, do you think? See anyone she knew?"

"I don't think she was embarrassed but she did see an old friend, Bill Lamson. He and a girl were sitting right in front of us."

"The devil he was!" Kirkland said bitterly. "I was sure she was all over that. This is bad news to me. Very!"

"No, sir," Paul said eagerly, "I'm sure you have that wrong. She told me all about Bill on the way home. She said it had done her pride good for him to see her out with an escort, like any other girl. I could swear from what she said that she has no feeling for him now whatever."

"Thank God!" Kirkland said, adding, "The young swine!"

"Quite," Paul agreed savagely. "But personally I'm glad he was."

"Anything else then," Kirkland probed, "did anything else happen which could have upset her?"

"Well," Paul answered, "when we got back, to the library . . ." He hesitated. "She is . . . very beautiful and I was holding her in my arms . . . I'm afraid I did let myself go. . . ."

Kirkland eyed the ceiling. His expression was far from condemnatory.

"I guess then that was it," he said slowly, "but just what her reaction means, even I would not dare to say. At least my boy, I'm in the clear now. I know where we stand, you and I, and I can't tell you the relief it is. I've been thinking pretty badly of you, and I beg your pardon. I guess we may have to do some waiting. Women, Anne especially, can't be pushed. But we can still hope."

He sat, thoughtful, and then went on.

"My father used to say there were two ways to take a fort. One was by direct attack and the other was . . ."

"By siege?"

"By withdrawing a little, concealing your forces and keeping the enemy guessing."

For the first time in days Paul laughed with normal young mirth.

"You're a good ally, sir," he said. "I won't accept the word *enemy*, of course, but otherwise the technique may have something in it for me. Somehow, you've cheered me up. Maybe a little relaxing will do me good just now."

They went on to talk of the coming primary. Kirkland was pleased over Paul's work in the evenings.

"It's the little groups that make up the big ones. Keep it up, Paul. We're pretty safe, but in this game you can't take a damned thing for granted. As soon as Halsey has the nomination, you can get into things, in earnest. Maybe do a bit of traveling about in this end of the state, at least over week ends."

Paul mentioned in detail the Memorial Day celebration at the Redstone Mines. "Don't book me up for anything else on that date," he said. "I'm getting quite warmed up over my speech."

"Can you throw in a plug for Halsey?"

Paul shook his head. "I'd rather not. You see I'm trying to sell them some ideas Johnny Bovard and I both hold about America. At first I meant to use them only for a jumping-off point. Now they are the whole speech and I'm deadly in earnest about getting it across. Later on, I can go to Redstone and talk particular politics, but not this time."

"Well," said Kirkland, "do as you think best. Just don't let Johnny Bovard carry you off your feet. He's got socialistic tendencies and he's not dry yet behind the ears. Now take this jamboree at Redstone. Ox roast and all that. Terrific expense to Bovard. I certainly don't care how soon he bankrupts himself, but it's all a crazy performance for those hunkies. Silly waste. Well, it has one good feature. It will get you known out there. Come in handy later on."

Paul thought for a long time that night when he returned to his room; then he wrote another letter.

Dear Anne,

Forgive me for everything, including the nuisance I've been making of myself in disregarding your wishes. I will not bother you for some time. Perhaps we both need to relax a little. As for thinking of you, I can't promise not to do that.

Yours always,

PAUL

In spite of the constant deep ache in his heart, Paul found a certain relief in the sudden cessation of his efforts to break Anne's silence. He began to eat and sleep better, to find new mental fertility in connection with his daily work and his outside activities. When Halsey swept the state in the party's primary, Paul had a strong feeling of personal elation. It was as though he, himself, had been advanced; and when Kirkland invited him to lunch with the new candidate he went with eagerness. He found Halsey a blond, heavyset, good-looking man of fifty-five, genial, socially polished, with keen eyes and a weak chin. In spite of the fact that he bore out Hartwell's description of him, Paul had a warm, pleasant feeling of sitting in the seats of the mighty as he chatted with the two older men.

"Mr. Kirkland tells me you're one of the men who are going to take the stump for me, Devereux. That's mighty kind of you. I wonder if we could outline your program a little right now?"

"Fine!" said Kirkland at once, as Paul hastened, also, to agree.

"Now, as I see it, I've got a good chance of carrying the cities," he glanced briefly at Kirkland, who nodded, "but my weakest spot may be the country sections, this county for one. My opponent, Thompson, is pretty strong here. So, if you could start work among the farmers and the small-town people at this end of the state, it would be fine, eh, Kirkland?"

"That's the way I've figured it. You see, Paul has the right background. He grew up in the country."

"That's right," Paul said, "so I can talk crops with the best of them. If you've once ploughed a field, you know, you've got the open sesame to a farmer's door."

"This is *wonderful!*" Halsey exclaimed. "My boy, you're a gift from heaven! I not only never ploughed a field but I'm a little shaky as to which is wheat and which is oats when they're first coming up. Rye is clean beyond me! Corn, now, I'm pretty sure of."

Paul laughed. "If you had ever hoed a cornfield as a boy, you'd be surer still!"

"We'll get everything lined up soon," Halsey went on. "Needless to say, I have the greatest confidence in Mr. Kirkland's decisions. By the way, how much time can you give to this?"

"I've got a job of course," Paul said, "in a law firm, but my bosses know my interest and are disposed to be lenient. I should say I could take off one day each week and I'm quite willing to use all my summer vacation if necessary—and of course most evenings."

"Good! Fine! We'll see you don't lose anything in the long run. Mr. Kirkland has told me of your own ambitions. We'll not forget you!"

So it had gone. Smoothly, pleasantly, and completely in accordance with his own desire. The candidate for governor—indeed one could almost say the *next* governor—was calling him *Paul,* was promising him aid in the future, indefinite perhaps, but still promising. . . .

When he repeated the conversation to Hartwell, the old man pulled his mustache ends down to two parentheses about his chin as he listened to the climax.

"Uh-huh!" he remarked. "First law of politics. You scratch my back, I'll scratch yours!"

"Well, what's wrong with that?" Paul asked a bit testily.

"Nothing," Hartwell replied blandly, "nothing at all. So far," he added.

With his summer's campaign work outlined and his vacation to be taken over by it, Paul decided to give himself a week end out of the city. With the full coming on of May he had begun to long for the country; besides he should, he told himself, check on the condition of things at the farm. There was still another reason. In his Memorial Day speech he had used the general theme of the early settlers of America as an introduction; how much better if he could make it personal and explicit. When he had rented the farm to the Oakeses, a kindly, thrifty couple he had known from boyhood, he had left most of the furniture in its place, only putting in the attic a few old pieces and some of his mother's books and papers. He remembered that she had written at one time a modest little family history of her people, the MacBanes, and he meant to look for it. It might give him just the springboard he needed for his speech.

He saw Kirkland just before leaving, for a moment. He had nothing new to report from home. Anne was quiet, pale and thinner, but made a great effort to sound normal when talking with him. He had discussed it all with Mrs. Catherby and she, too, was at a loss, for Anne had resolutely refused to confide in her also.

"The trouble is," Kirkland said, "that for as gentle a person as Anne, she has an amazingly strong will. We've got to get round her some way. She's looked really worse since you began your new tactics. I don't know whether to be relieved by this or more worried. It's hell sometimes to be a father, Paul."

Paul smiled grimly. "I don't want to sound impertinent, but it seems to me you have the easy end of it! I'll tell you one thing, though. As soon as this speech is off my chest I'm going back to a direct assault. And if it's any comfort to you, I'm not going to give up very easily."

"Good boy! Well, have a nice week end. I've been wondering about getting Anne away for a little change. We have a house, camp we call it, in the mountains. She's very fond of it. Maybe I can get her up there for a week or so."

"She's told me all about it and it sounds wonderful. I think your plan is fine, only . . ." He looked anxiously at Kirkland. "Only *take care of her, sir!*"

"You tell *me* that!" Kirkland burst out, and then laughed as he wrung Paul's hand.

The trip to the farm, the first he had made in his new car, was all pleasure. Gradually as the miles lengthened, the familiar rise and slope of hills, the wide bright levels of the new wheat, the green and flushing rose of the woods where as a boy he had trapped a possum and found the first arbutus—all this enfolded him and brought at once the sweet pangs of memory.

He drove along the lane at five o'clock past the old watering trough under the walnut trees, and up to the big clapboard house at the end. It had been repainted last fall by his order and he noted its white freshness now with pleasure. The paling fence had been done too, which gave contrast to the new grass inside. His mother had always liked the fence, so he had left it, contrary to Mr. Oakes's opinion. The barn would need paint in another couple of years, he surmised. An expensive job, that, but just now it looked well enough, and the barnyard was neat, just as his father had kept it.

A wave of homesickness swept over him as he parked his car and went toward the back steps. There was the big catalpa tree under which they had always sat on warm Sunday afternoons; there was the long low woodshed, and there the path down to the old spring-house! He had always loved the errands to it when he was a boy. He used to pause in its cool stone fastness, listening to the water running through its narrow channel, before he stopped to lift the lids from the cream and butter crocks standing in the clear stream. The little structure was rendered more cool by a huge willow tree which overhung it. It was still there with its wide branched seats upon which he had so often sat to dream boy dreams or read a book. He hoped it would still be tossing its green lace when *his* children. . . .

He brought himself up short with something like a physical pain in his heart, climbed the steps and knocked at the kitchen door. Odd, to come back after the separating years and knock at your own door! At least it opened now quickly for they were expecting him. Mr. Oakes was calmly cordial.

"Well, Paul," he said, shaking his hand as he transferred his pipe, " 'bout time you was showin' up here, ain't it? Been quite a while."

Mrs. Oakes gave him just the welcome he needed. She patted him with motherly affection, while her delight showed in her kindly face, flushed now with the excitement of his visit.

"My, Paul, I'm that glad to see you! And don't you look good, though! Handsomer every time you come. It's a wonder some girl hasn't snapped you up long before this! Now would you like to sit down right here in the kitchen for a minute where we can look at you! You're just a sight for sore eyes, ain't he, John? We've got a fire in the sittin' room if you'd rather. . . . It gets cool evenings."

"This is perfect, Mrs. Oakes. Just let me get the feel of it again. I'll go to the sitting room later. Oh, something smells good!"

"It's fried chicken," she reported, all smiles. "I do hope I done right. I studied whether you'd like that or ham best but I settled on the chicken today with ham tomorrow." She looked suddenly anxious.

"Wonderful, Mrs. Oakes. Say, I'm happy to be here. I want to see everything and I must leave Sunday after breakfast so I'll soak up as much of it as I can meanwhile."

He sat down in one of the wooden rockers in the corner of the kitchen, and drew a long breath which had in it a blood-drop sigh for the past forever gone, and the relaxing peace of the present. He eyed the old room. There still stood the huge oak sideboard with the deer head at the top; there was the table against the wall with farm magazines, the Hagerstown almanac, a radio and a Bible arranged neatly upon it; there was the extension table and stiff wooden chairs; there was the big coal range, and beyond, the pantry, where milk was strained and rougher work done. All the same.

Something rich and nourishing welled up within him drawn from the deep, permanent roots of childhood and youth. It was no effort to talk with the Oakeses, for he had known them all his life and could slip easily back into the farm vernacular.

When the early supper was ready he went up to the big spare bedroom above the parlor to freshen after his journey, and found everything there as it had always been, with his mother's best quilt on the big walnut bed. From the window he could see the wide fields, both green and freshly ploughed and beyond them the rise of Sugar Hill, colored now by pink sunset clouds.

He ate an enormous meal realizing how desperately sated he was with restaurant fare, and when the big white layer cake, and home-canned peaches from the orchard trees appeared, he told Mrs. Oakes solemnly that he craved no more of life!

"You're downright starved, that's what you are! If you'd just come up here for a few weeks I'd fatten you up. What about your vacation?" Selina Oakes inquired eagerly.

"Come along in harvestin' and I'll give you a job," John said. "An' right now, how 'bout milkin' a cow?"

Paul laughed. "Anything but that," he said, "but I'll watch you do it."

"We only keep two now—just for our own use—an' John does them in a jiffy. Go out along though, while I tidy up here. You'll want to see the old barn before dark," Selina told him.

As he walked out to it in the gentleness of that hour between afternoon and early evening, he wondered if any farm-bred man ever got over his love for a barn. For this building was at once the countryman's office, the center of his activities, the repository of his wealth, the concrete crown of his labors. And in addition to all this it was his refuge, his retreat, his sanctuary. He remembered his own father's habits. When anything went wrong he betook himself immediately to the barn, and found solace there. He felt this now, as he went in, the familiar smells of grain and hay and beasts all about him. He walked along in front of the stalls, stroking the noses of the animals, asking when the cows had calved, praising the size of the two work horses, still supplementing the tractor, looking about with eager, nostalgic appraisal. He climbed the stairs to the floor above to see the mows, remembering how they had been his own retreat in all boyhood troubles, and as the mingled odors of hay, grain and ancient wood assailed him there he felt a mist in his eyes, not so much for the memories themselves, as for the sudden realization that that boyhood had been sound, secure and blest. He went down the shallow stairs and sat on a feedbox watching John at his milking.

"At least I can carry the buckets back to the house," he said, "while you finish your chores here."

As he walked back, a pail in either hand, his eyes took in the beauty around him. The old orchard below the barn was clouded over now with the last white of the cherry and pear blossoms and the breaking pink of the apple boughs; above them a new young moon hung like a shaving of silver. All the subtle scents of the spring night converged upon him, along with old familiar sounds; the bay of a dog from over the hills, the muted bleating of the sheep; the twilight twittering of birds, especially the indescribably poignant note of the robin, and above these all in shrill, ecstatic chorus, the pipings of the young frogs in the lower meadow.

He set his burden down and stood thinking of his mother. Perhaps he had been wrong in feeling a bitterness because her great gift had not had complete fulfillment. Her name had never been in lights, as he was sure in other circumstances it could have been; but against the dusty theater and its captious applause, must be reckoned all this that he felt more sensibly now than ever before. There had always been beauty for her soul to feed upon, and more even than that, there had been other values. The truth came sharply home to him that no place, no profession in itself could effectuate a life; it was the individual perception, the insight, the grasp, the *quality* of the ecstasy and the pain that made it whole, that filled the cup.

He heard Anne's words again, "Oh, not wasted *when she had you!*" Then he heard nothing but that voice, he saw nothing but that face looking up to his in its eagerness, its tenderness. The longing for her swept through him like the wind . . . *Anne* . . . *Anne.* . . .

He went on to the house and deposited the milk in the pantry, listening to but only half hearing Selina's easy chatter.

When the Oakeses had retired at their usual early hour, Paul took a flashlight and repaired to the third floor. Everything in the huge attic was in order, with the stillness of disuse and the repose of the past upon it. He glanced around briefly and then crossed to the big secretary where his mother's books and papers were. He opened the doors and picked up volume after volume worn from much reading, accented with many underlinings which he picked out with his flashlight. There was Shakespeare, Thoreau and Emerson; there was Lawrence Sterne and Bunyan, Longfellow and Tennyson. There were a number of books of compiled *Platform Readings,* which even in the light of his recent thinking he could not quite bring himself to look at. Instead he went on glancing at the passages here and there to which she had evidently given special thought. They made him realize more than ever that in his careless youth he had never fully appreciated the quality of her mind. The last book he picked up was a small one, much worn and annotated. It was selections from the works of Stevenson, and one line, carefully underscored, struck him with violence. It read, *The lie of a good woman is the true index of her heart.* He put the tiny volume in his pocket, for later consideration.

At last, in a drawer, he found the real object of his search. It was a notebook with the words "A Brief History of the MacBane Family" written on the cover. He recalled reading it as a young boy, at his mother's earnest insistence. He had been cruelly indifferent then, at fifteen, to what must have meant much to her after years of careful work in collecting the material, selecting, and writing it down. How forgiving the heart of a mother! he mused, as he gave one more glance about him and then, with the notebook in hand, went back down the stairs to the sitting room. He drew the light nearer and began to read.

The first of our family to come to America was John MacBane, a Scot, who with his wife, Isabel, arrived in Philadelphia after a rough four weeks' steerage crossing on April 5, 1774. These facts are set down in an old Bible which used to be in my grandfather's possession. I still recall the brief notation underneath: *Infant child died at sea.*

Paul read on absorbed. The record dealt mostly of course with genealogical data but in between were inserted stories of pioneer days handed down from father to son, or taken from old diaries and letters which had been borrowed from here and there. The drama of these, set between the quiet statements of birth and death, was fiercely evocative. There were references to the war in which John MacBane with the other men (never more British than when they decided to fight for what they conceived to be their rights) shouldered their muskets and marched away, leaving their women to guard the cabins in the wilderness.

The story went on, with gaps here and there where records were lacking, but continuing the general trend. Later on was a reference to Gettysburg and much later to San Juan Hill and finally the Argonne forest. But these were strange and incredible breaks in the steady pattern of developing a vast new country.

At the very end there was a paragraph written in fresher ink and with a hand not quite steady. It was his own war record ending with the line: *He is now looking forward to the profession of law as a career. May God bless him in it.*

Paul's eyes were moist as he closed the notebook and sat thinking. This that he had read was not merely a family history; there was in it the story of America itself. And only here could such a saga have been written. There they were, his forebears: the pioneer, the minister, the carpenter, the blacksmith, the mason, the farmer and the judge—ordinary men most of them, but strong, determined builders of a nation. And he was of their breed.

At last he put out the light and started upstairs carrying the notebook reverently. He would take it with him and keep it always.

When he was ready for bed, however, it was the small Stevenson volume he took out and looked at again. That his mother, to whom truth was practically a fetish, should have underscored this line was mysterious indeed. He could remember her constant admonition to him not only in boyhood but through his college years: "Always tell the truth, Paul, no matter at what cost. It is the foundation rock of integrity."

He read the line again: *The lie of a good woman is the true index of her heart.*

With one of those flashes of insight that come unbidden he suddenly thought of an incident of his boyhood. They had all been invited by old friends of his parents in Ohio, to come out to visit them during the great occasion of their town's centennial. He remembered vividly the excitement occasioned by the letter. His father and mother planned at once for the trip, in the new Ford car. They would get John Oakes to look after the stock while they were gone; the other farm work was well on the way for the season; it could wait for a week. The letter of acceptance was dispatched. Then John Oakes had fallen sick. The other farmers were short of help and it was clear that while they wanted to be neighborly, it would be a serious inconvenience to them to take on anything more.

"I will stay at home," his father had said almost harshly, to cover his disappointment. "You and the boy go on."

It was then—as he knew now—that his mother had spoken the lie.

"No, you and Paul go. As a matter of fact, John, I haven't felt very strong these last weeks. I'm actually not too able for the trip and all the visiting. I'll be much better staying quietly at home. I'll do nothing but feed the stock and do the milking. In between all day, I'll rest and read and take me a little vacation all to myself. This would be best for me, John!"

Oh, the actress of her! His father had accepted at last after close questioning. She had waved them off on the day of their departure, protesting brightly to the last. They had driven up the lane and around the cornfield, when he had looked back. His sharp eyes had picked out her figure still in the front yard, only now her head was bowed on the fence post beside her. Even as a boy he had felt that attitude of utter dejection; but he had said nothing at the time and soon forgotten it. Now with maturity's clarity of vision he understood what he had vaguely guessed then.

What a visit it had been! His father had reveled in it and talked of it as long as he lived. But if the lie of love had not been spoken he would never have had that happiness which colored his even-tenored life.

So that was the meaning of the strange line! The only lie of a good woman was a sacrificial one and for love alone. There was a veracity then of the heart more true than truth itself!

He got into the big walnut bed and lay thinking in the dark. Could it be—oh, dared he believe it? That Anne's hard words belonged in this class? *I do not want to see him again,* she had told her father. *She does not wish to communicate with you in any way,* Miss Davis had reported.

He was all at once very still and relaxed. The faint bay of the dog over the hills only served to accentuate the lenitive quality of the quiet. A peace flowed over him. Coming weeks might prove this new interpretation to be a mistaken one, but for this night under his own roof, this tender, brooding springtime night, he was going to rest in hope.

6

‎ৼ৾ ON A BRIGHT May morning Arno rose early and spent the better part of two hours in dressing; as a rule he managed it in fifteen minutes. Today he showered and shaved with slow, meticulous care; he tried on three shirts before one suited him, and then was lost in endless consideration of neckties. The bright red, which he favored, was so striking that it would at once arouse the suspicions of Sayles, and he wished to avoid that. It was necessary to play along with her. At last he settled upon a light blue with a red diamond design. He tied it nattily and watched his reflection in the mirror with a certain complacency. Not bad, eh? Especially to call on a girl who couldn't expect anything better.

Ever since the day he had learned from Kirkland that the doctors said Anne would never walk again, a great determination had become fixed in his heart. Fate had played into his hands. From a height to which he could only regard her with hidden and impossible longing, she had been suddenly brought down by her incapacity to his own level. Even, judged by old Water Street standards, below it. She was helpless and he was a man, virile and vigorous. If he was willing to marry her as she was, wouldn't she have everything to gain? Every girl wanted to marry. This was his honest appraisal of the situation.

In spite of his inner elation and resolve he had let weeks go by before gathering his courage to do anything about it. After long thought he had decided to work it through Kirkland, himself. So a few days ago, after Sayles had left the office he had approached the Chief.

"You know," he began, praying the red would not come up in his face, "I keep thinking about Miss Anne's . . . trouble. I'd like to take her a few flowers some day. Do you think she'd see me? Around five, maybe?"

The Chief had looked at first startled and then greatly touched.

"Why, that's very good of you, Arno. Of course she'll be glad to see you. I'll speak of it to her tonight. I appreciate this myself, Arno."

"Just let me know the day and I'll be there."

So, this afternoon had been set and he hadn't been obliged to arrange it himself, thereby perhaps saying the wrong thing. He had ordered the flowers a day ago. They would be ready for him to pick up at four-thirty. Nothing but the best for Anne and besides it would do no harm to show her he had money, too—that he wasn't merely a hireling but a man in his own right. At the thought of the money, however, he instinctively drew his hand across his brow. That last set-to with Camponelli had been a close shave for him, all right. Before that everything had run as smooth as silk except for two uncomfortable questions. Once the Chief had said to him, "Say, don't you realize these fellows will have to shake down more for us if they expect to get their men elected?" And Camponelli: "Look, how much do you gougers think we'll stand for?" Along the way, Arno's various bank accounts had swelled slowly but perceptibly. Well, he had things under control for the present.

When he reached the office that morning Sayles took one look at him and her eyebrows all but met her hair.

"Well, where do you think you're going?" she said. "To the Wentworth tea?" She glanced down at the social page of the morning paper.

"Oh, I might look in and give them a break. And what's wrong," he added sharply, "in wearing a clean suit once in a while?"

Sayles eyed him with an admiration which did not escape Arno. He had always enjoyed feminine approval.

"You look pretty snappy, I must say."

"Well, thanks, and the same to you."

You had to keep old Sayles buttered up.

He went out at four as he often did on various confidential errands, while she was closeted with the Chief, and this time made his way to the florist's. The box was large and so was the bill. Very. But Arno paid it with a flourish.

"I hope you'll like the arrangement," the florist said. "You're sure we didn't misunderstand you? You didn't want a bouquet?"

"No, just spread out, sort of," Arno assured him.

"Well, looks like a wedding to me, anyway," the florist smiled.

Arno grinned back widely, and seemed to grow several inches taller as he left the shop. He managed to arrive at the Kirkland home at exactly five. *For afternoon calls with or without invitation to cocktails, five has become the generally accepted hour.* So said the etiquette book, which had recently become his nightly fare. Hackett, who opened the door, had two quite distinct attitudes toward those who crossed the Kirkland threshold. Both were unimpeachably correct, the contrast residing in subtleties which could neither be explained nor questioned. The one, however, made the guest feel that by right of birth he merited the world and all within it; the other, that the person arriving was an upstart whose entrance was permitted only by the completely undeserved grace of God and Hackett himself. As Arno inquired for Miss Anne he was treated to a liberal dose of the latter. As a result he felt as he was ushered toward the library that his tie was flashy, his face perspiring, and his knees unsteady.

Anne was seated in a low chair beside a table with a book in her lap, and Arno's heart turned completely over as he looked at her. She was thinner than when he had last seen her as she ran down the stairs that winter night in her red dress, and a little older looking, maybe, but oh, God, she was lovely. Not like any other girl he had ever seen. Sort of delicate and beautiful like something a man's hands could break the way he would a flower stalk. . . .

"How do you do, Arno? Father told me you were stopping in today. This is nice of you."

He was shaking hands, his face he knew, red as a turkey wattle. He could smell a sweet scent as he bent over her. It seemed to come from her hair. It, at least, was just the same. Goldish, with a shine on it.

"Well, how are you, Miss Anne," he heard his voice, a little too big and heavy. He was holding his box awkwardly and suddenly laid it on her knee. .

"I just brought you a few flowers . . ."

He stood while she undid the string and took off the lid. Within ranged row on row were white orchids. Her amazement was unfeigned.

"Arno! Oh, you shouldn't have done this! Why, I've never *seen* so many in all my life!"

"You haven't?" Arno asked delightedly.

"No, they're incredible! What a gift! How can I thank you?"

She looked up at him then and he backed away a little. He must watch himself or he might spoil everything. Her eyes. . . .

"Oh, it's nothing," he said. "I'm glad you like them." He couldn't keep the pride, though, out of his voice.

"I'll ring for my nurse and get her to arrange them."

Anne was looking back now at the orchids, still with a rather stunned expression.

"Would you want to pin one on?" asked Arno eagerly. "Or a couple maybe?"

"Of course," Anne agreed. "It's so wonderful that these are white. I have a regular *thing* about purple orchids. I don't care for them."

"You don't?" Arno was overcome with relief as one who has been too near a precipice. For he had thought first of the purple and had chosen the white only because they were more expensive. "Well, I'm glad you like these."

Miss Davis entered, introductions were made, and Anne selected one orchid which she fastened to her dress and handed the box to Davy with a steady countenance.

"Perhaps a wide, low glass bowl, and when they are arranged, would you please bring them back here? And oh, do sit down, Arno," she added as Miss Davis left the room with her exotic burden. "I suppose you and Father are busy running things as usual?"

"Well," Arno said, his confidence returning, "we manage to keep pretty busy. The coal works aren't going as strong as they did a few years ago—some of the veins are worked out—but it's still a pretty good business."

"And politics?" Anne said smiling.

"Oh, we still dabble in that a little. Just got our man nominated for governor. The Chief—I mean your father—he's always got a few tricks up his sleeve. I mean in a nice way, that is."

Anne laughed, and Arno felt a tremor go through his body. *Steady,* he thought, *don't go and give yourself away too soon.*

"I must tell Father how loyal you are! Have . . . have you any new bright lights showing up in the political field?" she asked, looking carefully at the bowl of orchids which Davy was placing on the table beside her.

Arno was pleased. It was a lot easier to talk to her than he had expected and she evidently *was* impressed with the flowers.

"Oh, I don't know. I guess young Devereux is about the only new one your father's got under his wing right now. Ever heard of him?"

"I . . . yes, I have," Anne agreed. "How's he doing?"

"He seems all right, though we still don't know too much about him. The way your father just picked him out of a hat from hearing him make a short speech surprised me. I suppose he knows what he's doing though. He usually does. And Devereux does have a lot on the ball. I'll tell you, though, the trouble with these *handsome* bright boys. At least the way I look at them."

"Yes?" Anne prompted eagerly.

"Well, you see, take a young, good-looking fellah like Devereux now. He thinks he's going in for a political career. But he's the kind that gets in the social swim sooner or later, gets married, and then as likely as not his wife won't like the political mix-up. She'd rather he stuck to law and made some money and stayed home nights. You know! I just think he's not the type you can depend on for *our* business. Of course time will tell."

"Have you seen any evidences of . . . of what you fear?" Anne asked, very carefully.

"Oh, *I* don't know anything about his private life. He runs around a lot with Johnny Bovard and he's in the social top drawer all right. And I've seen him out a couple times with Johnny's sister. Good-looking girl. Well, just surmise on my part, that's all."

Hackett came in with a tray and set it down condescendingly. There was more chat over the drinks and then Arno noticed that Miss Anne looked tired and very white.

"I guess I'd better be on my way," he said suddenly. "Hope I haven't stayed too long."

"Not at all," Anne said, forcing a smile. "And I do so thank you for the orchids. Wait till Father sees them!"

Arno left, in a near ecstatic state. It had all gone so much better than he had even dared to hope. Why, he could talk to her almost as easy as to old Sayles! He hadn't said anything about going back. He'd let things ride for a little while. Best not to rush it. Besides, with her, it was safe enough to wait. No rivals now. His breast swelled with his secret and his assurance. He'd heard about young Lamson, how he'd been practically engaged to her until the accident, and then dropped her like a hot potato. Well, in a way you couldn't blame him, young fellah like that. Now, as to himself . . . the hot blood rushed to his face until his eyes felt blinded by it. It wouldn't matter to him whether she could walk or not . . . if he could just have her. . . .

When he was gone, Anne sat very still in her chair, staring at the spot where Arno had been sitting. So, she had been right in her recent thinking about Paul. She had guessed it even before this man had pointed it up with his own observations. She should not be surprised. She was only thankful, oh *so* thankful that she had taken the initiative when she did. Now at least she had her pride left, intact, undamaged. Such a small, pitiful residue from the flame, but something. As to herself from now on—it was like the line of the old song: *All the tomorrows will be as today.*

White, cold, stone-still as an image, her heart dead, she sat on until Hackett brought the phone to her.

"Your father on the wire, Miss Anne."

She stirred and braced herself as she heard his voice.

"Oh yes, Jimmy."

"Mouchie? I'm at the club. I really should have dinner with a man, tonight. Pretty important. Will you mind?"

An immediate sense of relief ran through her.

"Not a bit. I think I'll retire early. From shock. I've had a big afternoon. Your minion called and guess what? He brought me *one dozen white orchids!*"

"What the devil. . . ."

"Yes. Sort of pathetic, wasn't it? He so wanted to do well by the boss's daughter. I feel like a bride or a corpse, I don't know which."

"Did you say *a dozen?*"

"Thirteen to be exact. Twelve in a bowl and one on my shoulder. But be sure to say the right thing to him tomorrow for he was *so* proud of himself. No wonder, at that price! The man means to be kind, Jimmy, I grant you that. Only please head him off if he shows signs of coming again. I couldn't take another batch of orchids."

"You're sure you're all right tonight?"

"Absolutely. As a matter of fact I may ask Gran to come over and see my floral display! She'd probably think of a poem to fit the occasion and it should be celebrated! Have a good time, Jimmy. See you at breakfast."

She hung up quickly before her voice broke. "On second thought," she murmured, "not even Gran. I'll have to fight this out all over again tonight. And it had better be alone." The trouble as she knew was that the battle was never won.

She removed the orchid from her dress and put it in the bowl with the others, then rang for Miss Davis. When she came Anne motioned to the flowers.

"For some reason, Davy, I can't look at them. Keep any you like for yourself and then take the rest to the kitchen. I have an idea the girls there would love them and they shouldn't be wasted. And Davy, could I have dinner in my room and just stay there tonight? Father won't be home."

Miss Davis looked at her with keen solicitude.

"If you wish," she said quietly, as she picked up the bowl of orchids.

Paul himself was having a somewhat disturbed mind over Johnny Bovard's sister. He had been invited to dinner at their home soon after he first met Johnny and it had been a pleasant evening. Janis was dark, vivid in coloring and full of vitality, with a frankness at once disarming and to some degree embarrassing. The dinner had been followed later by a Sunday buffet, and several times now at Johnny's invitation he had gone with a group to a night club, always being paired off with Janis, who made it no secret that she liked the arrangement.

One day at lunch with Johnny after he had come back from the farm he broached his uneasiness.

"Look," he said, "there's something I want to tell you. I'm not just in the open field. There is someone. It may never work out, but at least I'm pretty deeply involved."

Johnny looked at him keenly. "I could see the other night that Janis was rather throwing herself at you. And I might say there's nobody I'd rather have for a brother-in-law, but if that's the way it is, good luck, old man. I'll take care of Janis."

"She's a doll," Paul said, "and I feel like an ass saying anything at all to you, but I don't think I ought to keep on going out with her. The way it is with me."

Johnny squinted over his glasses.

"Funny about girls nowadays. Janis's all right. She's a good kid. Crazy and says what she thinks. But some of them! Egad, what a time I had last night! Gal called me up about six and asked if I'd take her out. She's good fun and I said yes. But before the evening was over I dumped her on the paternal doorstep and ran for my life. Disgusts you, sort of, doesn't it?"

Paul nodded soberly.

"Damned if I wouldn't like to go back for a while to the time when every girl was a pure, delicate lily who wouldn't even dance with a man who had liquor on his breath! Tell you one girl who had a good reputation among the fellahs. Anne Kirkland."

"So?" said Paul.

"Yep. They all said so right along the line. She never let down the bars by a hair's breadth. Nice to all of them but never *too* nice. And one of the most popular girls in college. Here in the city, too. Well, it just goes to show. Does the old man ever talk about her to you?"

"Very, very seldom," said Paul.

"Hmm. Suppose it hurts too much. Awful tragedy that. Well, now let's get down to business. The big shindig is just one week from today, I suppose you realize."

"And how! I'm scared and yet I still want to do it. I hope to heaven I don't let you down, after all the talking we've done about it."

"Not a chance. I'm going out early that day to see that everything's set up right. Can you come out before lunch? You might like to get the feel of things. Gosh, I hope the weather will be good. We've got a ratty old marquee if it rains, but it would spoil the fun, so keep your fingers crossed."

They were lunching at the Wiltshire, the city's most sumptuous hotel, because Johnny always proposed the extremes of social experience for dining. ("The one thing I can't stomach is mediocrity," he often remarked. "God save me from a tearoom.") Now, as they parted in the main lobby, Paul remembered suddenly that he had meant to get a haircut that day. He turned on his heel and went down the stairway to the hotel barber shop, regretting his decision as soon as he saw the luxurious setting in which he found himself. Oops, he thought, here's where they'll take the pants off you!

He sat down in the chair near the door to which he was assigned and looked interestedly into the mirror's reflection of his surroundings. Suddenly he stiffened. At one of the manicure tables sat a man whose full, fleshy face he now knew. It was Camponelli! He was smiling with bold assurance at the pretty girl who was working carefully upon his hands. As he watched, Paul was sure the man was trying to make a date with her. Though he heard no words he could see the little drama proceeding. *Nice kid, she looks to be, too*, Paul was thinking. *The dirty rat!* He noticed one other thing. Every few minutes Camponelli glanced up at a chair nearby where a man was being shaved. As the concealing lather was removed, Paul gave a start.

"If you please, sir, to sit still," his attendant requested, "and not change your position!"

"Sorry," Paul said. "But turn my chair a little more this way. I like the view."

The man being shaved was Arno! With a heavy weight of dismay upon him Paul saw what followed. Camponelli, following the evident female capitulation, grinned, studied his nails intently, handed a bill to the girl whose eyes widened as she slipped it into her pocket, and then got up and made his way to the washroom. A few minutes later Arno followed him. There it was, just that. But Paul knew, with an inner certainty that was absolute, that this was not coincidence. They had not come out when he was finished and left the shop. He walked slowly along the street, disturbed and uncertain. There was a hookup here, a live link between the numbers racketeer and Kirkland's right-hand man. Did Kirkland know it? Or was Arno working on some scheme of his own? Even this would be bad enough, considering Arno's connection with the office. Could the disappearance of the two into the washroom have been as innocent as that of any other two men? He wanted to think so, but could not. Some subtle current of reality transmitted without logical proof had struck him with violence and he could not shake himself free.

Back at his own desk he found a message from Kirkland asking him to call at the office that afternoon when work was over, so at five-thirty he presented himself. Kirkland was in fine fettle.

"If I were superstitious, Paul, I'd think our plans were going almost *too* well. Of course," he added, sobering, "on the one side we have enough worries to hold us down."

"Nothing new?" Paul asked anxiously.

"No, that's the trouble. Mrs. Catherby has been trying again to get her to talk about . . . well, about you, but it's no good. I've wondered sometimes if you called on Ellie—Mrs. Catherby—if maybe between you, you could think of something."

"I would be glad to, if she's willing."

"I always tell her she's magic. I get ideas out of the air when I'm with her."

"I'll wait one more week," Paul said, "and if we are still at an impasse I'll go to her."

"Good. But it wasn't that I wanted to talk about today. I've been in conference with Halsey and we've settled on a few high lights for your schedule this summer, beginning June fifteen. I'll give you a copy. But here's what delighted me. Right out of the hat Halsey pulled this one. He said he'd been very much impressed with you the day we lunched with him and that the capital needed bright young chaps like you. 'Ever think of him for a State Senator later on?' he asked. I kept a poker face and said that mightn't be a bad idea. Well," he added, giving Paul's shoulder an affectionate slap, "what do you think of that?"

"It sounds pretty wonderful," Paul answered. "If I can only make it."

"You'll make it all right. Now take a look at this," handing him a paper. "Brennen is my County Chairman with five hundred precincts under him. As soon as this speech of yours on the thirtieth is over, we'll get together with him. He knows this county like a book. As you go round making your speeches you'll get to know a lot of the committee members, little fellahs, most of them. They may not seem important to you, but you'll get the feel of *organization* from them. In politics you build from the bottom up or God help you! Well, I just had to tell you about Halsey's remark and that we're all set to go. Take these other papers along too and look them over when you have time. Platform stuff and all that. Fodder for your guns!"

As Paul left and went on back to his room, he thought earnestly of Kirkland. As a father his love for and devotion to Anne were beyond all question. She was, he knew, the center of his heart. And yet the strange game in which he was involved had the patent power to cause him to forget all other cares, all other joys. It was not just the normal concentration of any man upon his business or profession. With Kirkland there was an intensity coupled with a certain strange exhilaration which made Paul feel that the man might put this interest above everything else in a test. Would he? Would he, Paul, ever reach that point, he wondered uneasily? For he knew without learning that there was danger here. There was allurement, there was enticement, there was forever the temptation of the seductive fruit, the Golden Apples of power which hung before all whose imagination could envisage them, from the great manipulators down to the *little fellahs*, as Kirkland had termed them, sitting in smoke-filled back rooms behind village drugstores or barber shops. And he, too, had glimpsed the tantalizing fruit, else why was he started upon this amazing journey? His heart suddenly knew fear, and yet he also knew that he would not turn back.

After a half week of chilly showers, May 30, Memorial Day, dawned fair, warm and beautiful. As he dressed Paul thought of the observance of it across the land: the bright flowers on the sacred green grass; the fresh flag on the resting place of each soldier, the marching schoolchildren, and citizens and veterans; the sharp gun volleys over the graves and then the hush as Taps sounded in clear and sweet remembrance! The same pattern in every crossroads, in every town and city from one ocean to the other. An impressive thing, that, he thought, wishing he had incorporated it in his speech. Oh, well, he would add nothing now.

He would have preferred reaching Redstone when lunch was over but he didn't want to disappoint Johnny. Having promised Hartwell to drive him out, they went together, reaching the mines a little before noon. They passed slowly through the main street of the Patch, noting the flags and bunting flying bravely from most of the dull red doorways. The gaunt tipple and washer rose bleakly behind and the coke ovens stretched their sullen smoky length, which at night would turn to pillars of fire.

"It's a far cry from the mines as I knew them as a young man to a holiday ox roast and beer on tap," Hartwell said. "If the operators had done a little of this in the old days, along with a few other things, they might not be plagued with the union now. Ah, well, it's live and learn. If any of us ever do," he added. And then, "Highty-tighty, what a scene!"

On a level meadow just beyond the town was spread the fete. A crowd of men, women and children were milling about. A baseball game was in progress, a dozen groups of men were throwing horse-shoes, a merry-go-round was entertaining the children as its cheerful wheeze sounded above the other noise. In a huge depression from which pungent odors were drifting, the ox was apparently ready to be eaten. Rough tables and benches had been set up and at a side one, a row of chefs in white caps were busy setting forth the food on paper plates.

Johnny rushed up to greet them, flushed and exuberant.

"Quite a setup, what?" he asked. "Even Dad thinks it's pretty good. Come on and get a seat while you can grab one. I'm just about to ring the dinner bell." He flourished his megaphone and then sent his call flying over the countryside.

"*Come and get it!*" he bellowed, and at once there was a general rush for the tables.

As he ate, Paul studied the faces about him. Southern and central European mostly, with here and there a few Scots and Englishmen, he would guess.

"Magyars, Croatians, Poles, Czechs, Italians," Hartwell said softly in his ear. "The British cut down the wilderness, the Irish laid the railroads and these dig the mines, draw the coke and make the steel. And today we're all citizens together. Quite a thought, isn't it?"

"Quite," Paul said, his eyes fixed on a raised platform beyond the tables, with a sort of pulpit box decked with patriotic emblems. He had a sudden feeling of fright and weakness. This whole subject was too big for his puny efforts. He wished he could cut and run. But there could be no escape now for the time itself was approaching. The big pieces of pie were rapidly disappearing from the plates; the coffee cups drained.

When all were finished Johnny appeared with his megaphone.

"We will now have the exercises of the day, after which the games can begin again and last as long as you care to stay. Plenty of grub left, too, if you get hungry later. How do you all feel? Pretty good?"

A roar of satisfaction greeted this sally.

"All right, then, keep to your benches only face this way toward the platform. Will those taking part now please come forward?"

"Here I go," Paul said to Hartwell. "Wish me luck."

He mounted the platform along with Johnny and a young chap with a pitch pipe. It had earlier been decided by Mr. Bovard that it would be better policy for him to mingle quietly with the crowd and let Johnny run the whole affair.

There was first, now, "The Star-Spangled Banner," pitched by the young man in an accommodatingly low key. The children and young people sang lustily, with many of the older men and women joining in as they could. When they were all seated again, Paul moistened his lips and rubbed his chill, perspiring hands together.

The introduction was brief and in a few seconds he found himself standing at the loudspeaker behind the flag-draped box looking out over the faces raised curiously to his. He saw Kirkland sitting in a parked car at the edge of the field. This was a surprise to him. He waited for a breath or two and then, in the rich, moving voice bequeathed him by his mother, he began.

"One hundred and eighty years ago this spring my own ancestor left the old country to come to America. He and his wife and baby came steerage in a rough four weeks' crossing. Their little child died on the way over."

He could feel the sudden change from casual interest to profound attention. The eyes now seemed to pierce him through, for he had begun in the only possible way to make himself one with them.

Very simply then he began to tell them the story of America. First of the pioneers who had with their strong hands cut down the primeval forest. He told of the hardships, particularizing vividly from the history of his own forebears as he had so lately read it: of the little girl "captivated" by the Indians and never heard of again; of the bride found scalped on her own doorstep; of the boy clawed to death by a panther on the edge of the very mountain they could see rising blue in the background; of the woman fatally bitten by a rattlesnake as she went to the spring for water.

He went on. Under his dramatic description the listeners saw the wilderness tamed, and the gradual fields of grain spreading westward. Briefly, era by era, he showed how the men and women from the Old World, and their descendants, had built a new one, with heavy toil, with constant danger, but always with faith in their hearts. For there were wide spaces here, and freedom and always, summer and winter, the blessed sunshine which engendered hope.

At the end, he looked down upon the still, intent, listening faces. His voice took on a deeper timbre.

"I have tried to tell you the story of this land, the land that is now yours. The old first dangers have long since passed, but there are others, as you know, facing us now. This is a great country and dearly bought. Love it, work for it, believe in it, and keep it free for yourselves and for your children!"

He moved back and in the hush more eloquent than applause, Johnny quickly gave a signal for the audience to rise, and in a second the voices of all, rough, shrill, strident or sweet, swelled together and rang out over the quiet meadow, the Patch, the tipple and the coke ovens:

> My country, 'tis of thee,
> Sweet land of liberty,
>   Of thee I sing . . .
>
> Long may our land be bright
> With freedom's holy light;
> Protect us by Thy might,
>   Great God, our King.

Paul's own throat felt full as he sang, and to his surprise he saw here and there women with tears on their cheeks and men wiping their eyes with heavy hands.

Perhaps he had gotten his message across! Perhaps he had really made them feel it!

If he had any doubt of this it was dispelled by his reception afterwards, for the men crowded awkwardly around him to shake his hand and speak broken words of understanding.

"That's a-right, mister. This-a good-a country!"

"I come over, no can spik Engleesh. Now my boy, he take beeg honor in high school!"

"You talk right, mister. No scare here in America."

So it went. One woman made so bold as to edge close.

"I never hear about those first people that come from the old country before. We think we all the time work hard. But we don't have snakes and Indians. Mebbe we have it pretty much better as those first ones, huh?"

"I think we do," Paul agreed, smiling.

It seemed a long time before the crowd was willing to scatter again to their games. Their eagerness to speak to him, to shake his hand moved Paul greatly, and in proportion as he was touched by this, he was filled with a deep and humble elation. In his heart he knew as one old miner had put it that he had "done good."

When Johnny finally got to him alone, his face was so serious that Paul was startled.

"By golly, man, I expected a good speech, but I wasn't prepared for anything like that! I all but blubbered a couple of times. You had us in the palm of your hand. It . . . you . . . Oh, damn it, I can't say it, but it was great!"

Bovard himself was highly pleased, and Kirkland, getting out of his car and coming close, said in a low tone, "Well, that does it! I'll not stop till I get you in the White House!"

Paul laughed. "One speech doesn't make a President, I believe. But I've something important to ask you. Could you arrange to be away from home this evening?"

Kirkland's eyes narrowed. "I have to be," he said. "Why?"

"Nothing," Paul answered. "Just an idea."

Kirkland gave him a long look. "I'm going to be with Brennen to-night at his home," he said as he hurried off.

It was Hartwell's commendation Paul craved most, but the old man said nothing until they were back in the car. Then very slowly and with a slight break in his voice he said, "My boy, I'm very, very proud of you!"

And then they both hastened to talk of other things entirely, all the way home.

Paul made a pretense at eating dinner at the restaurant but his heart was beating too heavily for appetite. Johnny had clamored for a night's celebration but he had refused. The truth was that he had made a promise to himself that if the speech went well he would go that very evening to see Anne. He would allow nothing this time to deter him. If it took force to get in, force it would be. Eight-thirty was the earliest he could be sure her dinner was over, and what seemed a long waste of time stretched between his return to his room and that hour. He stripped, showered, dressed again with scrupulous care, sometimes muttering the refrain of a poem to keep up his courage.

> *But you'll n'er stop a lover—*
> *He will find out the way.*

Hackett was a big fellow, if he actually tried physically to block an entrance . . . Well, Paul muttered grimly, I'm a big fellow too.

At last it was time to go. All the cumulative tension of the day left him unable to bear firmly the fear of putting his fortune to the test as irrevocably as he was about to do. For a moment he stopped pacing the floor and sat down weakly. If Anne's strange behavior was caused by unselfish thought of him, if her hard words had been but the lie, sacrificial, then he was sure he could persuade her, could win her. In that case he would come back, rejoicing as a strong man to run a race. If on the other hand, she did not wish in her own heart to consummate their friendship, he would re-enter this room, lost and despairing. In how brief a time was destiny wrought! Between his leaving now and his returning, the sweet, the dear, the tender person of his beloved would be his alone or else lost to him forever.

He pulled himself together and went out to the car. He drove slowly, feeling the uncertainty more easily endured than the bitterness of a negative finality. Sensible of the beauty of the May evening as though for the last time, he guided the car up the tree-shaded driveway and parked in his usual place. As he crossed the porch a wave of fragrance from the locust blooms along the upper garden wall struck him with poignant sweetness, as though bearing the breath of all love of all the ages.

He rang, and Hackett opened the door.

"Good evening, Hackett. I'm calling to see Miss Anne," he announced firmly.

"I'm sorry. Miss Anne is not at home."

"I intend to come in!"

"Her orders are that she does not wish to see you, Mr. Devereux."

For reply Paul put a hand upon Hackett's chest and pushed, moving over the threshold as he did so. To his amazement a wide grin overspread Hackett's countenance as he allowed himself to be propelled farther backward.

"God knows I did my best to keep you out, Mr. Devereux. She's up in her sitting room," he added in a pleased stage whisper.

The surprise of the older man's reaction was so great that it sent over Paul a wave of optimism. He nodded his thanks and hurried to the stairway, taking in its incredible grace as always as he started up, and arrived in a moment all but breathless at the top. He could see Anne's sitting room door very slightly ajar. He reached it gently and pushed it open. Anne sat on the sofa beside the window, her head propped on her hand as she gazed at the garden below. Her whole attitude was that in which he had first seen her, one of utter sadness and dejection. With a cry he started toward her. She turned, shock written on her pale face.

"Paul! Oh, why did you do this?"

He was very close to her now, feeling the full weight of his passion. "Because I had to come! Surely you knew I would, sooner or later. Anne, why have you tortured me so? Why have you held me off? You know I love you, that I want more than anything on earth to marry you . . ."

Then he sank down beside her and his arms went round her. She tried to struggle against him.

"You are mad, *mad* to think of such a thing. I can't marry you. Surely you must know . . ."

Their broken words ran into each other.

"Do you love me, darling, oh, say you love me, that's all that matters . . ."

"I tried so hard . . . Oh, Paul, I fought so desperately for what I thought was your best good . . ."

"Do you love me?"

Suddenly all the tension went out of her body. As if in supreme giving she yielded to the urgency of his strength as she sobbed against his breast.

"Yes, yes! From the first, I think. But that last night I knew I must . . . Oh, Paul, I love you so terribly, so utterly. . . ."

For a long time the words were blurred and inarticulate and unnecessary. At last she raised her head. The tears were still wet on her cheeks and Paul tenderly wiped them away. She reached up to smooth his hair.

"I've always wanted to do that," she said smiling, and then a gravity fell fast upon her face again.

"But even so, Paul, even with all our love, how can we think of marriage . . . as I am?"

He had gone over his arguments so often in his mind that they poured from him now, with the fierceness of established conviction.

"I will tell you," he said, "just how it is on my side, for I know that is what troubles you. I love *you*, the essential you, your mind, your spirit, your body. The fact that you cannot walk does not alter that. Then there would be the completely selfish side of my marriage to you. I've known a number of unhappy husbands and in most cases it's because the wives get to leading their own lives. Take Harvey, our other senior partner, for instance. He can never get his wife on the phone. Just once I heard him make a comment when he didn't know I was within earshot. 'My God,' he said, 'is she never at home?' Now when we are married I would know that when I come back from work, you would be there, waiting for me, ready to listen to all my problems and the story of my day. I've dreamed of this. It may seem a small thing to you, but it's bigger than you know, even if utterly selfish on my side. You see the capacity to run about is not the supreme qualification for a wife."

Anne watched him, amazed, drinking in the words.

Paul went on. "And another thing. I'm not too athletic. I play a little golf but I believe I'd rather do that with men anyway. I like to play bridge. We can always do that. I love quiet evenings of talk or reading aloud—the sort we've always had. I hate cocktail parties like the devil. I like the theater. We can go, just as we did before. We can do so many things of that kind, in that way. As to my carrying you—I will be so proud to do it. I'll be always thinking as I hold you, *She's mine! She's mine!*"

"Don't!" Anne said brokenly. "Don't. You're so wonderful, it hurts!"

"So you see our marriage would be nothing strange or in the slightest way impossible. My heart will never stop aching for what *you* have to miss. But I will miss nothing important myself. Oh, my darling, I'll try to make up to you in every way I can, always, always. I'll try with all my powers to make you happy!"

As she was about to speak he broke in, this time embarrassed.

"One more thing I must say, before you answer. If you could get about normally I'm afraid I'd be insufferably independent, wanting you to live on my salary and all that. But I've thought this all through. My pride may suffer a little but that's really unworthy. The thing is I will probably just have to hang up my hat here, if your father doesn't object, and accept a good deal from him, or rather let *you* accept your life as usual. It's the only possible way for your comfort. You do understand this part, don't you, dear?"

She sat silent for a few moments and then such a radiance flooded her face that Paul felt dazzled. She could not speak, but she raised her eyes, shining with relief and wonder, and he understood. So, after the heartache, the uncertainty and the fear, there was lovers' heaven at last.

Sometime later Anne straightened as though coming back suddenly to reality.

"Oh, we must try to get Father at once! He'll be dumfounded, I know, but he'll be terribly happy. He likes you. I wonder where he is!"

"He's with Mr. Brennen. I'll look up the number."

As Anne held the phone she looked up innocently.

"Do you think he has the least idea about . . . us?" she asked.

Paul felt a miserable sense of deceit. "He's a pretty smart man," he countered.

When Kirkland finally spoke, Anne's voice was vibrant in reply.

"Jimmy? I've got the most wonderful, the most fabulous, the most *stupendous* news you ever heard! Hang on to your chair or something. Who do you think is engaged? Me, Anne, your daughter! Paul and I are going to be married. Can you believe it?"

Paul could hear the burst of Kirkland's joy from where he stood. It went on for several minutes, punctuated with Anne's happy interjections.

"He's thrilled," she said over her shoulder. "And I do believe he suspected all along . . . Yes, Jimmy? His speech? No, he hasn't mentioned it yet. We've had some other things under discussion. Yes? . . . He says you were wonderful, Paul, that you should have been an actor and that you could make anybody believe anything! . . . Well, he's made me believe he loves me anyway, Jimmy. I've never been so happy! Here's Paul now to ask you for my hand. Don't refuse for it won't do you any good. The young man, I find, is obstinate!"

Their conversation was brief and light, with Kirkland's "Thank God, my boy," spoken under his breath. It emphasized, however, the sense of concealment Paul had felt earlier.

"And now, Gran! Even if it wakes her up," Anne cried when he had finished.

If another drop had been needed to fill the cup, Mrs. Catherby's surprise and joy provided it.

When there was quiet again, Paul said, "And now, about the wedding."

A shadow like a dark cloud at noon fell upon Anne's bright face.

"The wedding," she repeated dully.

In the instant Paul saw what must be passing through her mind: the bride descending the beautiful stairway in her robes of white;

her stately procession on her father's arm up the flower-decked church aisle with her bridesmaids preceding her and all the gay world of her friends looking on as she approached the high beauty of the altar where he himself would be waiting. . . .

He laid his cheek against hers and his voice was infinitely tender.

"I know, my darling, I know. But we are two people pledged to think only of the essentials, aren't we?"

She kissed him for answer. "In the fall, do you think?"

"The fall?" Paul burst out. "Good heavens, no! I want to be married right away. Why on earth should we wait? A lifetime will be all too short to have you as my wife. Couldn't we be married next week? That would give us a little honeymoon somewhere before I have to start campaigning for Halsey. I can get that postponed for a bit since I know the Boss! *Please*, Anne!"

"*Next week!*" She drew back, startled, and then slowly began to smile. "You don't realize it, but everything you say seems to be just what I need to make me feel secure. I must get some new clothes, and think out just how we'll manage the ceremony, but after these endless months of nothing to do, it will be heavenly to feel rushed and flurried and absolutely *driven* for time. If you wish," she said the words slowly as though still weighing the incredible sound of them, "we will be married next week. We can go up to the camp for our . . . honeymoon. I love it and you will too, I know. It would be the best place for many reasons. I know we're both insane . . . but oh, let's plan!"

It grew later and later and then early before Paul left. When he finally reached the front door he found Hackett dozing in a chair. He touched his shoulder.

"I'm sorry to have kept you up so long, Hackett, but you can lock up now. Want to hear a big piece of news?"

The old man jumped. "Miss Anne?" he asked huskily.

"We're going to be married next week. Congratulate me!"

Hackett wrung his hand, while his eyes misted over.

"With all my heart," he said. "I've lived here for twenty years and I can tell you there's no girl like her. You never did a better job than when you nearly pushed me over! I've been praying you'd do some such thing. Well! Well! The Lord be praised and bless you, sir!"

The next day after a late lunch with Kirkland, Paul returned with him to his office to pick up some papers.

"I think I'll tell Arno and Miss Sayles," he said. "They've both been very kind to me."

"Good!" Kirkland said. "I almost told them myself, but decided you'd want to."

Paul went into the other office, where Sayles looked up frigidly from her typewriter and Arno rose in more than usual friendly fashion.

"Hello, Devereux," he said, "have a seat. What can I do for you?"

"Nothing, thanks," said Paul. "And I won't sit down, for my own work's waiting. I just dropped in to tell you both that Miss Kirkland and I are to be married Saturday of next week."

Miss Sayles's mouth opened and remained so. Arno's face went white and then scarlet with color.

"Not . . . Anne?" he brought out thickly.

"Yes, I'm a pretty happy and lucky man. Just thought you'd both be interested to hear about it. Well," as the silence continued, "so long!"

He closed the door behind him and chuckled as he told Kirkland.

"It surely bowled them over. They could barely speak. As a matter of fact Miss Sayles said nothing at all and Arno merely gulped something. Well, I'm still enough stunned myself to excuse other people for being so. I'll see you at the house, tonight."

Back in the office Sayles looked at Arno, who was standing motionless.

"Well," she said, trying to make the words light, "that was a piece of news if ever I heard one!"

Arno's knuckles were white on the back of the chair.

"The dirty, stinking bastard!" he gritted. "The damned low, fortune-hunting, scheming *rat!* He knows which side of his bread's buttered all right, the skunk!"

Sayles's eyes widened. "You're right! That's all it could be, the way she is. Well, her money's done her some good, I suppose, if she wants to buy *that* with it."

Arno turned abruptly, and went out.

Sayles sat very still. Her white blouse was immaculate as usual, her hair smooth perfection, her carefully manicured hands rested lightly upon the typewriter, but her normally inscrutable countenance was broken with pain.

So that's how it's been with him, she thought. *It's not believable, but then nothing ever is. It's hit him hard all right, poor Arno.* Then with a deep sigh she added half aloud, *And poor me!*

If Kirkland could have seen her then he would not have thought her sexless.

Anne had her wish. For the next ten days from morning until late night she was busier than she had ever been before in her life. But because of this and the joint advice of Gran and Miss Davis and the best Bride's Counselor in the city, there was going to be a real wedding after all.

"It's wonderful, under the circumstances, to do it this way," Anne told Paul the night before. "I mean when it has to be so different it's sort of dramatic to have it sudden and soon. And everyone is *so* excited and pleased."

"Including the groom. Only I've hardly seen you since the night you agreed to marry me."

Anne turned the shining diamond upon her finger. "I'll try to give you a little time, afterward," she said demurely. Then looking up with her heart in her eyes, "You're sure, Paul, I won't be a hindrance to you in your political career? We really didn't give that enough thought."

Paul's answer was thoroughly convincing.

On the evening itself, their closest friends, young and older, gathered in the music room, where an orchestra was playing softly, and upon the stroke of eight were ushered into the great drawing room, seldom opened, but now decked with flowers and shining with candlelight. At the farthest end sat Anne, radiant and lovely, in billowy white with a tiara of orange blossoms on her hair. Paul stood close beside her with her father near to perform his part, and the clergyman facing them. The vows were pledged, the prayers were offered, the rings exchanged, the blessing given, the nuptial kiss received. They were man and wife!

Then while the guests filed past, chairs and small tables appeared as by magic. The champagne was circulated, the elegant supper served, toasts were drunk, with Johnny Bovard in his finest form proposing all sorts of absurd ones, while Hartwell offered the most tender. The music played, the laughter and chatter grew louder and gaiety filled the room and flowed out through the tall windows into the dusk.

When the company gathered at last in the hall to watch the stairway, they found themselves outwitted. Paul with his sweet burden appeared from the small morning room, where Anne had changed, and in a moment was at the door. They all saw her say something to him.

"You're carrying me over the threshold in reverse, you know," she whispered in his ear.

For answer, as though no one were looking, he kissed her and then, both laughing, they moved quickly over the porch to the waiting car, where Hackett stood holding the door open. Paul set her in her place, ran around to his own side and they started. But slowly, for the young people gathered all about them, shouting their good-byes and good wishes, throwing their rice and confetti all the way down the drive. Then with a last wave, Paul stepped on the accelerator and they were off, into the warm encompassing darkness of the summer night.

7

꿏 IT WAS the last night of the honeymoon. They sat on the terrace watching the full moon rise above the mountain blanching the purple of the valley below to palest mauve. There was the beauty of completion, of utter fulfillment in the great golden orb which accorded with the mood of their own hearts.

The fortnight had held within it all the incredible felicities of which they had both dreamed. There had been little of awkwardness or discomfort. The camp, which was really a wide-spreading and finely built house, was now, with the new highway for most of the distance, only a two-hour drive from the city; they had reached it the night of the wedding a little after one. Davy, driven over by the Kirkland chauffeur, had left earlier, and was unobtrusively in her place when they got there. She and the couple who were year-round caretakers, attended to their physical comfort and in between times made themselves invisible; so the lovers had the feeling of being alone on the hilltop, with the warmth and sweetness of June enfolding them. There had been but one bitter hour. On the second day Anne had urged Paul to go for a walk while she rested. When he came back he heard the sobbing even from the doorway. He rushed across to their bedroom, where Anne lay in her desperate grief. Terrified, he drew her into his arms. She was trembling all over as if from a chill.

"Never to walk with you through the woods! Never to walk with you anywhere. . . ."

He did not try to offer fatuous words of comfort. He only held her close, speechless with anguished pity. When a tear fell upon her forehead, she raised herself and looked into his eyes.

"For me?" she whispered incredulously.

"*Only* for you."

With a long, shuddering sigh she became quiet. Her arms reached up to him.

"I can bear it," she said, before his lips fell upon hers. "I have so much besides."

They never referred to the hour again.

A lovely and satisfying pattern soon sprang up to fill their days. Paul took a long brisk walk in the morning while Anne, with Davy's help, was bathing and dressing, after which there was a late, deliciously delaying breakfast-luncheon on the terrace. Dinners were varied according to their impulse, sometimes stately with candlelight and Anne in one of her bewitching trousseau gowns; sometimes picnic fashion from the coffee table before the fire when the nights were unusually cool. In between they read aloud, played games and talked endlessly with open hearts. The days were never long enough except that with their ending came the mystery, the passion, the ecstasy of the nights.

It was Mrs. Catherby who had packed the books. In all the rush neither Anne nor Paul had thought of them, but with the luggage came a box of Gran's choicest with Paul's own volume which he had lent her among them. So in the warm murmurous afternoons on the terrace or perhaps in a deep chair in the evenings by the fire, Paul read aloud from them. They went back often to "Love in the Valley" describing over and over their own emotions as they had first shared the words. And one evening when the logs were almost burned out Paul suddenly opened a volume at a random page and then stared at it, startled:

"Why, here is the thing you quoted to me that first night I met you!"

He read, where his eyes fell:

> "THE MASTER OF THE CARAVAN
> Open the gate, O watchman of the night!
> THE WATCHMAN
> Ho, travellers, I open. For what land
> Leave you the dim-moon city of delight?
> THE MERCHANTS (*with a shout*)
> We make the Golden Journey to Samarkand.
> (*The Caravan passes through the gate*)
> THE WATCHMAN (*consoling the women*)
> What would ye, ladies? It was ever thus.
> Men are unwise and curiously planned.
> A WOMAN
> They have their dreams, and do not think of us.
>
> VOICES OF THE CARAVAN (*in the distance singing*)
> We make the Golden Journey to Samarkand."

"That's it," Anne said. "It's by an English author named Flecker, and I think this bit is from a play. It's beautiful and haunting, isn't it?"

"Do you think it's true?"

"I'm . . . not sure."

"Anne, do you have any fear about my own plans? In connection with us, I mean?"

"Maybe a little. Oh, not really. Just now don't let's even admit there are fears in the world."

"Or politics either!"

Paul rose, made the fire safe, put out the lights, and carried her to their room.

This last night as they sat on the terrace, looking at the rising moon and listening to the soft mountain sounds round about them which were somehow quieter than silence, Paul from the step leaned back against Anne's knees and her hand gently caressed his head.

"I hope," she said softly, "that as soon as possible I will have a baby. You know the doctor says that is one thing I should be able to do as well as any woman."

"You would have something better than Devvie to hold on your knee, then."

Anne laughed, then spoke seriously. "You really think it might happen, don't you?"

He turned slightly until she felt his lips smiling against her hand. "I should think there would be a very strong probability."

"Naughty!" she said. "You know what I mean." Then they laughed together from sheer overflowing happiness.

"But, really," she went on, "there is so much I could do for a baby, even . . . as I am. I could bathe it and dress it and rock it and sing to it . . . you know they allow that, now. Then later on I could read to them and teach them all sorts of things . . ."

"I note you have changed to the plural," Paul broke in.

"Oh, yes. I do hope we have several. Then, when they come in from school just as you said of me as a wife, I would always be home. Oh, I do think, Paul, I can still be a good mother."

He could not speak for a long moment. The tenderness of it all brought such a lump to his throat.

"The dearest, the best, the loveliest in the world," he whispered.

When they got back to the city, Kirkland's reception, for a reserved man, bordered upon the ecstatic. He seemed full not only of happiness but of suppressed excitement. When he could get Paul into his study he began nervously, "Of course it's too soon, I mean naturally some months may elapse before . . . What I really wanted to tell you is that I've already gotten in touch with Dr. Hertzog! He is most interested in hearing of the marriage. He has promised that later on . . . whenever the time arrives he will come over and be here for the . . ."

Paul was distinctly annoyed.

"I think that is all very premature. I may say that what you are thinking of is certainly not the thing uppermost in my mind at the moment."

"If you were her father it would be," Kirkland said, apparently not conscious of the edge in Paul's tone. "And I hope you will tell me . . . I mean when it *does* happen . . ."

"Anne is the one to do that," Paul broke in shortly. "And now what is the plan right now for me? I'd like to be briefed as soon as possible so I can get at my speeches." His voice softened. "As I guess you can well imagine, I haven't thought about them much these last weeks."

Kirkland's eyes suddenly filled. "I know, my boy, I know. She's very like her mother! I'm so thankful, so happy! Well, now to get down to business. We'd like you to start as soon as possible making one speech a week. Later there will be more. I took the liberty of lining up the first engagements round the county. If you have the pull I think you do, we'll send you out over the state later on. Good for your own campaign when that time arrives. Here's the line-up now."

They went over together the list of towns varying in size from one of fifteen thousand population to a country crossroads settlement.

"You can feel yourself out," Kirkland said, "and see where you go over best. By the way, how are you on stories? Ones for the public, that is," he added grinning.

Paul looked worried. "Not too good, I fear, and I ought to have a stock. Mr. Hartwell may be able to help me there. I'll talk to him."

As a matter of fact he was eager to see the old man again, and as he shook hands with him next day in the office, the feeling seemed mutual.

"Well, my boy, glad to see you back! I ought to sue you for breach of promise, though."

"How is that?"

"Just when you say I'm to be invited frequently to your bachelor quarters, you suddenly up and get married."

"But you'll come to dinner with us soon, won't you? You and Anne will be the greatest friends. You must come often to the house . . . it will be just the same!"

Old Hartwell shook his head. "Not quite. A bachelor and a married man are two quite different animals. But I'm glad you chose to belong to the latter breed. And I'll be most happy to go to dinner when it's convenient. Well, well, do you think you can bring yourself down to earth now?"

Paul laughed. "I've been up among the stars, all right, but I'll try to get back to business in a hurry. By the way, I need your help. I'm to start speaking for Halsey next week, and I suddenly realize I have no fund of stories. Mr. Kirkland thinks they're pretty important. Could you dig me up some that I could work in here and there?"

Hartwell stroked his mustache. "Use a Lincoln one whenever you can. That always goes over anywhere. You should have a few just for the country too. I'll see what I can gather up. By the way, we've run into a very puzzling case while you've been gone."

They settled then to talk it over, and Paul's face grew grave. It seemed that the firm of Willis & Company had put in their bid along with several others for the contract of filling in a dump on the east side of the city. It was a big project. Willis represented that his bid was for $100,000, which he considered a fair one. He would have given the city a good job and made himself a reasonable profit. He lost the contract but had learned later that the company that got it was to receive $180,000.

"How did he find that out?" Paul asked.

"Oh, the award bid is always posted. In any case he's determined to sue the city. I have a strong suspicion he has reason enough. We're graft-ridden certainly, but whether we can do anything about this, I'm not so sure."

"I'd like to sink my teeth in that," Paul said determinedly.

Hartwell studied his desk.

"Perhaps I should not tell you until our suspicions are confirmed, but we've been making a quiet investigation. The company that got the contract is a smallish one under the name of Betts & Bolton. They deal chiefly in slag, and we find most of it comes from the Kirkland mines."

"Well," Paul put in, "they have a right to get it anywhere, haven't they?"

Hartwell nodded. "But we are inclined to think Kirkland owns the company and operates it under this other name . . . a front, as it were."

"You have proof?"

"We have a good deal. What then?"

Paul got up abruptly. "Mr. Hartwell, I can't believe this! If it should turn out to be true and you take the case, it will hit me very hard. But let me know what happens. You can understand how I feel."

"I do, I do, my boy. Don't get excited. I doubt if we'll decide to go further into the matter at all though I'm strongly tempted to see what we could do with it. As I told you, the welfare of the city interests me. But you just forget it for the present, and go on with your speeches. I'll see what I can do for you in the way of stories. Well, it's good to have you back and I'm very happy for you."

It was a nice dismissal but Paul returned to his own office disturbed and perplexed. If Kirkland was really involved in this situation, which looked like city graft at its worst, did he dare refuse to acknowledge it? And if the firm took this case it would cause daily headlines for weeks. Being a member of the firm he would be in some sense associated with it all even if not actively involved. It was bitterly hard to run into a thing like this upon his happy return! He plunged into matters awaiting him on his desk, determining—rather weakly, he thought—to do nothing, to say nothing for the present until he saw how the problem developed.

Just before he left that afternoon Hartwell sent for him.

"I've thought of a Coolidge story you might use. When he was in the legislature there was a man who thought Cal was pretty homespun and was always trying to heckle him about it. One day this chap said, 'Mr. Coolidge, do the people where you come from say a hen lays, or a hen lies?' Cal looked up at him and drawled, 'The people where I come from lift her up to see.' You could use this to illustrate the point that a voter should find out the facts about a candidate. You, yourself, being the exponent at the time, of course."

Paul laughed heartily. "That's great, Mr. Hartwell. If you get me a few more like that one I'll have some real ammunition."

Each evening after office hours he rushed home to Anne, shedding cares as he went. The delight of her personality was ever new. Just now she was full of plans for converting certain rooms upstairs into a suite for themselves. Her sitting room across the hall would remain as it was for they both loved it, but her bedroom was being refurnished, "just to add a little note of masculinity here and there," as she put it, and the rather spacious writing room beyond converted into a dressing room and study for Paul. On the other side, as Anne shyly pointed out, a door could be cut into a guest room later on, and open into what would make an ideal nursery. Each evening she showed him samples of fabrics, of wallpapers, of pictured furniture and her own carefully drawn designs. He knew all this involved a large outlay of money and he hesitated how to approach the rather troublous problem. One night he felt he must speak of it.

"I would like to bring down the old secretary from home and perhaps a few other pieces for my room. Would you mind?"

"Mind? Oh, Paul, I think that would be lovely! I should have thought of it myself. Maybe we can decide on the carpeting first, and the hangings too—they should be simple but very rich, don't you think? And then when everything else is done, you can have your furniture sent down. I do want this room to be very, very handsome for you."

"There is one thing I must tell you," Paul said gently. "I will pay for everything in it myself. Your room—well, it's still really *your* room. I'll say nothing about that. But the expense of mine must all be borne by me. So, don't make it all *too* handsome, will you?"

Anne looked surprised and hurt. "Why, I thought we'd settled the wretched money business once and for all," she said.

"In a sense, yes. But it's bound to keep cropping up. There will always be things I will want to pay for if I can, and you must humor me. For instance, I want you soon to buy a hat, or something very extravagant, and charge it to me, so when the bill comes in I can hit the ceiling and make a scene like a proper husband—and then love writing the check for it. You see?"

They were sitting on the sofa in her sitting room beside the opened windows. She laid her head against his breast and his hand caressed the shining hair.

"You are so dear, so inexpressibly dear," she whispered.

It was long before they took up their planning again.

One thing which puzzled Paul during these weeks was Arno's attitude toward him. The first day he went into Kirkland's office the Chief himself was out so Paul went on through, smiling, to speak to Arno and Miss Sayles and receive their congratulations. These latter, however, were not forthcoming. After the barest greeting Sayles concentrated on her typing while Arno looked at him with a smile but what seemed like actual malevolence in his black eyes.

"How are you, Arno?"

"Why, pretty good, Mr. Devereux."

"How are things going?"

"Well, such as what?"

Still the smile but Paul felt the insolence. He met it with quick sarcasm.

"Oh, the weather of course. It's the only thing really worth discussing."

"Why, it's been pretty warm here these last weeks. I suppose where *you've* been, it was nice and cool."

It was almost a sneer.

"Do you know when Mr. Kirkland will be in?" Paul asked sharply.

"I really wouldn't know."

"Could you give me any idea?"

"Afraid I couldn't."

Paul turned on his heel and went into Kirkland's office to wait. What was the matter with the fellow? He had always been more than friendly before; now he was not even civil. He recalled Arno's face when he had told him about his coming marriage. At the time he had attributed his silence to surprise. Could it have been shock as well? And if so, why?

Kirkland came in soon, as Arno must have known he would. He closed the door between the rooms and then sat down with evident pleasure for a talk.

"Look," Paul said in a low tone, "before we discuss anything else, can you tell me what's wrong with Arno?"

"In what way?" Kirkland asked in surprise.

"He acts as if I'd just shot his grandmother. He was as rude as possible and he looked as though he hated me for something or other."

"I think you must have imagined this, Paul. Arno gets moody spells at times and he's likely in one at the moment. I have absolute confidence in him as far as our mutual affairs are concerned but I don't have any idea what his life is like on the outside. He's not married but heaven knows what entanglements he may have. He's probably just bothered about something of the sort."

"I have a feeling," Paul went on, "that his attitude is somehow due to my own marriage."

"Why, how on earth could that affect him?" Kirkland's tone was almost amused.

"He may feel that I was a little presumptuous in aspiring to Anne. Of course I feel so myself."

"Nonsense!" Kirkland still sounded amused. "Don't get ideas about Arno. I know him like a book. I'll speak to him now, though, about his manners!"

"Please don't. I beg of you don't let on to him about this. Just let things ride. I may have been oversensitive. It will all straighten out."

"Oh, all right," Kirkland agreed. "Probably the best way. Arno's a good fellow. I don't know what I'd do without him. Now I want to talk about Brennen."

They were soon deep in plans. Brennen was County Chairman and Paul would be working closely with him. They had lunched together several times and now Brennen would go along to the first meeting where Paul was to speak.

"I don't want to be underhanded about this, Paul. It's all for your own good later on so I'll tell you. I've asked him to be at this Citizens for Halsey dinner out at Rothbridge Friday night. I've asked him to listen to everything you say and watch everything you do, and then report to me."

"Good way to put me at my ease," Paul grinned.

"Oh, I'm not afraid of your getting stage fright. It's just that Brennen is an old hand at this game. He'll know what corners ought to be smoothed off you, if any. He'll know whether you need a little coaching in, well, discussing the issues of the campaign."

"You mean in *evading* them?"Paul asked, a little sarcastically.

"Well, now, I'll tell you. There is black and there is white. In between is a pretty decent, solid strip of *gray*. The older you get the more you realize that gray isn't such a bad color. And in politics you work with it or you don't work at all. But the trick is, always make it sound *white* to the voters. Well, you'll catch on. You've got brains and I think you've got the knack."

Paul was thoughtful all the way back to his own office. He dropped in to chat with Hartwell as he often did when the day was over.

"How's the speech going?" the old man began.

"Oh, it's fair, I guess. The hen story is perfect for a starter. Have you thought of any more?"

"I found a Lincoln one you may like. When Abe was a candidate for Congress back in 1846 he attended a revival service of Peter Cartwright. Cartwright called on all who wished to go to heaven to stand up. All rose but Lincoln. Then he asked all to rise who didn't want to go to hell. Lincoln still sat. 'I'm surprised,' Cartwright said, 'to see Abe Lincoln sitting back there unmoved by these appeals. If Mr. Lincoln doesn't want to go to heaven and doesn't want to escape hell, perhaps he'll tell me where he does want to go?' Lincoln slowly rose and said, 'I want to go to Congress.' Now, I've thought of a way you could work that in with . . ."

"Listen," Paul said, still laughing, "that's too good to waste on the governor. I'm saving that one for myself later on. That is, if I ever get the length of a candidacy. I'm a little low-spirited at the moment. Tell me, how do you like gray as a color?"

"I usually wear it in the daytime."

"I'm not speaking of clothes," Paul smiled. "I've been told that in politics you work with it alone. That black and white as such cannot be discussed with the voters. What do you think?"

The old man pondered gravely. "I take it you mean whether I think there should ever be compromise between right and wrong. In other words is there an absolute? Like truth. The older I grow the less sure I am that there is. Pilate's question on that still stands and only God knows the answer. That's why the whole question of compromise is such a difficult one. When I was a young fellow I sat in on a murder trial. A man had killed his older brother. No doubt of that. He was convicted and sentenced. But what came out clear as crystal, to me, at least, from the evidence was that this older brother had practiced a fine form of mental torture on the younger one for years, until he one day cracked under the strain and put an end to it. Now the fact was that the dead man was the real murderer and the convicted man an essentially good and decent fellow."

He paused thoughtfully. "But we have to have laws in this, our most fallible society. The apparent wrong must be punished, though the real truth lies below the fact. I'm afraid this isn't any help to you, though, in connection with your voters."

"It's interesting," Paul said, "very. I've often thought too, about whether a hard and fast line can ever be drawn . . ."

Hartwell leaned forward. "I didn't quite finish, and I don't want you to misinterpret what I've just said. No human being can adequately assess what we term *right* and *wrong*, any more than he can absolutely define *truth*. But what we can have are principles which transcend fact. And we've got to hang on to those at any cost. In other words, your personal honesty, Paul, your integrity, not the other man's but your own, is the thing that can never be grayed down, or compromised, or bargained over. That, I fear, is the only comment I can give you on your question."

As Paul rose to leave, Hartwell added, "We are not taking the case of which I spoke to you. I'm sorry to give it up but we haven't enough to go on."

"I see," said Paul briefly, a great relief flooding through him. At least there would be no public scandal, but he knew he must find out if he could about the real ownership of the firm of Betts & Bolton.

The facts came to him sooner than he expected. He had called Johnny Bovard upon his return but found him out of town. This week, though, they lunched together at The Dive, as Johnny called it. The latter, ebullient as ever, leaned across the table and beamed upon him.

"Well, well! And how's Benedick, the married man? Boy, what a fast one you pulled! You could have knocked me over with a wet pinfeather. How's Anne? How's everything?"

"Fine, fine, fine, to all three questions. I'm as proud and happy as is the lot of mortal man to be. Can't you come out soon to see us? Anne's busy supervising some remodeling upstairs but of course we live all over the place. What about dinner some evening? Anne can get a girl in and we can have a game of bridge later, okay?"

"Of course," Johnny said. "Wonderful." But something in his voice was not quite right. A little later he spoke slowly, looking down at the table.

"If it doesn't sound like a prying maiden aunt, could I ask you when you fell in love with Anne?"

Paul spoke earnestly. "The first night I met her. I really knew then, I think, though I wouldn't admit it. Then there was a terrible struggle in my mind. Her condition, you know. Not a barrier to my feelings, but to my being able to care for her myself. I had to fight it all out with my pride. Then I couldn't get her to accept me. She had her own pride and her fears, and I was sunk. But at last. . . ."

Johnny interrupted by reaching out his hand. "Let me congratulate you all over again."

Their eyes met. "You thought badly of me?" Paul asked slowly. "The whole setup bothered you?"

Johnny's honest face colored a little. "Not really," he said, "but let's just say I'm glad you've told me what you did just now. I'm happier than I can tell you about the whole thing. My word, what a beauty she looked the night of the wedding! And when you carried her out the door—boy, I choked up like a monkey. Envy, I guess."

The tiny cloud was gone and they talked on with their usual ease.

Johnny was deeply interested in the campaign work. His father knew Brennen and, in a slight way, Halsey.

"Dad thinks Halsey's a lightweight but the better of the two candidates. How do you preach the gospel, Paul? What can you find to say about the fellow? You know what I've often thought?" He went on without waiting for an answer, "I think if a strong man would decide to run for office, and then tell the voters the truth about everything—no pussyfooting, no political strings, just straight from the shoulder, honest-to-God stuff . . ."

"How would he get a nomination?" Paul asked.

"Yeah, that's a point. He might have to play Br'er Rabbit till he got that and then just let 'er fly."

"He'd be a voice crying in the wilderness."

"Could be, but I'll bet there'd be a darned lot of ears among the trees taking it all in."

As they were leaving, Paul had a shock. He all but ran into Arno, entering with another man. Paul greeted him and Arno smiled his strange smile.

"Who's the fellah?" Johnny asked. "The one with the grin."

"You noticed that?"

"Well, it did look a bit from the teeth out."

"He's Kirkland's right-hand man and I've a hunch he doesn't love me just now. Don't know why."

"I've seen him around, hangs out here a lot but I never knew who he was. That's why he's with Betts, then."

Paul pricked up his ears. "Betts?"

"Yep. Betts & Bolton run one of Kirkland's subsidiaries under their names. Say, don't mention that. Trade secret, sort of. We do the same in a smaller way. Kirkland's got a lot more irons in the fire, though, than we have, not counting politics."

"Johnny, walk along with me a little. I want to ask you something. Do you know anything about this project for filling in a dump over on the east side?"

"Sure do. We bid on it. Why?"

"Too high?"

"Well, we didn't get it anyway. There's usually some shenanigan. You can't tell about these city contracts."

"You know who got the contract?"

"Oh, yes. Our friends there, Betts & Bolton. We knew when they were bidding we hadn't a chance, but we didn't take it too hard. We have a lot of slag just now but we're more interested in some road contracts if we can wangle them without selling our souls. Oh Paul, you know sometimes I wish I was a nice clean dirt farmer. I wasn't born for intrigue. Well, here's where I've got to leave you. Love to Anne and tell her to ask me to dinner!"

It was all true then, Paul thought, as he went back to the office. Kirkland could call the tune at City Hall as well as in the state capitol. And threading through the background of events were certain figures now shadowy, only half descried, but which Paul feared, with a dreadful prescience, would become to him, at least, distinct and clear as time went on.

He stayed alone in the office after closing time that evening, sitting at his desk, head in hands. He still possessed the overpowering desire to continue what he had begun. The speech at Rothbridge had gone over well. He couldn't help knowing it even if Brennen had not told him. He *loved* speaking. It was meat and drink to him to gather the audience up skillfully in his hands and hold them there while he worked his will upon them. Over and above this was his steady ambition to become an integral part of the great political scene. Like a recurring mirage, which his will tried to dispel, was the thought of the governor's chair beyond the Senate, and even the pinnacle of the White House. Absurd to have those fleeting thoughts —or was it? Every ambitious man must dream, must aspire, must see an ultimate goal even if it was forever unobtainable. There was in Paul also a strange inherited quality of being without vanity conscious of his own potential. Added to all this upon the one side was his consuming love for Anne and the horror of bringing pain upon her.

On the other side were his growing suspicions of Kirkland's power and connections and the nagging voice within him that told him he should bring these into the open to be confirmed or denied.

In the end, however, hot and weary, he decided to go on as he was doing *for the present*. How many weak postponements had been made under that comforting guise, he thought, as he drove out home. And yet he was in honest doubt as to whether his course of action was motivated by cowardice or by sanity and wisdom. Then, at the end of the drive were Anne's waiting arms, her lips, her shining eyes —and the world without, well lost.

It was a hot summer. The mercury mounted and the city seethed and sweltered while the skies remained brassy bright and no rains came. Paul worried over Anne, who refused to leave for the house in the mountains except during the short week ends when he could go too.

"I'm perfectly all right," she insisted. "I like warm weather. The house is really quite comfortable and the garden is lovely. Mother always stayed on here except when Jimmy could leave too. I'm going to be just like her so you'll have to put up with my company. It's Jimmy who ought to get away. I don't know what's wrong with him. He's nervous as a witch. Have you noticed?"

"He's working too hard, though heaven knows why. He ought to slow up now and take things easier. Of course most of it now is pulling the strings for Halsey."

"I sent him over to Gran's tonight. She always does him good, calms him down. Besides I think we should dine alone sometimes."

They were eating on the back terrace, the candlelight falling on Anne's bare shoulders above a sea-green gown. There was the soft cool sound of falling water in the fountain and scented drifts of white flowers in the garden beds. A thrush sang in the rowan tree. Paul felt he had never known such delicate, such exquisite delight as this moment of early dusk, with the candlelight, the perfumed air, the fountain and the thrush.

"I'll tell you something," Anne was going on, "if you're sure it won't turn your head. Jimmy says you are the most marvelous speaker he's heard in years. He says you have the gift of swaying people, and Brennen says so too. He was telling me all this last night when you were out. He says Brennen told him one old chap came up after a meeting last week and said, 'Why don't you run this young feller for something? He can have my vote right now.'"

She paused a moment and leaned toward him across the table. "Jimmy says—I quote—'I'm going to swing him round over the state the last three weeks before election to all the doubtful spots.' Then he added, and I quote again—'I think next year he'll be a walkover for the Senate from our district and someday I'm going to put him in the governor's chair!' Unquote. And you'll have to forgive Jimmy for running things. That's his nature. Well, what do you think of all that, my fair young sir?"

"I'm a little stunned and of course it's quite exaggerated . . ."

"Jimmy never exaggerates."

"Oh, why should I try to dissemble to you? I'm tickled to death! I'm simply so pleased I don't know what to say!"

"I'll tell you something more," Anne said with a sweet gravity. "When Jimmy spoke about your being governor eventually it was just as though a dagger had gone through my heart—my condition, you know. Then last night as I lay awake I began to plan. I thought of all the things I could do even as I am. I could certainly sit in receiving lines. I could still entertain. I could even dramatize myself a little! Oh, Paul, I honestly believe I could get away with it! I could do my part! If the wild dreams ever come true."

He picked up his chair and plate and moved over to sit close beside her. Then he held her to him as he kissed her. When she could speak she whispered, "What will Hackett think when he comes out? You'd better move back to your place."

"Hackett likes me. Ever since the day I nearly pushed him over. Why," he laughed, "I do believe you've never heard about that! We were too busy then discussing other things."

So he told her of his desperation to get to her on that most fateful evening and of Hackett's delight in being manhandled. They counted over the happy weeks since their espousal; they talked with young guarded pride about what the future might possibly hold for them; then when the meal had ended he carried her to the big terrace chaise which held two, and there they lay side by side, close and silent for the most part, as lovers love best, listening to the fountain and their own warm beating young hearts.

A few days later Paul received a letter at the office signed by Benjamin J. Barker himself. It asked if he would be kind enough to call one day soon to discuss a matter of business. Miss Kern, his secretary, the note went on, would be glad to arrange an appointment mutually agreeable. Paul was astounded. What could the head of the great Barker Bank want to see him for? Then he whistled softly. They had backed the other man for the nomination and lost. They probably did not even now want Halsey to win. Could Barker be considering anything so crass as to attempt to "buy him off"? Hardly, but he decided to make the appointment.

When he entered the great private office a day later he had a feeling of awe. Here, so to speak, was the center of financial ganglia, the pulsing and compelling nerves of which reached around the world.

Mr. Barker was a small man with a cropped gray mustache, unimportant looking except for his eyes. These were gray and keen as steel.

"Mr. Devereux, this is good of you to come. I'm very happy to see you."

"I'm glad to meet you, sir."

Paul sat down and waited. The older man, to Paul's liking, went straight to the point.

"As you doubtless know, the interests of the Barker Bank are very far-reaching. Not only do we have branch institutions in most countries from China to South Africa, but we have connections with several railroads, large insurance companies, et cetera. This means that the legal aspect of our business is highly involved and very important. From time to time as a young lawyer of exceptional promise comes to my notice, I seek to attach him to our staff. It was for this reason that I sent for you."

Paul swallowed self-consciously. This was what he had not expected.

"I have known Mr. Hartwell for many years. I consider him one of the most brilliant legal minds in the profession. I know the training you will have had under him. It is unkind of me to attempt to take you from him, but"—he made a small deprecatory gesture—"all is fair rivalry in business. Would you be interested, Mr. Devereux, in coming into our organization at a starting salary of fifteen thousand? There would, of course, be steady increase in proportion to your ability."

Paul's head swam. *Fifteen thousand* for a start? He was making eight at the present. There was a snag here, somewhere. Something that didn't meet the eye. Without time, almost without thinking, he heard himself decline.

"I feel you have honored me, Mr. Barker, perhaps much more than I deserve, with the very fine offer, but the firm has been very good to me and I'm deeply interested in my work there. I'm especially fond of Mr. Hartwell, so I think I would prefer to stay where I am."

Mr. Barker's eyes sharpened. "Would you not be willing to give this some consideration? There would be, I should say, almost no limit to the possibilities here. Why not think it over a little before deciding?"

"That will not be necessary, Mr. Barker. I greatly appreciate your offer, but I would not care to leave my present work."

He was surprised by the firmness of his own voice. The goodbyes were pleasant but brief and Paul was soon on the street again. Once there the picture was clear to him. The offer had been on the surface a perfectly normal one, though the salary was high. Mr. Barker doubtless *was* from time to time on the lookout for new young lawyers. But underneath Paul felt the subterfuge. Barker was indeed trying to buy him off, though the iron hand was sheathed in pure velvet. Nothing as yet had made Paul so clearly realize his own latent power as this. Barker was afraid of him. He wanted him on his side not only now but in the future. For by the curious "grapevine" which obtains in the political world, he had doubtless heard that Paul was marked for the senatorship. He was not so much trying to wean him away from Hartwell then, as from Kirkland. The Barker lobby was powerful both in the state capital and in Washington, and Kirkland always opposed it! Well, Paul thought as he walked on, *I'm at least getting myself noticed.* He would have been less than human if he had not felt elated.

One thing disturbed him more and more as the weeks passed: Arno's attitude. It did not, according to Kirkland's prophecy, improve. If anything it was more unfriendly now than at first. The sneering smile was never absent when Paul spoke to him. Anything like the former collaboration had ceased to be. On a hot afternoon when the weather was sultry and tempers ran short, Paul made a decision. He left his own office a little early to get some information he wanted from Kirkland's files. He knew the Chief was not there, since he had left the night before for the capital, so this would give opportunity for a showdown with Arno.

Paul went in as always, his manner casual and friendly.

"Hello, Arno."

"How'd you do, Mr. Devereux," the sneer rampant.

"I would like to have the list of the county committeemen. I think I can use it to some advantage just now. Could you give it to me?"

"I don't believe I could lay my hands on it at the moment," he drawled.

"You're a liar," Paul said hotly. "Mr. Kirkland said you had it filed and would give it to me."

Arno only stared at him offensively. "My memory just fails me sometimes."

"Come into the other office," Paul said shortly, conscious of Sayles's intent glances.

To his surprise Arno followed him, and they stood facing each other.

"We've got to have an understanding once and for all, Arno. We can't go on like this."

"Like what?" He smiled.

"You know as well as I do. For two months you've acted as if you despise me."

"Maybe I do. I don't like a fortune-hunting rat."

Paul lunged toward him and landed a blow on his face. "Nobody will call me that!" he shouted.

Arno came back with the spring of a cat. He had not grown up on Water Street for nothing. They were fairly well matched, Paul taller and with some college boxing experience, but Arno quicker and more accurate in his aim. When they had been hitting at each other hard for five minutes, with Sayles's shocked white face peering from the door, Paul suddenly backed away and held up his hand.

"This is dreadful," he said. "We're acting like ten-year-old boys. I'm ashamed I began it, Arno, though you did call me a lousy name. Can't we get to the bottom of this without blows? I'm certainly no fortune hunter. I married my wife for the same reason most men do."

"Oh, yeah?" said Arno half under his breath. He turned sharply and walked to the window where he stood, breathing heavily, looking out. Paul waited, startled at his quiet. Arno's shoulders drooped, and something in the posture made him insignificant and pathetic. He faced about at last, touching a swelling eye, went into his office and returned with some typed sheets which he laid on Kirkland's desk.

"There's your list," he muttered.

"I'm truly sorry, Arno, that I started the fight."

"No need to mention this episode to the Chief."

"Certainly not. And I really want to be friends with you. I'll be needing your help. I'd like for us to be able to work together as we did at first."

Arno did not reply. He raised one hand in an odd gesture which might mean anything, returned to his own office and closed the door.

Paul stood a moment, then went to the washroom to bathe a bad cut on his chin. He did not, fortunately, show other outward signs of the scrimmage, but he left for home shaken up, and more, with a horrible tendency toward sickness at intervals for one of Arno's punches had landed in his stomach. Much worse than all this, however, was the fact that he felt humiliated, ashamed and completely uncertain whether matters were now better or worse between him and Arno. The picture of the fellow's standing there, looking out of the window, all his jauntiness and assurance gone for the moment, his shoulders pressed down as though by a burden, made Paul's own anger drain away.

As he neared the house he told himself with honesty that perhaps this sudden knowledge of his own weakness was good for him. He had been the object lately of general and rather extreme praise, Mr. Barker's offer coming on top of all the other commendation. He had felt he was maintaining his poise and perspective through it all so now it came as a shock to him that he could suddenly lower himself to the point of lashing out with his fists and blackening a man's eye! How mortal weak the human spirit! How vulnerable the armor of the soul!

He had meant to tell Anne nothing but she knew at once that something was wrong.

"Darling, whatever is the matter? Why, you look as though you'd been in a fight!"

"I was," Paul admitted ruefully. "I mixed it a little with Arno, of all people."

"*Arno!*" Anne's voice was amazed.

"Yes. I don't know what the devil's gotten into him lately. He's been the rudest possible to me, and today he called me a fortune-hunting rat and that just hit me on the jaw so I let go at him. He came back of course so we had it for a few minutes there in your father's office. I stopped first—that's the only decent thing I did—but I don't know where we stand now. And I can't figure him out. He's just been like that since our marriage."

Anne looked as though a light had broken upon her. "I think I know," she said wisely. "It's jealousy. You see, for all these years he's been closer to Jimmy than any other man. He's been his confidant and I imagine he's been pretty proud of it. Now, when you suddenly and without warning become the Chief's son-in-law, poor Arno's nose is horribly put out of joint. Don't you see? He would sort of hate you."

"That might just be the explanation," Paul said with relief. "I do see the point of it and it's perfectly logical. Poor cuss! Since I understand it now I can put up with it. More than that, I'll try to keep away from the office as much as possible. I can always discuss things with your father here. And I'll find ways to bolster up Arno's ego as much as possible. You're wonderful, Anne, to have thought of this! What would I do without you?"

"Your poor chin," she said, touching it. Then she laughed softly. "You know, I rather like the idea of my husband fighting for his honor!"

"Real he-man stuff, eh? Well, don't be too thrilled for I don't expect to make a practice of it!"

During October Kirkland carried out his plan for Paul's "swing around the state." It was all much more important campaigning than he had been doing in the county, usually a speech at a party dinner in a large city. The success of these was marked from the first. In a hotel room at night or lying wakeful in a Pullman berth he thought of the men he had met, key men in state politics, important business-men with large axes to grind. He thought of their friendliness, which was not merely the mechanical courtesy of the occasion. He knew—hated himself for knowing and yet still knew—that he possessed a certain magnetism, that most elusive personal quality of charm, which was invaluable in the sort of work he was doing. He tried to hold himself rigidly in hand, but a certain swelling feeling of ex-ultation kept rising within him.

During the month he had scarcely an evening at home. When he wasn't off at his overnight engagements, he was working not only on his speeches but even more at the desk in his office, making up for his absence in daytime. Anne was patient in the main, though once in a while as they sat at a hurried breakfast she looked very sober.

"Do bear with me for a little," Paul begged one morning, looking anxiously for the smile that did not come. "As soon as election's over, I'll be here all the time. I promise you!"

She put her hand over on his. "I hope so," she said. "But I know the pattern, darling."

During the last days Paul found himself in a whirlwind. He grew more eloquent, more persuasive in his speeches. He heard himself repeating extravagant promises for his candidate, picturing Halsey as a paragon of all virtues. It was done almost without his active volition. It was all a result of this tremendous excitement which caught him up in its vortex and which, with its relentless, fiery pres-sure animated him from without rather than from within. This was politics; this was manipulation; this was the delirious power of which the uninitiated knew nothing. Paul, now in the midst of it, realized it was to him congenial air and was happily intoxicated by it.

On election day Halsey swept the state. As early as ten o'clock at night his victory was conceded. Paul and Kirkland had been together all day, in the latter's office, and at Party Headquarters. Arno joined them there in the evening and was, outwardly at least, normal and civil. Paul was conscious, however, of his gaze upon him as Kirkland proudly introduced him to the men he had not already met. There was a bonhomie between Paul and many of the state leaders which

Arno was evidently observing with his sharp black eyes, but there was elation enough in the room for everybody, Paul kept thinking.

It was very late when he and Kirkland got home, but Anne was waiting up with coffee and sandwiches ready.

"Well," she said as they were finishing, "now that the thing you two have been working on to the exclusion of all else is a *fait accompli,* I intend to assert my claims as a daughter—" she paused, looking archly at Paul—"and as a wife. And I don't mean *maybe,*" she added inelegantly.

"You won't have to try very hard," Paul said, "on the wife part."

Kirkland gave them a quick glance, announced that he was dead tired, and left them alone.

And it was only a short time later that Paul was aware of a change in Anne. Her smile became less animated and more tender; she sat for the most part, quiet, listening contentedly while he or her father talked, her face touched with a soft glow from within. It seemed, indeed, as though sitting close to them she was yet living far away in a different world of mystery and light.

Two weeks before Christmas she told Paul that she was going to have a child.

8

▗ IT WAS a deliriously happy Christmas! They all, including Gran, confessed that they could not remember such a joyous time. Paul and Hackett put up the greens under Anne's direction: holly, ivy and pine everywhere, with the big tree in the music room, touching the ceiling, ultimately laden with color and lights, and poinsettias and red roses aflame in the big hall and the library. On the dining room table was the centerpiece made long ago by Alice herself for the little Anne and used every Christmas since: Santa Claus and his sleigh, airily delicate and alive upon their snowy mirror, with the name of each reindeer embroidered lovingly upon each tiny, straining, red-coated chest.

"Won't it be fun to show this to our children, Paul, and point out Dasher and Prancer and the rest, and read them ''Twas the night before Christmas' in front of the fire after the stockings are hung up? Won't it be wonderful?"

"Too wonderful to believe," he whispered, his lips against her hair. "I'm so happy it wakes me up at night!"

Anne laughed. "I'm so happy I sleep like a top. I . . . well, I've known a good many wakeful hours the last year and a half!"

"Darling!"

She hurried on brightly. "Have I told you about Gran? I'm so excited these days I'm quite loony. She always comes over the day before Christmas and stays till New Year's afternoon. Her one real visit with us. She began doing it right after Mother died and has always kept it up. She has the big front guest room and arrives with bags, boxes and packages as though she'd come hundreds of miles. It never ceases to thrill me just as it did when I was little, and it pleases Jimmy too. He's crazy about Gran. And of course *this* year . . ."

Ah, this year, with its quivering current of joy, evocative of all the tender symbolism of Christmas in all the ages!

It was Paul who thought of the *sing*. "Do you know," he said one night, "in the bottom drawer of the old secretary among Mother's papers are a lot of little carol books. She used them each year at the Grange social. Why couldn't we have some folks in. . . ."

It was all Anne needed. She began telephoning at once with the result that two nights before Christmas a dozen young people filled the wide hall with gay salutations and then very soon with Anne already seated casually at the piano, began to sing the familiar seasonal songs. Johnny Bovard had brought his fiddle by request and sawed away delightedly with more animation than technique, but no one noticed or cared. When they rested for breath there were doughnuts and mulled cider, but they were soon back on their feet crowding toward the piano.

"Here's one we haven't done yet . . ."

"And what about . . ."

"And oh, I *love* . . ."

So they hailed their favorites and began all over again.

It was late when they finished *O Holy Night,* which Anne had decreed must come last. As the goodbyes were being said, a slender young fellow with dark, smoldering eyes came up to Paul, and held out his hand.

"Thank you," he said. "This has been a beautiful experience. As cold water to a thirsty soul, so is an evening when no one gets high and no ribald stories are told and no one hugs another man's wife!"

Paul laughed. "Christmas comes but once a year, but if you like the quieter forms of entertainment, do come back again. That's the kind my wife and I happen to prefer."

"You're very fortunate. I'll surely come if I may. I'm a sort of city misfit. I grew up in the backwoods."

"As hick to hick, greetings. So did I!"

"No! I thought you had to go to New York to run into the real country-born. Everybody in this city seems to be indigenous."

"I know," Paul said, "I've noticed that too, but still there are a few of us strays. We ought to stick together."

"I would certainly like to."

"I'm sorry but in the madhouse at first I didn't get your name."

"David Laird. I'm an attorney with Reed and Dorrance."

"Well, well, we're lawyers under the skin then, too, as well as country boys. I'm with Hartwell & Harvey."

"So? Then you are the one who campaigned for the governor?"

"A little. Are you interested in politics?"

"Just academically. Well, thanks again and I'll give you a ring after the holidays. I want to say goodnight now to your wife."

There was a flurry in the hall. Johnny Bovard had opened the front door and came back with a shout.

"What do you know! It's snowing to beat the band! The ground's covered already. Yeah, boy!"

There was a wild rush for the porch, someone started *White Christmas* and above the noise of the cars the strains of it rode high upon the night as they all sang at the top of their voices down the drive and out along the street.

Later, Paul and Anne lay in bed in the darkness and talked of the success of the evening.

"Did you know the dark chap? Said his name was David Laird," Paul asked.

"No," Anne said. "I think he was Betsy Thorne's date. He has an elegant bass voice."

"He seemed to approve of everything. I'd like to see him again. I rather think we'd hit it off pretty well."

"It was all lovely tonight. I'm so glad you thought of it!"

There was the exquisite hush of the falling snow outside the opened window as they lay, listening. Anne spoke again with the happy anticipation of a child.

"And tomorrow morning Gran comes! And in the afternoon we'll trim the tree!" Her breath caught sharply. "I still keep forgetting. I'll watch while the rest of you trim it."

Paul drew her close. In his passion and his pity he wondered if he dared tell her of the faint, the evanescent hope that was now showing like a strange fire in her father's eyes and which kept recurring to him, himself, even though he fought against any real consideration of it. Should he share with her secretly this most tenuous presumption?

No, he decided, this would be unwise and even traitorous to the hope itself, which rested only upon the chance result of complete physical and emotional shock. Any foreknowledge would surely destroy even the possibility.

There was a quick gust of wind outside blowing the flakes before it, and a stirring in the wintry branches of the trees. Their own close warmth seemed suddenly more safe, more dear. Then the wind subsided, the trees became quiet, there was again only the soft breathing peace of the falling snow. Enfolded in each other's arms they fell asleep.

Old Hartwell had been invited for Christmas dinner. "We're so terribly short of family," Anne had told Paul. "Of course I'm doing the best I can to remedy that situation, but for the present . . . well, what do you think of having Mr. Hartwell? He's such a darling and alone."

Nothing could have warmed Paul's heart more than the old man's pleasure as he reported it to Anne.

"Oh, good," she said. "He and Gran will like each other. Davy is going to dine with us so that we'll make six and I'll ask Hackett to spread us out a little so we'll look even more. How I long for a whole tableful on holidays!"

It turned out an unusually congenial dinner group. Mrs. Catherby and Hartwell quipped and quoted to their hearts' content; Davy blossomed out from her usual professional reticence with a free and charming manner; Paul and Anne shed their own glow; and Kirkland, with a high florid color in his cheeks, talked a great deal, for him, and laughed recklessly even when there was no joke. There was no indication during the meal that Hartwell considered his host an unscrupulous man and that the latter knew it.

"You'll all have to forgive me," Anne said as dessert was over, "if I've gone traditional in a big way this year. But we've never had an actor in the family before—yes, you are, Paul, even though you aren't on the stage—so we're going to sit around the fire in the library with our coffee and have him read A Christmas Carol to us."

It was a truly happy day. When it was all over, the hour late, and Paul and Anne alone in the library, he put on a fresh log and stretched out on the hearth rug at her feet.

"Your reading this afternoon was simply marvelous, Paul! The characterizations were incredibly real. It almost frightens me."

"Why on earth?"

"Well," she said slowly, "you are a born actor. I believe you could actually make me think you loved me even if you didn't!"

Paul threw back his head and laughed heartily. "Now that's the greatest piece of casuistry I've ever heard! But what a compliment! I'm awfully glad you were pleased with my little performance. I enjoyed doing it. It's all been the most perfect day to me. Last year I had dinner at a restaurant and supper with Mrs. MacLeod. I'm not sure which time I was the most lonely."

"Poor lamb, how ghastly for you! I was lonely too in a different way. Paul, will you promise me something?"

"Anything, darling."

"You'll always tell me the truth?"

He sat up then, his eyes startled.

"I hope you don't need to ask me that!"

"I mean there won't be any concealment—oh, I don't know how to express it—but you have such a gift for acting, I know I sound muddled but surely you understand."

"What I understand is that you're dead tired and must get to bed at once." He rose and picked her up in his arms.

"But you haven't promised, and when you're about it"—her voice dropped very low—"maybe you could even make it retroactive, if that's the right word."

"Now what on earth do you mean by that?" He was still faintly amused.

"I'm not sure. It's just that I'm so happy in our love that it scares me a little. Could you promise?"

He was serious enough then. "Yes," he said, "a thousand times yes, past, present and future to every question in your foolish little heart. Is it all right now?"

"It's heaven," she said, as she clung to him.

During the week Paul became more and more conscious of Mrs. Catherby's influence upon the family, and even upon himself. She was wise with the rich wisdom of a finely cultivated mind and the long experience of the years. She was witty as well as wise and kind in addition to all. As a final link to bind them, her love of poetry equaled his own. She asked him once about his work and listened attentively. He found himself telling her Kirkland's remarks about what he himself called the politician's *color*.

"How, I keep asking myself, can I be honest and still get ahead in this game?" he confided earnestly.

Mrs. Catherby smiled. "That hateful, damnable monosyllable *how*, as Luther called it. It rises to confront us no matter what game we're playing. *How* did the world begin? *How* does it keep on going? *How* can we best serve its progress? Never any end to the *how's*, but they're always a challenge. And as to your particular one I feel you'll be able to meet it . . . you and Anne."

"You include her in it?"

"I think you'll discover you can't leave her out," she said quietly. And then, "Paul, I want to talk to you about the . . . baby. I'm disturbed over Jimmy's attitude. He's so sure this will be the miracle that will cure her. He told me last night that he's phoned Dr. Hertzog in Europe twice already. The doctor has made certain suggestions and has promised to come over, at the time. But I am afraid Jimmy is too confident of this. Of course," she added a little sadly, "I can't help hoping myself."

"Nor I," Paul answered, "but I don't let myself dwell on it, I'm worried about Jimmy too. Ever since we've been married, he seems to be under the pressure of strong excitement. It's not good for him. I tried to make him see reason once, but it was no use."

"I know," she said. "All his life he has been able to bend people and events to his will except in the case of those he loved most. My daughter's death was beyond all his power and wealth to prevent, and then Anne's accident. I feel the greatest pity for him. As I've often said, I don't *approve* of him and his methods but I love him deeply. Ah well," she sighed, "we'll all keep hoping. I'm a great believer in miracles myself, but try to hold him as steady as you can."

Then her face brightened. "To get back to poetry," she said, "do you know Ledwidge?"

"Never heard of him," Paul admitted.

"Then I must introduce you. He was one of the many young voices silenced in the First World War. I'll lend you my volume for they're hard to come by now. Listen to this. I put myself to sleep with the peace of it." She repeated slowly:

> *The sheep are coming home in Greece,*
> *Hark the bells on every hill!*
> *Flock by flock and fleece by fleece,*
> *Through the evening red and still . . .*

Isn't it lovely?"

"Beautiful!" Paul exclaimed. "There's economy of wording for you. He's caught the whole landscape, the whole mood in a few lines. Do you remember any more?"

"Just the ending:

> *Then sleep wraps every bell up tight,*
> *As the rising moon grows small."*

"The pure, musical *clarity* of it!" Paul said. "Why do so many of the modern poets seem to feel they must obfuscate the sense and torture their rhythm into crazy patterns? What's the reason for it?"

"Is it a reflection of our times?"

"God forbid, but what do you really think?"

There was always this quick, eager flow of conversation between them. And on New Year's afternoon when they all helped her into her car, Paul kissed her as tenderly as did the others.

The Christmas snow still lay white and the next week added more to it. Within the great house quiet reigned. All sounds from the street were now muffled and soft. The greens were down, the big tree stripped and removed, the tiny reindeer and sleigh packed carefully away. Anne, after a week of unusual gaiety and diversion for her, sat in her living room, bemused with her own thoughts as she folded and refolded the tiny garments that had been among her gifts. Paul was working late to make up for early afternoons during the holidays, Kirkland was closeted both at home and in his office with a variety of men who were part of the hidden and intricate machinery of political management, and Arno spent his evenings in a certain room above a tavern bar where a still different type of men ruled a kingdom.

Kirkland wanted Paul to go along to the capital for Halsey's inaugural but Paul decided against it, on account of Anne. He was finding plenty to do on Saturdays as a sort of aide to Brennen.

"All grist for the mill later on, you know," Brennen told Kirkland. "He's a comer, your young fellah. He's going places."

Because the firm had been so lenient with him during his campaign work, Paul tried now to give extra time to the office even during the lunch hour. He found not far away on the first floor of an office building a small hole-in-the-wall food bar which he began to patronize regularly. The menu was limited but good, the service quick and the man behind the counter jovial and efficient. The same customers seemed to come day after day to sit upon the high stools and partake of coffee and sandwiches. Paul with his usual interest in people watched them. Stenographers and elevator boys, he would guess, along with a few shabby older men made up the clientele. One man, whom he found it hard to place, was always on his stool at the farthest end. The proprietor was apparently known to all as Bill. With miraculous deftness he slung the food along the counter, then presented each customer with a check, gathered it and the money in with a swift sleight-of-hand movement, made change at the cash register and repeated the same performance over and over. He fascinated Paul, but more than that he felt certain undercurrents about him as he sat on his stool watching. He was certain that several times his eyes had caught a customer putting another slip of paper under the check as it was handed back with money to Bill; he had intercepted also certain looks between the latter and the man who always sat at the end. They were knowledgeable glances. Another thing interested him. Once a customer had come in in a high state of elation. No reason for it was given and yet Paul with his keen perception had a feeling that it was understood all the way around the high stools.

"Well, well," Bill remarked on this occasion, "certainly is nice weather we're having, eh?"

"Boy, you said it!" the happy one grinned at him.

Something—a tremor, a delicate shock, a responsive vibration—passed along the line.

One day, suddenly the truth struck Paul. Bill, behind the counter, was selling something more than ham sandwiches; he was selling policy slips; these customers were "writing numbers" and the man always at the end must be a so-called *runner*. After his endless coffee and pie, when the lunch hour was over, he would collect from Bill, go out to his car and probably betake himself to another gambling setup. For that, Paul was now sure, was what this innocent-seeming eating place was; it was a gambling center just as much as a circuitously reached back room filled with roulette wheels—or bird cages. This was one tiny manifestation of the big numbers racket of which Camponelli was the head.

Paul waited, loitering over the dessert to try to outsit the runner. But it was to no avail and he finally went back to the office and in at once to see Hartwell with his imagined discovery. The old man showed no surprise, he only nodded agreement.

"Quite likely," he said, "quite likely. The city is riddled with just such spots."

"But shouldn't I report it to the police?"

Hartwell smiled. "My dear boy, the police know all this better than we do. They give protection—for a consideration. Your policeman on the beat collects each week from the runners and gives it to the Precinct Captain."

"And what does your man on the beat get out of it?"

"Oh, he gets to write a few numbers himself! Once in a long time the Police Commissioner sends word down that there must be a show made of law enforcement, so one runner is nabbed. Probably the one the Precinct Captain thinks has been holding out a little on him. The matter gets well aired in the papers and then everything goes on as usual." The old man sighed. "I can tell you more of what goes on here if you want to know. I've lived in this city a great many years."

"What can be done about it?" Paul's tone was sharp with earnestness.

Hartwell made a gesture, half of despair. "I've told you, but I know you're not interested in city politics. If we could get one absolutely incorruptible and fearless man to head city government, he could go a long way toward cleaning it up in one administration. And if a single major city were once clean I believe the crusade would spread. Honesty is contagious as well as corruption. Well, does this answer your question?"

"I suppose so," Paul said slowly. "I'll have to think this over."

Hartwell leaned toward him and pointed a thin finger. "I'm just an old theorist," he said, "for I've never had the gumption myself to pitch into the fight, but I'll tell you how I have it sized up. Let's take an example. Here's a man who breaks his marriage vows and becomes immoral. He'll at once begin to practice deceit. Now my contention is that that particular breakdown in his integrity will spread in some degree through all the areas of his life. Bound to. And it's like that with these rotten spots in our cities. They *spread!* Well, it's foolish to belabor that point. The facts speak for themselves. And," he smiled, "I'm glad we've had this little conversation."

He has a genius for dismissal, Paul thought humorously, as he got back to his desk, *and he needs it with me, for I never get tired talking to him.*

The facts relating to the gambling setup in the lunchroom were not easy to put aside. Paul determined to get all the information he could concerning the "rotten spots," as Hartwell had called them, just as a matter of information. At least then he would not be naïve, ignorant. He talked with Johnny Bovard, who in his casual light-hearted way was a man of wisdom.

"Yep," Johnny said, "it's the big thing here, the numbers racket. The horses, too, of course, and the slot machines. It all seems almost like kid stuff when you think of it, but brother, it's tall enough the way it works out. The money those hoods take in is fabulous. And don't ever think they're not smart in the way they spend it!"

"Cadillacs and such?"

"Oh, sure, all that, and Miami Beach in the winter. That's where they all hibernate. But I mean real investments. You know this new hotel that's going up? The Mayfair? Well, I happen to know Camponelli owns two-thirds of that. Boy, they'll muscle in on everything, before they're done."

"How do you find all these things out, Johnny?" Paul asked curiously.

"Oh, I get around. In a mixed society. Maybe it's not to my credit but I shoot the breeze with all kinds. Of course I draw the line at the big, big C himself!" he laughed, then sobered. "How about your friend Arno? Isn't that what you called him? You know I've a suspicion he's running with the hare and the hounds both."

"How so?"

But Johnny would commit himself no farther.

"Oh, just a hunch. But if I were you, I'd keep my eye on him. He's a sharp-looking cookie to me."

At home these evenings Paul had other things to occupy his mind. Kirkland had let Anne assume that the suggestion came from her own physician, but it was in fact Dr. Hertzog who by transatlantic phone directed the making and installation of a gymnastic machine, the use of which would strengthen the leg muscles during this particular period. So aside from the daily massage and manipulation which she had had ever since the accident Anne now went, as she put it, "horseback riding" in the evenings when Paul was there to see. It was a new and clever device, with a comfortable seat, and motor-propelled stirrups which moved the legs in a short circular motion.

"You see," Anne told Paul, "as it stands, it's a *horsecycle*, only it should have a head and a tail to make it all horse. I love it! It gives me the greatest sense of normal leg motion and I'm going to keep using it even after the baby comes. You can't imagine how I enjoy it!"

Her cheeks were flushed and her eyes happily alight. Involuntarily she shook back her hair. He knew how she must have looked as she cantered along the country roads on summer days of old and a great pain clutched his heart. All in the moment he shared Kirkland's doggedly fantastic dream. Perhaps he had been too much the doubter, too afraid of a great consuming faith that the miracle would happen.

They talked long that evening about the pattern of the coming months and he explained to her in detail how his own time would be engaged. In April he was to begin campaigning for himself.

"Jimmy has done the impossible," he said, "and done it so well that nobody seems to recognize it. I *should* be running for Assemblyman. As I've told you it's almost without precedent for a newcomer to head for the Senate. But Jimmy passed the word around and I was accepted. Besides, there was nobody else in the county, I gather, that they were really itching to run for the office this year. So, here I go. Well?"

Anne threaded her slight fingers through his strong ones.

"I do so like your hands," she said tenderly.

"Of all the *non sequiturs!*" he laughed. "Thanks, of course, but haven't you been listening to me at all?"

She gave a small sigh. "Oh, yes. I'm not sure I like the phraseology, though. 'Jimmy passed the word around'; 'there was nobody else they wanted to run.' I should be used to this kind of thing but it's never come so close to me before. Paul, when you get into the Senate, and I am sure you will, what will you do? What is it you really *want* to do?"

He colored a little and told her the Lincoln story. "I guess at the moment I just want to get into the Senate! But once there I imagine I'll find plenty to engage me. I'm going to run on the straight party platform, of course, but this development of water resources in the state interests me a lot. I'll have to talk about lower taxes and lower cost of government in my speeches—that always goes over well—and pay my respects to the labor question, but then having got the usual things off my chest, I'm going to pitch into this water question."

Anne folded her hands in a pretty attitude of attention. "Now," she said, "I'm waiting to be informed."

"Well," Paul went on, "the idea's been growing on me ever since your father and the Governor talked to me about it just after election. They're both very much in favor of it and the more I've looked into the matter the more I feel I've got something important to talk about. You see all through the east we face the danger of future water shortage."

"Um-hm," said Anne. "I could *try* taking just one bath per week."

"No, it's really serious. Or could become so. Ultimately we may have to have all our water piped from the Great Lakes. But that's a long way in the future. What we need now is a huge state reservoir. Now you see I can honestly let myself go on this idea. I've studied up on it. I believe it's sound. It would represent a good, not only for the present but for future generations. Voters go for that kind of thing. It's a *natural* for campaigning."

"Paul!"

"Yes, darling?"

"That last is unworthy of you. I don't like it."

"Haven't I just told you I've studied the possibility, that I believe in it, that a state reservoir would be a fine thing! Well, then, isn't

it all to the good that it's the sort of project that has public appeal?
What's wrong with that?"

"I'm not sure," Anne said, "but I think it's one of the things you
should know in your subconscious but never admit to yourself, certainly not to anyone else. Oh, how muddled I sound again! I can't
explain it, but what you said jarred on me like a discord on the piano.
Paul?"

"Yes."

"You know how much I love Jimmy?"

"I've a pretty good idea."

"So it's a hard thing for me to say of him, but I don't think his
motives are always—well, what I would want yours to be. That's
one reason I hate politics as such. You'll watch out, won't you?"

"And not let Jimmy contaminate me?" Paul laughed.

But Anne was sober. "Perhaps that's what I mean. But oh, don't
ever hurt him, no matter what he does. He's been hurt so much
already. I couldn't *bear* to have anything else strike him hard. He's
awfully fond of you, you know."

"It's mutual. He's an amazing person and he's certainly been wonderful to me. If I ever get any political place in the sun I'll owe it
all to him. I just hope I can justify his confidence in me."

And then all at once they were wrapped in the dear delights of
their own hopes and plans. The baby would come in July, in the
very midst of Paul's campaign, but the wonder of the event far out-
shadowed all else as they considered it. Anne's face had a delicate
luminosity now that blessed it with new beauty, and her whole body
was rounded and alive as never before. Sometimes Paul thought he
might have loved her for her body alone, so fair it was in every
part. But added to this physical perfection was the grace of mind,
the radiance of the spirit. Often, even in the midst of daily work
he felt his love rise within him and the hot flame of his passion
color his cheeks. He knew it had been so with Kirkland himself in
his love for Anne's mother, and the knowledge made him deeply
at one with the older man.

Even politically he was feeling a close kinship with Kirkland during these late winter months as they planned together the details
of Paul's progress toward the State House and discussed the problem of water resources as Paul was to present it. Only once did he
have a sharp misgiving.

"Now, about the possible location of the reservoir," Kirkland said
one day, "you can just let a hint drop in more than one place that

the general locality in which you are at the moment would be a good spot for it. You see wherever it is—if it ever *does* become a fact—there will be a big temporary increase of jobs, general prosperity, all that sort of thing. Well, if you just word it delicately enough. . . ."

Paul looked him in the eye.

"I can't do that, Jimmy. I can't lie to people."

"Lie? Who's talking about lying? Nobody knows now for sure where the reservoir will ultimately be. You can point out good reasons why several places are suitable, can't you?"

"Well," Paul agreed slowly, "I suppose so. I'll have to study that for a bit."

One morning out of the clear he had a call from David Laird, the first time they had been in touch since the carol sing before Christmas. Paul had all but forgotten about him and was pleasantly surprised to hear his voice.

"What about lunch some day?" David was asking. "Just say when."

"Fine," Paul said. "I'm free today if that's not too quick."

"Couldn't be. I have my car so I'll pick you up at your office a little before one. Okay?"

"Wonderful," Paul said. "I'll be on the sidewalk."

He liked David even better than the first impression warranted. He was a serious chap with a fine, even brilliant mentality. His conversation sparkled, as his face remained sober. Toward the end of the meal which was in a quiet restaurant, David looked about him as though to assure himself no one could overhear and then lowered his voice.

"I've been wanting to see you again ever since the night at your house, but I do confess now I have an axe to grind. I want your advice and maybe your help."

"You flatter me," Paul said, "and I love to give advice."

"Do you do any church work?"

"I'm afraid I don't," Paul said, "though I was brought up to it."

"So was I. Well, I happen to live near St. Luke's out in the south side, so I got to going there and got interested in their older Young People's Group. A nice crowd chiefly between the ages of, say, twenty-five and thirty. We meet Sunday evenings, have devotionals and then a sort of forum where we discuss all kinds of subjects and then a short social time at the end. I've enjoyed it and been pretty active in it."

"Sounds good," Paul said.

"Now, I'll tell you what's happened. Last year we were approached by a representative of an organization called the Allied Youth Leadership, the A.Y.L. The idea was for us to join with this bigger, non-sectarian group once a month and have a speaker to discuss important issues of the day. We voted unanimously to join. Now, I'm not very happy about it. I'm even uneasy."

"You think," Paul said quickly, "that there may be propaganda behind it?"

"How did you jump to that? That's exactly what bothers me."

"Well," Paul said, "I've read up a little on the way the Communists bore in. The more innocent the *front* the better they like it."

"I was afraid you'd think me a fool," David said. "It's all so elusive, but I'm pretty sure there's something wrong. I don't want to talk to our own group until I have some sort of evidence, for a number of our members have thrown themselves into the thing. I did myself at first and now I seem to be drawn in more and more among the elect. I've played along these last months to see what was really happening. But the last speaker we had certainly smelled of Marxism all right. Also they've been giving out literature the last two meetings. Idealistic as the devil on the surface, but all the little punches are there."

"I know, of course, that this kind of thing is going on but I've never run into it myself. What did you think I could do to help you?"

"Well, it's like this. You remember last Memorial Day out at Redstone?"

Paul nodded.

"The man who led the singing that day is the organist at St. Luke's. Awfully nice fellow. I see quite a bit of him. He's told me more than once about your speech. He was very impressed. Now, the thought occurred to me that, if you were willing, maybe I could get you worked in to one allied meeting as the speaker. Then, you could give the same talk, let them have a dose of pure patriotism and see what the reaction would be. I believe we could pretty nearly tell the sheep from the goats. What do you say?"

Paul considered. His first thought was whether this could injure him politically. Then he felt ashamed as he met David Laird's earnest eyes. This was surely a call to render a patriotic service.

"If you think it would help, I'll be glad to try," he said slowly.

"Good," said David. "Thanks a lot. For some reason the key people in this association seem to have cottoned to me a little. I think

I can get you accepted. I'll not tell them what you're going to talk about, naturally. Can't I just say that you're interested in the welfare of the masses and your speech will have a sort of 'blood, sweat and tears' theme? That would be literally true and ought to go down with them if my suspicions are correct."

Paul laughed. "Word it any way you like. I only hope we're both barking up a wrong tree."

They switched then to personal matters and because David's dark eyes were sympathetic, Paul told him of Anne's condition and, hardly knowing why, mentioned the new exercise machine.

"She says if it only had a head and tail she could pretend it was a real horse," he added smiling. "She was very fond of riding."

To his surprise David considered this seriously. "What you should do," he said at last, "is find an old merry-go-round steed—they've got them here and there at antique shops—and then attach it. Has the machine a wooden framework?"

"Yes, it has."

"Then it would be easy. Are you handy with tools?"

"Not too much so, but I can use them."

"Woodworking is my hobby. I've got sort of a workshop in the basement where I live. Tell you what. If you find the horse I'll come up some evening with a saw and a hammer in my coat pocket and attach the thing for you. Would she like that?"

"She would love it. I know she's always been crazy about a merry-go-round. You know, Laird, that's most awfully kind of you! I'll tell Anne and she'll likely call you up. And I'll get on to the hunt as soon as I can. Really I appreciate this."

David was busy writing on a card. There was an intentness about everything he did.

"Here are the addresses of a couple of shops where you may have luck. And meanwhile I'll see what I can do about getting you on a program. I forgot to say the meetings are Sunday nights. Talk about appreciation! That's a mild word for what I feel about your agreeing to my request."

"If there *should* be something wrong at the heart of this group, as you fear, then I certainly have as much reason for doing my part as you have. I've got to go, but it's been great seeing you again."

"That goes for me too, and we'll keep in touch."

Paul was troubled as he went back to work. If this should prove to be a Communist organization and word got around that he had addressed it, it might wreck his campaign chances. On the other

hand no one hearing his speech could have any uncertainty about
his own beliefs, and if he refused for selfish reasons to do this thing,
he would hate himself. He decided to tell Anne about it, but not
Kirkland. Meanwhile he would cut his lunches short to look for the
horse.

And spring came again and sang through the city in late March
winds and the sweet stillicide of the dripping eaves in the April
nights. Anne from her windows watched the garden quicken with
swelling buds even as she felt the mysterious quickening in her own
body. A golden peace enveloped her, and each night Paul, a little
haggard from hard work and burdening problems, felt the haven of
it when he reached home. The relief of her presence and the joy
of their own love was so great that he spoke less and less to her of
his perplexities and relaxed for the brief hours they had together
in a sort of contented forgetfulness.

For the pressure of circumstances was strong upon him. There was
the regular law work which was in all conscience enough in itself
to keep a man busy; there were the forthcoming political speeches
which he kept turning over in his mind; there was the growing
knowledge, as he pursued his quest for it, of the city's dark and
devious corruption; there was the constant problem of Arno, who
now, incidentally, treated him with an icy civility almost harder to
bear than his former insolence; and there was the realization, still
not openly acknowledged to himself, but covertly waiting like a
wildcat to spring, of Kirkland's intricate and questionable involvements.

A few weeks before Christmas, a man whose uncle had been a
friend of Paul's father back in the country had come to the office.
"I need a lawyer," he began, "and I knew you were somewhere
in the city so I looked you up. It's sort of nice to do business with
somebody you know about even if we aren't acquainted ourselves."

He had started a small trucking concern some years before which
had now grown until he had a really sizable business in the dumping
of refuse. He wanted to get a charter for his company and had come
to get Paul to draw up the papers of incorporation to file with his
application. Paul took care of it, glad to be in touch even remotely
with old days at home, arranging as usual for the stock to be issued
for money *or services*. Sometime later his client had returned,
baffled and angry.

"A fellah called me up at home the other night. Wouldn't give his name, just said he was a friend. Said he'd heard I was forming a corporation and knew I'd have to negotiate a contract with a representative of my union and he just thought it would be smart of me if I'd get a man on my board of directors who had influence with the union. The dirty dog!"

"Well, go on. What more did he say?"

"He said he'd suggest I issue a nice block of stock to a fellah named Mallet. I've got the address at home. Lives down around Water Street somewhere. It's a damned holdup! He told me if I didn't, I might have trouble with my union. I'd like to knock somebody's teeth in. It's robbery! It's dirty, low-gangster muscling in, but I've got to do it or get out of business."

"You mean you can't fight this thing?"

"Brother, if you think I can fight this you don't know how this city's run. I'll tell you what happened to a pal of mine. He's got a trucking business too. Last year he put in a bid for a city contract. Had to have a performance bond to enclose with his bid. The bond was held up. He sent the bid on and was going to send the bond over by special messenger in time to put with it. The bonding company still held it up till the contract was awarded—to inside pals of course. Well, this fellah raised a terrible stink. He went to City Hall, he went to this Atlas Bonding Company and he told them plenty. Well," he sighed, "I suppose you can guess what came of it."

"No, what?" said Paul.

"They just about ran him out of business. His drivers got tickets from every policeman they passed. His trucks were pronounced overweight, or they said there were no tail lights on. Oh, all sorts of things like that. They made his life miserable. I tell you, you can't buck the setup. Not until all the mess is cleaned up, someday, if it ever is! I'll just have to issue the stock. Well, I was near here and I have to blow off steam to somebody, so I came in. Sorry I took up your time, but just thought you might be interested."

He got up. Paul was desperately in earnest.

"I'm going to discuss all this with our Senior partner. He knows more about city politics than I do. I'll let you know if we can help you. There ought to be some way . . . There's *got* to be!"

"Listen, son." The older man laid a friendly hand on Paul's arm. "There just ain't any way, so forget it."

But Paul had talked with Hartwell, at once. The old man shook his head. "Your man is right, I'm afraid. There's nothing we can do. What we need is a moral earthquake."

As Paul was going out he tossed a question over his shoulder. "Do you know anything about the Atlas Bonding Company?"

"Not too much. Good enough, I guess. They are subject to the State Superintendent of Banking and Insurance but of course sometimes . . . Kirkland is one of the officers, I know, though he may not be very active."

Paul did not reply. He had gone back to his desk and thought for a long time. But in the end he came to his usual conclusion. Not now, not with Anne in her present condition. But later on, he would gather together all the facts, all the vague suspicions and confront Kirkland with them. Find out the truth at last. But not just yet.

It was late in the spring when he had wakened suddenly one night, as one does sometimes, his mind fixed upon a thought which had never crossed it before. The trucking man had said the block of stock was to be issued to Mallet. Could it have been *Mallotte?* *Could it have been Arno?* Was he the link? If so, it would all fit in with what he already suspected. He lay, still and tense until the early light broke. His decision was this: when the baby was safely here, and Anne out of reach of danger, he would confront Kirkland and Arno both, and take the consequences.

One evening in May he and Anne were dining with Mrs. Catherby as they had often come to do when Kirkland was out of town. When the meal was ended Paul decided to include her in his confidence about David Laird's group meeting and to do so at once. He told them briefly then of Laird's request. Anne's reply was immediate.

"Oh, Paul, you can't do that! It might do you a lot of harm. People are so jittery about the whole subject right now."

"But if it would render even the smallest service to the country, how can I refuse?"

Anne's face was very grave as she sat thinking. "You can't," she said at last. "I see that, too. You've got to do it and give it your very best. I'm ashamed of my first reaction and I'm proud of you, dear. Only don't let's tell Jimmy. What do you say, Gran?"

Mrs. Catherby sat lacing her thin fingers together. "I'm proud of you both," she said quietly. "I always feel that one thing wrong with our present-day society is that the old word *duty* has been dropped from most people's vocabulary. In the older days it was spelled with capitals. I would call this that Paul has been asked to do, his *duty*, therefore he must do it. Besides, a speech such as he is going to give is exactly in line with what I believe should be done constantly throughout the country. The best corrective for the whole Communist movement here would be for Americans to keep shouting so loud about what they believe that it would drown the subversive voices entirely. It could be done!"

She paused apologetically. "I sound rather like a sermon, but I've thought a great deal about this. What we need is a soapbox for every citizen. We don't *talk* enough about our liberty, our blessed freedom! It's like religion. We seem to feel it's ill-bred to speak of it."

"I think you're right," Paul said earnestly. "When you come to think of it none of us talks as much about the good realities we have as about the bad possibilities we fear. Odd, that!"

Anne began to sing, half laughing.

> "*Accen'-tu-ate the positive,*
> *Elim'-in-ate the negative,*
> *Latch on to the affirmative*
> *And don't mess with Mr. In-Between.*"

"That's it, in a nutshell," Paul exclaimed. "Well, I can start putting our theory into practice in the speech at least. I admit I'm worried about doing it and I hate to go behind Jimmy's back. I'm glad, though, I have your joint approval."

"We had a professor at college who was an internationalist," Anne said thoughtfully. "He insisted it was pure chauvinism to love your own country best. He said that's what leads to wars and you should love the whole world."

Mrs. Catherby's normally gentle face was aroused. "Nonsense!" she said. "Absolute nonsense! You might just as well say it's wrong to love your own family best, and that you should love the whole human race impartially. I still believe in 'Breathes there a man with soul so dead . . .' If a man doesn't love his own country deeply, he *has* a dead soul, or at least a warped one."

Paul listened as the two women talked on, the old and the young. Then he smiled to himself. Perhaps between them—with Hartwell's good offices to boot—they could make something worthwhile out of him yet!

It was late when he and Anne got home, but they sat in their room still going over the conversation. Anne spoke of the plan for her and Mrs. Catherby to attend the meeting when it took place.

"I *so* want to hear you, Paul, and so does Gran. Couldn't she and

I go early and sit in the back somewhere? You wouldn't mind, would you? It wouldn't fluster you?"

Paul laughed. "Probably inspire me," he said. "I've got to bone up on the speech, though, for it's a year since I gave it. One more thing, I'm afraid, to fill up my evenings. You're a patient wife, darling. Don't ever think I don't appreciate it even if I don't say anything."

"You might say it now," she whispered, her cheek against his.

The next week Paul found the horse! A charming, prancing young steed, head up, nostrils wide, mane and tail flying, and only slightly in need of paint. He had a boyish feeling of excitement as he eyed it from all sides, paid the price and arranged for its immediate delivery.

There were so few surprises he could give Anne and this, he knew, would delight her. He telephoned David Laird, who was free and would come with his tools that evening. So with youth's ability to engage completely in the pleasure of the moment without probing the tragic actuality which lay beneath it, they laughed and joked and were hilarious while David and Paul sawed and fitted and pounded. At length the mechanism stood transformed into a carrousel figure and Anne's happiness in it was complete. David's face during the work had relaxed and even his dark eyes seemed to smile now as Paul placed Anne on her charger, turned on the motor and they watched the moving stirrups.

"I feel about five years old," she said. "At that age they couldn't get me off a merry-go-round! I can still see Jimmy's shocked face as he bestrode a giraffe in order to keep near me. How can I thank you both for my darling colt! And David, you have been too wonderful! First the idea of it and now your skill in putting it all together. Lift me off, Paul, now, won't you, since I've demonstrated, and we'll go down to the dining room for a snack. Besides, I want to show David the carvings, since woodwork is his hobby."

When he was leaving, David spoke to Paul at the door. "I've enjoyed the evening more than I can tell you. What a lucky man you are! About the speech, I've decided to wait until there is an emergency. I've told the leaders I know of a man who could fill in very acceptably if a speaker ever failed them at the last minute. This way they won't have a chance to look you up beforehand. If nothing happens in the next month or so I'll go off on another tack."

"You still feel worried about the setup?"

"More than ever. The inside ring seem to have me marked for

something. At least they've made casual but definite overtures in the form of giving me jobs to do. So far, as I told you, I'm going along until I get more proof. One other chap in our own church group has got the wind up about them. I'm glad, for now we can hash over it together. Can you really fill in on short notice?"

"As far as I know," Paul said. "Even if we're in the mountains for a week end, I could get here in a couple of hours."

"And you're still willing? The whole business, you know, is hot stuff. I do appreciate your attitude but I don't want to do you harm."

Paul said slowly, "I'm still willing."

"Stout fellah!" David said, as he left.

The emergency arose sooner than either had expected. In fact it came two weeks later, almost a year to the day from the time he had first given the speech. Paul had been out all day Saturday in the southern part of his district. When he got home late in the afternoon, Anne told him David Laird had been calling.

"He wants you to get through to him at once," she said. "Oh, Paul, I believe this is it."

It was. David explained that the speaker for Sunday evening was sick. The chairman, recalling David's suggestion, had appealed to him.

"I still didn't have to give your name, as the thing was so hurried, just said 'my friend.' Since they for some reason think I'm all right, they're accepting you. How about it?"

"I'll be there," Paul said.

"The meeting is in Gannet's Hall—you know, just behind the Arcade—at eight-thirty. We'd better get there just on the dot, not before. I'll pick you up. Okay?"

"Okay," Paul answered.

Anne was so excited Paul feared for her.

"You must be calm, dear. This isn't good for you," he adjured.

"But I've never heard you speak before!" she kept saying. "Besides, Gran and I plan to go early, sit far in the back and keep our eyes and ears open. It's just possible we may pick up something."

Paul saw them off Sunday night in Mrs. Catherby's car at seven o'clock, he himself leaving in David's a little after eight. They had to park a block from the hall and as they walked over they decided from the number of cars that the attendance would be large. They went in the side door as David directed, both nervous and jumpy.

"Well, here we go," David said. "*Ora pro nobis* and good luck to you! You're a brick to do this at all."

They moved swiftly up the side aisle, since the hour had already arrived, and in a moment Paul was shaking hands with the chairman, a pleasant, ordinary-faced chap who led them to the rostrum. There was ten minutes of "business" and then the brief introduction. Due to sudden illness the speaker scheduled could not be present, so at the last moment their good friend Dave Laird had arranged with a good friend of his, Mr. Paul Devereux, to pinch hit. It was with gratitude and pleasure, therefore, that they welcomed him, etc., etc. His topic would be "A Problem of the Masses."

Paul found himself on his feet, looking over the audience. It was, indeed, a fair-sized one and with no outward or visible sign of being anything other than normal. He began and there was at once the quieting of movement and the growing attention to which he was accustomed. Even as the speech progressed through the description of pioneer living there was still a close interest. But as the real theme of America developed, the free, the dearly bought, the object of her children's love and devotion, there was a change. Paul saw it and felt it at once. There were the many innocent, touched and eager faces of the singlehearted; but there were also the tense stiffening ones of those whose allegiance belonged elsewhere. With all his power of eloquence Paul proceeded, conscious now, clearly, of expressions of shock, displeasure or steely antagonism in many sections of the hall. There was even a hurried conference among those who had remained at the literature tables at the back. The chairman cleared his throat and looked openly at his watch. Paul went on to his conclusion.

When he had finished, there was a burst of scattered applause. As soon as it was ending Paul turned quickly to the chairman, already on his feet.

"Could we all stand now and join in singing 'My country, 'tis of thee'?" he said in a loud, clear voice.

This had been prearranged with David Laird, who, having brought Paul up to the rostrum, had without invitation remained there to have a view of the faces. The organist of St. Luke's was at the piano and at Paul's words at once struck the opening bars of 'America.' Paul raised his arms and the audience rose, some of them very slowly. There were others who left the hall, and still others, easily noted, who did not join in the singing. The chairman was one of these. But there were enough to make the words ring out.

> *Land where my fathers died,*
> *Land of the pilgrims' pride,*
> *From ev'ry mountain side*
> *Let freedom ring!*

The chairman was suddenly very busy after the meeting was over, taking time only to say brief and perfunctory thanks to Paul without compliment of any kind. There was a crowd gathered before the platform, however, as Paul came down—eager to express their appreciation, so on the surface everything seemed usual enough. But David, moving about among those who were still in the hall, had much to report when they drove away together.

"What a speech!" he began when the car started. "I congratulate you from my heart. I never heard a more moving one. And Paul, it did the trick! Nothing in the world could have been better for the purpose than the very words you said. I saw faces change while you were talking, didn't you?"

"I certainly did."

"But that was only part of the evidence. As I moved about afterwards, I made a point of talking to the key people I had the biggest doubts about. They were noticeably cool to me. *You* know. Once again nothing you could exactly put your finger on and yet you could feel it plain as a snowbank. I said to one of the men, 'A great speech, wasn't it?' He said it certainly didn't follow the subject announced. I told him I thought it had followed it perfectly—*the problem of the patriotism of the masses.* He gave me a stony stare and went on. But here's the payoff!"

David paused to get through a bit of traffic, then continued. "Here's the clincher, the concrete evidence I can present, now, to our own group. I'd been made a member of the publicity committee, a pretty important spot. Well, just before I left tonight the chap who asked me to take it came up to me and sort of hemmed and hawed a little and then told me that they had found another man who could give a little more time to the job than I had felt I could and perhaps I wouldn't mind being relieved of it. I assured him I didn't. With some warmth. Well, what do you think?"

"It looks pretty obvious to me. But what do you do now?"

"First I'll talk straight to our own group next Sunday night. Lay it on the line for them. I think they'll withdraw at once. Also I'll speak to the other young people's groups that I know are in it. Then I think I'll report my suspicions to the F.B.I. and that's all I can do. But I'll never cease being grateful to you, Paul. You don't know what good you may have done tonight over and above proving our case."

When they got back to the house Anne was excitedly awaiting them. She had something to add on her own. "You see," she said, "we left my chair out in a corridor and Hawley carried me in. We were practically the first people there so the ones who sat near us later didn't know I *couldn't* stand up at the end. Gran and I were too polite to applaud and then sat still during 'America' and the men just next us evidently thought we didn't approve of the sentiments. One of them leaned over to me and said, 'I assure you the committee knew nothing of this speaker. We took him wholly on Dave Laird's recommendation!' And then I said, 'Don't worry. I think he was simply marvelous!' and you should have seen his face!"

When David was gone Anne told Paul with tears in her eyes of her pride in him.

"I feel somehow that I know you better than I ever did before. Gran and I sat there holding each other's hands under the folds of my skirt and sometimes they both trembled. We felt it so. What you said, and then the thought that it was *you* saying it, was more wonderful than I can tell you, dear."

He kissed her for answer.

"It isn't vanity, heaven knows, but I'm glad you heard the speech and liked it. Your praise means more to me than anything else in the world." Then he fell silent.

"Paul, do you really feel the sort of thing we ran into tonight is dangerous?"

"I do, indeed."

She drew a long sigh. "I'm glad you said what ought to be said, no matter at what cost to you." She looked up with shy tenderness. "That is the way a hero behaves."

He drew her closer. "I wish I could feel heroic but I don't. I only feel scared now that it's all over. What if suddenly just before election someone comes up with the choice morsel that I addressed a Communist group? Then what? I'd be done for before I could explain it. What price duty?"

Anne's voice was low but very firm. "There is no price too high for that. So we'll have to take what comes—if anything does."

9

◄§ AND JUNE CAME, not with intolerable heat as in some years, but with a gentle effulgence that made even old and tired hearts bloom a little again. Anne sat each day in the garden under the shade of the rowan tree, setting in the last delicate stitches in the little garments it had been her pleasure to work upon. Patiently turning the imprisonment of her chair into the opportunity to create beauty for her child with her own hands, she had made the entire layette. Hackett, who, being English, loved a garden and spent his leisure hours puttering about in it when the regular gardener was not there, came over often to watch her deft fingers and gaze raptly upon the small bits of white.

"Doesn't seem as if anything livin' could be as little as that now, does it, Miss Anne?"

"I know," Anne would laugh, "but that's one reason babies are so sweet—the littleness, you know."

"I'm happier than I can tell you, Miss Anne," he said one day, "about everything—you and Mr. Paul and the baby coming. Sometimes I think I'm almost as excited as your father, if I may be allowed to say such a thing, only . . ."

"Yes, Hackett?"

"Only sometimes I'm afraid he's a little *too* excited, as it were. He's likely just nervous, but it occurred to me—if I may say so—that maybe you could say something to put him a bit more at his ease, as it were."

Anne smiled at Hackett's troubled face. "You know how he has always worried about me, Hackett. My grandmother says that when I had my tonsils out he made as much fuss as if it had been a major operation. I suppose you remember that too. But it's sweet of you to be concerned about him and I'll try to calm him down."

In one of the inner offices of Kirkland & Company at that very moment the same anxiety was being voiced.

Arno leaned back from his desk and studied Sayles thoughtfully. She had a new hair-do which softened her chiseled features greatly. She had taken also of late to wearing white blouses that could almost be called frivolous. Arno was thinking that if her nose were shorter she wouldn't be half-bad looking. He considered now for a few moments before he spoke.

"Sayles," he said finally, "have you any idea what's wrong with the Chief?"

Sayles also considered, warily.

"In what way?"

"Go on! You know as well as I do. He's nervous as a cat. He starts a sentence and he doesn't finish it. His face is too red. There's something the matter with him."

Sayles's own face flushed. She had been studying Arno these last months much more than she had watched Kirkland. Arno had changed. Maybe no one else had noticed, but she had. The lines were deeper in his face; there was a little gray now in his black hair; his sharp eyes sometimes looked almost dull and a certain devil-may-care assurance had departed from him. She missed that, most of all. Thinking back it seemed to her to have been absent ever since the day he and Paul Devereux had the fight. Just now she was uncertain whether to tell him what she knew or not. But Arno kept pressing.

"Listen, Sayles, I can read you like a book. You've got some information I haven't. Come on now, give with it." His voice was sharp.

"Well," Sayles said slowly, "he might just be sort of anxious. Men . . . fathers are, I guess. You see Anne's going to have a baby."

"When?"

"July sometime. He just told me the other day."

And Arno sat quiet, not speaking, only staring at the wall across from his desk.

It was this silence, this outward sign of the heart's bitterness which she alone knew, that made Sayles begin to say stumblingly what she had rehearsed a hundred times in her own room. *Someday*, she always assured herself, she would tell him, later though, not just yet. But now, almost without conscious volition the words were coming from her, uncertainly, tremblingly.

"Arno, there's something else I want to tell you though I guess it's a queer thing for me to do. But we've worked together here in the same office for over twelve years and as you say we do know each other—better maybe than anybody else ever would . . . and it's like this. You said once I was a . . . cold fish. I'm not, Arno. I'm not cold at all, I'm . . . Well, you see I know how to make a nice home and I can cook. I could make a man comfortable and I could make him happy other ways . . . *you* know. I could keep on working or I could stop. I'd do just like he wanted. I . . . I can't say it any plainer, Arno. . . ."

Her face was scarlet. She, too, watched the wall and the filing cabinets as though from them an answer would come.

Arno stood up and came to her chair while her heart stopped beating. He touched the top of her head with—was it his fingers or his lips? She would never be sure in the dark watches of the night. He spoke gruffly, thickly.

"You're a good kid, Sayles, but I'm not for you. I'm sorry . . . but just forget it, will you?"

He walked quickly to the door and went out. Then he opened it and Sayles's heart started to beat again.

"I'm sorry, girl, but it's just no dice!"

Then he was really gone, and there was no sound of any kind in the office.

It was that night that Anne had the accident. The doctor had ordered her to keep up what she called her horseback riding once a day. He pointed out that with the motor slowed down the exercise would be comparable to a short, easy walk, which if she were in normal condition, she would still be taking. This evening Paul had set her on the horse, secured the straps on her feet and was about to turn on the motor when Kirkland's voice came with some urgency.

"Can you come to the phone a minute, Paul, at once? It's important."

"Wait, will you, Anne, and I'll see what he wants."

Anne sat patiently for some minutes. Then as Paul did not return she looked toward the motor switch on the wall a little to the side and behind her. She had never, of course, turned it on; in fact Paul was, as she thought, unduly fussy about not only doing this himself but always being in the room when the device was in operation. She waited a little longer, then slowly reached back toward the switch. Her reach fell short. She leaned a little farther. Her fingers almost touched it. Lost in the possibility of the small triumph she forgot caution and stretched still farther. As she did so, she lost balance and her body fell over the side of the horse, her feet still pinioned.

Her first cries were unheard. Then suddenly there was the sound of frantic running steps. Paul and her father and Davy reached the room almost at once. Paul raised her, his face quite white. He loosed the straps and carried her to her bed. Kirkland was already calling the doctor while Davy rushed for whiskey.

Anne's tears were now half laughter but it was clear she had been more frightened than she would admit. She clung to Paul as she shakily assured him she was quite all right and it was all her own stupid fault. When the doctor came he was grave and careful. He ordered a strong sedative and suggested someone keep an eye on her all night. Outside the bedroom with Paul and Kirkland he was very candid. It had been a nasty shock, coupled with strain. It might induce premature labor. No one could tell. Keep her in bed for a day or two, continue the prescription he was leaving, and hope for the best. He would be in in the morning but call him and the ambulance at once upon signs of trouble. Miss Davis would know the symptoms.

"And look here," he said turning to Kirkland, "you're shaking all over, man. Brace up. I think there's a good chance all will be well. But you've got to calm down. Take yourself a good hooker now . . . and I think by the look of you, young man, you could do with one yourself . . . and," to Kirkland, "I'll give you a little something to make you sleep tonight."

"Not to me, you won't," Kirkland said violently. "I intend to stay up so I'll know exactly what's happening. And what should I do about calling Dr. Hertzog? You know he promised to fly over on a moment's notice. If there's the least danger now . . ."

Dr. Leyton put his hand on the older man's arm. "Try to take it easy. For tonight at least. This may have no bad effect at all. Don't get Hertzog over a month too soon, for God's sake. He's got more to do than fly the Atlantic."

Paul left then to go back to Anne but Kirkland continued down the stairs with the doctor. He thought as he went of the spring day over a year ago when he had made this same descent on the lightly curving steps, his heart heavy, awaiting the verdict. He saw vividly Dr. Hertzog's face as he had turned from the door that day and gone back to the library to tell him the strange story that had given him the fragile hope upon which all these later happenings had been built.

At the front door now, Kirkland faced the doctor, his face tense.

"We have gone over this before, I know, but now when her . . . when her time may be near I must ask you again for your promise that you will not in any way shorten her labor." His face twitched. "You know what I mean. Hertzog said that it was the extremity of pain which made that other girl he told me about get upon her feet without knowing she did it. The doctors have all agreed that Anne's paralysis *could* come from a hysteric block in the brain, caused by the shock. So, there is, you see . . ."

The doctor stopped him gently. "I know all that, Mr. Kirkland. We will do everything you have suggested up to the point of harming her or the child."

Kirkland's voice came in a hoarse whisper. "I would even sacrifice the child."

"You must remember," the doctor said sternly, "that it is not your child. Your daughter and her husband, I think, would not share that feeling." Then his eyes narrowed as he studied the man before him.

"There is something I wish you would do. Go to see your own doctor tomorrow! Have him check you over. You're running under pretty high steam, I think."

Kirkland made a gesture of annoyance. "Nonsense," he said, "I've never been sick in my life! I haven't seen a doctor for twenty years. And of course I'm anxious now. Who wouldn't be? But I'll tell you one thing. I'm as sure as I'm standing here that after the child is born, Anne will walk again. Hertzog said the cases seemed practically parallel, hers and this other girl's. He's so interested he agreed at once to come over when I first called him. If he hadn't been pretty confident in his own mind of the outcome, do you think he'd have done that?"

The doctor shook hands kindly. "We'll do everything we can and we will all hope. Now I must go, and you try to relax. I've never lost a grandfather yet, so don't let me down."

Kirkland smiled vaguely at the doctor's attempt at humor, and then hurried back upstairs. In the dim light of Anne's room he could see she had already dropped off to sleep under the opiate, and that Paul sat close beside the bed, watching her face.

"I'll be across the hall," Kirkland said in a whisper. "Are you staying up all night too?"

Paul nodded.

"Then call me instantly, if there is any . . . anything alarming. Of course I'll look in from time to time."

The next morning Anne awoke after a twelve hours' sleep, refreshed, normal and in fine spirits. In her most becoming satin and lace froth of negligee she ate her breakfast in bed and surveyed the haggard faces around her.

"I've never heard of anything so preposterous," she kept saying. "Davy was keeping an eye on me. So why you two blessed darling idiots should have sat up all night too is clear beyond me. If I didn't

love you so much I'd be very severe with you. Now you've both got
to get some rest."

Her brightness was suddenly clouded over by her solicitude.

"I'm really all right. I feel fine. I'll stay in bed today and loaf to
satisfy you all. But the rest of you *must* get some sleep."

"We will," Paul assured. "I'll take forty winks now before I go,
and tonight we'll go to bed with the chickens. What about you,
Jimmy? Can't you take the day off?"

"No, no. I have to go to the office. Got an appointment at eleven.
And a lunch date. I'll come home early though. Now you'll be careful, Mouchie!"

"I promise you I won't lift anything heavier than a powder puff.
Do come back soon, Jimmy. You look as though you were just home
from the wars."

When he had gone downstairs, Anne and Paul held each other
close, in a long, sweet, wordless embrace, before he went into his
dressing room to rest.

After four days had safely passed the doctor confirmed Anne's own
appraisal of herself. The accident had done no harm. All would proceed according to schedule and the baby be born sometime between
the middle and end of July. The Saturday trips to the mountains,
though, had better stop. So Anne once more spent the days under
the rowan tree in the garden, trying to learn contentment, to practice, even through the occasional dark inner floods of bitterness, acceptance of her lot. For she was all unaware of the hope that hovered
about her like an aura.

Paul's campaign was going (he felt superstitiously at times) almost too well. His opponent, Richard Kent, was an older and wealthy
man, a strong-line adherent of his own party and sound political
timber. But he was not an inspired speaker, and he was a conventional urbanite. In the larger towns and cities they did not run into
each other, but in the country they had had one or two encounters.
One hot day early in July, Paul was trying to cover an agricultural
section in the western end of the state. As he drove up one lane
to talk to the farmer who was an influential member of the Grange,
he saw a large car, chauffeur-driven, coming slowly along the broken
road at the side of the field. When it reached the pasture gate the
chauffeur got out, opened the gate, drove through, got out again and
closed it. The somewhat corpulent man in the back seat Paul recognized as Kent. He also saw in a distant field a man and a boy standing
by a big vat, observing the scene also.

Paul parked in the barnyard and walked toward the big car.

"How are you, Mr. Kent? I guess we make the same general rounds."

Kent was outwardly affable and rather assured.

"That's right, Mr. Devereux. It all goes along with the job of campaigning, as I guess you're finding out. Well, we'll be getting along." He lowered his voice. "You'll not get very far with that one," he said, pointing over his shoulder.

The big car moved gingerly on over the rough field road and out into the lane. Paul walked back along the field, his eyes still on the farmer in the distance who, he could see, was watching him. When he came to the pasture gate he vaulted over it and continued his way, coming at last to the man.

"Mr. Hartman?" he inquired pleasantly.

The farmer nodded. "That's right. I s'pose you're Devereux. I've seen your picture."

Paul smiled, and looked at the boy. "You've got a good helper, I see."

"Yep. This is my son, Jake."

"Are you having water trouble?"

"We sure are. Driest summer in forty years, they say. Bad enough for the crops but it's worse for the cattle."

"How many head have you?"

"Fifty. Dairyin' is more profitable now than dirt farmin', it seems."

"It's a good business. Where do you get your water?"

"Well, we've got a good run that's always full enough except in a summer like this. Runnin' low, now. We pipe it here to this main vat an' then pipe it down to the barn. We're havin' a little trouble with our force pump right now. Jake's been primin' it."

Paul looked it over. "We had one like this on the farm at home. When it got cantankerous, we found it saved time to get a real pump man at it."

Hartman shot him a swift glance. "You grew up on a farm?"

"Yes, I still own the old place. I've got a good man farming it. Up in Logan County."

Hartman put his foot up on the edge of the pump, pushed his straw hat back a little and eyed his caller appreciatively. The talk then flowed easily: cattle and crops, fertilizer and implements. Jake drew nearer and joined in too. They ended up with baseball, in which Jake was a local hero. Paul, who by now was hot and parched with thirst, eyed the clear water in Jake's priming pail.

"Mind if I take a drink of that?" he asked. The farmer shook his head. "I wouldn't if I was you. It's right from the run an' cattle tramp round in it, couple of fields back."

"Right," said Paul. "I'll be back in town soon. I can wait. Well, it's been nice talking to you, Mr. Hartman and to you too, Jake."

The farmer walked a little way with him toward the gate.

"When Kent was here just now, he was thirsty too. Thought that pail of water looked mighty good. I tried to explain but he thought he knowed pure water when he seen it, so—" he shot a sly grin at Paul, "I just let him go ahead."

After that Paul knew it was unnecessary even to mention votes. He shook hands and the farmer carefully wiped his forehead.

"I never was one to make promises but I'll say this. I know a good many folks in this here county and I'll do what I kin for you."

There were other evidences of Paul's growing popularity in the rural areas of his district. Tentatively at first but more surely as he went on, he put forth his own sound, conservative views on agricultural policy; he spoke eloquently of the water-resource question, and always everywhere in the country he gave proof at once he was farm-bred himself. Kirkland, who had feelers out in all directions, learned all this without Paul's telling him. He was enthusiastic about the whole campaign. In the urban sections, too, there was growing confidence among the leaders that Paul's election was assured.

"I tell you, Paul," Kirkland said when they were having a nightcap downstairs alone one evening, "it's going to be a walkover. And, my boy, it will be a very special victory to me. I never confessed before to a living soul that I would have liked to hold office myself, but I knew from the outset I was the wrong type. So I've had my satisfaction working behind the scenes. But to give you a leg up, and I mean *up*, will be even better than going it personally."

Paul was deeply touched by this wholly unexpected admission of Kirkland's. So, he would have liked to sit in the governor's chair himself! He, too, must have had those fleeting visions of the still higher seats of the mighty which occasionally crossed Paul's own mind until he banished them with something like embarrassment of the soul. He felt closer to Kirkland than he had ever done before; he forgot in the glow of the moment his dark suspicions; impulsively he reached over and grasped the older man's hand.

"We'll work it together," he said exuberantly. "I owe everything to you. Now I'll try to do my best to make our joint dreams come true. And," he added, seeing Kirkland's face light with rare pleasure, "when we're at it, why not make the sky the limit?"

"So you've thought ahead too," Kirkland said jubilantly. "It's just between us for the present and for a long time to come. But, my boy, it's all more possible than you could guess. These things are often planned by *somebody* a long, long way back. There's likely to be a man working, building up, pulling the strings, bringing events to pass for years before the big public figure emerges. Well, I'm that man. And you're going to be that public figure! It's a deal. Let's have another drink on it."

They had several, as a matter of fact, but at last they went back to the library, both in high spirits, to talk again about the last arrangements for the coming birth. In their present state everything was bathed in a roseate mist. All success was sure. All miracles not only possible, but imminent. Kirkland went over again in minute detail the arguments supporting his belief in Anne's coming cure. He even recapitulated all his thinking from the hour Dr. Hertzog had left after his strange confession and he himself had stood stricken at the foot of the stairs, through his evening with Mrs. Catherby when the great idea had come to him, his later struggle, his determination, his first talk with Paul, the confidence he felt in him even then, Paul's first dinner here at the house. . . . "And," he ended, "the rest you know."

Paul, in one of the rare alcoholic loquacities of his life, told his side of the story: his first shock at Kirkland's proposition, his dislike of even coming to dinner, his meeting Anne, his falling in love, his desperate problems, his despair, and then the final bliss. Never, even to Anne had he thus laid bare his soul.

They finally talked, not too coherently over a final drink, about Dr. Hertzog's coming. The uncertainty of the time presented the gravest problem, but Kirkland confessed now what he had done. He had offered Hertzog a month's vacation in this country for himself and his wife with all expenses paid and a fee besides.

"But we still may not hit the right time for him to be here even at that," Paul objected. "They say babies can be two weeks or more late as well as early."

Kirkland nodded wisely. "Not this one. This one will be right on time. Hertzog will be here. Everything's going to be all right! You know, Paul, I feel good tonight. Relaxed, like the doctor said. I feel fine! Everything's going to come out just the way I've planned it. I think if I go on up to bed now—damn it, I believe if I go to bed now I can sleep. Wonderful evening, Paul. G'night."

He rose carefully, balanced a moment and then went stiffly toward the stairs. Paul decided upon getting up that he needed some black coffee badly, and went on back to the kitchen to make it. When he opened the door of Anne's room softly, a little later, he found her sitting up in bed, wide awake.

"Wherever have you been?" she asked.

"Downstairs with your father, having, I fear, a few nightcaps too many. Still, I'm glad it happened for we had a great talk. I really never felt so close to your father before. Only now I have to be careful how I e-nunci-ate."

Anne leaned forward. "It all sounds queer to me, for Jimmy *never* takes too much. What on earth did you talk about?"

"Oh, it was politics first. Anne, what do you think? Jimmy always wanted to hold office himself but he felt he wasn't the type. He can't make a speech to save his soul, you know. Well, he decided just to pull the wires then, run things from behind, the way he's done. But it was a rev-el-ation somehow that he'd had all these other ambitions and no one ever knew. Till tonight."

"Dear Jimmy!"

"And now you see he's planning to live it all vi-vicariously if I should get ahead and . . . and go places."

"I suppose," Anne said quizzically, "that he's already decided what year you'd better run for President!"

Paul laughed. "You're psychic all right but I doubt if he has the year picked out. After politics we went on to something much more important. Give you one guess."

"The baby?"

"You and the baby. And how it had all come about, and all your father had thought of at first and planned and all I had thought and planned and the re—recapit-ulation of the whole story. Say, I still feel pretty fuzzy. Would you rather I kept my inebriacy in the dressing room tonight?"

Anne laughed. "Heavens no! You do sound funny in spots, but since neither you nor Jimmy is given to this sort of thing, I guess I can forgive you both. I wish I'd heard the talk though. It really must have been good if it had this effect on the two of you."

When all was dark and quiet Anne spoke again, thoughtfully.

"What did you mean about *all Jimmy had planned for me* and all you had planned too?"

But Paul was already asleep, and in the brightness of the new day she forgot the words entirely.

Kirkland's prophecy was correct in several particulars at least. Exactly on the fifteenth of July, Dr. Hertzog and his wife arrived in the country. When they reached the city, Kirkland was at the airport to greet them and to drive them to their hotel. The meeting was warm between the two men, though when they were finally alone for a few minutes, Hertzog spoke anxiously.

"I hope I have not in any way given you a feeling of assurance about the outcome of all this," he said. "I warned you at the very beginning . . . Indeed I have been ashamed in my conscience that I ever told you what I did, and yet . . ."

"Yes?"

The doctor smiled. "It is natural for all to hope. I do, myself, having once seen this thing happen. But only a hope as a *man*, mind you. Nothing as a doctor. Nothing. You understand?"

"Perfectly. Now for some details. I have not told Anne that I sent for you. I would like her to feel your being here is mere coincidence, and that I've casually asked you out to see her!"

"Very well."

"You have met the obstetrician, Mr. Leyton, over the telephone, but I'll arrange to have you get together at once. Meanwhile, until things begin to happen, I have tickets for you and your wife for all the best shows and I think you can find enough to entertain you during the day."

"Your kindness overwhelms me. Once again I feel my services are small in comparison."

Kirkland waved away the suggestion. "Just to have you here is worth more to me than I can possibly say. When you and Leyton get together you can decide on . . . I have told him I do not wish her labor shortened."

"You are a brave man," the doctor said. "For the possible chance of her ultimate good you are willing to go through hell with her. A strong man. I salute you. Tell your daughter I have come over to study some American methods and will give myself the pleasure of calling upon her."

Kirkland told Anne at dinner that night, keeping his voice carefully light.

"Oh, by the way, who do you suppose is in town? Dr. Hertzog.

You remember? He's over to study something or other and wants to come out to see you. His wife's with him."

Anne stopped eating and stared at her father.

"Jimmy," she said, "you may be able to play poker with men, I don't know. But you can't with me. Guilt is written all over you. You sent for him. Now just to save time, confess it."

"What in the world makes you think such a thing?" Kirkland exploded.

"Because it's true," Anne said calmly. "Only *why?* That's what bothers me. Why, Jimmy? Is anything wrong that I haven't been told about?"

"No, no!" Kirkland shouted. "I never could keep anything from you. It was my own idea. Leyton had absolutely nothing to do with it. He thought it was crazy. I liked Hertzog. He was interested in your case. He's had so much experience along every line. He told me about another girl just like you who had a fine baby. He helped attend her. I just thought we might as well have him over. . . ."

His voice trailed off and Anne laughed across at him.

"Isn't that too silly, Paul? But he's sweet just the same. I'll warrant, Jimmy, you would have had the Queen's own obstetrician too, if you could have wangled it. But aside from the foolishness of the whole business, I'll be glad to see Dr. Hertzog. I liked him so much." A slight shadow fell, but she brushed it aside. "We can talk more now than the last time. I'll call tomorrow and ask them both to dinner, how would that be?"

But there was not time for that. It was that very night that Anne woke suddenly from her first sleep, sat up in bed and snapped on the light. Her face was white with pain. She waited for a little and then woke Paul.

"I think this is it," she said. "Will you call Davy and . . . and do the things that have to be . . ."

She could not finish the sentence.

Paul sprang up, clutched his robe, called Davy and Kirkland and then dressed with furious haste. For ten minutes the telephones were busy, in twenty Anne was ready to go, in a half-hour the ambulance was at the door, for it had been agreed that means of transportation would be easier under the circumstances.

Paul carried her down in his strong arms, holding her face close to his own.

"Courage, darling, courage . . ."

"It's all right," she smiled though there was a sharp catch in her breath. "It's just a little more than I expected . . . at the start!"

Hackett in an ancient house gown, his face gray with concern, opened the front door for them and stood on the steps muttering, "Good luck, Miss Anne! Good luck, my dear!" until the ambulance had moved off and Paul's car with Kirkland beside him had followed it.

There had been a short dispute a little while earlier about Kirkland's going along. Somehow the matter had never been brought up before. Paul did his best, with nervous annoyance, to dissuade him but to no avail.

"I'm going," Kirkland said between his teeth that seemed inclined to chatter. "I'm going and I'm staying—till it's over, and hell can't stop me." So they rode together through the warm July darkness, each praying in his own way.

As Anne had told Paul on their honeymoon, the doctor had assured her there was no reason why she should not bear children like any other woman. What he deemed unnecessary to tell her, but what both he and Dr. Hertzog had explained to her menfolk, was that because of her enforced inactivity during the whole period of pregnancy the birth itself might be a very difficult one. It was this fact coupled with the decision to reserve any alleviation to the last possible moment that made the faces of the two men now white and tense even at the beginning of their vigil.

They sat in a small empty room of the great hospital on the floor below the labor and delivery rooms, feeling the vast, impersonal atmosphere penetrating every nook and corner.

"Ghastly place, isn't it?" Kirkland managed to bring out after a time.

"Not too cheerful," Paul agreed.

"Who was the she-devil that put us in here? The one that wouldn't let me finish my sentence!"

"I don't know," Paul said, smiling in spite of himself, "Some sort of floor superintendent I suppose. I gather we're lucky to be allowed to stay in here. Special dispensation."

"I'd like to see them put us out. How will we know how things are going?"

"Dr. Hertzog said he would look in on us at intervals and report. He said there would be nothing to say for some hours."

"Hours?" Kirkland barked hoarsely. "How long . . . that's one thing I forgot to ask about. Did they tell you? I mean give you any idea?"

Paul swallowed hard. "Oh, they never can be sure. Every case is different. The fact that Anne started out with such severe pain may mean it won't last so long."

Kirkland groaned, and began to move about nervously. Paul felt he would give all he possessed to be left quietly alone to dree his weird in his own fashion. At least he could grit his teeth and sit still. He wondered if he would have to endure the other man's furious restlessness for the whole time. His own hands gripped each other hard. Dr. Leyton had told him that fifteen to eighteen hours of labor was normal for a first child.

"I can't even remember now how long I waited when Anne herself was being born," Kirkland said later on. "That shows what time will do to you. How could I forget that?" he demanded.

"Do sit down, Jimmy. We've got to get hold of ourselves. We can't expect Anne to have all the courage, can we?"

"If it was an ordinary birth, if nothing more was hanging in the balance! How can you sit there like a stone image? How can you preach courage to me? Don't you *know* what may happen now? Don't you *care?* Sometimes I think you don't feel the suspense of it at all. At any minute now she may get up—she *may walk!* I've told them to come down and tell us at the first sign. Well, say you *expect* it, you *believe* it? We've got to, I tell you. What time is it?"

"It's two o'clock."

"Good God, is that all?"

He sank into a chair, the veins in his forehead showing. Paul watched him, anxiously. He was sorry he had not asked one of the doctors to give him some sort of sedative. He got up.

"I'm going to stretch my legs in the hall," he said. "I'll only be a minute."

He walked to the desk in the alcove. The woman whom Kirkland had dubbed the she-devil, sat there, starched and cool. She looked up distantly.

"My wife's in labor upstairs. Her father is down the hall there with me. He's not young and he's terribly upset. I'm afraid he can't quite take it. Could you give any very mild sedative for him. . . ."

"We give no medication without a doctor's orders."

"Well, could you let me have a couple of aspirins then?"

"I have told you we give *nothing* without doctors' orders."

"Isn't there a house doctor, then? Anyone you could ask?"

"I'm afraid not," she said. "This man is not a patient here. In fact we do not ordinarily expect anyone—except the husband—to be waiting in these cases."

"I suppose," Paul said icily, "it would not be too much to ask for a glass of water?"

She rose stiffly and went to the kitchen nearby, returning with the glass. Paul accepted it gravely and then stood watching her.

"Do you never smile, never give a word of encouragement to poor suffering mortals?" he asked.

She relaxed a little. "We have this sort of thing happen every day. Babies are born all right no matter how excited the men get."

"But you see," Paul began earnestly, "this case is different . . ."

She did smile then. "They all are," she said not unkindly, "to the folks concerned. Now just take it easy."

He went back to Kirkland, who gulped the water gratefully. Then they waited on. The dawn broke with a hot, misty sun rising from the clouds of night; then the clear early day and the rattle of the street noises. They both jumped as Dr. Hertzog's stocky figure appeared at the door. He motioned them back.

"Nothing actually to report, but I had a wish to see you and tell you to rest a little and have some food." He smiled into their dull, drawn faces. It was the patient smile of one who has known suffering and witnessed more. "You can really do no good here, but I know you wish to—how do you say it?—stand by."

"How . . . how is she?" Kirkland's lips were stiff on the words.

"She is still of course in labor."

"Is it . . . very hard?"

"Labor is always hard," he said noncommittally.

"There had been no . . . she has not moved?"

The doctor shook his head. "We are watching closely for the least sign. As I told you . . ."

Kirkland broke in. "I know. I know, but I'm still sure it will happen. Is Leyton with her now?"

"Yes. When I go back he will leave temporarily but will be in his office on instant call. I will stay all the time and we have an excellent nurse who understands the whole situation."

He paused and looked carefully at Kirkland. "Would you not be willing to go home and rest for a little? Stay there till toward evening, say?"

"Evening!" Kirkland gasped.

"We agree the child cannot be born before some time this coming night. Won't you rest a little in between?"

"No!" Kirkland shouted. "How can I rest? Is Anne resting? I've got to be here."

The doctor did not reply to that but looked at Paul.

"There is a little coffee shop on the first floor, I'm told, which opens early. Won't you both go down and have something to eat? Take a little turn in the air too? It will be good for you."

"We'll do that," Paul said, and followed the doctor out into the hall.

"You can tell me the truth," he said in a low tone.

Dr. Hertzog watched the young man's haggard face. "It is, as we expected, very, very bad—especially since she cannot move or walk to change her position. Aside from that, however, it is all not unique. Other women I have seen suffering as much."

"But in other cases you would give them something . . . something to help?"

The doctor nodded.

Paul felt a frenzy overcoming him. "I can't let her be tortured, doctor, even for this chance! Can't you see? I can't allow it! She's my wife. I have the right to decide."

Dr. Hertzog looked at him steadily. "I agree with your father. This chance we must take. We play for high stakes. But one thing I tell you. When we see she can endure no longer we shall give her medication at once. We will watch her every moment. I can promise you she will not be permanently harmed by this. I will," he added, a great kindness suffusing his face, "I will do to her as to my own child, no? Be brave now. Your part is hard but not the most hard."

They wrung each other's hands. "Give her my love," Paul said. Then in a moment he caught up with the older man at the elevator.

"Could you order something for Mr. Kirkland to make him relax a little? It's getting on my own nerves, watching him. I'm afraid he cracks under this."

"Of course. Of course. I should have thought." He led the way back to the desk, and spoke to the nurse there.

"I am Dr. Hertzog of Vienna. I am here in consultation with Dr. Leyton on a confinement case. I leave you now a prescription for the elderly gentleman awaiting news of his daughter with her husband here. Please to see that he has one tablet after his breakfast and one after his lunch. He refuses to leave the hospital. I thank you."

He wrote quickly and hurried off while the nurse stared at the paper and then at Paul. She did not smile but her face was respectful.

"Maybe your case is something special at that," she said. "I'll see to this."

Breakfast in the crowded little shop, a turn on the front pavement, and back to the small waiting room. It was Paul's turn then to grow respectful of the nursing profession. With complete control of the situation, a bright young thing in white presented Kirkland with the tablet, smiled with complete indifference at his violent opposal, placed it on his tongue, held a glass of water to his lips and was gone before he could speak. It had its effect soon. He leaned his head against the back of the chair and slept, exhausted. Paul now had a chance to be quiet. He tried to read but the words conveyed no meaning. He paced the floor; he prayed, he dozed; he went softly out and down to the street. Here for two hours he walked under the hot July sun.

There was no further report until after lunch, then Dr. Hertzog appeared again, once more giving a sign that there was no real news. He himself looked very weary.

"Things are going along . . . It is very slow as it usually is with a first child. I am watching her with the greatest care . . ."

"No . . . no *movement?*" Kirkland asked.

"None, so far."

Kirkland swallowed as with difficulty. "I believe you said that in the other girl's case it happened toward the end of labor?"

"It did."

Kirkland drew a quick breath.

"Be patient. Try not to suffer too much yourselves," the doctor said. "Fix your minds upon something pleasant . . ." He smiled. "As upon the child, for example."

Paul followed him outside again. He did not know that his grip on Dr. Hertzog's arm was painful.

"Give her something!" he said. "She can't go on like this. You said yourself it's worse for her than for a normal girl. *I order you!*"

The doctor's eyes behind his spectacles were compassionate, but unyielding.

"I shall do so when I know it is necessary and not before. I am used to responsibility, Mr. Devereux. I take it now. I do to her as to my own daughter. Control yourself. You must not be less brave than your wife."

He turned abruptly and hurried away. Paul went back to the room to find Kirkland still groggy.

"They must be giving me some kind of damned dope. You can't trust them in a hospital." He leaned his head back, then started up. "You see?" he said. "You heard him say it would happen toward the end? Don't let me sleep long. Any time now . . ." His eyes dropped heavily.

The afternoon was endless, the heat intolerable. Paul felt as though he himself had died a thousand deaths. As though he were also under an opiate his thoughts grew dull and confused. Kirkland slept on.

At five he saw a nurse pause outside the door and motion to him. His heart all but stopped as he hurried to meet her. She handed him a note, smiled and disappeared. He opened it with a shaking hand. It was from Hertzog.

> Dr. Leyton and I agree that medication must now be given. Her suffering will be greatly eased or nonexistent from this point on. But what we hoped would happen will not now occur. I will explain this to her father when I have the birth itself to report. It is better so—the good news with the bad.

Paul read it once and again, then went back to the room and stood by the window, staring blindly out at the street. The ghastly tension in himself as he had felt torn with Anne's suffering was released. Only the weariness now engulfed him, along with a black disappointment which amazed him. For he had steadily refused to think of the possibility of the miracle. It was as though he had felt that by keeping his mind free of it, even as Anne's was free, it was the more likely to happen. His hope had not been dominant, voiced and implacable, like Kirkland's. But he knew now it had been there, alive and waiting in his subconscious mind, an unselfish hope, that with the news of her child there could be brought to Anne also the radiant word of her cure. He stood there filled with a dull despair, for a long time; then he sank into his own chair, and slept.

He woke at six o'clock with the supper sounds in the hall. Kirkland was still asleep. He looked old and worn and for once—weak. Paul slipped out and down to the street for a turn in the air. He did not want to be away long, so he brought some food up from the coffee shop and ate what little he could in the room. He hoped Kirkland would sleep on until the final word came. A tremendous excitement within him now superseded every other thought. The child! His and Anne's! Would the word come now before midnight? Before dawn?

It came at eight o'clock. The two doctors arrived together, Dr. Leyton still casually fit and cheerful, Dr. Hertzog haggard but beaming too.

"You have a fine, healthy boy, Mr. Devereux. And your wife will be all right too. She's still asleep."

Kirkland started up at the voices. His eyes took in the smiling doctors. "It's happened?" he said. "She *has walked?*"

Dr. Hertzog put an arm about his shoulders.

"Not that, my friend, but listen to our news. Your daughter has been safely delivered of a son. You are now a grandfather! Is that not cause for rejoicing now? You must believe me."

Kirkland stood as though frozen.

"The child is born and she never moved?"

The doctor shook his head.

"Then," Kirkland said with sharp bitter emphasis, "there is no more hope. She will never walk again."

Hertzog made a motion for the other two men to leave the room. "I will talk with him alone," he said, adding before Paul could speak, "and go with him back to his home."

Once in the hall Dr. Leyton slapped Paul's back. "Well, your young man gave us all plenty of trouble, but what a beauty he turned out to be. Eight pounds and a half! Now, come along and have a look at him and then you can go into your wife's room and wait till she wakes up. Like to be the first to tell her the news, eh?"

And suddenly Paul felt all weariness leave him and all disappointments. He was no longer even a creature of earth. His feet were winged; his head touched heaven. He talked wildly to Dr. Leyton, who somehow seemed to understand; he said strange, foolish things to the nurse who showed him the baby, and she, too, did not act in any way startled. He tiptoed at last into Anne's room, took one look at the dear white face on the pillow, then burying his own in his hands he wept for the pain, the relief, the unspeakable joy of it, and the nurse there did not seem surprised either.

An hour passed and another before Anne's eyelids slowly opened. He bent over her.

"Darling," he whispered huskily, "can you understand me? It's a boy! We have a beautiful little son!"

Her eyes grew wide with wonder and joy. She could not speak, but she understood.

IO

◦§ AND NOW, more than ever before, happiness filled to overflowing the big house on the West Hill. All paths led to the nursery next to Anne's room as to a shrine, and the small creature there grew more beautifully engaging week by week. Anne herself bloomed in her motherhood, "remembering," as Dr. Hertzog had quoted to Paul, "no more the anguish for joy that a man is born into the world." Mrs. Catherby came over each day in spite of all advice to the contrary, insisting that the sight of her great-grandson put new life in her; and Paul understood, for he himself felt within him an upsurge of strength as though in thews and sinews, as in heart, he was now invincible.

There was only one unexpected cloud. Anne spoke of it anxiously to Paul one evening as they sat together in the nursery.

"Whatever can be the matter with Jimmy?" she asked. "I thought he would be beside himself with pride and delight and, you know, he really isn't. He comes in and tries to make noises like a grandfather, but they don't ring true at all. Have you noticed? Do you know what's wrong?"

Paul thought. There was no point now in keeping the facts from her. Very gently he told her the story while Anne listened in amazement.

"So, you see," Paul ended, "he is still feeling that particular disappointment. Just give him a little time, dear, and he'll be as excited over the baby as anyone."

Anne's eyes were wide with incredulity.

"He believed I would get up . . . on my feet?"

"Yes. He made himself believe it."

"And Dr. Hertzog actually felt there was a chance?"

"Not a strong one, but still a possibility."

"And you?"

Paul hesitated. "I tried not to think much about it, but of course I hoped—for your sake."

"And no one told me? I might have had the joy of hoping, too." Her voice was piteous.

"But you see, dearest, we *couldn't* tell you. We didn't dare. Your knowledge might have destroyed the chance!"

"I'm not so sure," she said slowly. "If I'd known, I might really have tried . . . No, I see what you mean. Only an unconscious reaction would have succeeded." She drew a long quavering sigh. "But I understand now about Jimmy. He cared more about my walking than about the baby." She looked up, meeting Paul's eyes. "You didn't feel too disappointed . . . afterwards?"

"I never even thought of it then," he assured her honestly. "I was too happy."

"I'm glad for that. It makes it all more bearable. But the whole thought that there really was even a grain of hope for me has shaken me a little. And poor Jimmy! Why, he would be thinking of this, then, all the months before! And this was why he had Dr. Hertzog over! Oh, I see it all now, and his ghastly disappointment. Paul, when did he first tell you about it?"

Paul hedged carefully. "When we got back from our honeymoon he told me how eager he was for you to have a child, and why."

Anne accepted this. "Well, knowing Jimmy as I do, this explains everything, even to his looking ill now. It's the reaction from all the strain. I believe, though, I'll get a doctor in somehow to give him a checkup. I'm sure he hasn't had one in years. Yes, I'll do that."

She was very quiet the rest of the evening and Paul's heart ached for her. He wished bitterly he had never told her of the hope at all. He felt now that it had been a cruel thing to do, even though all he had wished was to explain Kirkland's lack of enthusiasm over the baby. He tried his best now to divert her; but after they had gone to bed she wept wildly, hysterically against his breast and not all the outpouring of his love could calm her.

"I have to give way sometimes," she sobbed. "I try to hold it all in —deep—and I'm really happy—it's only now to think there was a chance. . . ."

At last Paul got up and went into the nursery. He lifted the sleeping baby, carried it into their room and laid the warm sweet little body in her arms. Then he knelt beside them, his grasp encircling them both.

"You have us, darling. We'll try always, always to make up to you for . . . the other."

She held the child close for a time, her cheek against the downy head, and then when Paul was again next her, she lay quietly listening to the tenderness of his voice. But she did not speak again. There was only the quivering, broken breaths, until at last she fell asleep. But Paul lay awake until the first pale light came flooding through the dark. He knew now what high fortitude, what resolute valor lay behind the daily brightness of her smiles which he had taken for granted. He knew, and his spirit bowed before it.

It was some weeks before a connection could be effected between Kirkland and a doctor, for at the first suggestion of such a thing from Anne, he had shied violently from it.

"I'm as fit as a fiddle! Nothing wrong with me. Just because the house is now lousy with doctors is no reason why I should get mixed up with them! And all this pediatrics business for the little fellow is nonsense, I think. Keep a baby comfortable, give it plenty to eat and then let it alone. That's my theory, but of course the modern way of doing . . ."

"Now, Jimmy, don't get yourself worked up. Just come and have a look at your grandson. Isn't he wonderful? Aren't you thrilled over him? Don't you want to hold him?"

"Not till he's a little bigger, and of course I'm thrilled. Why wouldn't I be? Fine child. Good head. Well, I must get along to the office. Goodbye."

He stopped and kissed Anne and patted the baby. At the door he looked back, wistfully.

"You're pretty . . . proud, Mouchie?"

"Proud!" Anne laughed back at him. "I feel as though the whole business of having a baby was my own private invention! As proud as that, sir! Now *please* don't work too hard, Jimmy. Come home early and have something cool to drink and meet the worshipers. They're still coming."

And they were. Those of Anne's friends and many of her mother's, who were still in town or near it, came with votive offerings to see the baby and rejoice with Anne, their normal interest quickened by the unusual circumstances. So her sitting room was likely to be gay from five o'clock on, with Paul's friends adding to its liveliness. Johnny Bovard kept dropping in, his pockets bursting with small stuffed animals, and David Laird brought a tiny chair he had made himself in his workshop.

"You two do the darndest nicest things," Johnny announced one day. "You have sudden surprise weddings, and carol sings, and *babies* . . ."

"All in the singular, so far, please," Paul laughed. "Well, why don't you old bachelors stir your stumps and do likewise?"

"'Pon my soul, sirrah, you make me think there's something to this marryin' business, after all, eh Dave?"

"Egad, could be," Laird returned with mock solemnity. "We'll look into it, study this particular case a little longer to see how it works out . . ."

"No need to do that with this pair. They're goners for good. Couldn't pry them apart with a crowbar. Say Anne, how about a look at the offspring?"

"Of course. Davy's in the nursery now."

"Come on then," Johnny said exuberantly to David and Paul. "Follow me, my lads. I've learned a thing or two these last weeks about child care. Mind you keep your big mouths shut if he's asleep. I don't trust the Senator here. He's inclined to go eloquent when he looks at his son. No modesty! None whatever! Well, damned if I blame him! Okay. Here we go! I've got a pink rabbit for him today, Anne."

It was the last week of August when Anne manipulated events so that on pretext of a slight cold she had their own physician at the house when Kirkland came home from the office.

"Just tell him, Dr. Scott, that you find I am worrying about him and for *my sake* you will go through the motions of checking him. I doubt myself whether there is anything really wrong, but my husband and I have been a little anxious lately."

The ruse worked. As always the love for his child overcame all else. He submitted to the examination in his own room, with poor grace, complaining loudly that a man couldn't call his life his own, when women got ideas, but yet he submitted. The doctor took a long time, then he stood off a little, surveying the man before him.

"I think," he said, "that you're used to giving and getting straight talk, aren't you?"

"I hope so. What do you mean?"

"I mean you're not in good shape. You've got a very high blood pressure and it's lucky we caught it now before it does any more harm to your heart. We can bring it down if you'll co-operate. But you've got to slow up."

"Now listen, doctor . . ."

"*You* listen to me. I'm not fooling about this. You've got to rest every day for two hours, eat the diet I prescribe and take *the medicine* I'll give you. And you must not for any reason whatever allow yourself to become excited. Is that clear?"

"Clear as mud. I don't intend to . . ."

"If you don't," the doctor said looking him in the eye, "I won't answer for the consequences. I'm giving it to you straight and I think you're smart enough to take it."

"Well, well," Kirkland said, looking abashed as well as stricken, "well, well, go ahead then. Fix me up."

"And you'll do your part?"

"Oh, I suppose so. I'll have to, I guess, for Anne's sake."

"Right! That's the spirit. Suppose you drop in at my office tomorrow for a few tests and then I'll have the directions all ready for you. And don't worry about yourself! Just do what you're told and we'll make a new man of you."

"No need to bother Anne about all this, is there? She's still nursing the baby and I won't have her upset."

"I'll have to report to her since she arranged the interview."

"Well, tone it down then. I want your word on that."

The doctor hesitated. "If you give me yours that you'll follow my directions to the letter."

Kirkland groaned. "I'm mad as the devil, you know, at finding there's anything at all the matter with me. But . . . I give you my word."

"Good. I'll have my nurse phone your office tomorrow morning and give you an appointment. Remember, ease up on everything, and *keep calm.*"

Anne was pleased with the doctor's conversation with her. "His blood pressure is up so I'll give him some medicine for that and some diet suggestions. That's routine, you know. And I've told him to take things easier. At his age that's always a good thing."

"And he'll be all right?"

"You just browbeat him into seeing me once a month and I'll keep him in hand."

"I'll do that, if I have to have him dragged there. And I'll see he takes the medicine and all that. Oh, I'm awfully relieved, now that you've seen him. Thank you so much, doctor."

She gave Paul the news that night and he, too, felt relief. "That's good, really. I knew there was something wrong but now that you've got the doctor on to him I'm sure he'll be fine. His spirits will come up, too. How's the young man? I've got the hardest work holding out till quitting time. I'm so anxious to see him. Has he done anything new today?" In a moment they were adoringly beside the crib.

Kirkland was as good as his promise. He took his medicine, he followed his diet, he came home early each afternoon and lay down till the dinner hour. Hackett kept an eagle eye on him, Anne fussed over him tenderly, and Paul noted his improved looks and congratulated him. He even himself admitted grudgingly that he was feeling better.

As September enfolded the city and the countryside, it was decided that the baby was old enough for week ends in the mountains. Anne was happy over going, admitting now how much she had missed the camp during the late summer. Davy and Hackett drove up one day to install some nursery equipment there, and on Friday Anne and Paul were to follow with the baby, with Kirkland coming on Saturday, since he wished to supervise some fall planting on the grounds before leaving. However the plans changed suddenly at the last moment. Paul was unexpectedly asked to speak at a Saturday night dinner. Since he already had contracted a cold he decided to stay home and nurse it till then. Seeing Anne's disappointment Kirkland canceled the tree planting and went off with her Friday in the later afternoon.

"I'll be up Sunday as soon as I can get there," Paul promised. "I guess it's as well for me to keep this wretched head away from you all till then. Be careful now . . . Goodbye."

He watched them wistfully as they drove off, but there was nothing else to do but work during the evening on his speech and doctor his cold.

About nine o'clock he wanted a book he had noticed on the desk of Kirkland's study. He hurried down, found it and was about to leave when the phone rang. He picked up the receiver. "Yes?" he said huskily, not realizing this was not only Kirkland's habitual way of answering, but that his own throaty voice sounded now much like that of his father-in-law.

"Listen, Chief, we've run into something with C. Those damned men of his we bonded have skipped and their bonds are going to be forfeit and C says . . ."

It was Arno talking very fast but at this point Paul broke in.

"This isn't the Chief, Arno. He left unexpectedly for the mountains. Be back Sunday night. Devereux speaking," he added.

He could feel the shock over the wire. Then Arno's voice came cool and casual. "Forget it!" he said, and hung up.

It was Paul this time who paused at the foot of the beauteous stairway as though he had not the strength to climb it. All the glad power he had felt within him these last weeks because of his fatherhood seemed to depart from him. He felt weak. All the straws of suspicion that the wind had borne to him before were as nothing compared to this crushing, unequivocal blow. For now there was no doubt. With his own ears he had heard the truth from Arno. There was a definite link between Kirkland, the state boss, and the numbers racketeer and his kingdom of corruption. This was more than the machinations of ordinary political intrigue; this was alliance with the lowest form of evil; this was partnership with the devil.

He finally climbed the stairs, but he did not sleep till dawn.

For the first time in his campaign he felt himself less than forceful Saturday night. His voice was hoarse for one thing and his heart was heavy for another. Though it was late when he was free he drove on up to camp that night. He felt physically wretched and as though he might have a temperature, but though he knew he must not go too near to either Anne or the baby, he longed to see her and hear her voice as soon as possible.

He let himself quietly in with his own key, snapped on a light and made his way across to the large first-floor bedroom fraught with all the sweet memories of the honeymoon. He opened the door softly and spoke. In a second Anne, roused, startled, at his voice.

"Paul, is that you?"

"Yes, darling. I drove on out as soon as I could get away. I don't dare come near you for I'm full of this beastly cold. I just wanted to get here as fast as I could. I'll go upstairs, dear, and see you in the morning. Are you all right?"

Anne had put on the light and raised herself in bed. The frill of her night dress dropped over one shoulder. "*We're* all right, but you look simply awful! I'm glad you came on tonight for you can stay in bed tomorrow and Davy will look after you. Are you sure you're not really sick? I *am* anxious!"

"Sure. Just a pip of a cold. How's the baby?"

"Good as gold! Wait a minute."

She had rung as she spoke and Davy appeared almost at once in her wrapper from the smaller room beyond.

"Look at this fellow, Davy! I think he needs some medicine. He turns up at this hour of the night white as a ghost one minute and scarlet the next. He thinks he should go upstairs. Will you look after him and dose him up?"

Davy took charge at once. "Come right along," she said to Paul, "and I'll have you fixed up in no time. We're as well stocked here as a drugstore!"

Paul still stood in the doorway after Davy had started upstairs.

"Good night, darling. I wish I could kiss you!"

"So do I! You're sure there's nothing wrong, Paul? Besides the cold? Your eyes look—I don't know—*worried.*"

"Just bunged up I guess. Now get back to sleep. It was a shame to wake you. Here's the best I can do at the moment," blowing a kiss.

Anne returned it and then called after him softly. "I love you." He turned back. "I'm better already. Did I ever tell you you look beautiful in bed?"

"It would be too bold of me to remember. Did you?"

He stood watching her as her face colored with a lovely flush.

"Beautiful, *beautiful!*" he repeated. "I guess I'd better go while my self-control holds out."

It was much easier, Paul decided next morning, to remain upstairs. He could not have endured a whole day spent in Kirkland's company. As it was he lay listening to his voice rising from the terrace mingled with Anne's laughter, and pondered on the mystery of the man. Strong, kindly, powerfully efficient, determined, passionately devoted to those he loved and capable of eliciting great love in return; but also relentless in his ambitions, and completely without principle or conscience in the execution of them. This was Kirkland. This was the "Boss." How was he to meet him with the accusations which were now burning his own heart? For he, too, more than he had realized, had affection for this man, and a certain strange respect which one must always have for power in any form. How could he make the attack upon him which he knew now he must make? How sever the link which he cherished and which he felt would be irretrievably broken? He groaned within himself and buried his face in the pillow. Anne . . . Anne. What of Anne in all this? He had waited for her sake; he had postponed a crisis; now there could not be much more delay. Not if he was to live in any sort of decency with his own soul. Through the long day he planned what he would say to Kirkland, how he would open the momentous discussion, how he would proceed. As to the effect upon his own career—he did not dare to think of it.

There would seem to be a law operating in human experience by which the mind once suddenly aware of a verity for the first time immediately encounters it again. This repetition of newly acquired knowledge, whether of word, face or fact, was one Paul had often noted with amusement or interest. So it was with a sort of fatalistic attitude that he accepted the following week's revelation. Their firm had been handling a big damage case for the Public Building Authorities. The matter concerned land taken for sewage disposal on the north side, and the attorney representing the group of property owners was Sheffkin, a very clever lawyer not noted for his probity. Paul had had tilts with him before and knew his shrewd but completely unethical ingenuity, so he had worked doubly hard on this case which was to come up at mid-September.

The first day he was able to be back at the office, a call came from Sheffkin.

"Hello, Devereux, how's tricks?"

"Pretty good, I guess."

"You *guess*. I won't buy that. I think you're always plenty sure of yourself. Well, I'd like to ask a favor."

"Yes?"

"I'd like you to agree to have time extended on this damage case. Some of my experts aren't ready."

"I'm sorry, but I can't agree to that, Sheffkin. The date for the hearing has been set and I want to stick to it. The fifteenth is the latest I can manage for I'll be running into some pretty busy weeks after that."

"Oh, yes. Your campaign."

"That's right."

"And you feel you can't agree to an extension?"

"No, I'm sorry, but I can't."

Sheffkin's voice grew uncomfortably suave.

"Well now, look here. Our office has done plenty for you in this campaign of yours. Surely you can grant us a little favor?"

"What do you mean by that?"

"Why, my biggest client has poured out plenty of money to finance the ticket. I suppose you know it *takes* some, don't you?"

Paul's tone was ice. "A great many contributions come in for expenses. That is no news."

"But what I'm talking about is different, my fine young friend. You wouldn't get to first base without my client's support, financial and otherwise. Now about . . ."

"Who is your client?" His lips were stiff on the words for he suddenly knew the answer that would come.

"Why, Camponelli. The big C. Don't tell me you're Kirkland's white-headed little boy and didn't know that. And, as I said, the stork doesn't bring the campaign funds these days. Now, Devereux, about this time extension, if you'll just okay it . . ."

"You've already had my answer on that," Paul said sharply. "I will not agree. I'm busy right now, Sheffkin, so if you'll excuse me . . ."

He started to hang up, but not before he had heard Sheffkin's heavy-breathed, "Why, you damned young fool! I'll apply to court for an adjournment . . ."

Paul got up at once and went into Hartwell's office. His white face startled the old man.

"What's wrong, Paul? Is it as bad as you look?"

"Bad enough. I found out accidentally last week that Kirkland is in direct league with Camponelli. Arno apparently operates as liaison man. Just now Sheffkin called me for a time extension on the damage case and tried to blackmail me into giving it because he says Camponelli's his client and has put money into the campaign."

Hartwell's face looked strange.

"You agreed to the extension?" he asked quietly.

"I did not. And I've got to have a showdown with Kirkland at once. There's no other way possible."

Hartwell let his eyeglasses drop on their black ribbon, pushed back his chair, rose stiffly, walked around the desk and held out his hand. His eyes were definitely misty.

"This, I think, is one of the best days of my life," he said. "I've hoped for this, waited for it, but I didn't expect it so soon. I suppose you realize this could affect your own ambitions?"

"I do."

"But you're going ahead in any case?"

"I've got to."

"Then bless you, my son," the old man said, and wrung Paul's hand.

"I probably have more information," he went on, "whenever you want it. I didn't feel free to offer it before."

"I'll take it all," Paul answered. "I'll need it now." Then unable to say more, he turned and went back to his own desk.

It was a beautiful late afternoon, mildly warm and mellow, with the approach of the year's fruitage in the air even in the city. Paul, country-bred as he was, sensed this acutely and longed for the farm as he drove back to West Hill. He had always loved the autumn months with peculiar intensity, feeling within them a sense of ful-fillment and well-being, as though life were pouring rich distillation into his cup. Last fall his feeling had had its climax in the unspeak-able joy of his new marriage; this year there was added another to make it complete—his fatherhood—with the possibility of his election in November to crown it. This is the way it should have been if the present problem of Kirkland's involvements had not cast its dark shadow over all. Why must life always be checkered? he wondered. Why could the human soul never enjoy pure and unmixed happiness? Was it due to the inherent complexities of man? Was it a reflection of Nature's dual capacity to produce and nourish and yet at the same time to rend and kill? Was it, perhaps, the design of God himself?

If goodness lead him not, yet weariness
May toss him to my breast.

These thoughts kept going round and round in Paul's mind, mingled with the distracting uncertainty of when to have it all out with Kirkland. It must be soon, and had better be in his office downtown, of course.

They were dining that evening, he knew, with Mrs. Catherby, the first time since the birth of the baby. He found Anne very bright and eager.

"I always love to go to Gran's," she said, "and I'm dressing up. She likes that. She doesn't demand black tie but I'd put on a dark suit if I were you. Jimmy always does, come fall. How did things go today?"

"Oh, so-so. How's my namesake?"

"Sweeter than ever. He laughed and cooed all through his bath. He loves it! I wish you could see him. Will you be home all this week end?"

"Most of it, I think. Is Jimmy all right?"

"Yes, he seemed in unusually good spirits, I thought. He actually sat down and played with the baby. Besides, he's like me, he's always pleased to be going to Gran's. She wants us early, dear, so maybe you'd better get dressed."

"Ten minutes first to rest my eyes on you?" The anxiety and fear in his heart made his voice more wistful than he knew.

Anne smiled up at him. "You're such a sweet, *sweet* silly! All right —I'll grant you ten."

When they reached Mrs. Catherby's apartment, as usual its peace lapped them round. It was not only the distinguished beauty of the furnishings, nor the perfection of the service which reflected long years of expert housekeeping; it was, more than these, the loving warmth, the rich intelligence, the charm and grace of a rare spirit that reached out to meet and hold them. Kirkland sank into a deep chair with an audible expression of satisfaction.

"Listen to Jimmy purr!" Anne said, laughing. "I honestly don't know how you do it, Gran, but your room is somehow more *comfortable* than any of ours."

"Wait till you are my age, darling, then you'll have learned just where all the kinks come in the human frame and have selected your chairs accordingly. We are having some cocktails out of respect to you two young things. Jimmy, will you join me in sherry as usual? And by the way, how are you?"

"Yes, sherry please. Oh, I'm all right. It's just this fool of a doctor that puts wrong ideas in my head. I've got to 'take it easy,' to 'slow up,' to 'remember I'm not as young as I was.' Makes me feel about a hundred. I promised him I'd follow all his confounded advice for a while, but if he thinks I'm going to keep it up indefinitely, he's crazy. You look fine, Ellie. You might give us your secret for that, while you're at it."

"Well," she said smiling, "the credit is largely due to Mr. Emerson, who gives better advice than the doctors, or at least more charmingly put. I've read it very often for years and acted accordingly.

> *It is time to be old,*
> *To take in sail:—*
> *The god of bounds,*
> *Who sets to seas a shore*
> *Came to me in his fatal rounds,*
> *And said: 'No more! . . .*
> *There's not enough for this and that,*
> *Make thy option which of two;*
> *Economize the failing river,*
> *Not the less revere the Giver,*

and so on. Isn't that in essence what the doctor told you, Jimmy? Only much more convincingly said, I think."

"Do repeat it again," Paul urged. "I've never come across it before. It's marvelous! Can't you say it all?"

Mrs. Catherby flashed her bright look at each of them. "How well you know how to flatter me! Just let me quote one of my favorites and I'm all set up for the evening. No, I don't remember it all, but you must read it for yourselves. It's called 'Terminus.' I've often recommended it to you, Jimmy. Just on the off chance," she laughed. "I know the last lines. I'll say them:

Lowly faithful, banish fear,
Right onward drive unharmed;
The port, well worth the cruise, is near,
And every wave is charmed."

"No," said Kirkland promptly, "that's not as good as the other. The first made sense. This sounds sentimental—just like a poet. That business of the port being worth the cruise, that's tommyrot. The cruise is the thing and we don't even know whether there'll *be* any port or not. No, your Emerson chap got off the track at the end."

"Of course we don't know about the port. Nobody does. But my feeling is that we live with miracles every day. Why doubt the final one? It just *could* happen to be the most reasonable of all when we get to it."

Paul leaned forward and set down his glass. "Do you know what I've often thought? If this *port* idea was something everybody dreaded instead of secretly tried to believe in, I've an idea a scientist or a psychologist would keep popping up every now and then with some sort of proof of it! The trouble is we're such a smarty, bull-headed race now we're afraid of a *happy* hope, aren't we? We're so scared of wishful thinking that we refuse sometimes to think at all. Well, anyway, the poem is wonderful, Gran, and I'm going to read it all for myself."

"Dinner is served, madam."

"How did we ever get on such a serious subject *before* dinner?" Mrs. Catherby asked laughing, as she led the way to the dining room. "We must make up by being extra frivolous later."

Before they left Kirkland threw a mild bombshell into the group. "I've decided to go to the capital for a couple of weeks. Leave tomorrow. There are a few little things I want to attend to there before election. A few little things," he repeated, looking fondly and meaningly at Paul.

"Jimmy, the glorified puppeteer," Anne said teasingly.

Paul's heart failed him.

"Leaving early?" He tried to sound casual.

"Yep. I want to get the eight-thirty train, so I'd better be saying goodnight now, Ellie. Wonderful evening as always. Fine dinner. Tell that cook of yours she improves with age. Well, you young folks staying on?"

Paul rose at once. "I don't want to tear you away, Anne, but I really should go too."

They made their affectionate farewells and were soon in their own car. Paul drove silently and Anne watched him with side glances.

"What's wrong?" she asked at last.

"You always know, don't you?"

"I should hope so. What is it?"

"I'm worried over something—I'll tell you later—but tonight I want to speak to your father."

"Oh . . . politics!" Anne said, drawing a long sigh. "Well, don't stay up too late the two of you. Or have too many nightcaps again," she added.

When Paul had seen her safely to her room he went to Kirkland's study and found the older man putting papers in a briefcase.

"I've got to talk to you, Jimmy," he said. "I wouldn't have chosen this hour but if you're leaving in the morning for two weeks I'm afraid it will have to be now."

Kirkland sat down and motioned Paul to a chair, eying him shrewdly.

"Go ahead," he said. "What's on your mind?"

Paul swallowed hard. All his premeditated approach left him. His heart was beating furiously.

"It's this," he blurted out. "I've discovered that you have a hookup with Camponelli."

He had expected Kirkland to show shock, shame, confusion. Instead he reached for a cigarette, lighted it and nodded calmly.

"I have dealings with him, of course."

"City or state?"

"Well, both, if it comes to that."

"And you take money from him? You've taken it for my own campaign?"

"Sure. And glad to get it. Now look here, Paul, just what are you driving at? I don't especially like being put on the witness stand like this. I know my own business and attend to it. Suppose you do the same."

"I tell you this *is* my business. When I accepted your offer I had no idea you were working hand-in-glove with the gangsters! I suppose Arno does the really dirty work for you while you sit back and take the money. The whole business is *rotten!* Can't you see that?"

"Now you just take it easy," Kirkland's voice was still calm but an ominous light was growing in his eyes. "You don't know how the whole setup works these days. I've got to play ball with Camponelli.

We've all got to take things as they are. We've got to be realistic."

"We do not," Paul cried. "Can't you see for yourself what you're doing! Here we've got a dreadful situation. By accepting it and playing along with it, you're making it worse. As for me, I can't be a party to filthy politics!"

Kirkland was calm no longer. His face was flushed and the veins thick on his forehead.

"Just what do you mean?"

"I mean what I said. I'm not going around making speeches to decent people on Camponelli's money! If I'm elected I give you fair warning I'm going to fight against this thing. I'm going to tell the people the truth from now on in the Senate or out of it. I'm going to stand on the side of clean government, and," his voice faltered, "if this means a break with you, then it will have to be."

Kirkland was on his feet now, and his breathing was heavy.

"Why, you young fool! You don't know what you're talking about. Without me, you'd be nowhere! You don't know this game any more than a baby. I've arranged everything! I got you nominated! If you behave yourself I'll get you elected! For God's sake, why don't you let me run things and keep your mouth shut?"

"Because I know too much about the whole setup now, and I can't go along with you if you stick to it. From now on—I'll have to go my own way."

They were both standing, Kirkland furious, Paul tense.

"You've taken everything from me," Kirkland shouted, "*everything!* You married my daughter, you live in my house, you eat my bread and now you turn against me! You'll block all we planned to do together. You're a damned, ungrateful . . ."

"At least I'm not a dirty crook!" Paul shouted back.

He thought at first Kirkland meant to strike him, but he wheeled suddenly, left the room and tore up the stairs faster than Paul could have done. A door slammed above.

Paul sank into a chair, his head in his hands. "What have I done! What have I done!" he groaned. "But what else *could* I have done?"

He sat for a long time, wondering how he could ever tell Anne. One thing was sure. In the morning, early, he would see Kirkland and apologize for his last words. He would retract nothing else but try to make amends for the harsh rudeness of his phrasing. After all, his indebtedness to the older man was indeed so great, he should have tempered his statements, he should have kept his self-control at any cost, he should not have angered him. Oh, the utter unpredictability of a quarrel! How inflammable words were to ignite each other until the blaze of them scorched and seared. This that had happened was catastrophic. Would there ever again be the same happy, easy-flowing days within this house? Would there ever again be an evening such as they had just had, the four of them, the two young people and the two older, fond and gay and *close?* He felt an intolerable weight of dread.

When he went upstairs at last he found to his relief that Anne was asleep. He undressed quickly and slipped into bed, lying tense and awake, his heart still pounding in his breast. A bitterness assailed him as he remembered Kirkland's last words. *He didn't have to throw up to me that I was eating his bread and living in his house,* he thought.

After an hour, however, he could feel nothing but distress at having caused the older man pain. His friend! Anne's father! He got out of bed cautiously and made his way to Kirkland's door. If he heard the slightest sound to indicate that the Chief, also, was restless and awake, he would go in and try at once to soften the memory of the blow though he could not recall it. But as he stood, holding his breath, in the still hallway, no sound came from within the room. He must, then, have dropped off. It would be wrong to wake him up to face disturbing thoughts again, if he had been able to sleep. He went back to his own room, and finally toward morning was wrapped himself in forgetfulness.

He awoke with a knocking at their room door, and the feeling that it must be Kirkland, stopping to say goodbye before he left the house. He was ashamed he had overslept and missed having breakfast with him. He opened the door quickly to find Hackett there, his face stricken.

"Mr. Paul," he said huskily, "I can't waken Mr. Kirkland. I'm afraid . . . I'm afraid . . ."

Paul brushed past him and entered his father-in-law's room. He lay as if in sleep, but one look, one touch was enough proof that the *port,* which they had all talked of so lightly, so conversationally the night before, had been reached, by him.

The great drawing room so seldom opened, was once again filled with white flowers and candlelight; but now there were no echoing voices as at the wedding, only the cold hush and the still, vast dignity of death. Within this quiet and utter detachment, Anne sat close to the one who for the first time in her life did not reach out eager

arms of love to her. In spite of all entreaties she would not leave
the place by day, and only under pressure, by night. Her grief was
stony, remote, absolute. After her first piteous cries to Paul when
the sudden and ghastly truth was broken to her, she withdrew into
her inner sorrowing as though by closing the door of her spirit to all
in the outside world, she could remain nearer to the one who had
passed beyond it.

Even at night when she and Paul were alone, her stricken reserve
did not change.

"I know—oh, my darling, I know what he has always meant to
you," Paul begged, "but don't put a wall between us now when I
long to help you, to share the sorrow with you. Can't you see I'm
suffering with you, especially since I. . . ."

"Don't," she said. "Don't remind me of that. I'm not putting up
the wall. It's just there. It's because no one of course can feel what
I do. I've got to get used to even the *thought* of life without him,
let alone the actuality of it. I knew he wasn't well, of course, but
I never once thought of a *serious* condition. I just wanted him to
feel like himself again. I can't accept this—I can't adjust—I can't believe it. Just let me alone, Paul. Please."

She did not, of course, know all, but she did know that Paul and
her father had had a sharp quarrel the night of his death. Through
her white lips she had uttered only one reproach. "I begged you,
Paul, never to hurt him." And from the depths of his own contrition
he had answered only, "I know, I know. I lost my head."

So there was no break in that silence of the soul which is more
still than lack of speech. Paul in his own pain and remorse had gone
to Mrs. Catherby. The shock had been very hard on her, physically,
and the doctor had forbidden her to leave her apartment; but her
spirit was strong and steady. She took one look at Paul's drawn face
and then put her arms about him as though he were a son.

"Poor boy," she said, "tell me everything. It will help you."

"But I'm afraid of doing you harm. I've done too much already."

"Dear Paul," she said quietly, "the human soul, by once suffering
as much as it is capable of, purchases a strange and terrible immunity
to all the rest of life's sorrows. This came to me when my daughter
died. Now it is not that I cannot know grief again. I do. At the moment I'm overwhelmed by it. But it is relative to a so much greater
one that it is endurable. It is bearable. You can't hurt me by telling
me the whole story of what happened that night."

So he told her, omitting nothing. Sometimes she asked a pertinent question, sometimes she said sadly, "I suspected this," or, "I was afraid . . ."

"So you see," Paul ended miserably, "there is no doubt that I really caused his death, and while I didn't tell Anne everything I think she feels this. Coupled with her frightful sorrow, it has made her withdraw from everything. Even our love," he added, half under his breath.

She sat, thinking. "I've been putting myself in your place," she said at last. "You can't help feeling this way now when your emotions are so shaken. But later on you will see it all in true perspective. The condition was there. The situation which you could not continue to ignore was not of your making. Poor Jimmy, *dear* Jimmy, for I truly loved him, was his own enemy. You must not blame yourself, Paul, and when a little time passes Anne won't either. Just now she is stunned, crushed. Jimmy was more than the ordinary father to her. He was mother too, and companion and friend. It was a beautiful relationship with all the best there was in Jimmy in it. Be patient with her, Paul. Be very gentle. She has had too much for a young heart to bear in a short space of time. Too much."

"I know," Paul said. "I realize that better than you might believe. She's been almost *too* brave up to this. I don't want her to break now. And I don't want her to shut me out."

"Just let her feel your love, but don't press it on her. A woman's heart and her body are very sensitively attuned to each other. Let her rest in her withdrawal for a little. She will come back to you."

"I will," Paul said, his face coloring a little, "and thank you for everything. I do feel better already and not so *lost* about Anne. When the funeral's over I want her to come here, alone, to see you. You'll do her good. Maybe you can even put in a word for me," he added, trying to smile.

She kissed him again when he got up to go.

"And your campaign?" she asked. "Will this change much in regard to it!"

"Time will tell," he said soberly. "The biggest change is in me. I've never thought of myself in the role of reformer before. I think I've just been a sort of selfishly ambitious person. But now, with all restraint lifted . . . There are some things I'd like to put my hand to."

"God bless you," she said.

And so once again the drawing room was empty, as was Kirkland's own room, as indeed was the whole house. Empty of the step of the master, and of the strong, virile, dominant personality which had filled it. It was strange, Paul mused each time he re-entered, that instead of feeling now more in possession, he felt more the stranger, more the interloper. Each time as he paused at the foot of the staircase watching its delicate curving, unsubstantial beauty, he was overcome by the feeling that he was in another man's home. Not his own. Ah, sadly not his own. And alimenting this sadness was Anne's continued attitude of estrangement, or at least of withdrawal. Once in the office when his thought was fixed upon the latter word he had aimlessly looked it up in the dictionary. The definition smote him: *the taking away of that which has been possessed.* The words kept returning to him with a significance the lexicographer had not intended.

But while he suffered for himself, his heart ached for Anne. He realized more each day what the relationship between her and her father had been. Small things taken for granted before stood out now in clear poignancy. The daily morning greetings for example.

"Hello, Mouchie. How are you?"

"Fine, Jimmy. Sit down a minute. You've got that green tie on again. It simply doesn't *go* with that suit."

"Okay! I'll change it. How about a red one?"

"I love a red tie on you. Are you having breakfast up here with us?"

"No, I guess I'll go down and look over the paper while I eat. Well, so long, Mouchie" (as he kissed her). "Be a good girl, now."

"Goodbye, Jimmy, dear. Don't forget the tie!"

Such *little* things but telling so much. All the tenderness of the years, all the familiar jokes and confidences, all the strong and fiercely devoted support to which she had been accustomed from childhood on, now swept away from her in a night. Her white face that even in a weeks' time looked thin struck him daily with anxiety. Against her loss he felt his own efforts to comfort her were impotent. Between them in the evenings words sounded forced and silences dragged heavily. Then at the end Paul would kiss her gently and go to his dressing room. Once wondering, hoping, he had said hesitantly, "Would you rather I stayed here, dear?"

But she had answered, "I think not yet," and the next week, too, had passed.

In the office Paul had turned to Hartwell. "There is no reason now why you should not tell me all you know."

"It was hard for me before, Paul. I'm fond of you, as you know, and I've grown very fond of Anne. And in a curious way that sur-

prised me, since I've been going out to the house I had come to like
Kirkland himself. So I kept quiet about many things. Now, for instance, this water resource problem that you've been letting yourself
go on in your speeches. You've been perfectly honest about that,
I'm sure."

"I certainly have."

"What you didn't see was Kirkland's angle to all that. If he could
have gotten that reservoir put through he would at once have bought
in land all around it cheap. There would be in that case water mains,
pumping stations, oh, a dozen related projects from which he would
draw his graft. In short, there would have been for him and his
minions what Dr. Johnson once called 'a potentiality of income beyond the dreams of avarice.'"

Paul groaned. "Is there no honesty, no integrity left for me to
stand on?"

"Yes," Hartwell said gravely. "Your own."

Brennen came to see Paul soon. He was all broken up. He had
been very close to Kirkland personally, but in addition he, like many
others, had felt his fortunes were linked with those of the Boss. Now
the king was dead and who was to succeed him? He presented all
this to Paul one day at lunch, asking him if he would join a small
group of leaders the next week to talk things over.

"I've been down to see the Governor already. He's pretty cut up.
Of course Jimmy put him where he is and would have kept him
there likely for another term at least. But every party man at the
capital is upset. The boys did anything Jimmy asked them, for he
did everything for them. He's the one they'd go to if they wanted a
place on a committee. Jimmy would give the word and it was done.
If a man wanted a higher post, say the speakership of the House,
he'd go to Jimmy. So you see when Jimmy backed a bill, by golly
they passed it. Why, once I remember when he needed more time
to sort of plot out some new strategy on a bill, darned if they didn't
recess a session for him!"

Brennen's face was a mixture of admiration and real grief.

" 'I have the votes,' Jimmy always said, 'and I elect my man.' "

Paul's own countenance was set. "Tell me more," he said. "This is
new to me."

"Is it really? Well, I guess there's a lot you can learn from him.
Nothing ever seemed to stump him. I mind one time there was a big
fight on and it looked as though we hadn't a chance. Jimmy suddenly
got one of his lobbyists to hand out fifty-dollar bills in the men's

washroom! Turned the trick all right. Yes, sir, he always had the answers."

"And I suppose the money came from Camponelli and his ilk?"

"Oh, could be. C wields a pretty big stick now. You have to play along with him but the dough's useful. Jimmy knew how to handle him. That's one big problem now. We've got to have someone else who can manage that end of things. Touchy business involved, you know."

"What about Arno?"

"Oh, well, he did the contacts for Jimmy but he has his limitations as far as our present need is concerned. We'll probably still use him though. He's smart and then he knows too much. Well, could you join us to sort of plan out your next weeks' schedule? Say, this coming Tuesday?"

"I'm afraid not."

"Well, we could make it Wednesday. I'll get in touch with the others at once."

"I'm sorry, but I couldn't join you Wednesday either."

Something in the tone made Brennen eye him keenly.

"Look here," he said, "are you trying to say you won't meet with us at all?"

"I guess that's it."

Brennen looked more puzzled than angered. "But I don't get it!" he said. "What's wrong? You're in this campaign up to your neck. We're all pulling for you. Now that the Chief's gone you've got to depend on the rest of us for a lot of things. These men I'm getting together know all the ropes. They'll steer you straight. We all feel you're a *comer*. We want to back you, but you've got to play ball with us, naturally. What do you say?"

"I'm sorry," Paul said slowly, "and I'm certainly not lacking in appreciation of all you've done for me. But I've got to think things out, for myself. I'm not going to follow in Kirkland's footsteps. In general policy, I mean."

Brennen's face was not only anxious but angered now as well.

"I don't get this at all. Here, we've been counting on you. Half a dozen men have said to me since Jimmy's death, 'Well, thank God we've got young Devereux. He'll bolster up the party in the state. He's going far.' That's what they all said. And now you lay down on us. You practically *quit* us. What in heaven's name do you propose to do?"

"That's it," Paul said quietly. "I'm not sure myself. But I'm afraid it won't be what you expect of me."

Brennen made an obvious effort to control his temper. He parted from Paul as from a wayward and misguided youth who was going through a troublesome period but would yet be brought to reason.

"After all," he said in parting, "no one's asking you to step into *Jimmy's* shoes. Nobody can fill them. Just keep on as you've been doing. Forget the meeting next week. After all you've been pretty hard hit—your father-in-law. That will make it easier to explain to the rest if you aren't there. Just take it easy for the present. Forget a lot of what I said if you didn't like it. Maybe I shot off my mouth too much. Well, I'll be seeing you soon again."

There was great relief to Paul now in talking everything over with Hartwell. From this point on he need hide nothing, and the reactions and advice of the old man helped his own inchoate thoughts to take form. For there was still a disturbing ambivalence about them. While on the one hand he felt a revulsion to the whole machine as Kirkland had manipulated it, on the other he felt a new and even stronger pull toward the political scene itself.

One day Hartwell asked him about Kirkland's will.

"Briggs was his lawyer, as of course you know."

"Yes."

"You've heard the will?"

"No, I haven't."

"Well, I think you should. Hasn't Anne been apprised of the contents?"

Paul hesitated. "She hasn't told me. You see—she's still so utterly crushed. But of course she must have heard it—or seen it by now."

Hartwell shot a keen glance at him.

"I should think she would need you very much in an advisory way. She has doubtless become now a very rich girl. If I were you, I'd go up and talk to Briggs. He's in this building, you know, sixth floor. Old friend of Kirkland's. I'd certainly talk to him about it. A will is no secret, and it may be easier for Anne if you know about it without her having to tell you."

"That may be so. I'll try to see him today."

He went up to the lawyer's office in the late afternoon. They had met before so there was now between them a degree of familiarity. Before Paul could get past the first amenities, Mr. Briggs had opened up the subject himself.

"I'm glad you dropped in," he said. "I've really been meaning to ask you to. When I went in my capacity of lawyer to see your wife I found her not only very sad but in what seemed to me an almost indifferent state toward the will itself. That was why I wished either to read it to you or tell you its contents."

Paul nodded.

"It is, I think, the shortest and simplest will I ever drew up. It states in the fewest words that after all his just debts are paid, his entire estate goes to his only child, Anne. That is all. No other bequests of any kind. He explained to me when he made the will ten years ago that he expected to make all gifts to charities or to friends, to some distant cousins, I believe, and to his secretaries, in his lifetime. I'm quite sure he did so, being a man of unfailing execution. As I suppose you must know, this leaves your wife a very rich young woman. It might be well for you to talk this over with her, and prepare her a little for the business responsibilities she will have to assume, or that you will assume together."

He paused and then went on: "I am the executor. Jimmy and I were friends since we were young men. I shall miss him greatly. As we set about administering the estate I shall be very grateful if you will work with me. There is the coal business. Will you want to hold on to it or sell it? It will not be so easy just now to market it well, and yet I fancy Bovard would give a fair price. Maybe you'll want to keep it and let this Arno man run it. I understand he's capable. Jimmy was very fond of him, proud of him, you might say, since he had made him what he is. As a matter of fact the only request he left in addition to the will itself was that a letter addressed to Arno be delivered by my own hand two weeks after his funeral. That," he added, glancing at the calendar, "will be tomorrow. I've no idea, of course, what it contains."

"No," Paul agreed vaguely, but with immediate uneasiness. "The thing is," he went on, "Arno and I aren't on very good terms. He just doesn't like me, to state the fact. Anne thinks he may have been a bit jealous when I came into the family. He has always, as you say, been very close to Jimmy and no doubt was proud of it. When I came along—well, you can see how it might have seemed to him. So I don't go to the office much. Haven't been since Jimmy died. I will go, though, of course, and discuss matters with him as soon as it is necessary. Meanwhile, thank you very much for this talk. I'll try to prepare Anne a little as you suggest, and needless to say I'll always be standing by—for anything. There's no immediate hurry about settlement?"

"Oh, no. We can let it ride a little."

"Good. I'm at your service in any way, and thanks again."

When he reached the house that evening Hackett greeted him with a faint attempt at a smile, "She's in the library, Mr. Paul."

Paul felt his heart thudding in his breast, for Anne had kept to the seclusion of the second floor night and day since the funeral. He hurried back along the wide hall, and paused for a moment in the library doorway as he had done that first evening he had met her. She was sitting on a sofa facing him, only now she looked up at once. She was wearing yellow, his favorite color, and her white face lightened as he came near her. He sank down beside her and kissed her gently, holding himself in check.

"Darling," he said, "is it—are you feeling better?"

She relaxed against him and as he drew her closer, he felt again the sweetness of her yielding body.

"A little," she said. "Most of all I suddenly felt how selfish I was being to you. But thank you, oh, thank you for being so understanding. It's just as though I had been very, very sick and was still weak and *bruised*, but able to sit up for the first time. *That* kind of feeling. As though"—she smiled a little—"this is mixing up the metaphors badly, but it's as if I'd been away in a far, desolate country and now at last had my face turned toward home. A little like that."

"Thank God," he said.

"I've a long way to go and I'll have many bad relapses, I suppose."

"Time will . . ."

"Oh, don't say that," she said drawing away from him. "I've heard nothing but that in all the would-be consoling notes that have poured in. 'Time will heal.' 'Time will bring its own comfort.' 'Time will help.' I hate the word. It's as though time was going to steal Jimmy from me completely. I can't bear it!"

"You have it all wrong, dear," Paul said quietly. "Time doesn't alter our love. It only makes the sorrow bearable. It gradually pushes down the bitterness of the grief and allows the happy memories to come to the surface. It's a blessed thing, really, time."

She leaned slowly back again against him. "Go on, Paul, talk to me some more. It helps. Please go on."

He talked on, smoothing her hair with tender fingers. At his suggestion they had dinner there, and then sat, still talking of many things, most of them unrelated to the past two weeks. At her request he read to her, old favorites and newer, among the poems they loved.

It was late when they went upstairs. They spent some time in the nursery, the little young growing life breathing to them of the hope and the sure gladness of the future; then at last when their own room was enfolded in darkness, they lay once more in each other's arms.

II

⊷§ The days since the news of Kirkland's death had been strange ones in the inner offices of the Company. While Sayles herself still looked sober and bewildered, it was Arno who was, of course, the more affected. There had been between the two men a bond stronger than that of patron and protégé or employee and employer; there had been a sort of rough affection, and understanding possible only between two natures essentially alike. The shock to Arno had been devastating. His world, so long now established and secure, had been rocked beneath him. His sense of personal loss was irremediably deep. He went about the management of Kirkland's affairs with efficiency and dispatch as usual but his throat still felt tight with an emotion he had never known before.

He and Sayles had both gone to the service in the big drawing room, for once together, according to Sayles's futile dream. Arno had strained his eyes to catch a glimpse of Anne's face through the opened door to a room beyond; but all he could see was her arm and Paul's face bending protectingly toward her. The sight of this had added the final bitterness to Arno's heart. In the cab which had borne them back to the office he and Sayles rode without speaking, since his set lips had warned her to keep silence. She broke it but once.

"Arno," she said, "did he . . . I mean did you get, did he ever give you something before? You know, stock or money or something?"

Arno nodded.

She sighed. "He did to me, too. And he helped me invest it. I'm sort of glad he did it like that. We don't have to wait and wonder now whether he remembered us in his will. Don't you think it's better this way?"

Arno did not reply, only kept staring out the window. But he agreed with Sayles. Maybe the Chief hadn't wanted them to have anything afterward to make them glad for his death. Even a little bit glad. Not that he would have been, but the Chief might have thought. . . . This way was better. No fancies running through your head, in spite of you, about a bequest.

So on the Thursday morning two weeks after the funeral he was the more surprised at a visit from Mr. Briggs, the lawyer. The latter did not leave him to wonder long.

"Mr. Mallotte, I believe?"

"Yes, sir."

"Attached to Mr. Kirkland's will was this sealed envelope addressed to you and the instructions to me to deliver it to you in person at the time specified. I hereby give it into your hand."

He passed him the letter. Arno looked at it dully. "Th . . . thanks," he stammered. "Will you sit down?"

"No, I must be going. I know this has all been a great shock to you as to all of us. He depended greatly on you. Well, I'll be in later of course when some decisions will have to be made in regard to the coal company. I am, as you may know, the executor."

"Yes," said Arno thickly.

"So, I'll say goodbye for the present."

When he was gone, Arno sat down at Kirkland's great desk. He had been working here for the last week, partly to keep from under Sayles's prying eyes and partly because being here seemed to bring the Chief closer. He looked at the letter, turning it slowly in his hands. It was so tangible, so objective, yet his name written strongly across it in the Chief's hand sent a small shiver up his spine. It was like wishing for a dead man's return and yet wanting still more to run from any evidence of it.

At last he carefully slit the envelope and drew out the single sheet it contained.

Dear Arno: (he read)

It seems pretty queer to be writing what will seem to you a posthumous note, if you ever get it. And yet we have to take account of what comes to all. As you know I am the only one who has the combination to my office safe. I will write it down here. If I get blown away at any time I want you to open the safe and go through the papers. Take out those you know I wouldn't want to have fall into anyone else's hands. You'll know the ones I mean. Destroy them at once, then give Briggs the combination and let him go at it. He's executor. Thanks, Arno, and good luck.

The familiar initials ended it. Below was printed carefully the combination.

Arno sat very still, reading over and over the short missive. The date was seven years ago. Anne would have been only sixteen then. That was the year he had first seen her, when she came into the office, her cheeks all flushed, and her gold hair curling on her shoulders.

"Is Mr. Kirkland here? I'm his daughter, Anne."

That was what she had said and he had heard the words in his mind night and day a thousand times since, and seen her smile. . . . How could he look at any other girl after that? And after the winter night when she had come running down the stairs at home in the red dress, her eyes like Christmas stars? Only three times he had seen her through the years. And yet, there it was. He loved her. And he alone knew how fierce and relentless that love was. A man who had never known the night would not feel so keenly the brightness of the sun. So with him, all the dark experiences of his youth in Water Street only made him more desperately, more cravingly aware of the beauty his man's heart had encountered. And because tenacity was a law of his nature, he could not relinquish it; he could not forget. Even in the utter hopelessness of the present, he could think of no other woman with the idea of love. Those he had, he had without seeing them, of necessity as with food or sleep. So now as he held the note, the date of which aroused the first memory of her, he felt the abyss of the lost closing in upon him anew.

He glanced at the safe. He should attend to the papers soon. He knew well enough the ones Kirkland meant. There was a faint swell of pride in his heart that he, Arno, was the closest after all to the Chief. Not Devereux, nor any other. He was the one who knew all his secrets, who now controlled their preservation. He decided to wait tonight after Sayles had gone and see to the matter. He put the note in his inside pocket.

"Aren't you leaving now?" Sayles said at five o'clock.

"No, I'm working on for a while."

"Anything I can do to help? I don't mind waiting," she added eagerly.

"No, not a thing. Go ahead."

Sayles slowly put on her coat and hat. With each new crisis, her heart stirred, waited, hoped.

"Well, see you in the morning."

"Right," said Arno, without looking up.

When he was alone he set the catch on the doors of Kirkland's office, drew out the note and went toward the safe. Slowly he read the directions, putting them into operation as he did so. The first time something went wrong, but the next was successful. The great door swung open and Arno began upon his task. It was not too difficult, for the papers were well sorted. Contracts and all business documents in one section; in the other, the ones that would be better destroyed. Arno read these latter over carefully, sometimes giving a low whistle. What meat these would make for the newspapers if the press ever got hold of them! What heads would fall, or at least be bowed pretty low. For many of them represented *deals* in the political world over which Kirkland reigned, the signatures on the papers being part of the price set. Even Arno was surprised at the careful wording in black and white. This was like the Chief, though, to leave no merely verbal streamers to blow away in the wind. Here he had it all, pinned down, solid.

There were other papers, more incriminating to Kirkland himself. These were notations of money received from questionable connections. These represented the "other sources of income" on the tax report. Arno whistled again. He and the Chief hadn't known *everything* about each other, that was for sure. He was a shrewd one all right. Or had been.

At seven o'clock Arno had completed his task. He took the papers one by one and burned them over the Chief's giant ash tray, then went back to close the safe. There was nothing in it of any nature which he had not gone over with scrupulous care, no shelf, rack or pigeonhole the contents of which he had not examined. Except . . . His eye was caught by something which looked like a tiny secret drawer at the top and back of the safe. Funny! He hadn't noticed it before. Looked as though it might be meant for jewels. He fingered it curiously until it opened. A small sheet of writing paper lay within. Arno took it out and read it quickly.

> To Paul Devereux: If after a period of three years the plan decided upon between us has produced no change in physical conditions, you are free of all obligation to me to continue in that status if you desire to be released therefrom.
>
> JAMES KIRKLAND

The word *copy* was scrawled in one corner.

Arno moved back to the desk and sank into the chair, his eyes glued to the paper in his hand. He read it again and then again; then sat holding it while all the blood in his body seemed to rise and pound in his temples. The meaning of the words, at first dislocated and uncertain, gradually clarified, phrase by phrase until the full import struck him as though with a physical blow.

"So it *was* a deal! I knew it. The dirty, scheming rat!"

It seemed natural to speak his thoughts aloud, so articulate were they as they crossed his shrewd and perceptive mind.

"I see it all like a book. The Chief thought she'd never marry the way she was. He wanted to give her a chance—kids and everything. He made the deal. He'd put Devereux where he wanted to be in politics if he'd give Anne the break. If she still couldn't walk after three years and he got fed up, the Chief wouldn't hold him to it. What a deal! What a bloody, lousy deal!"

He sat on for a few minutes, considering it as he fingered the paper. Suddenly a change came over him, as violent as from an electric shock. He held the sheet up before him, his black eyes staring at it as though it were a sentient thing.

"Ah!" he breathed. And again, "Ah!" almost in a whisper.

For in the moment the thought had come to him that here was an instrument fitted to his hand. Here, given him like a miracle was the means to his own triumph, to the fulfillment of his own desire. There wasn't a doubt of it! Out of the blackness and despair of the abyss in which he had been sunk, light broke like the blazing sun. Once again he was strong, completely sure of himself, invincible. He rose from the chair like a giant refreshed. Very slowly, and smiling, he put the paper in his inside pocket; then a shade unsteady as though intoxicated, he closed the safe, put out the lights, locked the doors and went out.

Down in the street he hailed a cab with the Chief's own commanding gesture. Once or twice as he rode he smoothed his coat above where the paper rested. He got out at a recherché restaurant where he had never eaten before. He had plenty of money with him. One of the first things he had learned from Kirkland was that a gentleman always carries enough money to meet any emergency. He went in with a faint swagger, eyed the check girl boldly, spoke with authority to the headwaiter and was seated at once. He ordered an elaborate dinner, and a bottle of champagne—not that he liked the latter particularly but that he knew it was the wine of celebration.

He ate slowly, savoring the viands and his emotions at the same time, and always with the faint smile still on his face. This paper would fix Devereux. Couldn't be otherwise. Put him right out on his ear. He'd been a phony from the start, just as he, Arno, had always

thought. Once he held his glass poised during a moment of inde-
cision. Would he take orchids with him again? No, he concluded, not
this time. There would be plenty of chances for them later. This
wasn't just a social call; this was more than that. His chest swelled
as he thought how much more.

When he got back to his room he smoked endless cigarettes, his
head dizzily going over and over again the past, the miracle this
day had brought, and the dazzling prospects of the future. He fell
into an uneasy sleep as the clock showed two. The next morning,
once more he dressed with the slow meticulousness of a ritual. At
last he could find nothing more to do, nothing else to change, and
set out for the office. Sayles noted his appearance with wide eyes.

"Going out today?" she ventured.

"Errand," he said laconically.

As soon as he thought Anne would be up he dialed the house number from the Chief's own phone with unsteady fingers.

Hackett answered.

"I'd like to speak to Miss Anne, please. I mean Mrs. Devereux,"
he corrected though the words stuck in his throat. "This is Arno
Mallotte from the office."

In a few seconds Anne's voice came.

"Yes, Arno. How are you?"

"Well, I'm fine. I . . . how are you? I mean . . . well, I know how
these last weeks have been for you."

"Thank you, Arno. I should have called you before to tell you how
I appreciated the fact that you're carrying on at the office. Later, of
course, we'll have things to talk over, I suppose."

"Yes. Miss Anne, I'd like to see you today alone, if I could. It's
important."

"Today? Would this afternoon at three suit you?"

"I'll be there at three. You'll be alone?"

"Yes, I'll be alone and in the library. I'll ask Hackett to show you
right in."

"Thanks, Miss Anne."

"Thank *you*, Arno. I hope it's something I'll understand."

"I think you will," said Arno, in an odd voice. "Goodbye."

He arrived on the second of three, having had the cab drive him
around the block until the hour, though the delay to him was
desperate. This time as he entered Hackett was distinctly respectful
for he realized now that Arno was running the business singlehanded,
for an interval at least. With his best air he ushered him into the

library, and then, in accordance with Anne's instructions, closed the door behind him.

Arno stood, his pulse throbbing, his eyes fixed on Anne, who sat watching him with a pathetic attempt at a smiling welcome.

"Do come in, Arno, and sit down. I'm so glad you have brought me a problem—as I suppose you have. Maybe something new to think about will do me good. Is everything going all right at the office?"

Arno made a slight gesture as though disposing at once of that routine.

"Fine," he said. "I mean I've learned to know the coal business pretty well through the years. As a matter of fact the Chief used to say I was his right hand in everything—politics too."

"I know, Arno. I know how much you meant to him and how much help you were to him. I do appreciate that."

Her voice was earnest, almost tender, and the cadence of it stirred depths in Arno's heart. It also made his approach more difficult. He wet his lips carefully.

"What I've come to see you about is not connected with the business. It's—well—it's pretty personal, you might say."

"Personal?" A wariness, a reserve, was in Anne's voice now. And at the sound Arno's resolution returned to him. There was no use beating round the bush.

"Miss Anne," he said, "—somehow I can't call you anything else— I've thought from the very first that Paul Devereux was after something when he married you. Money, or a boost in his political career, *you* know. I thought there was some kind of deal between him and the Chief! Your father would want you to get married like any other girl and as things were with you, there wasn't much chance so he . . ."

"Stop!" Anne cried. "How *dare* you say such things to me! I'll have Hackett show you out, and please don't ever come to this house again . . ."

"Just a minute!" Arno was on his feet now, standing in front of her. His black eyes were blazing. "Just a minute. There's more to this. I've told you what I always thought inside me, but I couldn't say anything. Now, I've got *the proof*. Right here." He drew the paper slowly from his inner pocket as Anne's eyes, wide with amazement and horror, watched him.

"In black and white," Arno went on. "In your father's own hand. He left me the combination of his safe. *Me!* I was the one he trusted to go through it and get rid of some papers he didn't want anyone

else to see. I found a secret drawer with this in it. Read it for yourself
if you don't believe me it was a deal. *Read it!*"

He thrust it into her hand and, breathing hard, watched as her
eyes followed the words. When her hand fell a little he bent over
her.

"Anne," he said thickly, "now you know Devereux has lied to you.
He never loved you. But I do, Anne! I've loved you since the first
day I saw you. As soon as you're free, I'll marry you and *I'll* not run
out on you in three years or in thirty whether you can walk or not. I
can manage the business for us both. I'll take care of you. I tell you
I love you!"

Interpreting her stony stillness as acquiescence he stooped, put
his arms fiercely around her and pressed his hot lips to hers with
all the starved passion of the years. Stunned at first into helplessness
she submitted, then moaning as if in pain she began to struggle, trying to push him from her. But Arno did not cease from the kisses he
had dreamed of for so long. With desperation then and a strength
born of extremity she fought him off with violence.

"Stop! Stop! Go away from me! I hate you! I *loathe* you!" The
words burst from her between his caresses.

At last, dazed and shaken she realized that she was free, that he
was no longer holding her. Instead, she saw him, his face white, his
eyes terrified, backing away from her as from a ghost. "My God! My
God!" he kept muttering as he turned, stumbled against the door,
clutched at it, opened it and left precipitately.

It was only then she realized that she was standing. A little distance from her chair.

Hackett found her as he came back anxiously to the library after
Arno's strange departure. She was lying on the floor, unconscious,
a paper near her hand. He lifted her to the sofa, rang for Davy and in
a few seconds her eyes opened upon their frightened faces.

"I knew he was up to no good. *Scum,* that's what he is!" Hackett
was saying. "Scaring her out of her wits about something. I never
should have shut that door on them. Then I'd have heard."

Davy's face was grave indeed.

"What happened, Anne? Can you tell me?"

"Just a sort of shock," Anne said faintly. "Can you get me up to
bed? I'll rest a little and be all right."

"Shall I ring up Mr. Paul?" Hackett asked eagerly.

"No." Anne's voice was weak but commanding. "I'll see him when he comes home. Don't call him."

Once in bed, revived with a stimulant, and with Davy temporarily satisfied, Anne lay alone, her eyes closed. It was as though the few minutes of unconsciousness had lifted the clouds from her brain, although nothing could lift the new weight from her heart. She lay thinking with anguished clearness of all that had happened. She had gotten upon her feet and walked. Only a few steps but still *she had walked.* That accounted for the blanched stare of Arno's face. He had seen what seemed to him a miracle, and was terrified of it. With a slow volition she allowed this knowledge to pass through and through her mind as waves might cover and recover an object on the sands. She had walked. The incredible, the prodigious, the inconceivable had happened. When she had deadened her heart to all hope, when her father had died despairing of it, the miracle had taken place. But it had been born not of physical travail as the others had watched for; this had had its cause and impulsion in an agony of shock still greater. She lay wondering whether to test the continuing validity of that which had occurred. At last, trembling all over, she tried to move one foot. It responded. Slowly she drew it back until the knee flexed. Then the other. Weak and shaken from the suspense and the realization, she rested again, still. It was true. Not only for a sudden moment of volcanic emotion, but now, as she lay alone and quiet, the paralysis was gone. The block, whatever it had been, was removed. She was free of her prison. She could walk, she could run, she could . . .

But oh, the poison in the cup which otherwise would have been filled with overwhelming, unutterable joy! She had pushed this aside for a little time until she had actually apprehended the truth and wonder of her cure; now, as one forced down again into darkness, she must consider this that had brought it about.

She drew herself up against the pillow and opened the paper which she had told Davy to give back to her when it had dropped from her hand. She read it again, the words searing eyes and heart together. Slowly, calculatingly, she forced herself to weigh the phrases, setting each apart from the other:

> *If after a period of three years*
> *the plan decided upon between us*
> *has produced no change in physical conditions,*
> *you are free of all obligation to me*

to continue in that status
if you desire to be released therefrom.

Starkly, unequivocally, the truth lay bare before her. The very clarity with which she saw it, seemed to make it more damningly unassailable. With Dr. Hertzog's story in mind, Jimmy had decided she must marry, must bear a child. He had offered Paul, the young political aspirant, the bribe of the Boss's help. He had made the deal, but left a way out for Paul *if after three years . . .*

It was so like Jimmy, so completely like him to do this that the wonder was she had never suspected before. But Paul! The darkness engulfed her as she thought of him. The past events flowed over her like drowning waters. The first night he had come to dinner, his insistence upon coming soon again, his talk with Jimmy in the study before he left! Oh, how the facts fit together! The steady pressure of his attentions upon her from the very start. His skill as an actor. *I think you could make me believe you loved me even if you didn't.* She recalled her words spoken once half in jest.

She thought of the night he had forced his way to her to brush all her scruples aside and ask her to marry him. She thought of her happiness then beyond believing, of her calling her father in all innocence as Paul listened close beside her, while she *surprised* Jimmy with her news. . . .

A slow scarlet of shame and of mortally wounded pride rose slowly until her pale cheeks burned with it. She, herself, her own body, had been bargained for. Sold in the market place when *the deal* was made. Her anger did not reach to the dead. She knew too well the relentless devotion of Jimmy's heart; but it reached to Paul. It reached to him and consumed him in bitterness. Whatever his feeling for her now, he had been guilty of deceiving her for his own selfish ends at the beginning. Of taking her love, so freely given in joy, for a *price.* And this she could never forgive. Her eyes fixed again on the word *copy* at the bottom of the paper.

In the lower hall Hackett was talking to Davy in suppressed excitement.

"And you see at the moment when I found her lying there, I never thought of it. But just now it come to me. She wasn't close to her chair. She was out a bit in the room. How did she get there? Had the fellow lifted her up mebbe? But he'd hardly let her fall, now would he? And his face as he rushed out was queerlike, to say the least. As if he'd seen something that scared him. So I just couldn't help but wonder . . ."

"What on earth are you driving at, Hackett?"

"Well, you know it leaked out that when the baby came this big doctor thought she just might get up on her feet when she was in pain, the shock you know might drive her. Well, it didn't then, but you see now . . . 'Just a sort of shock,' she said. So you see . . . and her being a little distance across the room and all . . . I couldn't help wondering . . ."

His voice broke with the stress of the thought. Davy stood silent.

"How far from her chair?" she asked at last.

"Come and I'll show you."

He marked off the space while Davy watched intently.

"It is strange, Hackett, but don't let's get excited yet. If anything really . . . happened, we'll soon know. Don't mention this to anyone else in the house."

When Paul came home that afternoon he was tired. He had come to a decision as to his course in the concluding weeks of his campaign. He was going to talk simply and truthfully about his own new desire to render honest service to his state and to do all he could to wreck intrenched evil, wherever it was found. The whole argument was working itself out in his mind. In addition to his weariness he felt irritated. One of their own witnesses on the damage case had been taken very ill. Hartwell had agreed that there would have to be a postponement. When Paul had called Sheffkin to tell him, the latter had been maddeningly complacent.

"Well, now this is better, Devereux. I sort of thought you'd see things differently when you thought it over."

"Listen, Sheffkin, get this straight. Our key witness is *sick*. Suddenly. The doctor says he won't be ready to appear on the fifteenth. That's the reason and the *only* reason we're agreeing to the postponement. I won't oppose it now and if you draw an order I'll give my consent."

Sheffkin's voice was honey and oil. "Why sure, sure! Of course, *I* understand. Well, thanks, Devereux. Thank you very much."

"Don't thank me," Paul had snapped. "I've told you the truth. Though you may not understand what that is. Goodbye."

"Sure! Sure! *I* understand. Goodbye, Devereux."

Paul felt he could cheerfully have throttled him. As he climbed the stairs a bit heavily that afternoon he tried to throw off his burdens and think only of the fact that the barrier between him and Anne had been immeasurably lifted. He knew by certain things she had said that her heart was still sore, not only from the sorrow but from the part he himself had played in Kirkland's death. She had spoken of this more freely last night than at any other time. He couldn't blame her for this particular distress. It was harrowing enough to him as he remembered; what must it be to her? Here again Time, the great mediator, would work, he hoped, on his side.

He hurried to the sitting room, where Anne usually awaited him. She was not there. He went toward the bedroom uneasily, opened the door and at once cried out.

"Anne, darling! Is anything wrong? Are you sick?"

He bent quickly over her and then realized with a pang that she was unresponsive to his kiss. Did she regret last night's reconciliation, he wondered? Had it been too soon after all? Gran had warned him. He should have been more patient.

"Anne," he repeated. "Are you all right?"

"Sit down," she said. "We have something that must be discussed between us."

He sank down in a chair close to the bed, his whole body taut with suspense.

"What is it?" he asked anxiously.

"Today I had a caller."

"Yes? Who was it?"

"Arno."

"What the devil did he want?" Paul said sharply.

"He had been going through the office safe. Jimmy left him the combination. He found this paper and brought it to me." She handed it to him.

Paul took one glance and then colored to the very roots of his hair. To Anne this seemed the final evidence of his guilt.

"You've seen it before of course."

"Anne!" he burst out. "This is *horrible!* I could kill that snake with my own hands for bringing this to you. Let me tell you . . ."

"I think I understand," she interrupted. "Do you have the original of this?"

"I do not." He fairly shouted the words. "I destroyed it at once."

"I can see how you would. But you did have it?"

"Anne," he begged, "listen to me! I'll tell you just how it all was. Your father practically forced the paper on me. I only took it to please him, and burned it as soon as I got back to my room. It meant *nothing* to me. It was all your father's idea. Oh, Anne, let me tell you how the whole thing happened!"

"I would like to hear it. From you." It was the quiet of her voice that was so deadly.

"Your father made me a proposition. If I would try to get you to marry me he would back me to the hilt in politics. I refused flatly. He seemed sunk. He begged me to come just once to dinner to meet you. I agreed. I came. The rest you know."

"Not quite," she said, still in the same voice. "After that first night at dinner, you went to the study to talk to Jimmy before you left. You remember? Just what did you tell him?"

Paul's look of embarrassment did not escape her.

"I told him I would . . . try to win you."

"You can hardly pretend that you loved me then."

"But I think I did. It's happened before. Plenty of men love at first sight. Oh Anne, can't you let this thing rest? It was your father's desperate desire to help you that brought it all about. What does it matter how we met? The point is we *did* meet. We fell in love. We are married. Can't you forget everything else? Surely you don't doubt my love *now!* Can't you believe that I wasn't really a party to the . . . agreement?"

"It is a little hard for me to believe that, considering this paper. And I have my pride."

He looked at her in a sort of anguished amazement as though he could not have heard her aright. Then the deadly coldness settled upon him also.

"What more can I say? I've told you the truth. If after all our months together, you still doubt me, I'm afraid I can't give you further proof. What do you want me to do?" he added almost under his breath.

She had spoken little up to this. Now, looking straight ahead she began, slowly, using Mrs. Catherby's very words at first.

"I've had too much, Paul. More than I can bear. Now this comes and shakes the foundations under me. It seems as though my pride, all my woman's dignity, all my faith has been dragged in the dust. I've got to have time to think it all through. I've got to be alone. I'm too *hurt* just now to keep seeing you every day. I . . . I would rather not."

"You mean you would like me to leave the house? To go away?"

"If you would. For a while."

He stood for a moment as though stunned, then turned and went into his dressing room. She could hear him moving about. In a short time he came back, a bag in his hand.

"I hope I won't need more than this," he said with a wry smile.

He went into the nursery and was gone what seemed a long time. Then he came out and stood looking down at her.

"I know you've had heavy blows, darling. Terrific ones. No one knows as well as I do what your courage has been. I think I can understand how this last one hit you. But Anne, you'll see it differently a little later. You'll get a new perspective. And you must forgive Jimmy for the original plan. It was his great love that prompted it."

"I have forgiven him," she said in a small voice.

"Then surely, *surely* you can forgive me!"

"That is entirely different. You must see that it is. Where will you go now?" she added.

"I can get a room at Mrs. MacLeod's again, I suppose. I'll let you know. I would give my right arm to save you from all this, Anne, but you must try to believe me. I love you. Isn't that enough?"

He stooped to kiss her but she raised her hand as though to hold him back. Her voice sounded choked.

"Paul," she said, "I haven't told you all. When Arno gave me the paper he evidently thought as soon as I read it, I would take steps to divorce you. So he told me he . . . loved me, would marry me as soon as I was free, and before I knew what he was going to do he had put his arms round me and was kissing me. It was . . . *horrible!* I didn't know what I was doing. I struggled and used all my strength and pushed him away . . . I was frantic . . ."

Paul's steady cursing interrupted her. She had never heard him really swear before and recoiled a little from it. "I'll knock his brains out," he was gritting through his teeth. "I'll beat him to a pulp! I'll . . . why didn't you tell me this at once? I'll find him tonight . . . I'll . . ."

"Listen, Paul. That's past. He will never bother me again. But that isn't all. Suddenly he fairly ran from me and I found then I was . . . was standing. On my feet. In the middle of the room."

He stared at her as though hypnotized and then his shout of exultation rang to the ceiling.

"Anne! It's happened! You walked! Oh God, I'm so happy! Oh, my darling! I can't believe it! Just the way we thought it *might* come! Now it *has* come! You're cured! Tell me again. How did you feel? Does Davy know? Have you walked up here? Oh, darling, get up now. Let me help you! Let me see you . . ."

She stopped his wild, incoherent joy.

"It's true. But somehow I can't grasp it yet. All I can think of is that Jimmy isn't here to know. And that I can't even talk about the wonder of it with you . . . the way I feel now."

He stepped back as though he had been struck.

"You mean you can't share this, *this* with me? Your husband?"

"Not just now." Her words were very low. "I'm too wretched. Too confused."

He stood for a long moment looking down at her as though at the end of love itself.

"I'll come whenever you send for me," he said, and went out without another word.

He talked with Davy in her own sitting room, giving brief, almost sharp instructions. Then as though to counteract the tone, he wrung her hand in a painful grip and went down the stairs. Hackett let him out, puzzled and concerned.

"You're not going away, Mr. Paul?"

"Just for a little while, Hackett. I'm counting on you and Davy to take care of my family."

"We'll do that, Mr. Paul. We'll miss you. Is . . . is Miss Anne all right now? She had a bad time here with that Arno person. I was very anxious."

"I think she'll be all right, Hackett. I needn't tell you that man is never to enter this house again under any circumstances!"

"I would have seen to that without you telling me, Mr. Paul, and good luck to you, sir, in your campaign."

His campaign. As he drove back across the city he forced himself to push away the torturing thoughts of the last half-hour and consider it in a new light. With the postponement of the damage case he would have now a better than three weeks in which to pour himself out upon it. He would ask to be relieved at the office. He would not wait for opportunities to speak; he would make them. He would go on an intensive tour of his whole district, laying bare the evils as he saw them, calling upon the decent people to support him. He set his teeth. He would cast aside every party prop. He would now be his own utterly free agent. He would publicly disclaim all dependence on Kirkland's machine. So if he won, he would win on his own merits, his own principles. And he passionately wanted now to win in this way. First because it was *right*, but also now because then Anne might believe that his honor was unstained.

By giving his days and his nights to this plan he would, he thought, save his sanity and keep his heart from despair.

When he appeared at his old rooming house, he had not thought of what explanation he would offer to Mrs. MacLeod; so when she met him he was embarrassed and stammering, as she gave him an eager, motherly kiss.

"Could you let me have a room for a little while?" he managed at last. "I'm in the last lap of my campaign for State Senator. I'll be working most nights till very late—" It sounded lame enough but he could add nothing further. She fussed over him in her old fashion.

"My, yes. Your old one's empty just now. I always hated to see anyone else in it. Just go right on up and make yourself at home." Fortunately she forbore to ask questions other than with her eyes.

He could not settle to work that night. Instead he paced the floor for most of it, his emotions too violent for sleep. He had no idea where Arno lived and the telephone directory was of no help. So that business would have to be left till the morning. He clenched his fists. Once he had finished with him, laid him low, the dirty, filthy scoundrel . . . giving the paper to Anne would have been hell enough, but laying his lecherous hands upon her . . . *daring* to force his kisses. Oh, when he had done what he intended to do he could at least breathe again. As it was now the very thought of it strangled him.

But most bitter of all was the realization that Anne *had walked*, that the cure had come; and yet they could not share the wonder, the rapture together. That once again he was lost, alone, shut out in what should have been their greatest moment.

He went to the offices of Kirkland & Company as early next morning as he thought anyone would be there. He found Miss Sayles alone in the inner office she shared with Arno.

Paul's greeting was brief. "I want to see Arno at once!"

Sayles looked very anxious. "He's not here, Mr. Devereux. I just got a note by special messenger. He says he's left the city on a month's vacation and to carry on. He didn't even give an address! I don't know what to make of it." She lowered her voice. "I'm scared for him. You know he *is* mixed up with C and those gangsters. You don't think he's . . . he's come to harm, do you, Mr. Devereux?"

"No," he reassured her strongly. "I'm sure he hasn't. I think I know why he left town for a while. Don't worry, Miss Sayles. You'll hear from him. Can you manage things here without him?"

"Oh, I guess so. Hartman in the outer office is good. If anything too hard comes up for us, I'll call you."

"Better call Mr. Briggs," Paul said shortly. "I may not be . . . available."

He felt actually sick as he rode down in the elevator. He had been keyed up to a physical encounter, the only way possible in his mood to settle with Arno. Now his strength and his tension were futile; he was helpless, impotent. There was no release for the swelling wrath within him. He wished as he walked along the street that it were possible to transfer this burning fiery fury to his speeches. . . .

In the weeks that followed, it seemed as though this had actually been accomplished. Released from work at the office until the election, he started upon what amounted to a crusade. It was only too easy, now that he wanted to know it, to acquire more evidence of the corruption that was eating away at the city itself and spreading its voracious power across the country. Hartwell had many facts to lay before him; Johnny Bovard had a different but no less damning set. Paul had his own. It was all more than enough for the present to talk about; though tight-lipped and determined, he registered a vow to probe still farther after election until he had learned by his own unremitting zeal the whole truth of all that lay beneath the surface.

He had a long talk at the beginning of his new course one night with David Laird, whose serious face showed earnest approval.

"I suppose," Paul said, "that what I want to do is to pull no punches these last weeks. Just let the people have the facts as strongly as I can present them. Tell them about the danger as I see it, and call on them to support me in fighting it. You see I know a lot now I didn't know at the beginning of the campaign. Take Kirkland himself. I had a very deep affection for him as a man. I still miss him terribly. But I've learned things about his methods as Party Boss that I've got to disclaim publicly, without mentioning his name, of course. The average citizen doesn't know who the Boss is anyway. There's a nasty stink in this state, Dave, and I'm going to let some fresh air in if I can. What do you think?"

"It's courageous and it's *right*, but won't this finish you?"

"I don't think so. I've got a hunch there will be enough people who can take the truth and act upon it. Anyway I'm going on with this. Look, have you heard any more about the subversive business?"

David shook his head. "No, except that the group we tangled with has entirely dissolved. Gone under cover. We did that much anyway, but I suppose they're just working elsewhere under another front. That's the devil of it, they're so clever in covering their wolves with sheep's clothing."

"I know," Paul agreed. "I've been wondering what I should do about the whole thing in these last speeches. I've had no repercussions as I feared from that one speech. What I've been doing so far, since I don't have enough concrete facts to give, is to put in a good plug in every talk for liberty itself. For individual freedom as we have it here. I'll try to make this stronger from now to the end."

"Good!" David agreed. "It's the positive approach, anyway, and may be the best. You know I admire you, Paul. You've got guts. If there is anything I can do to help you . . ."

Paul smiled. "Sure is. You and as many more as you can round up can get out and vote for me."

If the first months of Paul's campaign had drawn favorable journalistic comment here and there, these last weeks brought headlines! His meteoric swing around the district with talks to every kind of group made news. For they were not the patterned, political addresses to which the people were accustomed, even with eloquence thrown in; neither were they the harangues of a demagogue. These were the fearless outpourings of a man of conviction and of dedication.

He began each time quite simply by stating he had not known until recently that most of the money for the campaign had come from a great numbers banker . . . a racketeer! From that moment on he had rapt attention.

"And why," he would continue, "do the gangsters donate money for election funds? Because they want men elected whom they can count on to protect them. I want to tell you now that I am not, nor ever will be, one of their men. If I am elected, I will fight them in the Senate and out of it. And I may add that the money for these last weeks' campaigning is coming out of my own pocket, so I am free to say what I want to say, what I *must* say to you about the various dangers that threaten our body politic."

He would go on to particularize. "Do you know that the gangsters in this state not only have a tight hold on gambling and related vices but that they are moving in on legitimate businesses? Hotels, restaurants, night clubs, meat and provisions, automobile dealerships and even small steel companies? Do you, the citizenry *know* these things? Do you know too that there is danger, if we don't curb it in time, that the whole gambling ring will take over our state Senate? The problem that faces us is: *Can we continue to exist half underworld and half upper-world?*"

He spoke of the graft-ridden cities. "Do you know," he would press, "that countless city officials across the state who should be incorruptible are profiting constantly, if indirectly, in various ways from their offices? From insurance commissions on city-owned property, from insurance premiums on performance bonds for public works, from the awarding of contracts—to name only a few.

"Do you know that the tendrils of graft and corruption have become mighty interlacing roots so that even men who would like to be honest are tripped and trapped by them?"

Remorselessly, day by day, he kept piling fact upon fact and driving them home to his audiences, begging them to rally round those men who were known to stand for clean government and in particular to support him in his race for senator.

"If the good, the decent people in politics and out of it will only look these dangers in the face and then fight them, we can clean up our cities, our state, our country itself. For"—and here his voice always rang out with deeper eloquence—"do you also realize that steadily, insidiously, in all sorts of hidden and seemingly innocent guises, there press in upon us the machinations of enemies who would, if they could, overthrow our government by force? Are you, the average citizens, aware that these dangers are not far off but may be close to you?"

Then each time, whether he was speaking to a dozen or to a hundred, he ended with the same words:

"The Founding Fathers pledged their lives, their fortunes and their sacred honor to maintain this nation clean and free from foes without and within. Can we do less in these, our own critical times? For even more important for our protection than armament or bombs, is the determination of every individual citizen to do his best to oppose the evils that threaten us and to uphold in his own thinking and action the liberty which is our heritage and our strength.

> *For He who worketh high and wise*
> *Nor pauses in His plan,*
> *Will take the sun out of the skies*
> *Ere freedom out of man.*"

The headlines in the county papers grew bigger. Even city editorials began to appear.

The organization will have to do something about young Mr.
Devereux who is not as well trained at jumping at the crack of
the whip as the party machine would like. This candidate for
the state Senate has suddenly begun to speak quite out of turn
and with a force which is making certain strong men shiver at
his audacity. What the result of these wild utterances will be
on election day remains to be seen.

The comments varied from this near facetiousness to sober praise
or sharp rebuke.

His break with Brennen had necessitated certain mechanical
changes. Before, he had been using Party Headquarters; now he
must provide his own. At Hartwell's suggestion he took over a par-
tially unused room just behind his own office, and secured the services of a capable girl to take phone calls and attend to all the
multifarious incoming questions and messages when he was out. Certain campaign aids in the way of equipment were now cut off from
him—or rather he had cut himself off from them; but one small radio
station had offered him free time and for the rest he must depend
upon his unremitting speeches in every corner of the city and the
county.

Each night he called up Davy. Her replies to his questions never
varied, for of course the most important one he could not ask. Yes,
they were getting on all right. Yes, the baby was well. Yes, Anne was
walking about the house and the garden but so far seemed unwilling
to go beyond that. After such a conversation Paul would sit with his
head in his hands trying honestly to see Anne's side. It had always
been for him both a blessing and a curse (due no doubt to his
dramatic inheritance) that he could put himself in another's place.
He thought now of all that had happened from her point of view.
Her first incredulity that he would want to marry her, as she was.
Then, when he had overcome all her unselfish resistance there was
the wholeness, the beautiful, innocent rapture of her surrender, of
her giving. He groaned within him. The damning words of the paper!
The *three years,* the *plan agreed upon between us!* How could she
believe him completely after that, with the paper written in her own
father's hand? And by his own admission accepted by him, even
though he later destroyed it. What cruel havoc to her pride and the
tender faith of her love! It would indeed take time to heal that
wound. If it ever healed. He wrestled with despair.

One morning when he was back in the office going over his mail, Johnny Bovard called up. His voice was more than exuberant.

"Can I come over a minute? I've got to see you!"

When he entered the room a short time later, his face was like the risen sun.

"Yeah bo, I'm glad I caught you in. I just heard the news last night. It broke at a party and after that nobody talked about much else. I just haven't got the coin to say it right, Paul, but I guess you know how I feel!" He wrung Paul's hand. "This is the biggest thing since D-Day!"

"You mean . . . ?" Paul stammered.

Johnny moved back. "What do you mean 'what do I mean'? What do you think I'm talking about? *Anne!*"

"Yes," said Paul, trying to put life into his voice. "It's wonderful! It's incredible! I can hardly believe it yet, myself."

Johnny's smile slowly returned. "And I thought maybe I'd drop by tonight about the time you got home. Okay?"

"Well," Paul said, "you go on. Anne will want to see you. I won't be there."

"That's all right. I'll wait. What night will you be home?"

Paul stammered again under Johnny's clear gaze.

"I'm away most of the time . . . I . . . Oh, damn it, Johnny, you might as well have it. I'm not living at the house just now."

Johnny said nothing, merely dropped into a chair and stared out of the window.

"I'll tell you, Paul, if you didn't look as if you were dead and dug up right this minute I'd maybe have a big question in my mind," he said at last. "But anyone can see you've been through some pretty little hell all right. I thought at first it was just the campaign business. By the way how's it going? You're kicking up the dust with a vengeance. More power to you. You're prepared to lose over it, aren't you?"

"No," Paul said, "I'm not. I still have confidence that once the people know the true state of things they'll want to reform them. You see, people just don't *know* what's going on. That's what I'm trying to tell them."

Johnny whistled softly. "Go right to it. You're making a wonderful job of it. Only remember that voters are a darned undependable lot."

He sat still for a minute and then stood up.

"If I'm ever any good to you, political or personal—well, you know I'm standing by."

Paul couldn't speak for the tightness in his throat.

Johnny turned at the door. "What are friends for, by golly?" he said and disappeared.

One phase of his relations with Anne kept recurring to Paul with a sort of cumulative force. This was that now Anne in her own right had the wealth. Though this was not a comfortable thought, though it posed a heavy problem, he still felt that Anne could never feel he had been so low as to be influenced in his first decision to marry her because of the money. Bad enough, indeed, for her to feel that his political career had been the apple of temptation. But never the wealth. Somehow he was sure she would absolve him from any least mercenary suspicion. But there was still no word from her, and he still asked for Davy when he called up, for he, too, had his pride.

One night after a hard day's campaigning, he drove out of the city and on up to North Hill. He had read an article as he ate his restaurant dinner upon the possible annihilation of the human race. The author, a popular columnist, took a darkly pessimistic view. Not only did he feel this ultimate disaster was probable; he felt it might indeed be deserved. He was at pains to point out the enormous failures of mankind in general.

Paul parked the car on the crest and walked over to a lookout spot, from which he gazed down upon the million lights of the city spread like jostling stars in a firmament of darkness. Here before him, in miniature, lay the world; here, in little, was the human race. All the good and the bad, here they were in their little dwellings, under the eye of God. Were they perhaps his last and greatest experiment? Had myriads of other planets in their courses grown cold from God's despair? Would it be so with our own?

He stood looking down at the lights, thinking deeply. At last he raised his head.

"No!" he fairly shouted the word. And again, "No!"

With all the evil, some of which he was even now engaged in fighting, with all the greed, the selfishness, the colossal blunders of the race of men, there was still surely an overwhelming preponderance of good! As long as there was courage and love and sacrifice left in the world, it would not be annihilated. It did not *deserve* to be! A sudden picture flashed upon his mind. It was that of a slim, quiet young man who worked in the village hardware store back home. He had gone to war with the rest of them. Ambulance Corps. He had come back at last with the Bronze Star for courage far beyond the call of duty in bringing in the wounded under fire. He had come back, and slipped unobtrusively behind the hardware counter again. He was still there.

Somehow the thought of this quiet and outwardly colorless man with a hero's heart gave to Paul a confidence beyond all reason. He felt as though, like Abraham pleading for Sodom, he had brought before God Himself proof of the inherent greatness of man.

He stood on, watching the lights which signified all the diverse habitations in which families lived together, while a prayer rose within him for human kind everywhere; and then because the softness of the autumn night touched him like a gentle finger, he prayed for himself and his love.

During the last week Paul worked with frenzied zeal and a sort of sublime assurance in his cause. He was convinced that his last month's reform speeches, aided by the newspaper publicity, would make the victory Jimmy had predicted yet more sure. By election eve he was utterly exhausted but still confident, as he flung himself in bed, for once too weary to think of anything but sleep. When he first woke he looked out on a thin, dreary rain, the skies leaden, the last leaves stricken to the pavement. The sense that he could now do nothing more made him turn over again in drowsy relaxation. When he next woke he saw to his astonishment that it was noon. He got up hastily, dressed and went out to vote, barely in time to keep his appointment with the photographers. He lunched late with Hartwell at the latter's club but they did not discuss the day's cogent possibilities until they were ready to leave.

"I'm nervous as a cat," Paul admitted. "If a mere aspirant for State Senator feels this way at election time, how must a presidential candidate feel?"

"You might know some day," Hartwell said slyly.

Paul laughed the joke off and then turned suddenly sober as he recalled Kirkland's long-range plans for him.

"I suppose you'll be staying round at Party Headquarters all evening—this afternoon, too, for that matter," Hartwell said.

"Well, not quite," Paul answered. "You see after my various rounds with Brennen, and the sort of speeches I've been making, I'm really *non grata* to the inner ring. I'm a sort of hybrid. They don't quite know how to class me. If I win, they will be elated for the party victory, I imagine, and if I lose they'll be glad to get me out of their hair. I thought I'd stay with Johnny Bovard tonight and listen to the radio for the early reports, and then go over to headquarters toward the end. I'm in a funny position with the party," he repeated. "I started out strictly on the line, and I've ended up a sort of lone wolf."

"The only thing you must not forget," Hartwell returned thoughtfully, "is that politics is a complex game. You can't go it alone. You've got to work with other people. The big trick is to find the right ones. Well, after election you can take stock again. In any event I'm proud of you, my boy, and as the Psalmist says, 'Good luck in the name of the Lord.' "

During the afternoon Paul drove out to West Hill, passed slowly back and forth before the house and then ended up at Mrs. Catherby's apartment. She greeted him with her usual warmth, which in some measure comforted the soreness of his heart.

"Just let me visit with you for an hour," he said, "and maybe talk about the weather. It will do me good. I'm jittery today."

She eyed him keenly. "You've been avoiding me a little, haven't you? I've missed you."

"I've been busy every minute. Today will tell the tale whether it's been to any purpose or not."

The old lady shook her head. "No difference how the votes come in, you've done a wonderful thing, Paul. You've stirred people up out of their lethargy. I'm sure of that from the newspapers without having heard your speeches. You've been honest and courageous. Can't you take satisfaction in that?"

"I'm afraid I can't, unless I see results," he said.

They sat silent for some time and then she said quietly, "Do you want to talk about Anne?"

"I can't. I want to, but the facts must come from her."

Mrs. Catherby sighed. "She feels she cannot talk about it either, so I am completely in the dark about the new trouble, whatever it is. All I can do is love you both. The saddest thing of all to me is that the unspeakable joy of her cure should now be clouded over."

"I know," Paul said. "On the other hand, whatever unhappiness she is bearing, she has that to alleviate it. I've never seen her—walk. Has she been over here?" His voice was unsteady.

"Yes, several times. But I couldn't rejoice as I wanted to. 'The singing and the gold' is gone for her, Paul. She's changed. And she won't confide in me."

"I wish I could pour it all out to you," Paul said, "but I don't think Anne would want me to. You see how it is then, don't you? At least for the present?"

She nodded. "I'll just keep on hoping—and saying my prayers.

Now if you'll ring the bell, we'll have a good hot cup of tea and discuss the weather."

Paul felt better as he left. It was wonderful to feel that Gran blindly trusted him as she quite evidently did, even while grieving for her darling's pain. He went into a phone booth downtown and called the house. When Hackett answered he was about to ask for Anne when the old man interrupted. "I'll put Miss Davis on at once, Mr. Paul," he said.

His heart was beating fast but he tried to keep his voice calm. "Is Anne busy, Davy? Could I speak to her?"

"I'll see," she answered quickly. "Just a minute."

He waited, his hand gripping the phone hard.

When the voice came it was still Davy's.

"She is busy right now with the baby, but she said to tell you she wished you every success today."

He sat for a minute in the booth as though without strength to stand. This from her, and only this, coming out of the facts as she believed them, was a bitter message.

He got to the Bovards' at six-thirty and had sandwiches and coffee up in Johnny's room, while the radio's spattered comments kept coming over, some of them dealing with himself.

"A good deal of interest in this evening's returns centers around Paul Devereux, one of the candidates for State Senator. Young Devereux suddenly started on a crusade for clean government a month ago . . ."

"You're God's gift to the broadcasters, Paul," Johnny laughed. "They need filler-in material right now more than a cow needs a tail."

By seven o'clock one announcer had a bit more to add, of which he made the eloquent most.

"Returns from the little village of Denton in the northern end of the county have just come in, their polls closing at six o'clock. There were ninety-six votes cast. For State Senator, Paul Devereux received all *ninety-six!*"

"Hurray for Devereux!" Johnny yelled at the top of his lungs.

Paul felt an elation out of all proportion to the small fact itself. It showed he was right in believing that if the people only knew the truth. . . . Well, of course it was only a straw in the wind, and yet it *was a straw*.

By eight and eight-thirty the reports from the county and small-town polling places were coming in fast with Paul leading. By nine returns from larger towns and the city districts were mixed, of course, but with Paul still out in front and the party ticket as a whole running away ahead.

By nine-thirty Kent began to creep up; by ten he and Paul were neck and neck, by ten-thirty, he was in the lead; by ten forty-five, Paul stood up, his face tired and set.

"I'd better be getting over to headquarters now." He had hoped to make a late, triumphal entry there.

"I'll go along," Johnny said. "I'll admit it doesn't look too good, Paul, old boy. I'll tell you how I figure it. Of course you did upset the party apple cart a little. Then there wasn't time these last weeks for the decent people to get together on a reform vote, solid, you know, across party lines. But there *was* time for the hoods to get their word around. They've got a secret grapevine that would fool the Devil himself, and they control plenty votes. Don't ever think they don't. So there you are. Good try, old man, and don't be discouraged. Just up and at 'em again."

The headquarters room was in the old Masonic Hall building. When Paul and Johnny entered, they were for a moment unnoticed. The smoke was thick, the radios blaring, the ticker machines active, the men milling about, mostly in jubilant mood, for the party ticket was not only sweeping the county—all that is except Paul's place on it—but the state as well.

Brennen saw them first and came over. He greeted Paul more in sorrow than anger.

"Well," he said, "it's not so good to say 'I told you so,' but I warned you plenty. You've lost yourself a job and us the election for the Senate. It's too bad after the way you started out."

"I'm sorry, Brennen, but I had to do it. The thing's pretty well sewed up now, isn't it?"

"Yep. Afraid so."

"When should I send Kent a wire?"

"I'll tell you."

At eleven-thirty Paul conceded the election and sent the customary message of congratulation to his opponent, thinking as he did so, of the farmer and his pail of priming water.

Then he walked over to the window and stood for a moment apart looking out into the rainy night. The wet macadam of the street was shining with a strange black depth under the misted lights. But the darkness in his own heart was deeper.

~§ As THOUGH the elements had done their worst on election day and were now repentant, the next weeks melted into the warm, hazy effulgence of Indian Summer. The skies kept their rich October blue; the air was soft upon the cheek; and to those who had ever known the country, the autumnal nostalgia for lost childhood touched the heart. Out in the suburbs the last burning leaves rose in pungent smoke that mingled and drifted with the haze above the hills.

Paul was tired. He attributed it to the lazy warmth of the November days, to the hard work of his campaign, to his defeat. But he knew there were deeper reasons for the new lines in his face. It was his heart that was most weary, for there was still no word, no sign from Anne. One day he wrote a short note and sent it by special messenger.

Darling:

   Do you realize that if your father had never tried to make the "deal" with me you and I would never have met and loved and had our child? Have you thought also that if he had never written that paper you might never have walked again?

Love always,
PAUL

The reply came so swiftly back that Paul was shaken with hope when the note was delivered to him. But the lines were brief, without beginning or ending.

I have thought of everything but there is one bridge I cannot cross—yet.

He knew what that bridge was—the one leading to him and to their life together. He put the small paper next his heart, though there was little in the message to warm it.

In addition to his personal pain another haunted him. Defeat in itself was part and parcel of the great gambling game of politics. A man who could not accept it and try again was not of the stuff of which leaders are made. This, of course, he realized. Yet there was still in him a sense of disillusionment, of disappointment in *the people*. It was childish, he told himself, and yet there it was. Even reckoning with Camponelli and his underworld influence, it seemed to Paul that his four weeks of honest, vigorous laying bare the facts should have resulted in more votes than it had. Not for him personally, but for principle, for clean government, for the uprooting of evil. He recalled Johnny's summing up of the situation on election night and appreciated the truth of it; but still the perhaps unreasonable disappointment persisted. He was swept by new fears for his country.

The damage case came up at last and Hartwell & Harvey, with Paul representing them, won over Sheffkin. It gave a bit of salve to Paul's wounds, especially since it elicited from Hartwell one of his very rare professional compliments.

"Good work, Paul," he said. "You have the makings of a great lawyer in you if you ever decide to give up politics. It's only fair to tell you so."

"Thank you very much," Paul answered. "I've been wondering lately if I shouldn't just concentrate on the law and let the other go hang."

"I thought you were brooding along those lines. Only natural at the moment." The old man dangled his glasses on their ribbon. "But my advice is, keep an open mind for a while. Something may turn up to help you decide."

He could not have been more prophetic. It was the first of the next week that Paul received a phone call from Dr. Rollins, rector of the old downtown church of St. John's, which stood just across from the office building in which Hartwell & Harvey had their suite. Paul knew of him as perhaps the most influential minister in the city but had never met him, so the announcement of his name came as a surprise.

"Mr. Devereux," he was saying, "would it be possible for you to meet with a small group of men in my study on Thursday afternoon about four? We have a matter we are very interested in talking over with you."

"Thursday at four? Why, yes, that time is convenient."

If he noticed the slight hesitation in Paul's voice, Dr. Rollins gave no sign.

"Good! We will expect you then. Come in through the Parish House and someone will be there to direct you to the study. I will look forward to seeing you. And thank you!"

"Now what does *he* want?" Paul muttered to himself. Then a phrase of the conversation recurred to him. *A small group of men.* Ah, he thought, I smell a big church dinner in the offing, with me as the speaker. So, I'm to meet the committee—

He sat, staring ahead of him. The whole business of speech-making in which he had taken such satisfaction, even joy before, had now lost its zest. He felt as though he never wanted to "spout" again, as his father had termed it. And yet, a church affair— Probably he shouldn't refuse that. Oh, well, he sighed, he would wait and see. He hadn't been asked yet.

On Thursday afternoon he all but forgot the meeting. He had been working unusually hard upon an important brief and looked up suddenly to see his desk clock at four. He jumped up, straightened his tie and hurried over to the gray stone buildings across the way. An old verger met him at the entrance to the Parish House and conducted him to the study. The door was open so that Paul at once caught a glimpse of the men seated there. He had time to see Mr. Bovard, Johnny's father; Mr. Barker of the Barker Bank; and Joe Donnelly, editor and publisher of the *Daily Gazette*. In the split second he realized that this was not a committee for a church dinner.

Dr. Rollins came forward and greeted him warmly.

"Some of these men I believe you already know—"

When the introductions were over and they were all seated Dr. Rollins came swiftly to the point.

"Mr. Devereux, we along with many others, of course, followed the last weeks of your campaign with very special interest. We are men who in one line of work or another have deep roots in our city here. We have been increasingly concerned over local conditions. As you doubtless know a year from now we elect a mayor." He paused, smiled and then added, "To put it bluntly, we would like you to run for that office on a straight reform platform. We feel you can be elected, and we will back you with all the various resources at our disposal. While you are catching your breath I would like these other men to amplify what I have just said."

Mr. Barker spoke first in his measured voice.

"If we are ever going to clean up this city we've got to have a man at the head who is himself completely incorruptible. I had a little experience recently with Mr. Devereux which I think would be relevant to mention at this point. For certain reasons I wanted him in our organization. While I would not say that I was attempting to *buy* him, that element was perhaps present in my thought.

So I sent for him and offered him a salary most young men would jump at. He declined at once, refusing even to take time to think it over. I had the feeling he knew intuitively that money was being used as a pressure upon him and that he could not be influenced in this way. That, gentlemen, is, I think, a very important qualification for the man we are looking for."

"Mr. Donnelly?" Dr. Rollins turned to the publisher. "Will you give us your reasons for thinking Mr. Devereux can be elected if he's willing to run?"

Joe Donnelly removed his cigarette. "Well, now I'll tell you. As I see it from the publicity angle just merely a good, *incorruptible* candidate is not enough to swing this thing even if we all get behind him. This is going to be a fight and a damned big one. The reason I think we've got a chance with Devereux is because he's got the personality. He's got *looks*, too, and brother, that does no harm to the women's vote, I tell you! Don't let me embarrass you, Devereux," he added as Paul looked uncomfortable while the others laughed. "You only have to kiss the *babies*, you know! But seriously, Devereux here has a sort of dynamic, dramatic quality in his speeches that not only sways the people but makes what he says *quotable*. We can really make news of him as well as editorial comment. Our paper will support him, and since our reporters get into a good many back doors we can keep an eye on C and his rats as we go along. That may be pretty useful."

Mr. Bovard had little to say except that he felt things were going from bad to worse in the city and that while he was no horse dealer himself, he could at least put some money on the race. The other men smiled and Donnelly clapped him on the back. The fifth man, a Mr. Walters, also said little but the others appeared more than satisfied. He stated merely that since he had had some experience in local affairs he would be glad to help handle the proposed campaign.

Then Dr. Rollins summed up.

"Perhaps we have not been quite fair, Mr. Devereux, in letting you have no say up to this point. To be honest, we were all afraid that if you spoke at once you would refuse. Our feeling is that if we start now and work steadily for a year to build up a solid reform vote for you, you can win. My part, for example, will be to get as many church people as possible of all faiths to organize to this end. Mr. Barker and Mr. Bovard will see to the business and professional groups, Mr. Donnelly will handle the publicity and editorial buildup, and that's just the beginning, as Mr. Walters will tell you. Well," he drew a deep breath, "I guess we can delay no longer in hearing your reaction. You know the conditions here—what do you say?"

Paul's emotions up to this point had been tumultuous: astonishment, almost consternation, with pride also in the trust of these picked men and a hot desire to engage in this fight with them, as their leader. His lips opened to say he would of course need time to consider before giving them his answer. As he started to speak he met the cold keen gray eyes of Mr. Barker watching him intently. It had been his own immediate decision that day in the banker's office which had won the latter's approval and support.

Suddenly, to his own surprise he heard himself saying, "Gentlemen, I will run."

Back in the office he found a message asking him to call Briggs, the lawyer. Paul did so, mechanically.

"Oh Devereux, I just wanted to report that Mallotte is back in the Kirkland office. The woman there, Miss Sayles, has been quite upset these last weeks but now I trust all will go smoothly until you and your wife decide what you want to do with the business. I just thought I'd let you know about Mallotte."

About Mallotte. About Arno. He was back, delivered into his adversary's hand. Paul dismissed his secretary and sat thinking. He could go over to the office now and have it out with Arno. Knock his teeth in as he had burned to do. But somehow that fury was spent. He had no desire to harm him now; instead a strange pity for the man touched him. He himself of all men knew best the temptation of Anne's loveliness. It was even possible that Arno had cherished a secret passion for her. That idea had never occurred to him before, but it could be. If so—poor devil! He needed no further punishment—

With a gesture, as though brushing Arno aside once and for all, Paul sat hunched over his desk, concentrating on the momentous thing which had happened to him that afternoon. Perhaps because he had then been thinking of Anne he was struck with a new fear. He had just now pledged himself to run for mayor. He had done so without consulting his wife, without even telling her of his decision before giving it to the men. And this that he was about to enter upon was a very different thing from the race for senator with the beckoning, glamorous future, only half named and yet half acknowledged between them. This would be a grim and sordid fight with no great glory at the end even if he won, except the satisfaction of work well done. Yes, Anne had a right to know this, to be consulted. And yet—

even if she opposed it he knew he must go on. He must accept the challenge.

With his unfailing memory for verse there came back to him now the lines from the poem Anne had referred to the first night they had met.

THE WATCHMAN (*consoling the women*)
What would ye, ladies? It was ever thus.
Men are unwise and curiously planned.
      A WOMAN
They have their dreams, and do not think of us.
VOICES OF THE CARAVAN (*in the distance singing*)
We make the Golden Journey to Samarkand.

It was true. A man if he was to play the part of a man, must sometimes set forth, even though in one sense or another he left his dearest love behind him. Anne must have known this and dreaded it. How would she feel now? Especially since the only golden quality of this journey which he was about to begin would be whatever inner courage and integrity could be mustered by the man who made it.

He sat for some time thinking, fearing, wondering. At last he rose. There was one person by whom his news would be received with joy. He would go into the other office now and tell Hartwell.

In the big house on West Hill life had fallen into slow, patterned days. The first sharpness of her grief for Jimmy had merged for Anne into a steady weight of loneliness. This was entirely different from the anguish of her broken relations with Paul. This was a continual heavy-laden sense of loss. She saw her whole life against her father's personality: vivid little pleasures of her childhood which he had planned kept coming back to her; all the companionship of her growing years with him; the poignant tenderness of his constant care of her! She dreamed of him at night, and once when Hackett had knocked on her door early in the morning with a question she had roused herself just enough to call, "Come in, Jimmy," as she had been used to do. That had been a hard day.

She was half aware and yet unwilling to admit that she was using this natural sorrow for her father as a sort of opiate against the torturing confusion of her broken faith in Paul. She kept going on day after day unable to see or think beyond the first facts of their courtship as she believed them to be. Sometimes in the still darkness of the night she was overcome with shame because her love for him persisted—though wounded—passionate and undiminished in the depths of her being. But how could she take him back? How could she resume their life together when only the physical tie would be as before? When her mind and heart would constantly have in them the doubt, the great unanswered question? And the proof that he had truly loved her from the first, even with her handicap, that he had been entirely uninfluenced by her father's offered "deal" could be given only by himself; and the bitter tragedy was that he was the one person she was unable to believe. So in a prison of dull circling thoughts of pain Anne pursued her days, lightened only by the joy of her motherhood.

One feature of her altered life amazed her: this was her almost casual acceptance now of the wonder of her cure. It was so natural, so normal *to walk* that often for a whole day she forgot she had ever been unable to do so. She still dreaded outside contacts. She felt she could not yet bear the voluble and high-pitched exclamations and questions of her young friends. Hackett was, indeed, given an assortment of excuses to make for her when they called. She confined herself to the baby, to her music, to Davy; to the upper floor of the house and to the garden. Often with the child beside her, she sat for hours in the autumn sunshine limp and spent with too much feeling. But the fountain had been shut off early in the fall, by her order. She could not bear to be reminded by its soft raindrop splash of those nights on the terrace when she and Paul lay on the big chaise after dinner, listened to it, planning the future and telling each other their hearts' secrets.

She went over to Mrs. Catherby's frequently to dinner; but while it always lightened her mood temporarily, her inability to share her inner burden kept an invisible barrier between them. As always Gran had a poem to give her, and somehow this one kept recurring to her as time went on, like the incidental music of a play.

> *O hearken, love, the battle horn!*
> *The triumph clear, the silver scorn!*
> *O hearken where the echoes bring,*
> *Down the grey disastrous morn,*
> *Laughter and rallying.*

At first as she read from the slip of paper Gran had pressed upon her one evening as she was leaving, Anne felt the lines were oddly chosen for her; but gradually she understood the implication as Gran had subtly meant it. She, the woman, the wife, must take the initiative; must call out to her love the sound of triumph; must show faith in the ultimate "laughter and rallying," after the morn of disaster. But she sighed with the hot tears on her cheeks. She had no faith.

It was Sunday, and old Hartwell was coming to dinner. It had been upon sudden impulse that Anne had called to invite him and he had accepted with a touching alacrity. As she dressed she wondered what news he would give her of Paul. She would ask nothing of course, but it was inevitable that the old man would mention him. She wondered how much he knew of the estrangement. But since Paul had evidently confided no facts to Gran it was unlikely he would do so to Hartwell. Her hands trembled as she prepared to go down to receive him. For the first time since Jimmy's death she was using the dining room. It had to be done sometime and she had nerved herself to go through the ordeal today, only asking Hackett to make the big table as small as possible.

When she entered the library Hartwell was already there in his immaculate linen and finely tailored black. He rose stiffly to meet her, tried to be casual, but the first expression of shock remained on his face.

"You have been ill, my dear," he said gently.

"Not ill," Anne replied. "Only tired and very, very sad. I'm so glad to see you." A little flash of her old impulsiveness made her add, "Even gladder than I expected to be."

"There couldn't be a nicer welcome and I assure you the feeling is mutual."

They talked then over their sherry of the baby, of the weather, of Mrs. Catherby, who was to have come but was detained by a cold, and gradually of the election. Anne listened but said little. The generalities continued during dinner until it seemed when they were once again in the library with their coffee that there was nothing more of safe content left to discuss.

Suddenly, as though nerving himself for something which took courage, Hartwell set down his cup and leaned forward.

"My dear," he said, "I am very anxious about Paul."

Her face stiffened but she did not reply.

"I have not asked him about his personal affairs this time. His face forbade it. But I did once before when he looked as he does now."

"When was that?" Anne said quickly.

"It was before you were married. Before you were engaged. I was at his rooms to dinner. I had known for weeks that he was suffering, so I made so bold as to ask if he cared to confide in me. He did so.

That's why I'm anxious about him now. He looks the same as at that time."

Anne's voice was not steady as she spoke. "What did he tell you then?"

Hartwell looked up in surprise. "Only what of course now you know—"

"Please tell me. You can't understand how important this may be to me!"

"Well," he said, "your father had made him a sort of offer to help him politically if he would try to marry you. This was offensive to Paul and he told him so. Later, however, he met you and fell in love, but at this time of which I'm speaking you were refusing to see him, and he was quite in despair. I advised him not to give up—to keep trying—"

Anne had sprung from her chair and dropped on her knees before the old man, her arms about his waist.

"Oh, tell me everything," she implored. "*Everything*. This is life or death to me!"

His astonishment was evident, but he touched her gently.

"Why, my dear, I had no idea I was saying anything new to you. I don't remember the rest of the conversation except something I said of which I'm not too proud now as I recall it. I could see of course the tremendous advantage to him in a family alliance with—well, with the State Boss, so I asked him if his love for you *was* entirely independent of his affairs with your father—"

"Yes?" Anne breathed.

"He said, 'Completely! Utterly!' I remember the words."

She was on her feet, and the old man had the impression of a winged thing poised for instant flight.

"I must talk to Paul at once, if I only knew where to find him."

"He's working in the office all afternoon. I just saw him before I came. You can call him there."

"I must go to him," she said, and the look in her eyes made those of the old man mist over. "Won't you just wait here and read—and stay on to supper so Paul can see you too? And forgive me now. I must hurry—I must go—"

She was out of the room. Hartwell could see her running up the stairs, running down in a moment in hat and coat. He could hear her leaving the house, and in a moment the sound of her car in the drive.

He was still amazed and a little confused over what had happened; but one thing was clear. He, old, barren and childless, who loved them so, had somehow fathered their happiness. "*Nunc dimittis*," he murmured softly leaning his head for rest against the back of the chair.

Anne drove as fast as she dared. She parked in front of the office building, and found the outer door unlocked. The elevator of course was not running, but she scarcely knew she was climbing the stairs. On the third floor she stopped breathless before the chaste lettering of *Hartwell & Harvey, Attorneys-at-Law*. She opened the door softly. Paul sat at his desk intent upon his work, his face thin and lined. She went a few steps farther and he looked up. He rose, slowly, unbelievingly. She came close and laid her head against his breast. For a long time they stood speechless, feeling the rapture of each other's nearness—the touch, the kisses . . .

At last she looked into his face.

"Can you forgive me? Will you come back?"

His voice broke with tenderness.

"My darling, I've never really been away!"

He sat down, drew her to his knee and held her close while they talked of all that had happened during the weeks of their estrangement, up to this very day. He told her then of his new plans, hesitating as he repeated his promise to run for mayor. But Anne made no objection. They both knew that all the depths of their hearts, as yet unspoken, would be revealed later in the tender hours of darkness.

At last they rose to leave. At the door Paul looked down at her.

"Darling," he said, "I must warn you again. This may not only be a rough road I'm to travel but a dead end at that."

"I don't think so," she said. "It may be only the beginning. But whatever it is," and the light on her face blinded him, "I will be with you all the way."

They went down the stairs and out into the late afternoon light. As they approached the car Anne laid a hand on Paul's arm, as she looked across at the open door of St. John's.

"It's Evensong," she said. "I'd like to go. Today, after all that's past, wouldn't it be—fitting?"

"Very," Paul answered. "I would like it, myself."

They slipped quietly in somewhere near the back, for the service was already begun. The rich windows had caught the last embers of the day; the far white altar stood fair with its tapers and flowers. Anne and Paul knelt close, their hands clasped, their thoughts at first a mingling of their own happiness and the peace of the holy place. Then suddenly the words of the ancient Order of Evening Prayer struck their hearts and echoed there as though spoken to them alone.

O Lord, save the State,
And mercifully hear us when we call upon thee.

. . . .

Give peace in our time, O Lord.
For it is thou, Lord, only, that makest us dwell in safety.